LIVING SHADOWS
STORIES: NEW and PREOWNED

OTHER BOOKS BY
JOHN SHIRLEY

NOVELS
Transmaniacon
Dracula in Love
City Come A-Walkin'
Three-Ring Psychus
The Brigade
Cellars
In Darkness Waiting
Kamus of Kadizar
A Splendid Chaos
Wetbones
Silicon Embrace
Demons
The View From Hell
Her Hunger
...And the Angel with Television Eyes
Spider Moon
Crawlers
The Other End

A SONG CALLED YOUTH SERIES:
Eclipse
Eclipse Penumbra
Eclipse Corona

COLLECTIONS
Heatseeker
New Noir
The Exploded Heart
Black Butterflies
Really Really Really Really Weird Stories
Darkness Divided

LIVING SHADOWS
STORIES: NEW and PREOWNED

John Shirley

PRIME BOOKS

Prime Books
Rockville, MD
www.prime-books.com
prime@prime-books.com

"In the Road" © 2001 by John Shirley. *Darkness Divided*, Stealth Press 2001 | "The Gunshot"
© 1980 by John Shirley. *Oui*, Nov 1980; *Heatseeker*, Scream/Press 1989 | "The Sewing Room"
© 2007 by John Shirley. Original to this volume. | "Nineteen Seconds" © 2000 by John Shirley.
Horror Garage #1, 2000; *Darkness Divided*, Stealth Press 2001 | "What Would You Do For
Love?" © 1998 by John Shirley. *Black Butterflies: A Flock on the Dark Side*, Mark V. Ziesing
1998 | "Seven Knives" © 2007 by John Shirley. *Midnight Premiere*, ed. Tom Piccirilli, Cemetery
Dance Publications 2007 | "War and Peace" © 1995 by John Shirley. *Fear Itself*, ed. Jeff Gelb,
Warner 1995; *Black Butterflies: A Flock on the Dark Side*, Mark V. Ziesing 1998 | "One Stick,
Both Ends Sharpened" © 2001 by John Shirley. *Horror Garage #4*, 2001 | "Jody and Annie
on TV" © 1991 by John Shirley. *Cold Blood*, ed. Richard T. Chizmar, Mark V. Ziesing 1991;
New Noir, Fiction Collective 2, 1993; *Darkness Divided*, Stealth Press 2001 | "The Word
'Random', Deliberately Repeated" © 1973 by John Shirley. *Clarion III*, ed. Robin Scott, NAL,
1973; *Really, Really, Really, Really Weird Stories*, Night Shade 1999 | "Brittany? Oh: She's in
Translucent Blue" © 1999 by John Shirley. *Really, Really, Really, Really Weird Stories*, Night
Shade 1999 | "The Sea Was Wet as Wet Can Be" © 1999 by John Shirley. *Really, Really, Really,
Really Weird Stories*, Night Shade 1999 | "Blind Eye" (with Edgar Allan Poe) © 2006 by John
Shirley. *Poe's Lighthouse*, ed. Christopher Conlon, Cemetery Dance Publications 2006 |
"Sleepwalkers" © 1988 by John Shirley. *New Pathways*, Oct 1988; *Heatseeker*, Scream/Press
1989 | "Buried in the Sky" © 2006 by John Shirley. *Weird Tales #342*, 2006 | "Skeeter Junkie"
© 1993 by John Shirley. *New Noir*, Fiction Collective 2, 1993 | "Isolation Point, California" ©
2007 by John Shirley. *Horrors Beyond II: Stories of Strange Creations*, ed. William Jones, Elder
Signs Press 2007 | "Miss Singularity" © 2005 by John Shirley. *Outsiders*, ed. Nancy Holder &
Nancy Kilpatrick, Roc 2005 | "My Victim" © 2001 by John Shirley. *Cemetery Dance #34*, 2001;
Darkness Divided, Stealth Press 2001 | "Sweet Armageddon" © 1993, 2007 by John Shirley. *Air
Fish*, ed. Joy Oestreicher & Richard Singer, Catseye Books 1993

for Paula Guran...
a way to express gratitude...

CONTENTS

THE AUTHOR GNAWS HIS KNUCKLES:
A BRIEF FOREWORD

THE ASTUTE READER will notice that one of the stories in this book was co-written with Mr. Edgar Allan Poe. The author of numerous classic tales and poems, the inventor of detective fiction, and a great innovator of style, Mr. Poe died more than a hundred years ago—hence, the *particularly* astute reader will wonder how the author managed to collaborate with the gentleman. Some readers, having hit the bong or the bottle too often, will ask: Is the author far older than he appears? No. The author, unfortunately, is just as old as he appears. And despite appearances, that's not old enough to have known Mr. Poe. The truth is, a clever editor named Christopher Conlon took an untitled fragment of a story, an unfinished Poe manuscript, about a man perhaps going mad alone in a lighthouse. Conlon asked some modern writers, including me, to complete the story, each in his or her own way; the collected stories comprise an anthology called *Poe's Lighthouse*. Poe's unfinished story runs out after a few pages, concluding with: *The basis on which the structure rests seems to me to be chalk . . . . Jan 4.*

Everything before that, Poe wrote; everything after, in the story *Blind Eye*, I wrote. The anthology, a fascinating one, is available through Cemetery Dance Publications. I recommend it.

As for the rest of *Living Shadows*, there are old and new stories, here arrayed in two sections, complementary in tone. A few of these stories were taken from earlier collections of my stories because they fit the tone of *Living Shadows* and enhance its mood.

In the first section, the stories contain no element of the fantastic, though one or two may adumbrate the borderline paranormal, depending on your interpretation.

In the second section each story revolves around something that connects it to the realm of the supernatural, or the *slightly* futuristic, or the wildly surreal. I would deny, however, that they are genre stories of any kind—with the possible exception of *Buried in the Sky* which might be regarded as an example of "neo-Lovecraftian horror"—not, however, a generic one.

The last two stories of the first section are, in a way, subtly transitional to the second section; they ferry us across the river, into the fantastic. They are not fantasy *per se* but they contain elements—drawn from the subconscious, the hallucinatory, or perhaps some place beyond time and space similar to that of the Australian aboriginal Dreaming that resonates with the other-worldly. Hence their placement.

Some of the stories in this collection contain moments of over-the-top human intimacy; although nothing is dwelt on lingeringly, some of these moments may be distasteful to certain readers. But part of my purpose as a writer has always been to tell stories about people who don't normally get their stories told. We do not benefit literarily, nor increase our understanding of human nature, by omitting that which some may find offensive.

A few of the stories have been slightly updated, and edited. A couple of them were written long, long ago and showed my youth, overmuch in places, and that effect had to be muted. I could not have borne it otherwise. But they're all stories I feel are strong, meaningful, concisely effective, and they are all essentially the same stories they originally were.

For a time, I was skeptical, even dismissive, of the insights I had in youth. I have, however, come full circle, for the most part, and decided I was right after all.

J.S., December 2006

We flap, we flit, from one moment
to the next, like bats
driven and pursuing;
we're like hummingbirds
seen at dusk;
we're like moths silhouetted
against the moon:
we're living shadows.
The world of ideas casts
our tremulous shapes
onto this dusty stage.
We're here, we're not;
we suppose ourselves real;
a form failing to find light within
is only, is merely, is simply:
a living shadow.

*Verse by an unknown poet
written at an unknown time
translated by
an unknown translator*

1: A Few Blocks Down, Around the Corner

IN THE ROAD

1ST

CECILY'S MOM WAS in even more of a hurry than usual. She had to take Cecily to her tumbling class, and pick Eddy up at soccer, and then pick up Daddy at the airport. Daddy was always on his way to the airport or coming from it, and sometimes they had "time with him" at the airport itself, when he was there between flights. He was a Franchise Set Up Specialist; she didn't know what that was, except that it meant he had to crisscross the country, occasionally just passing through the town he lived in. But he was going to be here for Thanksgiving. He said he would play Monopoly with her on Thanksgiving.

Driving the Ford SUV down Burberry Street, Mom was spindling the little hook of auburn hair that followed the curve of her face and pointed at her chin, which was pointy also, and there was another hook of hair pointing from the other side of her face, so that was three points, Cecily decided; also the point of Mom's sharp nose: four. Mom's blue eyes, though, were soft and far away; they didn't exactly look at anything. Her gaze was passing over the Palo Alto cul de sacs and palm trees and spouting sprinklers on big green lawns, but never seemed to fix on anything.

Not quite thinking these things, Cecily was riding beside her mom, proud that she was old enough to do that now, it was legal and everything. "You have your creative crafts class on Sunday," Mom said. "Remind me of that so I don't forget to take you."

"'Kay." But Cecily resolved to forget to remind Mom, because she'd rather stay home and watch cartoons, and Yancy might come over and play Barbies.

"There's where my teacher said her sister lives," Cecily said, pointing at a side street. "She told me that when I told her where I lived."

"Huh yeah?"

Adults never seemed interested in things like that. But Cecily thought it was interesting.

There was something bloody in the road, up ahead. It was moving.

"Mom—oh!—what's that?"

Mom's sort of looked and her gaze flicked away. "A squirrel."

"It's sick. Can we help it?"

"What? No. It was hit by a car."

"So what, we could help it."

"It's not going to live, Cecily. It was hit by a car. It was in the road."

"It's still moving. It's trying to get out of the road. There was blood."

"It was in the road. Things get hit." She turned on the radio, the K-Lite station, which meant she didn't want to talk anymore.

Cecily looked out the back window but couldn't see the squirrel anymore; they'd gone around a curve and left it way behind.

2ND

NOT QUITE A year later, Cecily went to her friend Yancy's birthday party. Her older brother Eddy went too, sulking the whole time; he didn't want to go to his sister's girlfriend's party with a bunch of girls, but Mom needed him to walk Cecily home afterwards, because she had to go to her support group, and Dad was out of town.

At the party, Cecily felt let down. It was all sunny in the backyard and there was crepe twirling overhead and piñata candy and those little party bags full of cool junk to take home, and laughing girls, but Yancy was ignoring her. She hadn't said anything about the present Cecily had given her, she just opened it and went on to the next one, and now she was playing with Kathy and Moira, and hardly looked up when Cecily spoke. I'm supposed to be her best friend, Cecily thought.

She went wandering around the house looking for Eddy, to see when they were going home, and couldn't find him for a long time, then heard him yelling, "Whoa! Phat!" from upstairs in Yancy's house.

Yancy's half brother, a grown up guy named Vernon, was staying there, because he got kicked out of college and didn't have any place else to go—that's what Yancy said—and Eddy was upstairs in Vernon's room watching Vernon playing a computer game.

16

Vernon had long stringy brown hair and a goatee that was hard to see and skinny arms but a bulging middle. He wore a fading T-shirt that said *Id Software* on it, beginning to pop out holes along the seams. Eddy, who was thirteen, was perched on the edge of Vernon's bed; Vernon had let the sheets get rumpled onto the floor so there was just a bare mattress. Eddy sat leaning forward, staring over Vernon's shoulder, his buck teeth sticking out of his gaping mouth, twitching every time there was an explosion on the PC screen. For some reason, she thought of the squirrel in the road. She hadn't thought of it in almost a year.

"What do *you* want?" Eddy asked her, not looking away from the computer. He squeezed a pimple as he watched the game; he twitched.

"Just to see when we're leaving."

Eddy didn't answer her, instead saying to Vernon, "Whoa—you broke the skin."

"That's when it gets serious, dude," Vernon said, like he was sneering at Eddy. Then Vernon sucked some air through his clenched teeth, real hard and fast, like he was in pain.

She saw that he *was* in pain—there was a sort of clamp like a miniature bear trap with built-in metal teeth gripping his arm, and there was a wire running from the piston-driven jawlike device to the back of the computer. Whenever Vernon got shot in the game, the spikes clamped down and dug into his arm. Real spikes digging into his real arm. The toothy clamp looked like it was put together with duct tape and wires and little nails . . .

"The only way to play a killgame," Vernon was saying, "is on the hardest setting—ow, shit!—and with no saves, and with real pain. Then you're not full of shit . . . you're a real warrior . . . Shit, they got me . . ."

Her stomach lurched as she watched the toothy clamp convulsively bite down on his arm—with extra force when he was killed. It was like when Aunt Colleen's dog was shaking a dog-toy, growling and grinding it with its teeth. But it was his arm, not some toy, and it was grinding it up into hamburger, and blood was running down his arm, to drip off the elbow onto the rug.

"Whoa dude," Eddy said admiringly, as Vernon started the game over again. "You are serious."

Then Vernon's step-mom came in, and started yelling at him, so Eddy and Cecily went home.

Monday at school, Yancy made up with Cecily, and invited her over after school, and Mom said it was okay as long as she went to her jazz dance class before going to Yancy's, because Mom could pick her up at Yancy's on the way to the airport to get Dad.

Going from Yancy's bedroom, where they were dressing Barbies, to the bathroom, Cecily stopped in front of Vernon's partly open bedroom door—there was something she'd seen out of the corner of her eye that made her stop and look. It was the gun in Vernon's hand, one of those shiny silver revolvers. He was sitting on the edge of the bed, with his arm all bandaged up, twirling the revolver on his index finger. Hunched over the twirling gun, staring at it.

He stopped twirling the gun, and looked up, and scowled at her; reached out and slammed the door in her face.

That night, Cecily couldn't sleep. Her dad came into her bedroom to see her; he seemed relieved when she didn't want him to read to her. Him and Mom were having cocktails and watching the Spice Channel. She knew it was that because she heard the Spice Channel *oh-oh-oh* sounds when she went by the bedroom door. "Can't sleep, kiddo?" Dad asked, he was standing by her bed with his hands in his pockets, rocking on the balls of his feet.

"Dad?"

"What?"

"Yancy's big brother, Vernon, was playing with a gun today."

"Was he? What kind of gun?"

"A real gun."

"I don't think you'd know a real one from a toy gun. It could've been an air pistol. But then he's old enough to legally have a real gun, too. How was he playing with it?"

"Spinning it and looking at it."

"So? Guns aren't toys but . . ." He shrugged.

"He had this thing on his arm that chewed it up when he plays computer games. It was all bloody."

"I know about those—Eddy bought one from some kid and I took it away."

"Vernon's, like, sick or something. He's . . . I mean . . ."

She didn't know how to explain. She was sure of it, but didn't know how to say it so it sounded real.

"Forget it. He's a loser, that boy. Not our problem."

"What if . . . he's going to die."

Dad looked out the window; Cecily followed his gaze. The bushes moved in the wind, seemed to nod in agreement with Cecily.

"Well, Cecily—there's nothing we can do about it if he's going down. That's his mom and dad's problem."

"Can't you talk to them?"

"I don't know. We'll see."

But she knew that meant *no way*.

Dad didn't talk to Vernon's parents. Three months later, Vernon shot himself dead.

It was their problem, Dad had said. But they went to the funeral, and at the funeral she heard Vernon's parents say they didn't know the boy was that despondent, and Cecily heard her dad say, "Don't blame yourself, there's no way you could have known."

3RD

TWO DAYS BEFORE Cecily was to graduate from middle school, she heard that Harrison and the jock kids were planning something for Goop.

Goop was a seventh grader, whose dad had insisted his boy be allowed to play basketball in the intramural games. He was a whip-thin kid, with a long neck; his posture drooped, and his chin was weak, his eyes really big—"like an alien from *The X Files*," Harrison said—and he had a tendency to laugh at things no one else laughed at. Mr. Conners the English teacher said that Goop, whose real name was Christian Heinz, was "the very imp of unpopularity"; said it laughing and shaking his head. Mr Conners had once gotten in trouble with some lawyer for pulling several tufts of those soft little hairs from the arm of a seventh grader to punish him for talking back.

Goop had wanted to try intramural basketball, because he'd been practicing shooting baskets for hours, and they hadn't wanted to let him do it, especially because the Surfers were expecting to win the school trophy against the Shredders, and he would be in the Surfers basketball team because of which PE teacher he had. But Goop's dad insisted and insisted some more and the principal spoke to the PE teacher—so they let Goop play in Harrison's team: The Surfers. Only, shooting baskets alone is different than shooting them when someone is waving their hands in your face, and in the championship game Goop kept tensing up and missing when he got the ball. But he kept trying, just insisting on trying, when really he should've just hung back and been a guard and stayed out of the way. But "he was, all, trying to prove himself," Yancy said. And he just proved he was still the Goop.

Harrison's team lost the school trophy, and it was, anyway, just this stupid little four dollar fake-gold trophy, but Harrison took it really seriously.

So, as curious as anyone, Cecily was there, after school, standing in the very midst of a cool June late afternoon. She was waiting, with about thirty other kids, by the small wooden bridge over the creek behind the school; Cecily's big brother Eddy had even come over from the high school to see. The sun came and went and came again through the patchwork of clouds skimming across the sky, as Goop plodded obliviously up the path between the track and the football field, toward the little foot-bridge, carrying his books. He was staring at the ground, as he went, sagging like the books he was carrying had their weight multiplied by his misery.

He stopped and stared, just before the bridge, seeing Harrison leaning both forearms on one of the metal, concrete-filled yellow posts that blocked the bridge; the posts were to keep people from driving cars or motorcycles over it. Harrison was a tall kid with bright but empty blue eyes and skin that looked so smooth it was like doll-skin to Cecily—she was having trouble with acne then—and his cheeks were always more red than a boy's cheeks should be. But he was a tall, cute guy, who was good at sports, the hair on the side of his head cut into corn-row patterns, and everybody approved of him.

Goop put up a hand to hood his eyes so he could see against the glare; then the sun went behind the cloud and he saw all the kids waiting there, all watching him raptly, many of them grinning. He said,

"Okay, I'm stupid, okay." He turned to go back the other way—turned clumsily, in a hurry, so he dropped some of his books and the papers loosely piled in his binder and they went scattering all over the ground. Everyone laughed.

Goop bent over to pick them up.

Shaking his head in disbelief—as if he couldn't believe Goop would let himself be that vulnerable now—Harrison set himself athletically on his left foot, poised like a goalkicker, and slammed Goop hard in the tailbone with the point of his right Nike high-top, and the boy pitched forward onto his face, yelling in pain.

"You asshole," Harrison said. "You fucked everybody up."

Harrison grabbed Goop by the ankles and dragged him toward the bridge. Goop twisted this way and that like a fish on a hook. Harrison laughed.

Cecily got a twisty-tight feeling in her gut. She thought she saw Mr. Conners over by the bleachers, picking up some baseball equipment—he had been assistant coach besides teaching English—and she found herself walking over to him, after being careful the others weren't watching her. They weren't taking their eyes off Goop and Harrison.

She looked back when she was about halfway and saw that Harrison and two other kids, including her own brother, were kicking something in the grass by the bridge; the other kids starting to get looks of panic, backing away.

Mr. Conners was only about forty yards off. She was surprised he hadn't noticed anything going on. He was closing a duffelbag when she got there, and looked up, ran his fingers through his thinning, shoulder length brown hair; his crooked smile crooking a little more as he recognized her. "Cecily, isn't it?"

"Yeah. Um—I think Harrison's, all, beating up on Goop?"

"Goop? Oh—the Heinz kid? They fighting on school property?"

"I think it's off school land. It's by the creek. But they're not fighting . . ."

"Well if they're not fighting, what are we talking about?"

"Goop's not fighting. Just Harrison. I mean, he's hitting Goop."

Conners snorted. "I don't blame him a whole lot. The kid would go on shooting. Trying to show off, when he knew . . ."

"Yeah. I just . . . But . . . Harrison's, all, kicking him."

"Well, it's not on school property."

" 'Kay."

She turned, hesitating, drawn to see what was going on by the bridge—they seemed to be down at the creek now, she could just make out the tops of their heads over the grass, because they were all standing on the bank of little stream.

But she turned and walked the other way, to get the number thirty-four bus to the Tae Bo class she was taking with her mom.

It wasn't the slugging or the kicking, really, that did it, she found out, a few weeks later. A friend of Mom's was married to a doctor who'd worked on Goop at the hospital, after the incident at the bridge, and they found out from him: it was the lack of oxygen. Goop had fallen with his head in the water, face down, his body slanting up the bank; his weight holding his head down. He was dazed and weak and not able to get himself out of that odd position.

And the kids had left him there, assuming he'd get out. That's what Eddy said.

Goop didn't die, though. It was just brain damage.

He couldn't remember how to read and write, and he walked almost sideways, after that, and one of his eyes was blind. But it wasn't the hitting, so much as the oxygen loss and the brain cells dying. No one went to jail, but there was some kind of settlement, or something.

4ᵀᴴ

IN A THICKLY-HOT early August, when Cecily was fourteen-and-a-half, she was getting ready to go to her singing lesson, when the thing happened with the ice cream man. She was yelling at her mom, "Mom where's that Mariah Carey songbook? I need it for the lesson!" when her own shout was almost lost in the yelling from the street.

For a couple of minutes some part of her mind had noticed that the ice cream truck was in the street, or close by: she'd heard the amplified tinkling of the song the truck had played for years now as it cruised slowly through the neighborhood: "Yankee Doodle". Like a giant rolling music box, it played "Yankee Doodle" over and over and over and over, the end looping into the beginning. She'd often wondered how the guys who drove the grubby little white trucks with the stickers on them could stand the same sound going on and on and on for, what, nine hours a day. It would make you into a psychokiller, she thought. But maybe they didn't really hear it after a while.

It was annoying enough, anyway, just hearing it drive through the neighborhood, Mom had said once. You heard the song coming, and you heard the song going.

What Cecily had noticed, as she was looking through the pile of stuff on the little table in the front hall for the Mariah Carey songbook, was that the song had cut off suddenly. A moment later there was all the yelling.

She found the songbook on the floor, leaning up against a table leg, and yelled "Never mind!" at her mom, and went out to get the bus to her voice lesson, and then she saw all the people in the street gathered around the ice cream truck. It was really hot, and the air conditioners weren't working, because the electric company had shut down their neighborhood for a couple of hours—rolling intentional brownouts due to excessive electricity use in hot weather, it was called—and everyone was sweating and squinting; the heat rippled up from the asphalt.

She recognized Mr. Farmer, from across the street; the red-faced man who worked on classic cars from down at the dead-end; the two Italian sisters who lived together from the split-level on the corner; those four college aged-boys who liked to sit in their cars and listen to loud hip-hop in the driveway; Mr. Hinh, the Vietnamese man who owned the liquor store; that fat guy who collected old Harley David-sons; and two big blond men she didn't know. They were all in a circle around the little Pakistani guy who drove the ice cream truck up and down all day. And there was a seven-year-old girl with greasy black hair who looked delighted by all the adults yelling.

Cecily walked over to see what all the commotion was. Mr. Farmer was arguing with some of the others. "I just don't think you should hit him again—"

"I'll tell you what," the fat guy in the Harley T-shirt was saying, "this guy and his people have been warned again and again. The kid gives him two dollars for a dollar-fifty ice cream, he gives the kid the ice cream and fifty cents worth of junk candy instead of change—more like ten cents worth, he's *calling* fifty cents worth. It's stealing from children."

"And sometimes," the red-faced man chimed in, "he doesn't give any change of any kind. They know the kids won't say anything usually if they just keep the change."

"Sure," the taller, gray-haired Italian lady said. "They sell this horrible junk that makes sores in the mouth—they did this to my niece, candy that made her sick. And they lie about the change all the time—"

Cecily saw, then, that the little Pakistani guy was breathing hard, with a hand pressed to his nose; blood streamed through his fingers. Twice she saw him try to push through the circle of people to get to the truck—twice the men pushed him back against the sticker-covered side of the truck; against Dream Cream stickers and Frozen Three Musketeers Bar stickers and Sweet Tart stickers and Eskimo Pie stickers.

"Cocksucker is stealing from children!" the red-faced man shouted.

One of the Italian ladies escorted the little girl—who didn't want to leave—away from the truck. The girl went but kept looking back, grinning. She'd complained or something and it'd led to all this, Cecily guessed.

"My boss they tell me do this!" the Pakistani guy said, in a piping voice. "They tell me, my uncles, it is not my truck, they say no change, only candy! I don't steal but they tell me—!"

"These people are not honest!" Mr. Hinh said, "they deserve to be taught something!"

"It is not me—they make me do this! It is my only job!" the little man wailed.

"You see, it's a goddamn *policy* of ripping off kids!" the biker guy said. "Fuck you, pal, you didn't have to go along with it!" And he straight-armed the Pakistani guy against the side of the truck.

The Pakistani man gave a high-pitched cry of anger and fear and—the action almost spastic—kicked the biker in the crotch. The big man bellowed in pain and clutched at himself and the Pakistani tried to rush past him, but Mr. Hinh tripped the Pakistani and as he fell one of the college boys from down the street brought his knee up sharply into the falling man's throat, so that you could hear cartilage crunching, and he fell choking. The crowd backed away from him, and after a moment began to move off, shaking their heads; except the red-faced man and Mr. Hinh and the biker; they shouted at the little man, things like "You tell those people we don't want your thieving Paki ass in here anymore!" And the biker, as white-faced as the man next to him was flushed, kicked the Pakistani hard, once, in the side of the neck, and then turned and marched away. The others followed, muttering; shrugging. There was just Cecily about thirty feet away from the little man, who was spitting blood, coughing, gurgling.

Cecily didn't need to hear her mom shouting at her to get away from there. She knew what to do. She walked off, on her own, to the bus stop. She'd practiced the Mariah Carey song all week and she thought she had it down.

About ten minutes later, as the bus carried her around a corner, she looked back and glimpsed the man lying still in the middle of the road next to his truck. She was surprised to hear no ambulance coming.

Mr. Farmer had thought about calling it, he told her mom, but he'd heard you could end up having to pay for the cost of the ambulance if you called. Mom later said she thought that wasn't true, but she wasn't sure. Cecily heard, later, he choked to death on blood.

"Huh," Cecily said, when she heard that.

5TH

CECILY WAS DRIVING her small blond daughter Shelly to her first Kids Kreative Klass at the Montessori school, on a wet day in February, when Shelly pointed at the small white dog twitching in the road up ahead.

"Oh—I'm glad you saw that, hon," Cecily said. "I might not have seen it—"

As it was, she was able to drive around it with no trouble. It might've gotten on her tires.

"Couldn't we see what's wrong with it?" Shelly asked.

"No. Do you want your juice packet? You didn't have any juice for breakfast."

"Why not, why can't we?"

"Why can't we what?"

"See if the dog . . ."

". . . It's not our dog. It was in the road. It was just in the road. Do you want this juice or not?"

"'Kay."

They were on time for the class, but Shelly would've preferred to stay home and play videogames.

THE GUNSHOT

SHE PADDED BAREFOOT into his study, approaching him soundlessly from behind. He knew she was there, though he didn't look up from the video editor. Huysman hunched over his workbench as if to say, *Leave me alone.*

She placed her hand on his right shoulder, her fingers resting softly there and he reacted as if someone had dropped a lump of concrete on his back.

He whirled in his swivel chair, shaking. "Don't do that when I'm working!" She shrank back. He sputtered, "I'm—Jeez, I'm trying . . ." His voice trailed off. He stared, his face blank except for a shadow of horror around the edges. He stared into the middle distance. He was looking at her . . . no, he was looking *through* her.

She was a tall woman, but oncoming middle-age showed in her round-shouldered stoop. Her right hand was raised and trembling. In her left hand, there was a prescription bottle. She hoped he'd ask her why she was taking the pills again. Her doctor had ordered her to rehab from tranquilizers. She was hoping he'd get angry over the pills. Shout at her. Berate her. Notice her now. He only watched the circles under her large brown eyes coursing with tears that ran down to trace the faint face-lifting seam along the underside of her jaw. She burst out, "You're faking all this shit to get away from me . . . just another excuse . . . you haven't spoken to me in three days except for 'Gotta run, babe. Fall season hanging over my head, doll.' You insular son of a bitch."

Huysman had slipped from his chair and was kneeling, eyes wide, murmuring wordlessly, his gaze fixed at something unseen, his hands crossed over his belly, clutching himself like a wounded man trying to hold his entrails in place.

She looked over his head at the editing machine. One of his TV-movies was playing. "Looks like the end of the picture, Reggie," she

27

said. "Judging by the spouting blood, the bodies . . . Ah, right, there's
the triumphant master criminal standing over the millions of dead
cops he's wasted. Christ, no wonder this stuff's banned from the
airwaves—ought to ban it from cable, too." She didn't really think so.
She was trying to get a rise from him. He seemed not to hear her. She
continued, "There, now the triumphant master criminal walks off with
the girls . . . The End. A Reggie Huysman Production."

He blinked and looked up at her, seeming to see now.
"Sandy . . . the . . ."

"Yes?"

"The gunshot . . ."

THE RAISED BLACK lettering on the door said: Imaginaction
Productions—R.G. Huysman, President.

Straker studied the sign on the door. It was a little pretentious,
almost defensive—as if Huysman were saying, *ImaginAction is a
respectable business.*

Maybe Huysman was not as unaffected by the criticism as he
pretended.

Straker opened the door and entered the office. A petite brunette
secretary sat behind a translucent desk, keyboarding on an off-brand
'processor. Her fingers paused like a small animal awaiting an order as
she smiled. "Mr. Straker?"

"Uh-huh?" He smiled only as much as was needed.

"Mr. Huysman is expecting you. Please go right in."

"Thank you." He moved toward the door behind her, then hesitated.
He was close enough to her to smell her strawberry perfume when she
turned. "Mr. Straker?"

"Yes?"

"Your organization . . . it's called Intimate Investigative Therapies—
Inc.?"

"Yes."

"Um, what *is* that? Intimate investigative, um, therapy, I mean."

"Psychological detective work. We go into people's lives to see what's
bothering them. Our theory is you have to get involved with someone's

life to really have empathy, to really help them. You seem more than just curious. Do you need help with—?"

"No, no!" She glanced toward Huysman's private office. "I'm worried about Reg—Mr. Huysman." She smiled sheepishly. "I guess I take a kind of maternal interest in his feelings. He hasn't been happy. I just hope you can help him. He's tried everything."

"What have you noticed that makes—"

Just then the frosted-glass door to the inner office opened. Straker recognized Huysman instantly. He was a big man, a head taller than Straker. His weight lifter's build had begun to go soft in the middle, and the skin around his neck was starting to sag. His complexion was ruddy—until recently, most of his spare time had been spent outdoors, rock climbing, surfing, lifting weights in his vast, park-like backyard. He wore army fatigues, a khaki shirt and army boots. His blue eyes flashed as he looked down at Straker.

Straker—short and narrow and dark, his face softly Slavic—was Huysman's physical opposite. And there was another contrast: Huysman was afraid of something; his insecurity showed through his bluff expression and his bullish stance as he silently, somehow defiantly, took stock of the visitor. For his part, Straker seemed poised, confident and loose.

Huysman made a brusque gesture, and Straker followed him into the inner office.

Beneath a polarized picture window there was a mahogany desk with a polished leather inset; large easy chairs faced it on either side. There were a few books, some photos of Huysman with various vidstars and a fireplace that had never been used. This was an office for receiving people; it was too pristine for real work. A small video-replay machine was set up next to a low leather couch; Straker had requested it.

Straker sat silently on the couch. Huysman sat stiffly on the edge of his desk, facing Straker but not looking at him.

Straker took a palm-sized videocassette from the inside jacket pocket of his three-piece suit. The suit was thirties revival, pinstriped in black and charcoal-something. Fred Astaire might have worn on a date with Ginger Rogers.

Straker slid the tape into the player and watched the small rectangular screen rez up. He scanned the first page of a file report on Reginald Granger Huysman; his posture was relaxed, friendly without being presumptuously languid. "Now, as I understand it," Straker said gently, "you're suffering from hallucinations, yes?"

Huysman frowned, flicked his hands as if dispensing with nonsense. "Hardly. Not hallucinations. Hallucinations are qualitatively different. As different as a snapshot's different from a TV image. This . . . I've toyed with drugs, and I've had my share of hallucinations. This is something unique in my experience . . . Uh, you are Straker?"

"I am." Straker smiled almost meekly.

"Well, these . . . I think of them as visions. Or . . . they're just not like anything else. Unique."

"Everyone likes to feel unique."

"So, okay, maybe it isn't unique—because it's like a dream. It's hypnagogic, I think. Or eidetic. Pictures. I see it clearest with my eyes closed. It's like a waking dream. But more solid than a hallucination. It's—" he almost smiled "—it's cinematic."

"And this is something you want to be totally rid of?"

Huysman hesitated. Probably, Straker reflected, he disliked admitting his fear of it—or of anything. "Obviously," he said finally, defensively.

"Can you call it up whenever you like?"

"Not exactly. But it's predictable. It comes when I think about certain things. Sometimes it comes on its own. I wish it *would* come at night. But it doesn't. Only when I'm awake, so far."

"So you think about certain things and that brings it on?"

"Not quite so cut-and-dried as that. It's usually a sequence of . . . well . . . "

"Tell me, please. Go through the series of associations that bring on this, uh, vision. If the vision occurs, describe it to me."

Huysman began to speak. As he did, Straker entered notations on the videoplayer's keyboard; the transcript would be added to Huysman's file.

"Almost involuntarily, I'll start remembering the women in my life. Like Jenny Quinlan—that was twenty years ago in Vegas. I was directing a series of variety shows for NBC then. She was a dancer in the show. I was twenty-three. The golden boy of television. The prodigious wonder. Everybody wanted to hire me." Huysman's tone was bitter. He seemed to have forgotten his mistrust of Straker. He closed his eyes and continued. "At first, Jenny and I were mutually infatuated. She'd fallen for me badly, but I tired of her in a month. I led her on with talk of marriage, then I dumped her—left for Europe and said I'd be in touch, but never was. She wrote me twelve letters. I didn't answer a single one. Hurt her terribly. The next year, there was a scriptwriter, Lola Cassavetes. I led her on. We played. I dumped her. There were two more. When I finally recognized it, the pattern disgusted me, so—I married Sandy. We're still married. Eleven years. And I did it to prove a point, not because I loved her. Not because . . . shit . . ."

Not because . . . shit . . . appeared on the small screen and was transferred onto the cassette.

Huysman continued. "Sandy soaks up love like a sponge. She needs affection, she needs someone to play the husband role backward and forward. I played it for eight years. And then I couldn't stand it anymore . . . I feel strangled, oppressed, but I can't divorce her. The company is in her name, and she'll never agree to sell out to me. She'll drain me for alimony; ruin me somehow. Hell, I got into producing cable-drama by marrying her—her father owns the largest cable operation in the US.

"So I'm thinking about Jenny and Lola and Elaine and Gemini and Sandi and then the thing hits me. Listen, have you ever been walking over a bridge and, for no reason, you get an urge to jump? Or look over the balcony rail of a high building and get an impulse to just vault it? I don't mean a suicidal urge out of depression. What I'm talking about happens to the happiest people. It's a fleeting urge. A momentary impulse. Maybe it's why people go to see horror movies. You sort of . . . *revel* in an attack on yourself for no other reason but pure goddamn perversity. Well, this waking dream of mine feels like that . . .

"I'll be directing something when, suddenly, the world around me vanishes. In its place, I'm in a little room—the room's fuzzy, but I sense concrete walls and metal rafters overhead. There's a kind of tension in the air, like someone is blowing a dog whistle in my ear. I'm walking along one of the walls, in profile against it, and a sort of shadow falls over me. I turn around, my back to the wall, and everything goes slo-mo . . . like one of my cable-dramas when we slow things up, unnaturally slow, to emphasize the action, enhance the purity of the violence. When I turn to face the source of this shadow, I see a gun in someone's hand. I can't see who it is because there's a flash from the gun. It's a big pistol, a .357 Magnum. There's a roar . . . but by the time I hear the boom of the gun going off, I'm already bouncing off the wall, my guts opening up under the impact of the slug. The force of the shot slams me up against the wall and I bounce off. Looking down, I see my body exploding outward at the middle—a spray of red and a glimpse of entrails. Those Magnums, they practically cut you in half with one shot. I'm not feeling any pain yet, and I'm starting to fall forward, clutching at my middle when—*flash*—the gun goes off again. The gunman is only six feet from me—*flash*—three times, *wham, wham, wham*. I'm banged against the wall three more times. I can feel the chips of concrete from the wall behind me flying off as the bullets go right through me and smash into it. And here's the part that scares me, Straker . . . "

Huysman paused to glance at Straker; he seemed disappointed that this narrative had had little observable effect. He continued. "What gets to me, thinking about it afterward, is that—*I get off on it* when the bullets blow through me.

"And you know something else, Straker—the whole damn dream, if that's what it is, is directed. Cinematically, teleplay style. I see the thing from different angles: closeups, reversals, zooms, cutaways; all nicely edited to give a total picture of the action—except that the gunman is blanked. That gave Tolliver a big jolt. He said—"

"Tolliver?" Straker interrupted. "Who is Tolliver?"

"A psychoanalyst. He tried to help. Got nowhere. He tried the repressed-fag angle first. You know, sublimation of a desire to be penetrated. Then he started playing up my directing the bloodiest teleplays in the business. He said that the fact that I write the action scenes myself is the source of the whole thing. Claims I feel guilty because so-called TV-violence contributes to juvie crime, blah, blah, blah. But, hey, I've been insisting for years that I only give the public what it wants, and I've made the violent scenario a great art form. I still insist that's true. I *believe* it."

Straker politely said nothing.

"Tolliver," Huysman went on, "is full of shit. What do you think?"

Straker shrugged. "I'm not sure yet. I have to spend more time with you. Maybe when I watch you at home—"

"At home—?"

"Didn't you read the orientation materials? That's how I do it. I move in with you. It's the only way to get to the heart of things. You won't notice me after a while. You've paid for the treatment already, Mr. Huysman. It's expensive and we don't give refunds." Straker smiled apologetically.

"I don't like it. It's bad enough with Sandra . . . but, well . . . okay. This thing is interfering with my work. It's got to stop. It's even creeping into the shows."

Huysman was shaken. He went to a wall cabinet, opened it, and pressed a toggle. A wall slot dispensed a neat whiskey in a plastic shot glass. Sipping, his back to Straker, Huysman said, "Take your file cassette out and press the red button. it's cued."

Straker recognized the footage; he'd forbidden his daughter to watch it the night before. It was called *The Cop Hunters* . . . .Three black sedans following a police car. The sedans pursue it in a ten-minute chase through a warehouse district and into the suburbs. They corner him in a deserted housing project. The patrol car overturns. Cop gets out, bruised but whole, and runs. The six men in the sedans leave their cars and take up the chase on foot. They trap the cop in a half-finished, roofless garage. They close in on him, he tries to run, they push him back, he falls, they laugh, he gets to his feet, reaches for his gun . . . someone shoots him in the stomach with a .357 Magnum from about eight feet away. The details are grisly, in vivid color . . . gut exploding under the impact of the high-caliber slug, an out-splash of red, the cop bounces from the wall, begins to fall forward, three more shots throw him back, each bullet's impact shown in immaculately complete detail. Straker had to look away. But not before he'd seen the parallels.

Huysman stood beside Straker, impassively watching the choreographed butchery on the screen. "People who don't know any better say my shows are all more or less alike. But no two gunshot scenes are the same. And when we show someone getting their head hammered in with a two-by-four, we do that distinctively. No two are quite alike, though there are a lot of similarities. And I can tell you that this one is almost exactly like my dream—if it is a dream—but it was made after I started having the visions."

"How long have you been seeing this scene in your head?"

"Oh . . . three months. It's gotten more intense lately. Worse and worse. It's already happened four times today. Once at home, once in the studio cafeteria, twice in the office . . . "

"If it happens again while I'm with you, try to tell me. Try to describe it as it happens."

"You'll know when it happens. I'll be staring into space like I'm being goosed by a ghost. Shocked look, frozen. But I can't talk during it—Hey, I gotta go to the studio."

"I'll come along."

Huysman scowled, then sighed and said, "Yeah, OK . . . but stay out of the way."

"That's my policy," Straker said quietly.

"C'MONNNN!" HUYSMAN ROARED. "Get it set up! I want the tail end of that Harley pointed at the goddamn moon!"

Standing well out of the way, Straker watched as Huysman's burly assistants jammed a huge motorcycle into the windshield of a semi-truck that, moments before, they'd crashed into the base of a cliff. The dust was still settling, and a few grenade-sized rocks were tumbling from the cliff above, bouncing off the hood of the semi, narrowly missing the crews of cameramen, sound men, lighting men. The late-afternoon sun, distended like a hunger-bloated belly in the silt-thick Los Angeles smog, threw a bloodied light on the derricks, hoists and camera machinery crowded over the truck.

"Gedduh close-zup of the hand on the hood of the semi! Get the angle seddup—here lemme see that—" Huysman shoved the befuddled cameraman aside, climbing onto the metal platform to look through the eyepiece at the dummy hand, severed at the wrist, lying in a pool of blood on the hood. "Get some more broken glass around that hand—hey, get the fuck outta the way, Henry, you're throwin' a fuckin' shadow on the *hand!* And you—huh? All right, what you want, kid?"

A message boy from the studio stood nervously to one side, squinting up at Huysman. "It's Mr. Drummond, Mr. Huysman. He can't make it to the afternoon shooting." The cast and crew fell silent, watching Huysman expectantly, waiting for him to boil over in fury. Drummond was the star, but he'd missed three shootings that week. Because of Drummond, they were behind schedule.

"So Drummond isn't coming today..." Huysman said softly, dangerously.

Straker watched Huysman—expecting something other than an outburst of anger. He waited for Huysman to lapse into his "goosed by a ghost" look; this was a moment of great stress for Huysman. If the vision was a breakdown under stress, as Straker supposed, it should come now.

It didn't. Instead, Huysman shouted, "Aw right, we put up with it once more and then we find a replacement and start shooting from the beginning and he can eat his contract! Get the double in here!" The noise and bustle resumed.

Straker watched Huysman, revising his theory.

Two hours later, during a break in the shooting, Huysman and Straker sat together at a table in the studio cafeteria. Huysman drank coffee, Straker mineral water. Straker watched Huysman without seeming to. Relaxed, faintly smiling but never supercilious, Straker put Huysman at his ease.

Huysman stared moodily into the tarry depths of his cup and said, "I dunno. Straker, if she'd leave me alone a few days a week, I think I could stand to spend some time with her." He swallowed, shrugged.

"How much time," Straker asked breezily, "would you spend with your secretary?"

Huysman looked up at him, "Dana? How'd you get onto that?"

"I read it in her face this morning."

Huysman nodded distantly. "Sure, OK, but keep it under your hat, all right?"

Straker smiled as if to say, *How could you doubt it?*

"Dana treats me right, Straker. She doesn't beg me for more time. She doesn't go out with other people just to try to put me in my place. If she does mess around, she doesn't let me know about it, anyway, and that's close enough to fidelity for me. She's a good woman. She doesn't try to use her influence with me to get parts. She doesn't want parts. I'd love her for that alone."

"Do you love her?"

Huysman frowned. "Well . . ."

A shadow fell over the table. Straker looked up to see Sandra Huysman—he recognized her from photos in Huysman's file—standing just back of her husband.

"Going to tell him about Dana, Reggie?" She attempted to make her tone icy, but it overflowed with hot currents of hurt.

Huysman sat frozen, staring at his cup, his face empty.

"Mind if I sit, witch doctor?" she asked, glancing at Straker.

"Please do," Straker replied tonelessly.

"Sure, I know about her," Sandra murmured, puffing smoke at Huysman's down-turned face. "No big deal. Just like you, Reggie." She adjusted the lapels of her dark suit. Her face was clownish with too much makeup; her blonde wig set at an unconvincing angle.

"Stop trying to get me angry with you, Sandy," Huysman said wearily.

Sandra's blasé veneer cracked. Her eyes brimmed with tears.

Huysman looked at her. Then beyond her. His mouth opened, his eyes widened. He fell backward out of his chair and began writhing on the floor, his hands clutched at his belly, and he whimpered.

Faces turned to watch, but no one got up to help. Word of Huysman's "fits" had gone round the studio.

Sandra stood over him, shouting, "It's not gonna work, you bastard! Stop acting like an infant! You—" She lost her voice to sobs, and threw his coffee cup at him. The dark liquid splashed over his middle like a bloodstain.

THE GUNSHOT
• • •

HUYSMAN STOOD IN a place that was dark except for one harshly bright light in the center of a metal-raftered ceiling. He leaned against a concrete wall. He closed his eyes. Make it gone, he prayed. Eyes closed, eyes opened—it made no difference.

He turned to face the figure silhouetted by the glare of the bulb. He looked down to see the gun in the soft white hand . . . a big nickel-plated .357 Magnum.

SANDRA HUNCHED OVER Huysman, whispering in his ear, as the crowd gathered around them, arguing about what to do. "Should we call an ambulance?" Someone said. "Maybe this time it's his heart—"

"No, I'm a doctor," Straker lied. "I'll take care of him." He knelt down to hear what Sandra Huysman was saying. "I know who it is, shooting you in your dream, Reggie," she murmured. "It's me. I'm gonna kill you."

THE HAND HOLDING the gun came into sharper focus this time.

He could see a wedding ring on one of the fingers below the trigger guard, a ring he'd bought and paid for eleven years before.

"Sandy . . ." he whispered. "The gunsh—"

He was slammed against the concrete wall, pitched forward, smashed back by another bullet, and another, another . . . his whole being exploding outward from the middle, broken open, splashed . . . and this time he felt the pain coming, bearing down on him like an express train.

"I SEE IT DIFFERENTLY now, Straker," Huysman said thickly, trying to sit up in the bed. "It's a premonition—that's what it is."

"I doubt it, Huysman. I confess to being a little worried, though. I think your wife would like you to think it's a premonition. She knows you're vulnerable now."

Huysman rubbed his forehead. "Gotta bastarduva headache. Get me get me, uh, beta-endorphin. It's in the medicine cabinet. Down the hall to the right."

Straker stood and nodded. "OK. But listen—maybe we should get you into a hospital, after all. I'm not so sure your doctor did you a favor, having you brought here. He's right—it's nervous collapse, not a stroke or something. But I think you should be in the hospital—and I don't mean an asylum—for observation."

"What the fuck for?"

"Because, my friend, I'm afraid you're going to hurt yourself. The timing and sequence of your visions make it clear to me. You see, you've got a festering guilt complex over the women you've hurt. All of them. And to make it worse, you're making your wife miserable by ignoring her, even now. She's still fixated on you, no matter what she says. You sense that. You sense you've hurt her. You're punishing yourself with this vivid vision of your own assassination. What's more, your guilt over your lovers is linked to another festering complex about TV-violence. No one can be accused as often as you have been and remain totally untouched by it. The two complexes simply reinforce one another. You've directed your own waking nightmare. We can wean you from it by bringing you to a gradual confrontation with your guilt feelings— Huysman, are you listening?" For the first time, Straker's manner was forceful, commanding.

Huysman flinched. He sat in his underclothes, the bedspread thrown back, his head in his hands, shoulders shaking. "I dunno," he said weakly. "I can't think now. My head hurts too much. I dunno what you're talking about, Straker. She's going to kill me. It's a premonition—"

"Huysman, listen to me. A great many physical diseases are caused by a kind of psychic urge to self-destruct. A cellular despair. Cancer, particularly, shows up more in emotionally disturbed people than anyone else. And there's a malady called cynophobia, which produces the symptoms of rabies up to a certain point and is caused by the fear that you're going to have rabies. The victim becomes very sick, even dies, because of his pathological fear of rabies, though he doesn't really have it all. Your body responds to your mind that thoroughly. Hypnotists make their subjects stop and start bleeding from a small cut when trance—"

"For God's *sake,* get my pain pills!"

"All right. But you've got to stop believing this assassination scene of yours is real or, somehow—maybe a tumor, maybe a stroke—you'll live out a self-fulfilling prophecy and make yourself sick from it."

Straker left the bedroom, hurried down the hall to the bathroom, fumbled through the medicine cabinet. "Why am I hurrying?" he thought. "Why am I so afraid to leave Huysman alone?" He found the bottle marked BETA-ENDORPHIN, and hurried back to the bedroom. It was empty.

The covers were thrown back, the sheets still warm. Still clutching the bottle. Straker moved to the hallway and called uncertainly, "Huysman?"

He heard a sound from the direction of the garage.

It was empty except for a set of rusty barbells, a gasoline can, a workbench holding a few power drills that were collecting dust—and Mr. and Mrs. Huysman.

"That's right," Sandra was saying, "up against the wall, motherfucker. Now turn around to face me . . ."

Shaking, white, mouth hanging slack, Huysman obeyed her.

She wore the same dark suit. In her right hand was a large, nickel-plated .357 Magnum revolver.

The only illumination came from a single bright, white light bulb in the center of the garage, just behind her head.

She raised the gun. "Now you'll *feel* the bullets, Reggie," she said, almost lovingly.

Straker started toward her, opening his mouth to shout at Huysman.

She pulled the trigger. Huysman screamed. She squeezed the trigger three times more, and he collapsed in a welter of blood.

The blood from his burst stomach splashed Mrs. Huysman's pants. She stood with the gun hanging in her limp right hand beside her thigh and stared numbly down on him, an enigmatic smile flickering across her lips.

Straker took the gun from her hand. He was shaking himself. *So shaken up, I didn't hear the shots?* He looked at Huysman.

Huysman was quite dead, sprawled on the dusty floor with his head propped against the concrete wail. His eyes were open, locked on the spot where the gun had been when she'd pulled the trigger. His abdomen had been ripped open. From the inside.

Straker opened the gun. Nothing . . . no cartridges, no shells.

Empty.

THE SEWING ROOM

———

"We only have one computer hooked up to the Internet," Judith said. "We couldn't have two lines."

"This is . . . 2019 Coolidge? Roy Breedlaw lives here?" The man from the Internet cable company, looking closer at his clipboard, was a chunky Hispanic guy with a round, pleasant face and a mustache that made her think of her father—who'd been dead forty years. His soft voice made her think of Dad too, especially because it was March. Dad had died in the frozen lake, back in Minnesota, one unseasonably cold March.

"Yes, that's the right address, Roy's my husband—but we don't have a cable line for the attic."

"Says here you do. Anyway I can see the cable there. You see it, there, ma'am?"

She covered her eyes against the drizzle and squinted up at the eaves over the driveway. "Oh gosh . . . You sure that's what that is? Maybe it's the other line, that just passes through there."

"No ma'am, that one's over there, you see?"

"Oh." So Roy had installed an extra line without telling her. This man must think she was clueless. It made her stomach clutch up to think about it. "And you need to go up into the attic?"

"Yes ma'am. The box's got some kind of short in it. Probably water leaking in. Your husband asked to meet me here, on Monday, but you know how hard it can be for us with the timing. We missed him, so I came back today."

"Yes, yes I . . ." Monday, she thought, when she wouldn't be home. She was working three days a week now at Ronald Reagan Elementary. Mrs. Ramirez had physical therapy three days a week for the rest of the term. Roy knew she was gone on Mondays. He didn't want her to know about the cable in the attic. He didn't like people up there. "I'll get you a ladder, it's the only way to get up there. You have to climb up from the outside."

41

"From outside of the garage? That's unusual."

"I . . . He took the original indoor ladder out, to keep the kids out. He was afraid they'd get into trouble there." As she said it, she was conscious of how peculiar it sounded. She decided not to tell him about how Roy had rebuilt the attic just to house his model shop. Most men would have simply done the work on a bench in their garage—which was meticulous, uncluttered, with plenty of room to work.

"Not a problem, ma'am, I have a ladder, but thank you."

"Oh wait—it's locked. I do have a key . . . ." Should she give it to him? Roy said to unlock it only if there was smoke coming out, a fire of some kind. Otherwise no one was to go in. But there was a short, which could cause a fire. That's what she would tell Roy, anyway, when he asked why she'd given the man the key.

She took the key ring from the pocket of her housedress, twisted the padlock key off, and gave it to him. He took an extending ladder from his truck, leaned it against the house and climbed to the little door over the deck, in back, that led into the attic room over the garage.

Judith waited at the front porch, watching the cat melting in and out of the geraniums, imagining what it would be like to be married to this Internet cable man. He probably liked to barbecue with the family, take little camping trips. It'd be nice.

She kind of wished the weather would just get on with it and rain. But it didn't rain that much, after February, this side of San Francisco Bay. She started to pull weeds from the garden, almost haphazardly, wondering why it bothered her so much to give someone permission to go in Roy's attic. It was ludicrous, really.

The Internet cable man was smiling when he came back out front, chuckling about all the models that Roy kept up there. "Someone sure can craft models. Airplanes and every sort of thing." He handed her back the key.

"Yep, my husband doesn't care, just as long as it's a good model." She'd actually seen only a few of them. Sometimes he brought one down when he was finished, to show, for a few seconds. No one was allowed to touch it, though.

The cable man tilted his ladder and collapsed it down so he could carry it to the truck. "I guess the kids have a good time with that too," he said, easily taking the ladder under his arm.

Almost immediately she said, "Oh sure, they have a good time with that."

She didn't want to tell this stranger that Roy wouldn't let the kids up there, didn't ever put models together with them.

Brandon would have liked the models, but Roy wouldn't let him near them. *For heaven's sake, Judith, the kid's autistic, he'd only destroy them.* Cherie had never seemed interested in doing things with Roy. It was enough if Cherie's step-dad came to her performance at the high school talent show, and only because she wanted two parents there. Of course, she'd have preferred her real father, Barry. But after Judith had divorced Barry he'd moved to Los Angeles to be with the woman he'd had the affair with. They didn't see him much. Roy didn't like him coming around.

Judith waved as the cable man went to his van. She watched him drive away and then she went to get the ladder Roy used.

"MRS. BREEDLAW?"

"Hm?"

"Paper or plastic."

"Oh—paper . . . Um, no—plastic. Plastic's fine." Judith had noticed a flicker of irritation on the bagger's face when she said *paper,* because they already had the plastic bag laid out in a little metal frame, and it was easier for them. So she went with plastic, though she preferred paper bags. Maybe I should just up and say "paper" and the heck with him, she thought. Joe Gorris, at the school, said she wasn't assertive enough, especially with her students. He claimed she "let them run roughshod" over her in class. She knew she tended to be that way.

She looked to see if Brandon was still staring at the small, shiny toys in the gumball machine, things he'd have swallowed and choked on just a few years ago when he was going through his swallowing phase. He was still there, his lips moving silently. A small black girl in corn-rows and a Sponge Bob T-shirt came to stand near him, admiring the

HomiePals dolls in the machine: wizened little hip-hop figures on shiny keychains. The girl turned to stare at Brandon, maybe puzzled because he was a tall thirteen, too old to be enchanted by the machine. It was one of his autistic things—he didn't do it so much as he used to, though.

"Brandon, let's go!" she called, pushing the cart up near him, on the way to the door.

He didn't acknowledge her directly, of course, but he turned to go toward the door with her, and they walked side by side without speaking. He didn't ask for shiny things from gumball machines any more. The shiny things he looked at now were on MTV: Christina Aguilera especially. It kind of broke Judith's heart to see it. Even if Brandon had a girl, not just a pretty girl like that but any girl, he'd probably be afraid to let her touch him.

Brandon was getting better, she reminded herself. He was more in control of himself. He didn't do that spinning around anymore; he answered questions, most of the time. Brandon's progress was something good to hold onto. The therapist she'd gone to for herself, before Roy had decided it was too expensive, had said she should look at the positive things going on in her life, to break up that depression spiral. She didn't get depressed much anyway, now, with the Prozac. It was a low dose, but it worked well enough.

She and Brandon went out to the Explorer. It was still misting outside. About halfway through loading the groceries, Brandon started to help her.

The wind was rising, she noticed. She hadn't gotten the palm trees clipped and they'd be throwing their old branches at the house again. *Fronds,* they're called, she reminded herself. But they were five and six feet long, with a piece of wood on the end, when they dropped off, more like branches to her.

She hoped Roy wasn't home when she got there, though she wasn't sure why she hoped for it.

JUDITH KEPT A damp cloth in the freezer for her hot flashes, and she was pressing that to her head when Roy came in the front door. She could tell by the abruptness of the door opening and closing that it was him, and not Cherie. She put the washcloth back. When Roy saw her treating her menopause symptoms in any way, he acted as if she were trying to prod him into some outburst of sympathy. "I don't want to hear about it," he'd say. "If you need to go to a doctor, go, but all women dry up that way . . ." That last remark had been a stunning new level of insensitivity, even for Roy.

Now he came into the kitchen, frowning. "Has someone been up in the attic?"

How had he known, already? she wondered, drifting out to the living room. It was a bigger room—she didn't like being with him in so small a room as the kitchen. She was glad of the menopause, in a way, because before the change she'd felt more like being in bed with a man; someone, but not with Roy, and now she didn't much feel like sex with anyone at all. Roy hadn't asked for a long time, and it was just as well. She didn't know if she could stand another of those sessions where he rubbed himself on her till he got excited, squeezing his eyes tight shut so she could tell he was picturing something else, and then pumping her like an oil-derrick. He'd made her feel like there was something wrong with her, when she'd tried to talk about their sex life. She had shrugged and accepted him that way—she hadn't married him for sex, anyway. And she couldn't go through another divorce.

"The cable man said there might be a short there or something, so I gave him the key," she said, sounding as reasonable as she could. "You were going to have him up there anyway, on Monday."

She could tell by the way her husband was moving around the room, almost running as he went from object to object—flattening wrinkles on doilies, wiping dust from the tops of picture frames—that he was going to start shouting. She noticed that he'd changed the part in his hair again, switched it to the other side. Every so often he shifted the part, and when he parted his stiff brown hair on the right side of his head it looked all wrong, somehow. His eyebrows were too light for his hair and it was always difficult to see what color his eyes were, because of his heavy lids; you had to really look close to see they were greenish brown. When they met he'd looked slightly odd and the oddity had grown over the years, till it was as if his face were put together from parts of the faces of three men. He'd grown into his penchant for khaki pants and those golf shirts with the little alligators over the breast, too. He even wore that outfit to church.

He never missed church, though he'd given up the choir. He had a nice singing voice, a pure alto. It seemed more than fifteen years since they'd met in the choir. He'd come over to practice parts, and she'd play piano, and they'd sing. They started doing show tunes, and then he'd asked her out. He'd had a sense of humor, in those days.

He'd sold the piano, four years ago, to help pay for suing a man who'd sideswiped his car. He'd stopped singing in the choir about the same time.

"You were told: *no one goes up there unless there's a fire,*" Roy was saying, adjusting the shade on a lamp.

"I was afraid there could be a fire, because he said there might be a short." Change the subject, she thought. "We got calls from some attorney's office asking when we're going to make a payment on his legal bill? I didn't even know you'd sued another person else till she said—"

"Have those kids been moving things around in here?" he asked suddenly, the volume of his voice elevating two notches. His eyes darted to the ceiling, in the direction of the garage. "That chair wasn't so close to the wall." He moved it six inches toward the center of the room.

By "those kids" he meant Brandon, chiefly. Cherie generally managed to not be home when Roy was there.

"No, Roy, the kids have hardly been here. Now please—how are we going to pay for this lawsuit? We can't pay for it by winning it, they told me you've basically already lost it. I mean, did we have to . . . ?"

"The man was letting his bushes grow over our fence, and it was dropping seeds all over our land, and sending up shoots, and the roots from them damaged our pipes!"

"It just doesn't seem like . . . like a priority thing, Roy—"

"Are you telling me what's important in my life?" he demanded, turning to her, commencing the brittle monotone shouting that she'd known was coming.

When her first husband, Barry, had shouted at her, he looked right at her and it'd felt kind of good, because she'd known he was just letting off steam and afterward they'd make up and even make love. When they were signing the divorce papers, he'd said he was sorry he'd ever yelled at her. Funny time to say it.

Roy's yelling was so much worse. He shouted at her but never looked at her as he did it.

"I have to ask, Roy, because we don't want to have to move again."

"I'm getting a settlement, is that what you want to hear? Well I am, a settlement from the county on that other suit, and you're driving my blood pressure up, you're trying to kill me!"

She instinctively reached to pat his arm because the high blood pressure remark made her want to help him calm down, but he pulled away, shouting at her to keep the kids away from his things.

She decided she had to talk about the other Internet line. "You didn't tell me we had another computer in the house. A second line."

"What is it, because your last husband had an affair, you're putting that on me? Did ol' Barry meet his slut on the Internet? That's not me. I am not him. Okay? I am researching things, the law, things like that. That's what I need it for. I want to be able to do that research undisturbed. I told you about the line—you just weren't listening. I have to research this, it's complicated as all hell . . ."

He lectured her about the newest court case for a while, and how he wasn't going to let people damage his property. Judith was relieved when he finally went up to his attic.

He could claim she hadn't heard him, but he'd never told her about the extra Internet line. She was sure of that.

She went to the family room, where Brandon was playing videogames. She leaned against the doorframe and watched him play. It was a game with a Chinese name she couldn't remember, where you had to move a doll-like man in a gaudy warrior's outfit around, so that he fought giant wizards and dragons. But sometimes the hero could interact with friendly figures, and Brandon was making him approach a voluptuous big-eyed girl wearing a scaly looking bikini and boots. He made his hero do a kind of dance-step near her, so that she jumped back.

Then his character leapt backwards, and that made her jump toward him. It didn't seem to advance the game, but he kept at it, making the characters dance together as best he could.

Judith went to Brandon, and kissed him on top of the head. He took one hand off the controller, reached out, and patted the toe of her shoe, then went back to playing.

She smiled, feeling a little better, and went up to the sewing room she used as an office, to prep for class. It felt good to be teaching. If she could find a way to pay for night school she could get a teacher's certificate, work with special ed kids full time. Roy didn't want to pay for the classes though. Money going to lawsuits couldn't be spared for classes. Maybe she could sell the Explorer, make do with the bus. Roy had his own car, after all. But he'd want to use the money from selling the SUV to pay for his lawsuits.

Maybe she could get a second job.

LATE AFTERNOON, COMING home from work, she looked at her watch and decided Roy wouldn't be there for at least an hour. She had time to look at the attic one more time.

She actually went *into* the attic room, this visit. After the cable man had left she'd gone up to lock the door and, really, to have a look inside. She just looked around at the models, and confirmed for herself he had a computer in there she didn't know about. A Dell laptop connected to an HP printer.

On the right side of the garage attic Roy had set up a big, thick piece of fiberboard over two sawhorses. It was bright with coronas of spray paint, but all Roy's modeling tools were neatly lined on it. To the left of the workbench, under the nailed-shut half-moon window with the frosted glass, a cable ran to a laptop computer on a small workstation desk that looked like it had come from Staples. She'd never seen the desk before.

Bent over, under the roof, she slipped down a narrow aisle between the dangling models and sat on the old piano stool he used for a seat in front of the laptop table. You had to sit or stoop, in here.

This time, looking around, she realized she just didn't want to be around Roy any more than she had to, not because of the things she knew he was prone to do but because he really was a stranger, and she was afraid of feeling she was alone in the house with a stranger. Strangers might do things you couldn't anticipate.

People talked about finding out that they didn't know the people they were married to. But she didn't think they were experiencing it as completely as she was. She'd been married to him for ten years and she'd created a sort of model of him, her own glued-together model, in her mind. She used that model as her Roy. But that wasn't him.

Looking at the models, now—by Revelle and Astra and PlasCo—she felt like she was in some kind of Indian medicine man's cave. She didn't know exactly why, but it felt that way, like something she'd seen on the Discovery channel. Maybe it was partly the way the wind groaned over the roof. So much louder than you'd hear it downstairs. It sounded angry.

The models were hanging from the inverted-V ceiling on fishing line, some lines longer than others so the models were all at about the same level. Even the ones that weren't models of flying things, like the PT boat from World War II, hung dangling from the ceiling. Lots of the models were from World War II, but some were from the Vietnam War, like the MiG and a helicopter gunship. The Monitor and the Merrimac were from the Civil War. There were some cars, too, hanging from the ceiling. Who would hang cars from the ceiling? But plastic models of cars rotated slowly in the dusty air: a GTO and a Mustang and some kind of Mercury she wasn't sure of.

All of the models were perfectly made, without too much glue, without fingerprints; with smooth, expert use of modeling spraypaint, no paint where it shouldn't be. He trimmed the parts with emery boards and one-sided razorblades when they needed help fitting together. And all the parts fitted together exactly.

But what especially made her think she really didn't know Roy had to do with the miniature plastic people on the models. Roy had gotten them at Kroner's Hobbies, probably, and he'd gotten a tiny little paintbrush, with just two hairs on it—she could see it on his work desk—and he had painted a crooked line across each figure's neck. Every single one of the tiny figures, women in the cars and men in the planes and on the boats, was painted to show a purple and red line across their tiny little throats. The line was the color of a bruise.

She reached up and idly tapped one of the planes; she thought it was a B-52. It spun around, with its tiny little man in the roof gunner's bubble staring out at the whirling attic, showing the mark on his throat when he turned her way, spinning to look at the other models, showing the mark again. She reached out to stop the spinning and there came a loud crunching bang from behind her and she reacted, her hand knocking into the B-52 model so it rocked violently into the back of the dangling GTO. The little plastic trunk of the toy GTO popped off.

She sat with her fists balled white in her lap, staring at the broken model, listening. But she knew what the bang was, it was the frond from a palm tree shedding in the high wind. There were serrated edges, like little shark teeth, on each frond and they came down hard on the roof like a drumstick on a tom-tom, the whole house vibrating when they struck. She was glad Brandon was at the training center, the thumps always scared him.

She shook her head, feeling sheepish. The branch hitting the roof had scared her. It had made her feel like Roy was shouting at her for being in his sanctum, for touching his things.

She looked at her watch, as she waited for her pulse to slow. It was four o'clock. Roy wouldn't be home, likely, for another hour and fifteen minutes. Because of his blood pressure, Roy was only working part time. His job for the county, assessing road damage and repair, was kind of dicey right now, since he was also suing the county, claiming they'd given him a disability—she didn't really understand the claim. But there was no talking to him about his lawsuits.

Letting out a long breath, Judith got up, careful not to bump her head. She found the trunk lid of the model GTO on the floor. It looked like it would fit neatly back on the car. But when she went to put it on, she saw a papery something rolled up in the trunk of the slowly-spinning model car. She hesitated, then plucked the paper out, using the tips of her fingernails to get at it. She unrolled it, and held it to the light. It was a small cutting from a digital-photo printout, clipped from a bigger picture.

It was a photograph of a girl in the trunk of a car. She had a ball-gag in her mouth and her arms and feet were tied with rope. That was Roy's car. You could see the outline of the Taurus's rear fender, and you could just make out the top of the bumper sticker that said: *WWJD? What Would Jesus Do?*

"I TOLD HER no way was I going to get into the play but she said, 'Oh just audition' and I did and they gave me the part of Betty Rizzo and it's like the second best part in *Grease*—Mom are you listening?"

"What? Yes! Oh my God that's so great, you got . . . Betty Rizzo!"

Cherie laughed, not something she often did spontaneously, and flipped through the script in her lap. She was a bottle blond, she had that straight hair with just the suggestion of a curl at the bottom that celebrities had been affecting last year, but to Judith it looked like a haystack. Her acne had broken out again, across that slightly-too-small nose she'd inherited from Barry, but she wasn't an unattractive girl, and she had a decent singing voice. Her blue eyes—Barry's eyes—shone with a kind of derisive joy now. "Mom! You don't even know who Betty Rizzo is! You don't even know that musical!"

"It's true," Judith said, "I've never seen it, but I'm going to learn all about it—I have to help you memorize your lines!"

She had found a picture in each of four other models, the ones she could open without leaving an obvious trace. Four different young women, about Cherie's age. All were dead now.

"Mrs. Duwitt said it's the biggest play the senior class has done in years, and—*and!*—Nathan's in it!"

Roy had killed all those girls, and some others. She recognized one of the girls from her picture in the paper, two years ago. Missing, foul play suspected.

"*Nathan?* Oh my gosh! Do you think . . . do you think you guys'll get back together?"

"I think so. I think he wanted an excuse to. I'm not mad at him anymore. I don't think he was really into Miranda."

It all came together now. A thousand little suspicions, like loose bricks suddenly flying together to become a house. She had thought for a long time Roy was hiding things, more than just lawsuits. She'd thought it was an affair. But then she'd wondered about worse things. Could he be stalking someone? Taking pictures in some girls' locker room? Something. But this . . .

She remembered when he'd taped the news shows, for a long time, for months. He'd said it was so he could talk to Cherie about current events, but they never talked about them. At about that time, more than half the news shows contained something about the SP Killer. *SP* for "Smile Pretty", because the killer would take photos of the girls, tied up and terrified and about to die. The first of them had been anonymously sent to the police, with the caption "Smile Pretty!" printed on it.

Roy had taped more than just the shows that mentioned the SP killer. He'd been careful to do that. But he'd gotten all the SP stories, she realized now.

There were some closed boxes in the attic along one wall. He must keep the videotapes in there. What else was on the tapes? She really didn't want to look.

"Are you okay, Mom? You're not doing those afternoon cocktails again."

"What? No, you know I gave up drinking. I . . . why?"

"You're so, like, distracted."

"I'm just so amazed by this great development for you."

Brandon came into the room, not looking at his sister, but he'd been listening and he said, as if to the air, "Great development. Cool Cherie."

Cherie smiled. "Thanks Brandon."

The papers speculated that the SP Killer met the girls on the Internet. All the girls had been doing Internet dating or hanging about in chatrooms. But so far no one had traced the murderer that way. They'd tried everything to catch him. He was careful. He tortured them to death. But he was careful.

It wasn't careful, though, to keep the pictures. But then, all those kinds of people . . . it was hard to even think the words *serial killer* . . . almost all of them kept trophies. She'd seen a show about it on *CourtTV*. Roy had watched the show with her. He'd watched silently, closely. Annoyed when she ventured a comment.

"Tell Dad," Brandon said, looking into the air.

Startled, Judith looked at Brandon. Brandon was trying to say that Dad would be proud of Cherie, Judith supposed.

Cherie snorted. She knew better. Judith said, "I sure will tell him. We'll both be there on opening night."

She should go to the police right now. He was out tonight. He was supposed to be bowling. He did take a bowling bag with him when he went out. She'd never met the guys he bowled with. As far as she knew, Roy had never gotten a phone message from them on the answering machine.

Roy was out there right now, with that bowling bag.

"And it's just so cool," Cherie went on, crossing the gap in her happiness, the "tell Dad" lacuna. "I've got two songs with Nathan, we have to rehearse together a lot—"

Roy had tried to talk to Judith, once, about two years ago. Maybe he had been trying to tell her about his compulsions. *Do you ever feel, Judith, like you're already dead in your coffin and you're just remembering your life? You're laying in your coffin rotting and your ghost is stuck in there and whatever seems like it's happening to you now is just that dead person remembering this day. So you have to find some way to get out of the coffin, any way you can. You might have to be real destructive to get out . . .*

"*No,*" she'd said. "*I can't really imagine that.*" She hadn't encouraged him to go on. She'd been terrified by this sudden confidence, the unmitigated blackness of this disclosure.

She should have drawn him out, she saw now. This was her fault.

"And Nathan loves to do choreography—are you listening, Mom?"

"Yes! Yes I am. So you'll be dancing with Nathan as part of the show?"

He would tie them up and slowly strangle them, very slowly, the coroner had said. Making those red and brown marks on their necks, like the ones he'd painted on the miniature plastic people. *Very slowly.*

She had slept beside him for years.

"Mom? You are totally spacing on me. I'm gonna go call Lina anyway, she doesn't know, she's going to freak!"

She was sure there was a picture in every one of the plastic models, even the ones she hadn't opened up.

He was out right now with his bag.

She should call the police. She could call them right now.

ROY DIDN'T SAY much when Judith told him she had decided she was going to sleep in her sewing room, "for awhile." She would never be able to sleep beside him again.

He accepted her explanation about the hot flashes making her thrash around. Not wanting to disturb him. "Whatever, whatever," he said, taking a new Revelle model, some kind of dragster, out of a paper bag. "I'm going to work on this model." He folded the paper bag, put it carefully in the little kitchen closet he kept folded paper bags in, then carried the model out back, and set up his ladder.

She could hear him crossing the roof over the deck, and going into his attic room. He hadn't taken the bowling bag with him. He had stashed it somewhere else. He must have the digital camera in his coat. They were small devices.

She went to her sewing room and pulled out the bed in the compact sofa. The wind was still pushing at the house, outside. The walls creaked with it.

Judith locked the door, and lay on the sofa bed, stretched out, with just the small lamp beside her sewing machine turned on. She lay on her back, looking at the ceiling, wanting a drink so badly. She didn't care about getting started drinking again, but she needed to think with clarity now. She couldn't afford to be drunk.

Had he killed someone tonight? Was he printing the murdered girl's picture now?

Judith remembered watching her father die, on the frozen lake, in Minnesota. It had been dusk, in early March. She'd been ten years old. Her father had been out on the lake, trying to fish through a hole in the ice with one of his friends. They'd had too much beer and they'd started pushing each other, laughing and floundering around, and the ice had broken. Only her daddy had fallen through.

Emergency rescue had been sent for and people tried different things to get him out. Her mother had kept her back from the lake but she'd climbed a tree to see what was happening to her daddy and from up above she could see the blurry outline of a man thrashing around under the ice, drifting too far away from the hole he'd fallen through. People were yelling at him, "Don't use up your strength trying to crack the ice, Jim! Don't do that, just tread water! Tread water and wait, you'll make it, we'll get you out in a minute, we're gonna cut through! Just hold on—*don't do that, Jim!*"

But Dad panicked and couldn't keep himself from trying to break through the ice. He kept trying to hammer at it but his efforts were carrying him farther and farther from the hole and he was getting more and more exhausted and then he sank down, out of sight, and they didn't get his body out for a couple of days . . .

Judith could hear her daughter in her bedroom, muffled through the wall so she couldn't make out what she was saying. She was on her cell phone to one of her friends, telling them about being in the show; telling them every detail. The happiness was apparent in her voice, even if the words weren't coming through to Judith.

Most of the time, Cherie was morose. Now she was going to be happy, at least for a while. She had a part in a musical at school, and the guy she wanted to get back together with was in the play, too. She might never be happier in life.

If Judith turned her husband in, that would end. Everything good in Cherie's life would end, maybe forever.

Brandon was getting better. Measurably, anyhow. He had a really good special ed teacher who spoke warmly of him.

If she'd tolerated Barry's affair, it probably would've run its course, and they'd still be together.

But this wasn't like finding out about an affair. This was finding out your husband was a monster. She had to stop him. She had to turn him in.

Of course, with her husband in the papers and on the TV news, she would probably have to move away. Living here, with everyone knowing her husband was the SP Killer—unbearable. They'd have to start over someplace else. If the police allowed them to leave. They'd want her around to testify.

They'd have to sell the house to pay for lawyers. Roy would never accept a public defender. She paid for Brandon's teachers, now. The public schools had done so little for him. Brandon would lose that.

The police might not arrest Roy instantly. He might take revenge on her. He might kill her and Cherie and Brandon. Especially Cherie. She wasn't his daughter. He'd probably thought about killing her. But if he'd killed her, the police would look at him too closely. If she looked like she was going to turn him in, he'd have nothing to lose. He might kill them all.

And the people. *"She married the SP Killer. She had to have known. Some way you'd have to know. How could you not know? Come on. She knew. She knew!"*

She loved being a substitute teacher. That would end. The principal would be apologetic, but he'd let her go. *"The parents get freaked out, Judith. You understand."*

She'd never be hired to teach again.

She ought to go to the police. Already someone else might've died because she'd delayed. If she knew and didn't tell, she was in complicity, whether the police found out about her knowing or not. It was moral complicity. She was helping him kill those girls. There was a greater good. She had to go to the police.

A *thump!* from the roof. The palm tree had thrown another clublike frond at her.

If she turned Roy in, Cherie would know that her step-dad was the SP Killer and she'd always have to live with that and it would ruin Cherie's life. There was no telling what effect it could have on Brandon. How could it be good?

What else could she do? She imagined herself killing Roy—putting a pillow over his mouth as he slept. Putting all her weight on his face.

She wouldn't mind that, not at all. If she thought it would work. But she wouldn't be any good at killing him. He'd wake up and he'd grab her and he'd realize she knew and he'd kill her and then maybe Cherie and Brandon.

So she had to go to the police.

Cherie's voice was still coming through the wall from her bedroom. It was wordless and happy. Like a song hummed instead of sung by someone happy to be alive.

Maybe the girls her husband had killed had felt the same way, before he'd kidnapped them. Judith's sobs were long and slow and deep, they were honking sounds from the lowest places in her gut and each one wracked her whole body. She sobbed for a long time. It was like being beaten. Finally she lay still, and thought again of her father.

Judith's father had thrashed and struggled and tried to break out of the ice. The cold water had borne him down and they'd found him face down, floating in a layer of muck near the bottom.

He should have just gone on treading water till they'd gotten him out.

She could do that. She could tread water. She could tread water until some chance came to get out of the frozen lake. Cherie could be happy until then; Brandon could go on as he was until then. Maybe Roy would stop killing. He might. Sometimes they did. She'd read that. They stopped eventually.

She wasn't murdering those girls. Roy was doing it. He was the one doing it. And, after all, most of these girls were either prostitutes or slutty girls he'd picked up on the Internet. They shouldn't be meeting men on the Internet.

If a few more had to die, that had to be all right. She had to let it happen. She had to keep treading water. The lake was cold, and dark.

It was him. Not her. It wasn't her doing. She could sleep in the sewing room.

NINETEEN SECONDS

SOMEONE NUDGED ALAN from behind. In his turn, he nudged his little brother, ahead of him. "Move up." Two more steps up the stairs had opened when another kid or two had gone down the Drain.

"I timed the slide," Donny said, moving the two steps. "It takes about nineteen seconds to go down the Drain, if you're laying down when you do the slide. Sitting up after the tunnel, it's about twenty-one or twenty-two seconds . . ."

How many seconds in a year, Alan wondered. *How many seconds have I been alive?* Alan was fifteen today. His dad had arranged the birthday party. Alan hadn't wanted a birthday party at the waterslides, that was something you did for a ten-year-old, or twelve at the oldest. It was just one stroke up from jumping into a bin of plastic balls at the Kiddie Zone.

Donny, his brown hair thatchy from repeated wettings, was staring deeply into his watch, his lips moving, practicing the stopwatch mode.

Trying not to think about the spider, or his asthma, Alan wondered why kids around ten and eleven got into timing things. How fast to run ten yards, how fast to go down a slide. They loved watches with built-in stopwatches.

Donny was nut-brown—he had his dad's skin, seemed to tan easily. And he had Dad's easy carriage, his coordination. More than once Alan had caught the look of relief and hope in his father's eyes when he watched Donny play softball: This one wouldn't be a disappointment.

The line of chattering, squinting kids in bathing suits was moving slowly up the wet, winding fiberplastic stairs: step, step, stop—wait—step, step, stop—wait. Alan and Donny were two thirds the way up the stairs edging the Drain, the fastest, twistiest waterslide in the Wet City waterpark. Alan felt the Central California sun pushing on him, its heat seeming to ricochet directly at him from the flat, dusty fields around the waterpark. He savored the occasional gusts of chlorinated mist from the little waterfalls feeding the blue and green fiberglass tubes of the waterslides. The dust, the heat, the unseen clouds of pollen threatening to close off his chest again, and he was afraid of having an asthma attack in front of the others. He'd left his inhaler down at the picnic table—he'd look like an even more pathetic geek, carrying it around in his swimming trunks. The rest of the birthday party were local kids his father invited, high school freshmen like him; they'd said yes just for a free trip to the waterslides—last chance to get wet in the heat before school started. He didn't want to crumble in front of them. Yancy Stephens and his girlfriend Lani and that Danya with the twisty little smiles when she looked at you, like she was trying not to laugh. If he crumbled in front of them, with an asthma attack, or lose it to his fear of spiders and toy animals, they'd all try not to laugh. Like they had when they'd seen him come out of the changing rooms, long and skinny and pallid and reeking of the strongest possible sunscreen. And they were good at things that people cared about, they were not defective, it was as if all their parts worked so smoothly together, inside them, they were smoothly functioning machines, there was nothing wrong with them. They were even good enough to try not to laugh.

"I'm gonna push, see if I can get it down to eighteen or seventeen seconds," Donny said.

"Could depend on when you manage to look at your watch, after you crash into the pool at the bottom," Alan said.

Donny made a disgusted face; Alan was raining on his parade.

"You could keep your finger on the clicker thing on your watch and hit it just when you hit the water," Alan suggested.

"Hey yeah . . ." Donny brightened.

They were on the top level now, a few minutes from making their plunge. You could see the whole park from here, twenty-five acres of what used to be a wheat field, now it was nine waterslide structures and the Wild Sprinkler area for the little kids to play in. The waterslides were eccentric, complex structures, looping blue Dr. Seuss edifices, an apparent whimsicality underpinned with engineering rigor; flashing streams and waterfalls, laughing voices merging with rushing water.

Sometimes a vagrant breeze invaded the chlorine and sunscreen smell, betrayed the rot and blood of the slaughterhouse, down the highway a few miles.

Alan was increasingly aware that the asthma threat—the tightening in his chest, the shallowing of his breath—was entwined with naked fear. This particular slide, the Drain, scared him as no other did and for no good reason at all. He liked roller coasters, he liked the Top Gun at Great America, which could prise tooth fillings loose with its sudden G-forces. He liked the other water slides. But the Drain seemed to be designed by whoever had designed the night terrors he'd had, when he was ten and eleven. It had an innovation: those animal faces that popped out at you, and three short waterfall drops. Then there was nature's own innovation: the black widow he'd seen just after the Tunnel of Darkness, as his brother called it. The spider that no one else had seen.

"When I go through the Tunnel of Darkness, this time," Donny said, his voice given a kazoo quality by the finger digging in his nose, "I'm gonna make myself really straight like those luge guys so I just shoot through like a bullet through a barrel . . ."

"What kind of tunnel, anyway, isn't a tunnel of darkness," Alan said, eyeing the entrance to the slide as a blonde girl in a bikini, her breasts just big enough to justify the top, if you squinted, hesitated in its entrance until her friend gave her a shove and she went squealing down . . . maybe to run into the black widow. "I mean, it's redundant. All tunnels are dark, pretty much."

"Redund—what?"

"Never mind."

"You're getting a burned spot in the middle of your back, dude."

"Great. Just great. That's the spot I couldn't reach . . ." Usually his dad or mom would've put the sunscreen on his back but there wasn't a chance to do it without the party-guest kids seeing and he'd look even geekier getting gunk smeared on his back like a baby getting baby oil.

They were only five kids away from the top of the slide. A bored college jock in shorts and shirt, whistle on a string around his neck, was supervising the kids going down. His nose was peeling from sunburn and he kept gazing longingly over the alfalfa fields around the waterpark toward Sacramento.

The little farming community of Central Corners, where Alan went to high school, was about thirty miles from the outskirts of Sacramento, the nearest big town. Everybody knew everybody, and everybody knew that the teenagers all wanted to get out of town.

Two kids now. "You didn't even see a shadow hanging in that bush over the slide, that could be a spider?" Alan said suddenly, looking at the dim mouth of the tunnel opening of the slide.

"Get over that spider thing," Donny said, too loudly. So that the two middle school girls in front of them looked at them, then grinned at each other.

"Shut up, fag-ass," Alan said, his face reddening.

"You shut up, Shovel Boy," Donny retorted.

"Shut up about that," Alan muttered.

"Then you don't call me names neither."

Shovel boy. He'd spent half the summer shoveling manure for the Corral of the Doomed, as the local kids called it: the pen where they kept cattle for a couple of days, waiting to go into their own chutes, their wooden slides into the slaughterhouse. The cattle lifting their heads, smelling blood in the air, lowing, their eyes rolling. Knowing.

The idea had been to earn enough money for a car, but they paid you by the loadful, and it was a lot harder than he'd thought. He'd quit after six weeks with only seven-hundred-forty bucks. And what could you buy with that?

Now it was Donny's turn to go down. "Okay, checking watch," he said, climbing up onto the little launching seat at the tunnel mouth. "Okay, checking watch, checking watch, five four three—"

"You're holding up the line," the jock said.

" . . . two one!" And then he was gone, Alan's little brother sucked laughing down a drain into the darkness. Maybe it would get on Donny.

The jock glanced at Alan, made a keep-it-moving motion with his hand. Alan bit his lower lip, and told himself, in his mind, *Get over it, dude, for real.* He climbed up onto the seat . . .

Shit, you know that the fiberglass bears and cougar are the park's lame attempts to copy something the owner saw at Disneyland and they don't even scare three year olds . . . And the spider isn't—

"You going, dude, or what?" the jock asked.

Alan held his breath, which was his first mistake, and leaned back, pushed off with his hands, onto the stream of water and down the blue fiberglass slide, into the tunnel.

Big fucking deal, in nineteen seconds . . .

Down into darkness of the slide, slipping through his mother's fingers, like in the night terrors—later he'd worked out that each incident in the hollow crackling pith of the night, each night terror lasted maybe two minutes and seemed like hours . . . and hours.

Alan eleven years old, waking for the fourth time that year with what one doctor had said, later, was "classic night terrors" and what one had said was "sleep apnea complicated with a mild seizure of some kind", for him it was being awake in a body that was going on a shambling ride without him, feeling like his blood had been replaced with hot wax that was cooling, thickening; and as he sat up in bed, watching the pee welling out the side of his underpants, seeing it as if it were something completely different, just a phenomenon of color and liquidity, an expression of his insides, coming in pulses that seemed completely disconnected, though he could feel each pulse of release; and taking so long, an hour it seemed to him. Then he found himself up and walking down the carpeted hallway, trudging away from the taste in his mouth, but you couldn't get away from a taste, it was like metallic shit with burning electricity in it, that taste, and it was spreading through his jaw, making his jaw soft as it spread so that when he tried to shout for someone to help him, the bones of his jaw flopped around, only gargling noises coming out, and the trudging went on for hours, till he felt that coldness dripping from his scalp and he started to touch the back of his head but stopped when he realized the back of his skull was gone, and his brain was exposed, wet, don't touch it, you'll break something and make it even worse, just get down the hall to the trapezoid of yellow, but now something was oozing from the dark borders into the trapezoid of yellow, like a stain of motor oil (he could taste the motor oil) spreading into the urine he'd let go, now the spreading stain was taking shape, was a silhouette of a bear, a man in a bear suit, or just the bear suit alive, yes just an empty bear suit, empty but alive, turned half away from him; it was the mascot of that team that his dad and his brother watched on TV, its head revolving slowly on its shoulders toward him, its face trying to find an expression, contorting as it tried to make a beckoning grin, but its horrible, diseased nature forcing the expression into a murderous leer, one glassy bear-mascot eye drifting way higher than the other. And Alan rooted himself in place, in the hallway, so he wouldn't get any closer to the bear, but the floor was moving like one of those slow-moving rubber sidewalks in the airport drawing him toward the bear which was splitting open down its fat middle to rattlingly spew the white granite gravel that Grandma Ellsby had fallen on when she was coming out to the car to shout at his father and she had that stroke that killed her two weeks later, when he was seven, he could only see, out the car window, with his mother pulling him back, Grandma's hand clutching the gravel. Her yellow hand opening and closing. His mother was yelling at him with a megaphone voice, distant and fuzzy like the voice of the vice principal at school coming through the intercom, when you could only make out every third word the vice principal said except you could always hear him say, at the end, You are expected to remember this.

"AlAn, dAmMit, lOOk AT mE, WhAt aRe yOU DOinG!"

His mom's teeth seemed yellow, mossy, in her mouth; extending to become an endless wall of mossy teeth stretching away into the yellow trapezoid distance, the teeth curving around to wrap his head, thousands of crooked, green-yellow teeth in a rippling, dancing ribbon, and the smell of burning iron; then the smell of that "just a little off" hot dog he hadn't wanted to eat that his dad had made him eat because he thought he was just being "a prima donna about his food again" that had given him food poisoning, the teeth dancing, his mother shouting—

He was slipping to his wobbly knees as Mom shook him, in that hallway; he was sliding through mom's fingers, and he heard himself saying, "I had a service station man putting teeth, putting teeth, if that

bear comes, the smell of Mr. Green Things for a thousand points . . ."
He was trying to say something else, not sure what, but that's what
came out, and then sinking to the floor and jerking upright as his dad
poured ice water on him to shock him out of it . . . The sudden blaze of
the hall light as his dad hit the switch . . .

. . . Blaze of sunlight as he came out of the first set of waterslide
corkscrews and rushed feet-first toward the end of Donny's Tunnel
of Darkness, the urine-yellow light up there—something sliding into
it from the side, running along a web, taking on shape as it lowered
itself, dangling, quivering down: the black widow, seeking, perhaps,
to extend her web, her bulbous abdomen no bigger than a cherry-pit
but it seemed to swell in his sight like a black balloon instantly expanded on a balloon-filling machine, as she dropped lower and he
kicked at her, missed, and then she dropped on an unseen thread at
his crotch—some part of his mind noticing that all this was taking
too long, though it must have been under a second from seeing the
spider and seeing her drop, it seemed to take five minutes of rushing
toward the spider, his limbs leaden-heavy as he tried to move to avoid
her, the weight of slowed perceptions fighting high speed—then she'd
dropped—

She must've missed him, must've gone under him, when she—

Dropped, down the first waterfall, the slide angling enough so it
wasn't a complete drop but a sudden plunge into steepness, the sunlight exulting in a blast of rainbows, clouds of mist, and his heart gave
a leap, the protraction of time now a kind of grace as it opened up his
plunge into this pool of shine and cerulean water, the thought that he
was getting past his fears, he was halfway through the slide, he could
hear music echoing from somewhere, celebrating him, singing *You got
past the spider—!*

Then he was plunged again, was twisted to the left, slamming his
left shoulder on the smooth, gripless surface, as suddenly jerked right
with the switchback to slam his right shoulder and cheek achingly on
the wall, yelling at the unexpected pain. A mouthful of water, tasting
chlorine, swallowing it, coughing—what if the black widow were in the
water and he swallowed her alive—

Another plunge, a spin past the herky-jerky movement of the leaping plastic cougar, which looked to him not threatening but scared itself, as if the cougar were running from the next thing to come, warning him of the next plunge, even as it came, thump and choke, and there! the rearing animatronic bear, too much like the mascot bear, muzzle wrinkled in fury as it jerked toward him on its turntable; he saw Grandma's hand reaching from a split at the lifesize plastic bear's middle, plaintively reaching out, the hand no more yellowed or clawlike than it had been in that final year of her life, skin the color of tobacco stain, trembling out for him: if he could grab her hand he could pull her out, he clutched but missed and he heard her reproachful cry as he passed, and then the bear's icy shadow falling over him, from the trapezoid of yellow, its face meshing with his father's face, shouting at him, *Cut this bullshit out Alan,* and then the sinking into the rug, with the sinking a great weight on his chest, closing around his bronchial tubes, the wheezing begun, and as he opened wide on the final spurt of the drainslide he saw a long black spider's leg extruding from the edge of his bathing suit, she had—

She had got on him—

She was on him—

And the knowledge was stronger than the time he'd thought his hair was on fire, had awakened slapping at his hair, convinced, sure with a noontime certainty, that his hair was aflame and he was going to burn to death starting from the top—

More certainty than that: Knowing that the spider was on him as he spun through the blue half-tube, shouting, clawing at himself, someone laughing on the stairs beside the slide, Alan trying to shout *Get it off, get it off,* his mouth too heavy; if only the bear would call its spider back, the spider was one of the bear's eyes but with teeth to bite . . . Each breath so far from the last one, farther yet from the next, as he clawed his trunks off him and ripped at his crotch with his fingernails, maybe the black widow has got under his foreskin, she was going to get up his—*Get it off*—

A sweeping, slushy swish, a single low bass note, and then he was in the pool at the bottom of the slide, turning over in water only three feet deep, thrashing, seeing his feet above, they were framing the sun and a black crinkled spot on the sun—a spider sunspot—

The spider—!

The bear gripped his upper arm, yanking him upright.

No. It was a tall girl in shorts and 49ers T-shirt and short red hair and quizzical look and a whistle around her neck, "Whoa there guy," she was saying, leaning back so she could lift him to his feet . . .

Yancy, Lani and Danya were standing in a group beside a mortified Donny, near the edge of the landing pool at the bottom of the Drainslide; Donny's mouth open, he was staring as if he'd forgotten how to blink, Yancy and Lani and Danya were trying not to laugh, Yancy not quite succeeding, shaking his head, silent laughter—

Alan knowing he'd clawed off his swimming trunks, was standing there naked and bleeding, looking down to see his foreskin torn, clawmarks on his stomach.

He tried to say, *There was a black widow, look, there it is, floating in the water! I had to get it off—*

But he was wheezing with the asthma attack, crumbling in front of them, unable to speak and the turbulence in the pool had swept the spider into a little black dot that was sucked, as he watched, into the filtering trough, along with his swimming trunks.

He looked at Yancy and Lani and Danya and knew that his insides had become transparent to them, they were looking into him, seeing the disconnected parts inside him, and knowing, the three of them, forever knowing with a concrete certainty that he was fundamentally defective, he was defective, he was just defective.

WHAT WOULD YOU DO FOR LOVE?

LATER, WHEN HE was thinking about what it would be like to take a bullet in the head, Darry found that, even then, he couldn't blame Marla. He thought: Marla was only one part death.

Three parts of her were something else. Somewhere in her was a kind of mythic terrarium, where she kept another Marla, a little mental doll that moved with the power of imagination through a clean landscape, a place where neither fear nor pain could take root.

He taught high school, American Lit. He met Marla in the El Loro High School parking lot when she came to pick up her niece.

HE STOOD ON the front steps in front of the school office, beneath the flagpole; not wanting to stay, not wanting to go home to Bette. It was almost winter in El Loro, but it was Central California and the trees had shed only an outer skirt of leaves; the sky showed blue through fissures in the smears of number-two penciled clouds. His name was Darius; he went by Darry, and didn't like that much either. He stood in a wind that smelled faintly of leafy decay, watching Marla get out of the car.

Marla's niece, Cecily, was a pretty girl, except for the weak chin. He thought of Cecily as a student who sometimes tried. She wore baggy overalls, one strap deliberately left hanging, and a Pearl Jam T-shirt. Her hair was teased over to one side; there was a touch of irony about the coif. When Cecily saw her Aunt Marla coming to get her, instead of her Mom, she got a look on her face he knew from a thousand displays of adolescent embarrassment: Oh Gawd, not her.

But Darry felt a bittersweet tightness the first time he saw Marla. She wore a taut leopard-print blouse, black vinyl skirt not-too-short; a black butterfly tattooed on one ankle; around the other a charm bracelet. Her lips were full, voluptuous with shiny burgundy lipstick, but her mouth seemed not quite wide enough. Her nose was small, her eyes were a goldflake green; it was only later that he saw one eye was just a little higher than the other. Her hair was an unnatural shade of blond, cut close like a Roaring Twenties flapper, and you were *supposed* to notice that it was an unnatural blond; and her earrings were little silhouettes of Queen Nefertiti. There was a half-faded tattoo of an ankh on her forearm. And her feet were packed into almost vertically elevated spike heels. They looked at least a size too small.

"You like to look *close!*" Jan said, stepping up beside him, smiling to show she was Just Kidding. Jan taught computer science to juniors.

Darry realized that Jan had caught him staring at one of his students' female relatives. And with his mouth open, just a little.

He shut his mouth with an almost audible snap, jerking his gaze from Marla, who was standing on the school steps with Cecily. "Well she's . . . striking."

He smiled, hoping she took the remark and the smile as condescension toward the woman in the leopard-print top; the woman who wore black onyx beads, he saw now, glancing back at her; who was looking past Cecily, back at him.

Snap. Look back at Jan. She was a small, tidy woman with mousy brown hair; narrow in the shoulders and broad in the hips. She had large, pretty brown eyes; she wore contacts to give her best feature its best shot. He hoped she wouldn't press another behavioristic computer-model questionnaire on him. She had a fetish for computer-modeling behavior with artificial-life analogs. But she was saying, "Oh most definitely, she's a prize. I can almost read her rap sheet from here."

"Now that could be a little uncharitable, Jan."

"I guess. I feel like I knew her from gym class at my own high school. She reminds me of the one who put pepper in my brassiere. How's your Bette?"

"Bette's . . . she's good." Someday he was going to learn how to talk about his wife to people without it sounding like she was dying of something. She wasn't dying. She was just sort of housebound. Sort of. His looming sense of their mutual decline was almost certainly exaggerated. They were only in their forties. True, the American Association of Retired People had sent her a sample newsletter, because she was two years older than him and had popped up on some AARP databank; but he hadn't got one yet. Not yet.

"How's sophomore English?" Jan asked.

He managed to stare at his shoes and not Cecily's aunt. He had heard Cecily say, moments before: Oh no it's my Aunt Marla oh Gawd she's so . . .

So . . . what?

He managed, "How's sophomore English? . . . Um, in one word: apocalyptic."

Jan laughed. "I'd call you melodramatic except I know better. Try juniors and computer science." She'd been married once. The guy had just disappeared one day. Story was, she'd had a single, apologetic postcard from Florida and no other word, for years. And there was a rumor she was quietly rich from designing computer software and didn't need to work here at all. With modern kids, teaching for the love of it had always seemed incomprehensible to Darry.

He knew she had a crush on him. He could feel it like something sticky on his shoe. Sometimes he was tempted. She seemed willing; she seemed sympathetic but he wasn't sure what she was sympathetic about. What did she know about his marriage?

"Sophomore English, sophomore science—both oxymorons."

"But keep in mind—"

"I know: our teachers thought were a hopeless generation too. Et cetera. Sure."

She sang softly. "'Why can't they be like weeee were, perfect in every way' . . ."

"You have to pretend not to remember that musical, so it doesn't date you!"

She laughed. He watched Cecily argue with her Aunt Marla.

What are you so embarrassed about, girl? Just get in the car . . .

Jan was murmuring, "Well . . . I guess . . ." She was trying to think of something else to say, to keep him here. She'd prod him about the computer modeling questionnaire, and would he fill out another. But school was out and there were no meetings for once and he could go home; see his dog, avoid his wife. Marla was taking the reluctant Cecily to her mom's car. The aunt looked only ten years older than the niece. There was some story or other behind that, he thought.

He said: "Well—papers to correct—"

"Me too."

But as he started to turn away she thought of something. "You still writing that book?"

"Oh—perennially."

"If you sold it, would you quit teaching?"

He'd asked himself that a dozen times but he said, "Not a chance. I don't jump without a parachute. I'd quit if I got a half million dollar advance but—" He paused to chuckle. "I don't think it's that kind of novel. I think it's maybe a three-thousand-dollar-advance novel. Or maybe a 'paid in contributor's copies' university press novel."

"Your mistake is getting literary. Not enough shootings." She looked at him, then looked away. "Or enough sex."

"You're . . . probably right. I'm afraid this is more like a *Lucky Jim* for secondary school."

"Uh oh—anybody I know on the faculty get brutally caricatured?"

"Wha-a-at? Me? Write about anybody I know?" Darry winked. "Give me some credit."

She gave a brittle little laugh. He thought he needed another excuse to leave; he could tell her he had to feed his cats. But that would seem like no priority at all to her: he'd heard her say she didn't like animals. He didn't trust people who didn't have pets.

Inexorably, she said, "I do have one more questionnaire for you—"

"You know, those questions are getting a little personal."

"Sorry. Computer modeling knows no boundaries. I mean it is, you know, behavioristic. But it's all very anonymous and 'hypothetical person number thirty-nine' and . . . "

"Am I number thirty-nine? I'll do one more for you, tomorrow. Well . . ." He glanced at his watch. "Whuh-oh."

"Me too!" she said chirpily, just a flutter of regret, and backed away, smiling goodbye, then hurried off, briefcase swinging.

Darry saw Marla looking at him as she maneuvered to get out of the stunningly-illegal red-zone parking spot she'd picked, between two smallish handicapped-student shuttles. She backed her car . . . right into his Mitsubishi. Both cars rocked. She made a big show of grimacing.

He smiled sympathetically and his heart leapt as he walked over to the car and looked at the bumpers. She got out and looked too.

"Eek! Is that your car?"

"Uhhh—"

"I know it is, actually." She talked fast, which didn't sound right with the mild Texas accent, at first. "Cecily told me right before I backed into it. 'That's my English teacher's car and he's watching so don't—' And, you know, wham! And not even a bam and thank-you-ma'am!"

"Gawd, Marla!" Cecily said, with exquisite misery, getting out.

"It's your fault, girl," Marla said, shaking her head slowly at Cecily as she spoke. "You got me all tense saying—" She did a little mimicry of Cecily saying: " 'He's watching so don't back into it'. And then of course I get tense and I—"

"It's okay, really, there's no damage done," Darry interrupted.

"She scratched your bumper, Mr. Bentworth," Cecily said, rolling her eyes.

Marla was looking at his wedding ring. She looked up into his face. "Really? 'Cause see, I don't have any insurance—"

"Ooh big surprise there," Cecily said.

"—and I don't know how I'd—"

"Seriously. It's okay."

Marla cocked her head and the mimicry this time was of a you're-my-knight-in-shining armor look; an irony meant to show real gratitude.

"Well thanks. I owe you one. For true."

He hadn't noticed her fingernails before. They were the same color as her lipstick and shiny as a beetle's wing, about an inch too long, long enough to curl a little, and on each one there was little quarter-moon of spangle.

"Can we go, Marla?"

"I don't even know the man's name! Ex-*cuse* me!"

Cecily gave a sigh; he heard the sigh at least half a dozen times a day from various kids. *The world on my shoulders is more than heavy, it's flawed, and it's all I've got.* "This is Mr. Bentworth, Marla."

He shook her small hand; the long nails reminded him of seashells in his palm. "Darry Bentworth."

"Darry?"

He shrugged. "It's short for Darius. My old man was into Hellenic history." He almost added: *Actually that gives the impression that Darius was Greek whereas in fact he . . .*

Stopped himself in time.

Cecily was looking anxiously at passing teenagers and pulling her aunt by the arm. "I think I'm being summoned to the car, Mr. Bentworth . . . Darry . . . but I do, I owe you one!"

She waved with the tips of her fingers, her curved nails, and they got into the car and after backing and filling four or five times, they got out of the spot and drove down the street, only about ten miles an hour past the speed limit.

BETTE WAS STILL in her nightgown and pink slippers.

He heard the TV when he came up the walk to the condo. What was it, Rosie O'Donnell? Rikki Lake? It was a talk show of some kind. Then it abruptly cut off and he knew she'd seen his shadow on the window shade as he'd stepped onto the front porch. When he came in she was poring over bills on the coffee table.

He debated telling her he knew she hadn't been working on bills, she'd been watching TV, and she'd switched it off as he'd arrived to make it look as if she wasn't just watching TV all day. But he knew where that would end.

He stood in the archway between the dining area and the living room, looking at her. Seeing her, in that moment, as if seeing a stranger. He felt almost that he'd intruded in someone else's house.

She looked up from the phone bills. "Oh hi. I didn't hear you come in."

Uh-huh.

"Hi."

"You okay?"

"Why wouldn't I be?"

"You look funny."

"You're pretty funny-lookin' yourself." He smiled so she'd know it was a joke.

She looked back at the bills. He wondered how her calves got so big and so white. Her cheeks were round and white and heavy. She'd remembered to put on those half-glasses she wore for reading as she pretended to squint at the bills. Her long black hair was stringy, its washing at least a day late.

Think how you're perceiving her, he told himself guiltily. It isn't fair. It's your mood. And she's not at her best. The ashtray beside her was brimming with cigarette butts.

Irma, their miniature collie, lying at Bette's feet, woke up when he came near the sofa. She leapt up to stand on her hind legs, put her front paws on his knee, gazing raptly up at him. He laughed, reached down and grabbed her nose and shook it, making her snuffle.

"She's been flirting with that dog next door again," Bette said, smiling at Irma.

He sat on the arm of the couch, petting the dog. "Didn't you tell her she's been spayed?"

"She's ready to party anyway, I guess. I don't know where she gets the hormones. Today she ran down the walk after the postman—and she's always been nice to him, he's never been scared of her, but I was afraid he was going to mace her."

"Why?"

"She jumped up and grabbed a cardboard box that had some kind of sausage sample in it, right out of his bag!"

They laughed, and he patted Irma. "You're the lady pirate, Irma."

For a moment there was a warmth between him and Bette; the dog was the medium for it. He thought: We relate to each other through the dog or not at all . . .

He got up and went into the kitchen, opened the refrigerator. It was amazing how something so stiff and crispy as celery could become as limp and droopy as one of Dali's watches, hanging over the edge of the metal fridge tray. There were some moldy pickles; lonesome condiments; two cartons of half-eaten Chinese food that'd been there for two weeks. Nothing else.

"I'm sorry," she called from the living room. "I forgot to shop."

"You forgot?" He closed the fridge door.

"Yup."

He went to the door, looked through the dining area at her, still on the couch in the living room. "You've forgotten for a month. I always do it or we order out."

"It hasn't been a month."

"Yeah it has. Want to go over some receipts together?"

"Not necessary, Inspector Clouseau. I'm sure I must have . . ."

"Bette—you haven't gone out in a month. I've even taken the garbage out." He thought: Don't say it. But he took the leap. "Does the word agoraphobia speak to us at all?"

She stared at him. "You're saying I'm mentally ill because I've been a little depressed and haven't gone out much?"

"Depressed? Agoraphobia is not depressed, it's a step beyond it. It's fear of going outside. And it's not in the mental illness category. It's just neurotic. But you could get a little therapy or Prozac or something."

"Now you've gone from Inspector Clouseau to Dr. Kildare."

"God. No one remembers Dr. Kildare."

"You spend too much time around high school students."

"Yeah, well, that I won't argue with."

"You know what, I could take a shower, put on my special nightie—"

"Don't put yourself out."

He regretted it as soon as he said it.

Her face crinkled up. "You're right. You're right." She made gulping sounds as she cried, her head bowed; her hair drooping. "You're right I'm just . . . I'm a lump. I'm a fucking lump. I'm neurotic and scared and I'm a lump. You should leave me." The crying went into a higher gear.

He wanted to go to her and tell her it wasn't so but he was too angry and he was surprised at how angry he was. It wasn't like this was unusual or anything.

"Look—just . . . calm down. Have some of that calming tea, watch one of your shows, I'm going to the grocery store, get us some stuff. I'll make some soup, you'll feel better."

76

It was a way of trying to make up to her for provoking her to tears and then not comforting her. And he was hungry.

"No, I'll go."

But he knew if he waited for her to go, she'd make excuses and then it'd be ten PM and she still wouldn't have gone and there'd be no dinner and they'd both be in foul, low-blood-sugar moods and it'd escalate into a huge fight.

As he went into the bedroom and changed his clothes, he thought: *I ought to be able to do something more to help her.*

But there was something between him and what he knew he should do to help her, and he couldn't see what it was and he couldn't get past it. It was like one of the force fields in a science fiction movie. He felt a burning when he tried to cross it, to get to her, and he knew the burning was all in him.

"I can't even have a baby, I just have bloody pieces of baby," she sobbed.

He didn't want her to talk about the series of miscarriages. He very badly didn't want her to talk about it.

"Hon—just . . . take it easy. I'll be back. Bring you some ice cream."

Just what she needed. Ice cream.

Oh come on, he thought, as he went out the front door. She's only fifty pounds or so overweight. Some people at the mall, you couldn't believe they could get into a car to get there.

He stopped at his little blue Mitsubishi and looked at the condo. It was attached to the other condos, same shape and color, a deep red brown that was supposed to look foresty somehow, and there were little leafless trees in front of it; the little trees were the same size as TV antennas and almost the same shape. People had stopped using TV antennas, he thought, so the antennas had disguised themselves as trees for survival.

He got into the car and drove to the mall.

"EL LORO MEANS 'The parrot'," the bartender told Buck.

"No shit." Buck ran his hand over his bristling jaw. Two days short of a shave, he thought. "I wonder why they'd call it after fuckin' *parrots.*

Parrots don't come from California." He drank some more of his rum and coke.

"People let their parrots get out and they get wild and we end up with quite a few wild parrots. Maybe named after that, some of them local wild parrots. The town is only about thirty years old, see."

It was one of those Howard Johnson's bars attached to the Howard Johnson's restaurant, which was attached to the Howard Johnson's motel where Buck was staying. Usually nobody was ever in those bars except for traveling salesmen, fat and sullen.

But sometimes you could get some pussy there: somebody's runaway wife, or whatever. They go right to the motel bar from their room.

Buck liked the Howard Johnson's because you didn't even have to leave the motel to get your food. The less you had to leave, the more you could leave when you didn't have to. Good to remember. Crimebuster tip.

In the joint, in Vacaville, they'd loved it when he'd say "I gotta crimebuster tip for ya" and then he'd tell them how to slip the cops.

Of course the inevitable question would come up.

Why you here, if you so smart motherfucker?

Because, he'd said, every time, assholes like you need my help. It's charity, why I'm here.

Usually got a laugh. A motherfucker was laughing with you he wasn't sticking a piece of tape-handle shit-metal in your back.

The bartender, here, he was an old guy, kind of guy who lived to get away to Vegas when he could.

"You in town looking for work?" the old guy asked.

"No. Why?"

No particular belligerence in the way Buck said it, but the bartender could tell Buck didn't like the question about work. It implied more, unspoken questions, like: *Where do you get your money, and what have you been doing recently, and are those jailhouse tattoos on your wrist?*

"I don't know," the bartender was saying, "there's some work at the motherboard plant, lot of people come here to try and get some of that . . ."

"What's a motherfucking motherboard?"

The bartender tossed his head the way some people did instead of laughing. "A computer part."

"Oh, sure, that's right. No, me, I work in construction." Last job he'd had, ten years before, that'd been construction. He'd got seven hundred dollars for the company's truck and tools, when he left. "No, I came to town to pick something up belongs to me."

"Get you another rum and coke?"

"Nope."

Buck was looking out the window. A cop was rolling by. The cruiser went on, two small-town cops with their dicks in their hands.

Buck decided to go back to his room, look through the phone book.

THE MUZAK WAS playing the "left the cake out in the rain" song, and there was a sale on Lunchables on aisle three. Darry was trying to remember what else they needed at the house. Dog food? Probably. Ice cream? Definitely.

Then Marla came wheeling fast around a corner of the aisle and ran her cart broadside into his.

"Oh my god—twice in one day! It must be destiny!" She laughed and he had to laugh too. She saw he'd changed his clothes, he was wearing an *X-Files* T-shirt one of his students had given him, only because it had been clean, and she burst out, "Where'd you get that tee! I haven't got that one. I thought I had all the *X-Files* T-shirts!"

"Umm—one of my students gave it to me. He's kind of a fanboy or something . . ."

"Oh you're a fan of the show too, oh my god, that's so—what's your sign?"

He blinked. Had he said he was a fan of the show? He'd seen but one episode of the show, which had seemed pretentious to him—pretending it wasn't ordinary TV when it was—and . . .

And he said . . .

"Oh yeah I love the show, never miss it." He hoped he sounded sincere. Uh—my sign is . . . Scorpio." Actually his sign was Libra but Scorpio sounded sexier.

"Oh . . . my . . . god I knew you had to be a Scorp . . . So am I! I could see all those Scorp fires in you, seriously, I mean I know how that sounds but it was just like you were one of those gas fireplaces."

"Uhh . . . Hell yes, my gas is burning, you bet. Especially after the school cafeteria."

She laughed. Her cart contained Lunchables, a half gallon of tequila, chicken wings with a packet of barbecue sauce, pork rinds, Doritos . . .

"You know what I don't have anybody to talk about *The X-Files* with . . . "

. . . Oscar Mayer franks, white bread, a twelve-pack of Budweiser . . .

"Well—one of these days we should—"

What was he doing?

"How about now!"

"Um—" He felt like a crevice had opened up in the tile floor of the supermarket and he was pitching into free fall, as he said, "What the hell, yeah."

Something in him knew: It was happening so fast.

He found himself following her to the checkout. She was saying something about having to drop off all this stuff and did he have anything to drop off and he said no, don't worry about it.

In the parking lot he thought he saw Jan, she of the questionnaires, sitting in her minivan, watching him as he walked out with Marla. So, let her look.

In a kind of dream, Darry drove behind Marla's car—her sister's car—to a flaking white crackerbox house between two enormous pine trees; there was a silt of red needles on its roof.

He parked well back from the house, at an angle, as she drove into the driveway; she ran over the wheel of an overturned bicycle. She carried the bulging bags to the house, one in each arm, with no visible effort.

He thought: I should have carried them in for her. But he was hoping Cecily wouldn't see him out here, let alone in the house.

A police car cruised slowly by, and the crewcut young cop riding shotgun looked at him. Darry became uncomfortably aware that he was parked crooked, rear end of his car sticking out into the street.

But the cops cruised on, slowing in front of Cecily's house but not stopping. They turned the corner and were gone and then Marla came running up from the house, grinning. She'd left the two bags leaning on the front door.

"I don't have a key and my sister's gone and Cecily's gone but they'll be back soon so I guess the stuff'll be okay." All this as she opened the door and got in. "Well let's go!"

They went. She seemed unaware of the bike wheel crimped under the car she'd left in the driveway. He decided to say nothing about it.

They drove to the town's main drag, Silbido Avenue, and he turned right and immediately regretted it, thinking someone who knew his wife was sure to see him on this street. But then, who knew Bette, anymore?

"Um—where we going?" he asked, smiling, trying to make a joke of his vertiginous uncertainty.

"I should've brought the tequila. Well, let's go where we can have some drinks. Any ol' place. You know what, I don't watch *X-Files* all that much, really, some of them kind of bore me, I just like the alien ones. My favorite show is *Sightings*."

"*Sightings*. UFOs, right?"

"Oh yeah UFOs bigtime, man, but for real, and they also have, you know, ghosts and bigfoot."

"And the ghost of bigfoot?"

"I didn't see that one. They had this one where they showed a crop circle getting made, this light was flying around over a field and this crop circle appeared . . . "

He'd read about it. The film had been analyzed and it was a hoax. And he thought about telling her this. But he could see her cleavage, from where he was sitting.

"Oh I know," he said. "That was mind-blowing. You'd think the president would say something about all this. Flying saucers. I mean, it's evidence."

"Oh exactly, I'm so glad you think so. I really think I was, you know, from there, in my last life."

"From . . . ?"

81

"Another planet. Well, I think it was Mars because, see, Mars used to be this really green planet thousands and thousands of years ago but then they had a catastrophe? And what they had there, you see, was an Egyptian civilization, and they brought it to Egypt, but see the first pyramids and sphinxes, they were on Mars. That's why I've got this Egyptian jewelry, because really it's my connection to Mars."

"Yeah? How about this place? I mean, for a drink. 'Shady Corners Bar and Grill . . .' Most places that say 'Grill' don't have a grill though . . ."

"Whatever. And they had a catastrophe on Mars? And the people all went underground . . . and all that's left is that Face on Mars thing . . . But see I was one of those people in a past life . . . "

"Did you have, uh, hypno-regression, whatsit, to find out?"

"No. I don't think so . . . "

They got out of the car and he looked around at what the neighborhood was like, and he checked twice to make sure he'd locked the car doors. She was already on her way into the bar.

He followed her in. It was dim inside. There was a juke with colored lights in it. The place had a collection of beer signs on the rafters. There was a lifesize cardboard cut-out of a sunnily-smiling Dallas Cowboys Cheerleader in a bikini; the bikini was made of Budweiser labels. There were no windows that he could see. Only one customer; an old man— a shaking, sunken-faced barfly—sat at one end of the bar, talking to himself or maybe to the TV set tuned to an afternoon talk show. Darry felt a twinge of guilt, seeing the talk show. Knowing Bette was probably watching the same show, right now.

"Um . . . two margaritas," he told the lady bartender. She was about fifty and wore a remarkably short skirt, gold-mesh hose, and had a bell of yellow hair. Her swooping eyebrows were cartoonishly inked in.

"We don't do margaritas, honey," she said, as Marla put on a song from a solo album by Stevie whats-her-name from Fleetwood Mac.

"Tequila-up for me!" Marla yelled, punching more buttons on the juke.

"Ummm . . . for me too," he said.

They sat in a booth and drank and Marla told him a rambling story about why she'd left Texas. A boyfriend she'd been with five or six years: he'd abused her, knocked her around, and he sold her big-screen TV one day when she was at work, and he talked her into ripping off her boss and got her fired, but it was a sucky job anyway, working in one of those little glass booths at a gas station. But it wasn't so much that kind of thing. If she just knew where he was going to be on Christmas eve and on her birthday because on your birthday a person should, you know . . .

Darry agreed with her completely. She'd done the right thing, going to live with her sister to get away from the guy. Sounded like an abusive jerk.

"Oh he wasn't so bad, some ways."

And she told him about the dreams that had informed her she was a reincarnated alien princess, and he acted as if it were entirely believable, and they danced, and he drank several more tequilas, and he'd begun to get the spins halfway through "Hotel California" and then he'd run to the bathroom and when he came out she handed him some little white pills and said these'll fix you up and for some reason he took them and, after the glass of water she made him drink, he surprised himself by drinking more tequila . . .

They talked about favorite bands, and then the pills hit him, and his blood came up into his ears into a kind of roaring high tide, and the beer-signs seemed to be grinning conspiratorially at him, and then she was pulling his arm and he was throwing a twenty and a ten at the bartender and then they were in the car, and the car blurred into the grubby little office of the Happy Now Plenty Motel, which was run—and apparently named—by some Vietnamese people who scowled a lot when he and Marla signed in, and she astonished him, as they went into the equally grubby little motel room, by referring to the people in the motel office as "fucking slopes, excuse my language", but then they were kissing on the bed and his hard-on was like an open pocketknife blade under his pants . . .

. . . then she jumped up and turned on the wall-mounted TV and he was surprised, once more, to see they had a pornography channel here, that this was an adult motel, and she was laughing at the girl blowing the black guy, "little cunt polishes that nigger's knob like she had a lot of practice" and he felt he ought to say something about these racist remarks, enough was enough, but then she had given him more small white pills and another tequila . . .

. . . and then he was throwing up again in the little bathroom and in a fit of giddiness deliberately aimed a stream of vomit at the cockroach on the floor and he had to spend ten minutes cleaning it up with a towel which he felt compelled to get rid of so he threw the soiled towel out the bathroom window into the airspace and then he had to rinse out his mouth with the Lavoris that was on the bathroom shelf which had to be the single worst-tasting mouthwash in the history of oral hygiene and then . . .

. . . Then she was pounding on the door and saying she really had to pee but . . .

. . . as he was going out the bathroom door, thinking that his head felt like a beach ball with dozens of little race cars spinning around on its inner surface, she said, "You don't have to leave while I pee, we can talk. We don't need to stand on ceremony . . . You know what, why I think I started doggin' on you, because you remind me of this English teacher I had when I was in ninth grade, I wanted to fuck him bad but he wouldn't even talk about it, but he was so cute . . . "

And he stood awkwardly, hands in pockets, trying to look out the little bathroom window, rather than stare at her as she talked on and tried to pee, with her red lace panties down around her ankles, sitting on the toilet smoking a cigarette, and he thought:

We just met . . . she's the aunt of one of my fifth period kids . . .

Then she said, "I can't pee yet . . . come here . . ." And she took his hand and pulled him down beside her and put his hand between her legs and he gasped and she said, "Rub to help me . . . help me pee . . . rub to . . . " And almost immediately he felt a warm aromatic stream twining his palm, his wrist, ticking onto the porcelain, and she pulled him close and peed into the toilet and on his arm and kissed him on the mouth; she tasted of cigarettes and tequila.

She dropped the cigarette into the metal trashcan, and pulled him to stand in front of her and drew his dick from his pants and laughed when it jumped springily at her and then her mouth was on him, he could see lipstick on it, and she was still peeing, and he almost came that way, but in a few minutes she had led him into the other room and he was on his back, his hand still wet, and she was straddling him, with her skirt still on, her panties in one hand, a cigarette—when had she gotten another cigarette?—in the other hand and she pushed the panties into his mouth as she bounced on his dick and he clawed her blouse down so he could weigh her breasts in his palms and she said, "Pinch the nipples, pinch 'em, pinch 'em, come on . . . shit, pinch 'em, yeah . . ." And on her breasts were tattoos above each nipple: *sweet* and *sour*. There was a name in the cleavage, two letters curving down one tit *BU* and two more curving up the other *CK* and then he came in her and he felt sick and wanted her to get off him and she just laughed and kept rocking on him and—maybe it was the pills—he stayed hard and then . . .

Can't remember . . . can't remember . . .

He first thought about Bette and how late it was when David Letterman came on the little TV.

"Eleven o'clock . . . " he muttered, seeing Letterman.

Marla was sitting up beside him, eating the Chinese food she'd sent out for. Sweet and Sour pork. He hadn't been able to eat any of it. She was wearing the panties now, and the leopard pattern blouse. He could still taste the panties.

She put the Chinese food on a cigarette-burned lamp table by the bed, under a lamp shaped like a glass swan. She lit a cigarette. Marlboro Lights. "You haven't said much for, hell, hours," she said, reaching for the channel changer. There was an old cigarette burn on the channel changer. "David Letterman, I just don't git him. Let's see what else is on. Oh, Jay Leno, I like him . . . "

"Yeah, he's . . . "

Eleven o'clock. Bette would be looking out the window.

Good. Looking out the window was almost as good as going out the door.

"You should have somea that Chinese food, slopey little fucks did it up good."

He winced. "What's up with this racist stuff, Marla?"

"Ooh, Is that not politically connected?"

"You mean—politically correct?"

She turned a look on him that would have set him on fire if he'd been doused with gasoline.

"I guess you think I'm just a stupid kinda bimbo?"

"What? No! I mean—if you have some prejudices, everybody gets, you know, conditioned somewhere . . ."

"Conditioned. Con-ditioned. Somewhere. 'She's conditioned somewhere'. You saying I'm white trash? My mama was a racist?"

"Um—no, I'm just . . . hey, forget it. I have my kneejerk responses to stuff, you know. I mean, the irony is that my objection to racist comments is a reflex of my class status . . . It's itself, um, 'classist' and . . ."

The look she gave him now would have set him on fire without the gasoline.

You dumb shit, he told himself. Patronizing fuck.

"I'm sorry," he began, "I'm just . . . babbling. Drunk. Still drunk. Those pills—first they get me high, then, you know, confused."

"You don't know what drunk is, faggot." She got the fifth of tequila they'd sent out for and poured him four fingers. "Go for it."

"I don't wanna throw up again."

"You're past throwing up. Listen to Mama Marla, she knows."

He drank about half the tumbler. His stomach burned. He laughed. She drank the rest.

A thumping came on the door. Marla sat up straight. She was like a cat hearing the call for dinner; looking around to see where it came from.

"Marla?" A low voice from the door.

Darry felt a long, shimmering chill.

"Marla!"

She was up and he was standing, the room spinning, and only then did he realize he had on the *X-Files* shirt but no pants, his scrotum banging against his thigh. He looked around blearily for his pants, thinking maybe it was just her sister's husband. Obviously she did this sort of thing all the time and they had to fetch her home . . . And everyone would hear about it from the disgusted Cecily . . .

Marla was talking sweetly through the cracked-open door, the brass chain locked over it. "I'll meet you downstairs, baby . . . " Deep basso mumbles and rumbles from whoever was out there. "No baby . . . I wasn't running from you, I just needed some, you know, breathing space. Didn't you get my note?" More mumbles. The word *bullshit*. Rumbles. ". . . no I meant it, I was coming back . . . "

Darry had found his pants and was pulling them on but it was the wrong leg and they faced backwards so he had to start over.

". . . No baby, I'll be right down because someone might—Buck, baby, don't be stupid . . . "

Buck. *BU* on one tit, *CK* on the other.

Each of Darry's blood cells iced over individually.

"No, baby, you'll attract—"

Then the door gave out a thud and the chain snapped and flew across the room and Marla was sliding backwards across the floor on her butt and the door was slamming and Buck was there, big tattooed guy with his hair shaved off on the sides and long on top, little pony tail. His lower lip hung a little bit too far. He wore a guinea tee and oversized jeans and Nikes. He was looking at Darry with his mouth open, looking more stunned than angry. But his hand went behind him.

Marla shot to her feet and went to him, hands raised in front of her. "No you'll get 'em all over us—"

He straight-armed her so she flew with her feet six inches over the floor, smacked into the bathroom door and slid down it.

She sat there panting. Darry realized that she was aroused. "Okay, baby . . . okay, baby . . ."

He reached behind him again and drew the gun out, slowly. It was a .45 automatic, blue steel.

"Hey, no problem, I didn't know she was your girl, I'm outta here . . ." Darry said, desperately sorting words in the hope of coming up with the combination that wouldn't set him off.

As he spoke, he walked past Buck, his neck prickling, and got all the way to the door.

"He's the kind of guy, might call the police, Buck," she said. "That's why I wanted to meet you downstairs, he might get 'em down on us—"

Darry turned to stare at her. Had she really said that? He jerked at the door handle—

Darry felt a big hand on the back of his trousers, flew backwards, off his feet, flung to the floor much the way Marla had been. Found he was sitting on his ass, his back against the bed. "You get some good pussy, you punk-ass motherfucker?" Buck asked, his voice a rasp. His expression unchanging. Sort of flat, vaguely curious.

"Um—no we just—"

"He's so full of shit. He did me hard, Buck."

Darry gaped at Marla.

She went on, chattering happily, hugging her knees against herself like a Campfire Girl at a sleepover. "But he was such a fag about it, I had to lead him along by the dick and he let me sit on him . . ."

Buck laughed. "You rode him like a donkey?"

"Shit yeah!"

They both laughed. Then, almost affectionately, Buck turned and grabbed her by the hair and pulled her to her feet and back-handed her, knocking her back to the floor.

She was weeping now, weeping happily. "I deserve that. Running out on you and fucking this asshole. I do."

"You deserve a lot worse."

Darry began to see the depth and width of it. He jumped up and stumbled to the window, tried to yell for help. "Hey! Somebody call the police! Hey—!"

He heard her small footsteps behind him and heard a crash through a sudden burning in his scalp and he fell through the sensation, fell backwards, onto the bed. At the end of a tunnel very far away he saw her standing over him with a broken table lamp in her hands. "That's my girl," Buck was saying, as the tunnel shut down, and Darry lost consciousness.

He heard them talking for awhile, before he really completely came to. His hands were tied behind him with lamp cord. He couldn't feel his fingers. There was something jammed in his mouth: his own salty socks. He kept still and listened.

"For real, you're right over there in the Howard Johnson's?"

"For real. One block down the fuckin' street."

"We almost went to that one! But I think the cheap fag wanted to save money."

"You like assholes like this? Full-of-themselves assholes with Ph.Ds and shit?"

"Lord no, baby, you know I don't. I just wanted to go out and I didn't want nobody like you because it would just, you know, make me want you. You went to my sister's house?"

"Yeah she saw you leave with some asshole. She thought you was going to the motel strip. I ask a few people and, guess what, you stand right out. 'Yeah that little slut's over in that shit hole right there, I seen her go in'."

"Well I guess I surely do stand out! It's not like I was hiding that much, baby, don't you git that? If I wanted to hide from you, would I come to my sister's?"

"You got any more of that speed?"

"Right here, darlin'." He heard her rummaging in her purse. "Here you go . . . I mean, baby darlin' if I wanted really to get away from you would I go to my sister's? Like I didn't know you wouldn't look there?"

"Stupid little cunt you should've picked some place closer. Drove my ass three nights getting here."

"You drove all that way? But you see there, now I know what you'd do for love, to come out here and get me . . . "

"I start to come onto this speed I'll show you what I'll do for love you stray bitchin' dick dogging whore."

"Say that again." Her voice husky with arousal.

"You heard me. Dick dogging whore . . . turn your ass over . . . "

"Just don't break nothing please baby . . . " The sounds of slapping and her grunt of tearful happiness as he sodomized her.

Darry tried to wriggle around, get to the door, but he felt Buck fishing for him, felt callused fingers on his scalp, twisting his hair, jerking him to sit up, and then Buck was banging Darry's head on the wall beside the bed with one hand, while slamming himself into Marla, another fuck and a slam, a fuck and a slam, Darry trying to pull loose but kitten-helpless, a fuck and a slam, Buck's fingers around her throat from behind, jerking her back onto his dick with that hand, the other slamming Darry on the wall, Darry starting to swallow the socks, realizing he was going to choke to death like this, a fuck and a *slam*. "How's that feel, you two bitches, both of you bitches, how's that, how's that—"

That's when the door opened and shut and Darry heard Buck shout "What the fuck—?" And Buck let go of him, Darry rolling onto his back to see the police—

It wasn't the police. It was . . .

Jan? The computer science teacher from school. Was here in the room with him.

"Hi, Darry." Jan had a snub-nose .38 in her hand. She held it very steadily.

"You know this bitch? This your old lady?" Marla asked, with real wonder. She had separated from Buck; the two of them turned to look at the door; she reached down and pulled the socks from Darry's mouth. He gasped, and found his voice.

"Jan—run for the—" He gagged, and tried again. "—the cops!"

Jan shook her head. "I don't think you really want the cops to find you like this . . . Your wife would have to hear about it and everyone else too . . . " She was still in her school work clothes. She was smiling, very gently.

Marla and Buck were naked, on the bed. Buck made a grab for the his .45 but Jan was already scooping it up and stepping back from him. She pointed the .38 at his chest as Buck got ready to lunge at her.

"I took those classes for women—the ones where they teach you to be aggressive, to fight thieves and the like," she said, looking him in the eye. "They taught me to aim and to shoot. I really will shoot. And there's no reason for that to happen unless you insist. You're not going to jail . . . "

Buck sat back on the bed. "You his sister or what?"

"I'm a friend. I knew he was getting into trouble. He was due for it. Exactly due. I've been following him since the supermarket. When I saw him leave with her. I've sort of been expecting her . . . Can you stand up, Darius?"

"Uhhh . . . I think . . . oh shit my head hurts." A sob escaped him. Blood trickled hot on the side of his head.

"You see? He's such a sucky little shit," Marla said.

Buck laughed. "He is that, ain't he?"

Darry felt a rising fury. He pictured getting loose, getting the extra gun, shooting them both.

He wobbled over to Jan and turned his back to her. "You take off these wires?"

"No—turn your back to the bed. Marla? Would you do the honors?"

Marla looked at Buck. "Go ahead, darlin'," Buck said, grinning.

Marla untied Darry and feeling came painfully back into his hands. But they continued to hurt and so did his head and all his muscles. His heart was hammering; his stomach lurched. He wanted to throw up. But he managed to get his clothes back on; one of the most painful things he ever had to do. He found his wallet; they hadn't emptied it yet.

"We'll get you checked for a concussion," Jan said. "You got your wallet? Good . . . Come on . . ."

"You in love with him, huh." Marla said, lying back on the bed, eyes wide.

"That's right."

"I like that. That's romantic. See what she's doing for love, baby? I'd do that. I'd do way more than that."

Buck put his arms around her and said nothing, just watching the other two balefully, like a half tamed lion, as they backed toward the door.

"I need some money," Buck said. "He took some pussy off my woman."

"No," Darry said. "You took it out of me already."

"Best to leave everyone feeling equitable, Darry," Jan said. She handed Darry the smaller gun. She reached into a skirt pocket, pulled out five twenties. Darry realized she'd had the money ready for something like this.

The guy hammers my head against the wall and we're going to pay him too.

She tossed the money on the bed. Darry suddenly became aware of the agreeable weight of the gun in his hand. He came close to shooting. His fingers tightened.

But the fury was dissolving. *I like that. That's romantic.*

Buck looked at him and knew that Darry was thinking about shooting. "You one lucky motherfucker," Buck said. "I was going to kill your punk ass," deliberately pushing Darry.

Darry turned away and Buck smiled.

Jan ejected the clip from the .45, checked for bullets in the chamber, tossed it back to Buck.

Darry looked at her. "You're going to give him the gun?"

"He can't fire it now. He can get a new clip. Those things are expensive. I respect guns. I respect these two, really. Except he shouldn't be beating that girl up."

"I know I shouldn't," Buck said, evenly. But without sorrow.

"He knows he shouldn't," Marla said, nodding. Without judgment.

Darry couldn't stand it anymore. He lurched out the door. Jan came after him and closed the door behind her. As they went down the stairs she took the .38 from him and discreetly put it in her purse and they got into the minivan.

He retched in the minivan, as they drove to her place, but nothing came out.

"Was it the models?" He asked, after he was done retching. "You did that detailed a computer model of . . . of my behavior . . . my life?"

"Yes. I knew you'd get in with someone like that. And that she'd have someone like Buck. I modeled most of it—roughly what'd happen. So many variables, it's hard to be sure. It might not've happened. But I'm right about sixty-three percent of the time, computer modeling; projecting from personality with behavioral spreadsheets and probability ratios, weighing in primary environmental factors."

This kind of talk, just now, was ungraspable for him. All he understood at the moment were things like *I was going to kill your punk ass.*

"I called your wife, just before I came in, and said I heard you were the victim of a hit and run, and you weren't hurt bad, just stunned and wandering around, but I thought I knew where you were and I was going to get you to a doctor. She was interested but not, you know, frantic."

"Jesus. What a story. You should be the writer, not me."

"I'm taking you to my place to clean you up, then you go home to her but . . . Do you want me to tell you what you should do then?"

"What the hell. You just saved my 'punk ass'."

"That's the Darius I love. Well—you should divorce your wife, but see to it she has therapy first. She doesn't want to be married to you. I got her to do the questionnaires too."

"No, come on."

"Oh yes. Came to the house. Had to, to get your model right—you weren't detailed or honest enough. I used to bring her treats. Pastries and lattés. Told her not to tell you . . . She'll have a series of crushes on therapists and then she'll find someone amenable. She'll lose weight, too. She wants to be as free of you as you are of her . . . "

"Really?"

"Fifty nine percent probability. And then you should . . . You sure you want me to go on?"

"Yeah. It takes my mind off the way my head feels."

"You should live with me for awhile and see if you're ready to be serious with me. We'll be traveling. We're going on one of those cruises to Alaska first. I always wanted to see Alaska."

"Cruises?"

"We're quitting our jobs."

"We are?"

"I only stayed there for you."

"You're kidding."

"Nope. Not kidding. I don't need to work. I don't really like teaching all that much. I've got $680,000 in the bank. Plus another half million in shares. Software royalties."

"You're shitting me."

"That's such a revolting expression."

"Sorry . . . Alaska? All this sounds . . . "

"Like I'm as crazy as Marla in my way. Not really. Only a little. But we're such a good fit, you and I. Now me, I want, um, to take care of someone, very completely take care of them, and you, well, you really, really like to be taken care of. You're quite . . . passive, honestly. Deep down. You want excitement but you don't want to . . . to be the leader in getting there."

He didn't like that. He didn't really admit that it was true till about five months later . . .

. . . when during the day they watched an iceberg shuddering parts of itself into the sea, shattering in the spring wind: Temporary gems of ice falling, splashing in evanescent transparent lace.

And Jan's lace . . .

Her lace was black, in their little ship's cabin, at night: Narrow shoulders, wide hips: *holy shit, she fucks like a goddess!*

. . . and only then could Darry admit that it was true . . . when they were on the cruise ship, and Jan was bouncing on his dick, and he asked her to stuff her panties into his mouth.

SEVEN KNIVES

"I HEARD IT's based on a Hitchcock story that never got produced," Beaumont said, staring at the brutal props on the sound stage. He went closer to the iron maiden—a copy, anyway, of the medieval torture device. "That iron maiden's a beauty." This variant was shaped of metal bands in the rough outline of a woman, the blades pointing inward from the bands to penetrate the victim placed inside. "Who else is coming to the meeting, do you know?"

"All I know is the fax said we meet here and Dirby is directing. I mean, Lemuel Dirby, hell, that's enough for me," Rosano said. "And it's called *Seven Knives.*" He looked at Beaumont, and snorted. "Oh I get it. 'That iron maiden's a beauty.' Funny, Chris."

What was Rosano's first name? Beaumont was bad with names, but he knew that Rosano liked to maintain that 'we're all friends here' Hollywood mirage. Brian, that was it: a superficially jovial, half-Latino guy, his trainer never quite keeping his plumpness under control; a very expensive haircut and tailored shirts, brown leather Italian jacket, matching Bruno Magli shoes.

"Well it was a sort of joke but that iron maiden is really crafted like a son of a bitch, Brian. I used to do research for Stuart Gordon, before I got into scripting . . . Although there are some differences—odd little variations . . . "

Their voices echoed slightly in the dim room. Only two overhead lights were switched on, at this end. Beaumont peered into the deeper shadows of the sound stage. Except for the few props, and two folding wooden chairs, the concrete room was empty, the corners grimy. Squinting, he could just make out the heavy padlocks and chains on the corrugated freight door in the farther end. It was clammy here, all angles and dust like a crypt. It'd been used mostly for television work for decades, out here in the Valley, then low-budget films, some of them pretty respectable. There were ceiling lights on rails overhead spotting the props—the iron maiden, a rack complete with the spoked wheel, a couple of sharpened meat hooks, like talons, hanging from a gibbet, and a tin "executioner's ax" in a fiberglass "wooden block". The iron maiden was the most realistic looking. "On the other hand," Beaumont muttered, "this executioner's ax looks about as real as Joan Rivers' face." There was little else in the room, which was about as big as a Methodist church's nave.

As Beaumont looked around, the sound stage seemed increasingly oppressive. He thought of dozens of minor actors working here—and minor writers, sometimes, called in late at night; their hopes coming to nothing but instantly forgotten television filler. The thought came: Without the cinematic illusion, this room's as bleak as fate.

He felt like saying something just to shake the feeling of cold implacability. "This is cute having the first meeting with these props, since it's about a psycho obsessed with the Inquisition. *If* that's what it's about. I dunno, my agent just gave me a log-line. Meeting here's kind of a hard-sell way to get the thing going but more fun than one of those stifling offices on the Paramount lot."

"Was it really a Hitchcock project, back in the day? That'd explain why Mr Lemuel 'Art House' Dirby is doing a thriller . . ."

"Closer to horror, from what I understood. Maybe why Hitch never got it made."

"I'm glad to see you're here to do the scripting, man," Rosano said, sitting on the table of a prop torture rack. "Shit, I heard they were getting John Shirley to write."

"I don't know him."

"Oh man, when I was producing the remake of *The Seven Faces of Dr. Lao*—trying anyway, we never did get it produced—he was hired on as the writer. Mr. 'don't lose the original vision or it won't work'. Pretentious crap like that. He's over-rated. I heard Dave Schow did most of the writing on *The Crow*—"

The far door to the old soundstage was opening: Door Five—it had a big "5" painted on the outside of it.

Beaumont stared. Did he know this guy? He was familiar . . .

"Jesus," Rosano breathed. "It's Kenny Kaldren."

A compact guy in jeans, white button-down shirt, sleeves rolled, short sort-of-gay haircut, dyed brown. Wiry but with a very clearly defined pot-belly and sunken chest; he looked like he might be in his early fifties, but, remembering who he was now, Beaumont realized he was actually only around forty-two at most. Maybe booze or something had aged him.

Beaumont glanced at Rosano. He seemed almost scared, staring at Kaldren that way. The kind of scared that was so mingled with angry you couldn't tell them apart.

"Are you two the only ones who showed up?" Kaldren asked, his voice silken. He looked at them, at the iron maiden, around the sound stage. Back at the iron maiden.

"Who else is coming?" Beaumont asked. Rosano was avoiding Kaldren's gaze. Was looking at the door as if thinking of leaving.

"Mary-Beth Delmora," Kaldren said, "and Jim Perth."

"Jim *Perth* for Chris'sakes?" Rosano said.

"So you're . . . producing on this?" Beaumont asked, as Kaldren walked over to the iron maiden. And Beaumont noticed for the first time that the iron maiden's blades had knobs that stuck out a little from the bands they transfixed, and some of the knobs looked to be recently painted red. Seven or so of them. Maybe he was going to use exactly that prop in *Seven Knives*.

"Dirby could get a nice shot from inside this thing, with the iron bands criss-crossing the frame," Kaldren said, running fingers over the iron maiden. He chuckled—and the chuckle somehow decayed into a soft whimpering sound. It made the skin on Beaumont's arms tighten to hear it, though he wasn't sure why.

Kaldren reached out and, very deliberately, put his left hand around one of the blades, and squeezed. His shoulders tensed. Then he turned back to the Rosano and Beaumont, his hand dropping by his side . . . dripping blood. Copiously.

"Jesus, Kaldren," Rosano said.

"Come on, it's fake, Rosano," Beaumont said. "Comes out of those hollow prop knives."

"Yeah, prop knives!" Kaldren said, not quite laughing. Something flickered in his eyes, and was hidden away again.

Beaumont walked over to the iron maiden and touched the edge of a couple of the knives. "These are . . . they seem real—" He broke off when something dripped on the back of his hand from one of the knives. He drew his hand out and looking at it, feeling the still lingering warmth. He was almost sure it wasn't fake blood. He sniffed at it. "This is blood . . ." He looked at Kaldren who was staring at the door, then walked over to him and took his wrist, drew it close, stared at the coursing red ravine in the small pale palm. Beaumont could make out yellow fat and white bone in the cut. "Jesus. That's deep, Kaldren."

"That's too deep to be an accident," Rosano said, making an almost exaggerated face of disgust that made Beaumont think of the tragedy mask that hung, with the comedy mask, over some old stages. "He did that shit on purpose. He's going to have one of his big melodrama moments. This is bullshit." He stood up, zipping his jacket, preparing to go.

Beaumont dropped Kaldren's limp hand, as the blood started to drip onto his own fingers, warm and sticky. He shook his hand at the floor to whip the blood away. "You'd better go get that bandaged up. Stitched, in fact."

"Not much point in that . . ." Kaldren looked at Beaumont. "Get it?" He didn't laugh, or even smile. Blood dripped from his slashed left palm. He just let the hand dangle, bleeding, like that was what you did with a slashed hand. "I can't really feel much, anyway. Not . . . not easily." He shrugged. "It'll clot up . . ."

"Fuck this guy," Rosano said. "I didn't know he was involved. I'm out of here."

He started toward the door—but then it opened for Jim Perth. He was a tanned, blond actor-turned-producer; blond rinse by this time, judging by the deep lines in his face. Perth was executive producer of a low-rated cop show, *Waikiki,* a kind of unofficial remake of *Hawaii Five-O.* He wore a Hawaiian shirt, too, Beaumont noted. Parrots against red tropical flowers.

Perth looked at his watch, glanced around, "I haven't got a whole lot of time, we have a season premiere—" He broke off, seeing Kaldren. Who was staring back at him.

Perth seemed as stunned as Rosano to see Kaldren.

"Your show is going to be cancelled, Perth, that premiere is just a formality," Kaldren said mildly. "Everyone knows that. Which is why you're here, get another iron in the fire."

"Don't tell me you're in this, Kenny," Perth said, his voice a toneless, rapidfire clip. "Doing what?"

"I'm the whole thing," Kaldren said.

Perth snorted. "You haven't changed—the instant recourse to sneering rudeness. You alternated between that and flagrant ass kissing."

"No ass kissing today, Jim."

"Well— I'm going to split . . ." Rosano said once again. And again broke off as the door opened again.

Trying to manage an entrance without seeming too obvious about it, Mary Beth Delmora breezed in Door Five. Her straight-cut red-blond hair caught the light as she approached. She wore skintight blue jeans, deliberately contrasted with her red pumps, her rust-colored, low cut Armani blouse.

Not quite like she was coming down a modeling runway, Beaumont thought, but almost. And as she got close enough so they could smell her perfume—gardenias—he saw that her lips had been recently pumped with collagen. They were now slightly too puffy for her faun-slender face. He had an absurd urge to reach out and squeeze them to see if they were really lumpy. The skin on her face was drum-tight. She was forty-two trying to look twenty-three.

Beaumont was thinking: What subtle grotesqueries were engendered by cosmetic surgery.

"And here's our *star*," Kaldren said, smirking.

"Mary-Beth!" Perth said, his nostrils flaring. "You're looking . . . is it politically incorrect to say *hot*?"

"Hey, I didn't vote for Schwarzenegger, but screw it, say I'm hot. No groping, though." She smiled with some of her old charm, a light in her famously blue eyes.

Kaldren waited till she had reached the little group, then with his intact hand he plucked a remarkably small cell phone from a shirt pocket, hit a speed dial and said, "Te? My man! Go ahead."

Moments later there was a click from the door.

"You didn't just fucking have somebody lock that door," Rosano said.

"You bet I did. My good friend Te did it for me. I haven't even got a key. We both work here—I'm the clerk who rents the stages, nowadays. He's security. Nice Vietnamese kid. He thinks it's like I'm setting you guys up . . . for a pitch. Locked door, torture instruments, all part of the pitch. The good old-fashioned Hollywood movie sell-job."

"Oh!" Mary-Beth said, pointing at his bloody hand, smiling. "And blood capsules! I got here too late for the special effects knife!"

"You're not too late for the knife," Kaldren said. "Ironic, that—when one thinks of your surgery bills. I don't think you even remember me."

She looked at him, blinking. "Um . . . No. But Jim's right, you're rude. Oh!" She compressed her lips—it was an odd effect. "I do remember now . . ."

Beaumont said, "Is there some history here I should know?"

Rosano said, "You shouldn't, Beaumont, because then you'd know this little bitch Kaldren like I do. A clerk who rents sound stages! That's who called us here! I'm going."

"You've been saying that . . ." Kaldren said.

The others stared, embarrassed, as Rosano started for the door. Perth looked like he was about to follow him. "Is the door really locked from the outside?"

Rosano reached the door, tugged on it. "Yeah but big deal! I'll pound on it, or call security." His voice came to them filtered through space and echo. "I can get the number . . ." He took out his cell phone, started dialing for information.

"Rosano!" Kaldren called out, sudden and sharp. "You hid three hundred thousand dollars from the IRS and I know where it is."

Rosano stopped dialing.

Well, Beaumont thought, that got his attention.

Kaldren went on, "I had a . . . a lover who worked for your crook of an accountant. You skimmed money from the studio too . . ."

Rosano glared at Kaldren. "You little prick."

"Is this all part of the pitch too?" Mary-Beth asked, with an uncertain smile. "The locked door? You being rude? Hints of blackmail? All part of some mood-setting thing?"

"Sure," Kaldren said, "it's part of the pitch. That's part of the story, for sure."

"There isn't any pitch," Rosano shouted, stamping his way back to them. "This little weasel . . ." Rosano was leaning forward as he came, so that his face emerged from the shadows first: lean, tense, focused on Kaldren. "I'm gonna clout the little blackmailer . . ."

Beaumont said, "I'm not down with anybody getting violent here, Rosano." Beaumont stepped between Rosano and Kaldren, and put up his hands. "Take it easy, bro. Just wait . . . a bit."

"He made all this shit up, you know that don't you, Beaumont?" Rosano demanded. "I mean—this whole meeting is bullshit, if he's behind it. He's a pathological liar."

"Well it's true that I fabricated those faxes," Kaldren said, lifting his hand so he could gaze at the still-welling rift in it. "I had William Morris stationery from when I worked there. When I applied for a job on the lot I swiped some Paramount Executive Offices letterhead. When I called your agents, I pretended to be an assistant to Joel Silver on the phone. Fake confirmation calls . . ." He grinned, pale and sickly, and put on a younger voice: "'Hi I'm calling from Joel Silver's office, Joel wanted to talk to you about appearing in a new production to be directed by Lemuel Dirby, there'll be a preliminary meeting on soundstage five at . . .'"

Mary-Beth's mouth hung open.

"There's no Dirby in this?"

"No Dirby, but . . ."

Then her eyes crinkled with something approximating merriness—Beaumont was afraid the skin might tear—and she laughed. "This is great, I can improv with this." She put on an actorly face of concern, a breathless voice. "'But if you aren't really part of the new Dirby film, what are you doing here?'"

Rosano groaned. "Mary-Beth, he's not . . . it's not . . . no . . ."

"Oh!" Mary-Beth said. "Rosano is part of it!" She laughed with real relief. "I was getting really freaked out. So is *Seven Knives* like a picture about movie people? Like *The Player*? Or do we . . ."

Perth shrugged. "I don't care if there's a deal or not, I'm not into this kind of manipulation." He was all low-key, calm dismissal. He took out his cell phone, dialed Information, started walking toward door five. Then changed direction, moving toward the freight door in the shadowy end of the room. "Make more noise banging on that freight door . . ."

Rosano was tapping his own cell phone on his teeth. Still looking like he might hit Kaldren.

"I'm not going to blackmail you, Rosano," Kaldren said.

"You just did."

"Not really. I just wanted you to wait a moment. Hear me out, that's all I ask . . ." Kaldren turned toward Perth, who was pounding on the corrugated freight door with one fist, holding his cell phone to his ear with the other. "Perth—you remember I have the rights to Graven's Merlin Steele character?"

Perth stopped thumping on the door, a statue in the shadows. At last he pressed a button on the cell phone, put it back in his pocket, and started back toward them, frowning.

"Whatever you think you know about my . . . my tax situation, Kaldren," Rosano said, "you got it wrong."

As Perth joined them under the lights, Kaldren shook his head firmly, and said, "I don't think I'll have to mention any of your underhanded dealings to anyone, Brian. You need a break too badly. You've got a nice, big façade but you're in debt and you can't bring that money out of hiding yet. Everything you've tried to produce has gone south, for two or three years. I'm going to give you a chance to get the rights to Merlin Steele. You need a break. You all need a break. So . . . listen a minute. That's all I'm asking."

"What's a little listening, Brian?" Perth said.

Mary-Beth looked back and forth between them, blinking in confusion. Not sure yet this wasn't some kind of dramatized pitch.

Rosano seemed to chew it over, glaring. Then he nodded once, and put his hands in his pockets, and looked at Mary-Beth, then at the floor. "Spit it out then."

Kaldren pressed his wounded hand to his shirt. Strangely indifferent to the stain, for a guy neat as a pin, Beaumont thought. "Here's the thing," Kaldren said, almost dreamily. "Paramount has the rights to the Merlin Steele books. I have the right to the original short story that created the character—rights that my dad got. Along with the other Graven property he had . . ." He paused, tilted his head, and looked at them sidelong. "You remember that Merlin Steele story—*Pilot Fish?* You were all on that production! Beaumont was originally going to write—Mary-Beth was going to star. Perth and Rosano were two of the producers."

"We made that film and we're not going to do a re-make," Perth snapped.

"I'm not talking about doing that film. I'm talking about the three Merlin Steele books they have the rights to at Paramount. They bought the books and then found out they can't do those movies without the Steele character—a magician detective, hunting down demons . . . it'd be obviously trampling on my rights. Because I own the first short story. But Paramount wouldn't make a deal with me. They wouldn't cut me in. They dispute that I have the rights to the character. It's been in court for years. Now look at the papers on the floor inside that iron maiden . . ."

Beaumont went, opened the door of the iron maiden, swinging spikes toward himself. "I didn't see those." He picked it up. "Looks like a will."

"It wills the rights to "Grey Eyes", the first Merlin Steele story, to you three. It specifies you get those rights no matter how I die, even suicide. Which is how my death today will look. You're going to kill me and we'll make it look like a suicide. And you can make the movie."

They stared at him in silence. Beaumont could hear Rosano breathing.

At last Mary-Beth clucked her tongue, shook her head, laughing. "Oh—he's got you guys really going!" Perth looked at her, shook his head, then looked back at Kaldren. She made a sound of exasperation. "Jim—I mean, come on . . . This isn't . . ."

Then she broke off, gaping as Kaldren took off his pants. First the pants, underwear scooped off at the same time, then his shirt. "I think I'll leave my shoes on. My feet are cold." Now he was naked but for loafers with little tassels on them. He just stood there with his slumping shoulders and little round stomach, hands dangling at his sides, his dick angling at his crotch. Wearing nothing but the shoes and a Mona Lisa smile.

"Oh for Christ's sake," Perth muttered.

"Okay," Mary-Beth said, taking a step back, "Brian, you were right: he's . . . out of it."

"Put your fucking clothes on, Kaldren, shit!" Rosano snarled.

"You all stripped me naked," Kaldren said, his voice breaking. "All but Beaumont here. He left before most of it came down . . ." He turned to Beaumont. "You were on *Pilot Fish*. You left before I was shoved off the production . . . forced off . . ."

Beaumont nodded. Kaldren's father had been a friend of the widow of the famous horror writer, Graven. She'd sold him two key Graven properties, cheap. "Grey Eyes" and "Pilot Fish". But the elder Kaldren had died, a suicide in the midst of the production, leaving the rights to his son.

Till then Kenny had been a sort of pilot fish himself, following the sharks of the industry around, feeding off their leavings. Production assistant, assistant to the director, script supervisor. One unpaid Associate Producer credit. Nothing you could thrive on. Year after year after year, never getting any farther. Then he'd come into "Pilot Fish" . . .

"It was all I had." Kaldren was saying. "I couldn't do anything, I had no talent, none of the survival instincts that executive types in Hollywood use in place of talent. I had nothing else . . . And they took the picture from me."

"You're fucking nuts," Rosano said.

"I know exactly what I'm doing," Kaldren said, his voice gone suddenly soft, not quite child-like. He turned and walked to the iron maiden, opened the door, got in . . .

He stood there with his hands clasping the metal cage—seeming about to pull it shut on himself. He tensed . . .

"Don't do that!" Beaumont shouted, his heart leaping. Stripping naked in front of them, Kaldren had clinched the diagnosis: he was crazy enough to do anything. Beaumont took a step toward the iron maiden.

"Stay back," Kaldren said, "or I'll close it on myself right now. And you checked it out, Beaumont—some of these blades are real."

Beaumont stopped where he was. "Kaldren—what the fuck?"

"I bought the prop at a studio auction. Ran up a couple of credit cards getting it redesigned. It locks when you close it. I won't have to pay off the credit cards. Suicide's faster than bankruptcy."

He pulled it toward himself—

"Don't!" Beaumont said.

—but didn't quite close it. He shivered—and smiled.

He'd pulled it just close enough to score his skin; mere nicks, really, from seven bladepoints across his chest, belly and groin. The other knives were the original prop fakes. Blood started to trickle down from the seven little marks.

"He's really getting cut, Beaumont?" Mary-Beth asked, putting a hand to her mouth, adding vaguely: "I was just thinking it might be one of those reality shows . . . where they set you up with hidden cameras . . . like that *Punk'd* thing." She looked around for the hidden cameras. Maybe in that one dead track light?

Beaumont grimaced. "I don't think it's a set up—before you came I checked the iron maiden. At least some of the blades are real."

"Look!" Kaldren said. "Mary-Beth's going to 'cry'. Method acting! Maybe if she thinks about something bad that happened to her—like when she was passed over for that part that Julia Roberts got—maybe then she'll actually manage some tears. Crying for herself."

"But why this?" Beaumont asked. "Why hurt yourself? They did you some kind of wrong—forced you out of something. Okay, I see that. But . . . this?"

"I need . . . " Kaldren seemed unsure how to explain. "I just . . . need to . . . I had this habit—I would cut myself, see, for all my failures, for letting them kill my dad—"

"Kill your dad! Now what the hell are you babbling about?" Rosano demanded. "He killed himself!"

"Yes, enlighten us, 'Kenny'," Perth said, his eyes glittering coldly. He took the will from Beaumont's hand—scanned through it as Kaldren went on.

"Yes my dad killed himself. He was a fragile person. Like me. And you people told him you were taking the production away from him. You got him to sign a contract that made him a figurehead and gave him a little money and you lied to him about his title. He was no professional in the business. And he started drinking again and that brought the depression on . . . and he killed himself." He ran his thumb along a blade, watching it produce a thin line of glittering red.

"So you blame us!" Rosano said, rolling his eyes. "Your dad was as nutty as you. He kept changing his mind about the production. I'm sorry about what happened to him but it wasn't our fault. We tried to make him happy. Told him you could work on the production—take over for him—and you were worse than your old man."

Kaldren ignored Rosano, and went on, speaking to Beaumont—but it was as if he was looking through him. "All those people who loathed me—I knew they were right because when I came on the production, I just . . . I betrayed my Dad. I tried to fix everything and just made it worse—and they kicked me off the production too. And Dad killed himself. Maybe better he didn't see the movie—it became this stupid thing—an embarrassment. Hated by critics and audiences. And I let that happen . . ."

Rosano rubbed his forehead. "You're giving me a fucking headache. You're fantasizing that we're going to kill you—that's going to ease your guilt?"

"It's your fault and my fault, what happened. I can punish me and I can punish you—by making you kill me. It'll be such a relief to me. To finish it. To really feel it. To not imagine you're stabbing me—I imagined it so many times!—but to feel it for real. When you push the knives in the rest of the way. I want to feel it . . . when you do it. Feel the . . ."

"You really think we'd do that?" Mary-Beth asked. "Kenny . . . please!"

"Yes. You all will," Kaldren said, with fatal conviction. "I remember how you stood by, Mary-Beth, and you even justified what they did . . . when they took over the production. I was a producer. I wanted to keep control for Dad's sake—but because I wanted to fire Mary-Beth Delmora . . ."

"That was you who wanted me fired?" Mary-Beth said, with a voice that, for the first time, seemed somehow real. "I didn't know who, Jim just said that someone . . ." She gave Kaldren a sub-zero stare—a look from deep inside her, Beaumont thought.

"You weren't an actress, you were a theatrical machine . . ." Kaldren's voice seemed distant, as if he was shouting from the far side of a canyon. "I wanted . . . someone in touch with real life, with the suffering of real life. But you were sleeping with Perth . . ."

Perth and Mary-Beth glanced at one another, and looked quickly away.

". . . and he made sure you had the part . . . and Perth and Rosano—they used a clause, something I'd never understood, to push me out, give me that meaningless associate producer title . . . I lost all the rights—they said I was . . ."

"You could have kept the rights," Rosano said, through clenched teeth. "Goddamn it—but you kept after us! You had to have your own director, your own writer, your own actress and you started to follow us around away from the studio—"

"You stole it from me—and my father!"

"Insanity forced you out," Rosano said in a growl. "We got the police reports, you watching my house in your car—that was enough. Your stalking, your threats, your crazy emails. You had no talent, no savvy for the work, and you kept pushing and demanding . . . and whining."

"Oh yeah," Perth said, with a soft snort. "It was the whining I couldn't stand."

"I'm going to die today," Kaldren said. "And all that matters is that I understand why."

"Ohhh-kay, that's all," Beaumont said, taking his own cell phone out. "This has gone far enough, I'm definitely calling for someone to help us."

"No!" Kaldren yelled, his voice shrill."Look!"

And Kaldren swung the door of the iron maiden shut with a clang.

As the knives went home, he made a high pitched sound that went on and on, "Aa-a-a-ahhhhh . . . aa-a-a-ahhhh . . . "

They could smell the blood. They could see the wounds, deeper wounds now, four on Kaldren's chest, a couple on his belly, one piercing his groin. They all stood there, staring and listening to their hearts beat.

But they weren't killing wounds, Beaumont decided—deeper than before but, stepping close, he could see that the blades had gone in only about half an inch.

Kaldren stopped his moaning. He cleared his throat, breathing shallowly, raggedly.

"Oh God," Mary-Beth said.

Beaumont pointed. "Look closer—they're not stabbing deep into him . . . But they're deep enough he could bleed to death. And if he doesn't stay still he could push the knives . . . even deeper."

"Not yet . . ." Kaldren whimpered. Speaking made the blades dig into him a millimeter or so more. Breathing seemed to widen the wounds.

He stood there with the tips of seven knives in him. His body quivering, his knuckles white on the metal slats of the iron maiden. The other knives were plastic, spring-loaded blades receded into the hollow bases of their lower shafts under pressure from Kaldren's skin.

Tears streamed down Kaldren's face. But there was something else—a look of sleepy relief in his eyes, his drooping mouth.

Beaumont stepped closer and tugged on the door of the iron maiden. Locked.

The red knobs, Beaumont saw, were now sticking out a bit more— several inches that hadn't obtruded before. As if ready to be gripped, like the hafts of daggers. "I can pull them out. Hold still, Kaldren."

"No . . ."

Beaumont tugged on a knob. It wouldn't move.

"Oh . . . my." Kaldren lowered his voice to a near whisper. The others had come a few steps closer to listen. Staring in sickened fascination. "Beaumont," Kaldren rasped, "the . . . knives have ra-ratchets on them. Can go deeper. But . . . can't pull out."

"We'll get paramedics—the jaws of life'll get you out of there."

"No!" Kaldren deliberately squirmed so the knives were twisted in his wounds. Crying out as he did it: sobbing. He wailed with the multiple hurt.

"Stop that, dammit!" Beaumont shouted.

Kaldren sagged back a little, panting. "Then don't bring anyone." He had to pause, draw a careful breath; each time he spoke pain lanced into him. "Or . . . I'll do it again and again . . ."

Beaumont looked the device over. "Opening the door would pull them out. There must be a way to pop the door open." Beaumont looked around the back of the device, the sides, finding nothing like a spring release, a triggering flange.

"No, Beaumont," Kaldren said, almost whispering. "It doesn't. Designed my way."

"God he's a sick little fuck," Rosano said.

"A self-mutilator," Mary-Beth said, as if thinking aloud. "I did it a little, for awhile. Anorexic people do it. I got some meds . . ."

Beaumont nodded numbly. "Self-mutilation. Associated with BPD. Borderline Personality Disorder. They're feeling this horrible dysphoria and it's the only thing that eases it. Relieves pressure, creates some kind of weird endorphin rush . . ." Beaumont felt paralyzed, unsure what to do. If he tried to call anyone, break Kaldren loose, he'd impale himself. Finish the job.

Perth nodded, seeming very self-contained—and at the same time Beaumont thought Perth might kick the iron maiden over. "What I hear, for a lot of people it's narcissism . . . they feel abused, so their narcissistic response is to act it out . . ."

Kaldren tittered at their diagnoses—and then groaned when the small fluttering laugh drove the knives minutely deeper. And then tittered again. Blood flowed more thickly; ever more brightly against his pale skin.

Beaumont glanced at the others. Mary-Beth seemed to be crying for real now—it was hard to be sure. The tears were there. Only, Beaumont thought, watching her, they were tears of rage. "He's just a fucking masochist," Mary-Beth sobbed, fists clenched. "It's making me want to throw up."

"Like when you were . . . bulimic?" Kaldren said, his voice barely audible. Staring into space as he spoke.

Mary-Beth threw Kaldren a look like an eighth knife.

Beaumont found himself looking once more at the knives in Kaldren's wounds. Whenever Kaldren breathed, the knives dug in, widening the wounds a little, making them deeper, a millimeter here and there. Seven little wounds leaking blood. One of them almost gushing. It'd hit a large vein. Beaumont breathed in, his ribcage and belly rising to meet the blades. He breathed out, and the knife blades seemed to draw back just a little. But staying in the wounds. Kaldren shuddered faintly with each breath.

Beaumont realizing he wasn't breathing himself, and he forced himself to look away, and take a breath.

"The will seems real," Perth said, musingly, turning pages.

Beaumont stepped behind the iron maiden where Kaldren couldn't see him and took out his cell phone again.

Rosano went to Beaumont, put a hand over the phone. "No. Don't call anybody, Beaumont. Let's think this through, look over the will . . ."

"This is not a good time to talk about paperwork," Beaumont said sharply. Feeling claustrophobic, indefinably desperate. He felt as if he were the one in the iron maiden and not Kaldren. "I'm going to get out of here, someway, get some help."

"If you do . . ." Kaldren said. And he squirmed against the blades again. Gasped with pain . . . making fresh blood run.

"All right, all right!" Beaumont hissed.

"Just wait, Chris," Perth said, frowning at him. "We really have to think about this . . ."

"Rosano . . . Perth . . . come over here, put your hands on the knives—grab the . . . oh God . . . the handles . . ." Kaldren rasped. "Come on . . ." He paused to give a bubbling gasp. ". . . Mary-Beth. The . . . knives go in . . . they'll go in farther, all the . . . the way in . . ."

Beaumont came to look him over. "Shut up, Kaldren, for God's sake! You're just hurting yourself when you talk!"

Blood was streaming more heavily from the seven wounds now, running down to twine Kaldren's legs, the streams merging to pitter-patter from the open grating at the bottom of the device.

A movie prop, altered to be a medieval torture device, Beaumont thought. They didn't have to do much to make it real. Just a few small modifications . . .

Kaldren eased, shuddering and grimacing, against the back of the torture device. It was as if he found a kind of ecstatic release in the blades—and at the same time found them hard to bear.

"When the little prick was stalking us," Rosano snarled, "I remember his weird emails—threatening—turning up at my sister's wedding to harass me there . . . saying if I pushed him out he'd punish me . . ." He shook his head at Kaldren. "You're the only one being punished you little freak. You want to die, then do it yourself. I'm not going down for this . . ."

Kaldren shook his head like a man in a fever. Licked his lips. His voice a croak. "Designed so . . . look like suicide . . . like it happened . . . when I slammed the door closed . . . that's what you'll say . . . all of you . . ."

"I'm not going to do it, Kenny," Beaumont said. "Okay—you hate these people. You want to punish them and yourself too. And you fantasized this way . . . but you're hurting me too. And I never did anything to you."

"Beaumont . . . closer."

Beaumont stepped nearer to iron maiden. Smelling blood and sweat and imagining he could smell Kaldren's pain. That it smelled like metal and decay, at once.

"No . . . .Beaumont. You were . . . kind . . ." Kaldren's teeth were chattering now. He had to work hard at it to speak. "I wanted someone who cared, once . . . to see . . . to be here . . ."

Beaumont looked Kaldren in the eyes. "Kenny? You're using me like the others . . . pushing me—"

Kaldren's febrile, hooded eyes gazed back defiantly at Beaumont. "Pushing you, Beaumont . . . to just where . . . you already are. A business that'll do anything to anyone . . . to win. A business that makes money . . . from nightmare. You already are . . . one of them . . . what about Chase Morgan?"

What about Morgan? Beaumont tried to think of a reply to that one—and nothing came, for once.

Morgan. The young actor who died when the production Beaumont had worked on, *Blue Blazes,* had started cost-cutting. Including cutting the stunt safety specialist. Morgan did his own car chase—and the car hadn't been inspected closely. Later they found oil dripped onto the tires. He spun out and burned to death—a week after the safety specialist was canned.

And Beaumont thought about the people who died on *The Twilight Zone* movie. On other productions. How hard had anyone really tried to make sure everyone was safe? Only as hard as it was inexpensive.

"You're only hurting yourself, Kaldren," Rosano said.

"No, you'll see . . . I'll punish your souls . . ."

"Our souls . . . ?" Mary-Beth repeated, her voice almost as small as Kaldren's.

"Beaumont . . . what kind of people produce horror . . . something in them. Some . . ." He stopped talking and then . . . started to titter. High pitched, fluttering laughter, high in his throat. "Oh!" Kaldren hissed. "There it is! It feels good! It's good!" He was staring into space.

What was he seeing? Beaumont wondered. Seven knives, rigid and shiny, in the yielding, wet wounds?

"This can't go on," Perth said.

Beaumont nodded. "We've got to do something . . ."

"No!" Kaldren said, writhing in the woman-shaped cage. And fresh blood spurted from his wounds. "Ah-a-a-ahhh! Now it's hurting like hell . . . and—you are forcing me to cut myself more! You can stop it by pushing the knives in the rest of the way!"

"Stay still, goddamnit!" Beaumont shouted.

"Push the knives in! End this pain! Push them in!"

"Oh screw him, let him cut himself up," Rosano said.

Beaumont found himself glaring at Rosano. It didn't feel right to be angry at Kaldren—and he felt a need to let off steam at someone. "Rosano, you just want him to keep his mouth shut."

"Hey fuck you, he was lying about everything . . ."

"No, Rosano, you stole . . ." Kaldren broke off, choking.

"Shut up you lying little masochist!" Rosano shouted, stepping in to thump a fist on the iron maiden. The vibration transmitted to the knives, making Kaldren groan.

"Back away from him, he's sick but he's got a right to survive," Beaumont said.

"Does he?" Rosano demanded, spinning to face Beaumont. "He's torturing us! Don't you see that? Us, not himself! With guilt! And getting a sick thrill out of it!"

"Then don't play along with it by flipping out." He leaned toward Rosano, whispering. "Go off behind him—call the police. Paramedics. I'll keep his attention . . ."

Rosano hesitated—then turned to Perth. "Did that will look real?"

"Sure. We can say we found him here . . . we can say the will came in the mail—we'll say it came whatever day tomorrow is . . ."

"We could just let him bleed to death," Rosano said.

"No," Mary-Beth said reasonably. "They might save him. People will say why didn't we get help sooner. And—we all do need those rights . . . I could play Steele's wife, Chloe."

Beaumont felt a chill like a current carrying astonishment and disgust. "You're fucking kidding."

Perth spoke with concise rationality. "He's going to kill himself anyway, if not today, sometime soon. He'll continue to harass us. He may even try to kill us. Look how crazy he is. I say let's . . . put him out of his misery. And with him dead, the rights to those stories will be settled—everyone wants to make them."

"Our prints will be on the knives," Mary-Beth said.

"We can wipe them—or say they're on there because we tried to pull them out."

"Seven knives . . ." Perth mused. "One for each hand, for the three of us on *Pilot Fish* with him—and one for Beaumont. Like he figures Beaumont only half killed him."

"Beaumont . . . to finish me . . ." Kaldren said. His head drooping now.

"Hey whoa," Beaumont said. "Seriously . . . you can't . . ."

"He's right, Beaumont—we need this," Rosano said. "I need it. I know a guy at the studio—this'll end the Merlin Steele litigation. It'd probably not be resolved any other way . . . not so the movies could be made. And you Beaumont—you haven't had a significant deal in what, three or four years, right? A fat screenwriting deal! At least half a mil. At least."

"Maybe we could get Dirby," Perth said.

"Fuck this . . ." Beaumont said. He circled the props, moving out of Kaldren's line of site, and quietly took out his cell phone, tapped in 911.

"We have to do it now," Perth said, to Rosano and Mary-Beth. ". . . right now, we don't have any time to think about this, after this call goes through. Now!"

Mary-Beth chewed her puffy lips.

Perth took her hand, gently. "What was that crack he made about your surgery bills? About the bulimia? Anyway, you'll be doing him a favor . . ."

She nodded, just once. Then she led the way, striding over to the iron maiden. Her slim, prettily manicured fingers hesitated over the knife handles. Head drooping, Kaldren groaned. She got a good grip . . .

"Wait . . ." Kaldren's voice was faint. "Maybe . . . don't wanna die . . . wait . . . "

Beaumont pressed the cell phone to his ear. He could barely make it out. "Please hold, all emergency lines are busy, an operator will be with you . . ."

Beaumont smacked almost threw the cell phone across the room in frustration. "Goddammit! Listen—Mary-Beth, Perth—hey—don't!"

But they were crowded around the iron maiden now, Perth and Rosano and Mary-Beth, taking the knife grips into their hands.

"Wait . . . don't . . ." Kaldren rasped. And louder. "Wait, waiiii—" The word stretched out, taut, like a violin string—and became a scream as even from where Beaumont stood he heard the crunch of six blades on bone and cartilage, the slither of steel in meat. Kaldren made a squeaking sound, and made it again.

"There's a seventh, Beaumont—!" Rosano said. "One more knife! And he's still alive!"

Alive, screaming, gurgling, writhing. The seventh blade was right over his heart.

"No!" Beaumont shouted.

"Please hold, all emergency lines . . ."

"You have to, Beaumont! Or you'll tell someone—you'll turn us in! You have to!"

"No fucking way!"

"God, do something, Jim," Mary-Beth wailed. "He's just . . . he's shaking, he's getting blood all over . . ."

"I'll do it," Perth said. And he drove the seventh knife home.

There was a long, tattered gasp, and then silence.

They stepped back from the iron maiden. Mary-Beth turned her back on it. "What about him?" Perth asked, after a moment, nodding toward Beaumont.

Rosano put his hand in his coat. "I had some death threats. So I carry a .38. But . . ."

Beaumont shook his head. Then he spoke into the phone. "Yeah uh –hi. We're on soundstage five, at Dennison Studios, over on . . . right, that's the place. Yeah we came to a meeting and found a man dead—a suicide . . . it's hard to describe, just please . . . send . . . send some help . . ."

Beaumont hit the red button. Put the cell phone in his pants pocket. His hands shook, so it took more than one try to get the phone in.

Well. Making movies was like war, Beaumont thought. There were casualties. People died. Souls died.

And the thought came: Could you feel it, when your soul died?

He took a deep breath. Half a million, maybe?

"Better hide that will," he said.

WAR AND PEACE

BUTCH STARTS FUCKING around with the dead girl's body "Butch," I tell him, real dry, "I'm pretty sure that's not standard police procedure." This, see, was two years ago; the first time I looked at Butch different.

Butch has pulled on the rubber gloves. I knew a cop got AIDS from touching a fresh stiff; cop with a cut on his hand turning the dead guy's bloody face for a better look: Boom, an officer's ass shriveling up with HIV. We put on the gloves now.

This stiff is a Chicano girl, big breasted, and she has a little horizontal knife cut about two inches long in the top of her left tit, and there really isn't much blood, I don't know why, but most of the bleeding was internal. But somebody has . . .

Butch says it out loud. "Long thin blade ri-i-ight through the titty and ri-i-ight through her itty-bitty heart."

She's propped up in bed in a motel, wearing a black leather skirt, one red pump, no top, one eye stuck open, the other shut, like a baby doll. There's some ripped clothes lying around.

Butch reaches out and runs the rubber-covered tip of his thumb, real slow and tranquil, along the lip of her wound. Then he pinches a nipple. This is making me nervous. I mean, we're a couple of white cops in the Hispanic neighborhood, shit.

"What the hell, Hank," Butch says to me, grinning. "Let's pump a fuck into her. She's got one more in 'er."

You get into gallows humor, this job, so I grin back and says, "She's still warm and soft."

But he isn't kidding. He starts playing with her titties, even the slashed one, and lifting up her skirt. "You can turn your back if you want, or not, I don't care," he says, his hand on his zipper. I get this feeling he's hoping I won't turn away. "Come on," he says. "She was a fuckin' whore anyway. I got a condom so I won't leave no DNA."

"We don't know that, Butch. All we know's a motel manager found a stiff." But he goes on playing with her. "Butch—no fuckin' *way*," I say. "They called her family from the ID in her purse, her fuckin' *mom* might show up and come in and see that shit. 'The white police officers were fucking my dead daughter, Mr. DA! I'm suing the department's ass!' I mean, Christ, are you . . ." I didn't finish saying it.

He steps back, the same cool grin, but then he catches the tip of his tongue in his teeth like he was just kidding. "Fuckin' with ya. Gotcha didn't I." He walks out past me. But I see him re-arrange his dick in his pants as he goes. He has a hard-on.

BELIEVE IT OR not, I read about it in the papers. No one called me. I'm just coming off vacation but, shit, somebody should've fucking called me. Della, Butch's wife—the wife of my partner, my best friend—turns up dead in the trunk of her own car, and no one calls me.

Now I'm over at Butch's, just being there with him. Making us some coffee. It feels funny, looking at Della's stuff in the kitchen. My own wife Jilian gave Della those dish towels; Love Our Planet machine-embroidered on them. Some kind of soybased dye used in them. My wife goes on these spending sprees in Berkeley.

Della not long ago re-did the kitchen, and put everything in its place, and picked out the curtains and the other new gewgaws about two weeks before; spending too much money, Butch had said. But the kitchen now looks like a picture out of *Ladies' Home Journal*. And then some dirtbag strangled her, and her new kitchen things all seem like placemarkers for her going. *You knew me for years. I babysat your kids. Where am I now?*

I'm just a patrolman, but I see dead people all the time, mostly old people that croak out, and I got to make a report. But this is different: Butch's wife Della, she baby-sat my kids, made me and my wife dinner. She could be bitchy but Jilian liked her and Ben liked her and Ashley liked her and we were used to her. And some bug killed her to make a point, and put her in the trunk of her car. I was glad I wasn't on the detail that found her, after two days . . . the smell of someone dead two days in a trunk; someone that you fucking went *golfing* with.

I look through the door at Butch sitting on the couch quiet as a
mannequin in a store window. Butch wears a yellow golf shirt, and tan
Dockers pants, and brown loafers with tassels, and no socks. He has
that same butch haircut, going a little gray now, that got him his tag,
which he says he wears just because you pretty much never had to comb
it. Although I think he wears it because his dad had one, his whole life.
His dad was a Marine Corps flyer, stationed right here in Alameda, a
real big old hard-ass who shriveled up with cancer and died whining. I
shouldn't talk about him like that, but I always hated the old fucker.

The Gold Tins are searching the house. Just a routine, but it ticks
Butch off. "Treating me like a fucking suspect," he says. "God, Della."
Starting to cry again. His eyes are still red, from crying for two days.
He was talking about Della for hours, what a patient woman she was,
how she put up with all kinds of shit being a cop's wife, worrying about
him, and it ends up they got her and not him, and how it isn't right. The
captain was there for an hour or so of that, yesterday, a hand on Butch's
shoulder, sometimes starting to cry himself, and later on the captain
tells the reporters from the *Oakland Trib*, "This is genuinely tragic. Officer Behm feels it so deeply. He's got just about the biggest heart of
anyone I know." And he talks about Butch's work with the Eagle Scouts
and the vocational fair, lots of good stuff he's done.

I tell Butch. "They're looking for stuff that could connect your wife
with a killer, like a letter, say—I mean, no offense but they got to consider
maybe she had an affair, Butch, and her boyfriend did it. You know?"

He snorts, "Boyfriend. Not Della, not ever." There might be a little
contempt in the way he says it. He starts to say something, doesn't say it,
then he goes on, "What the fuck is the point of looking for a boyfriend
when they got the message painted right on the car?"

Meaning the spray-painted graffiti on the side of her car. They found
her car, her body in the trunk, in the Oakland ghetto, right there in
gang-banger country, and spray-painted on the side in red was "WAR."
And the killers sprayed a little circle around the bumper sticker that
said, "OPOBA." Oakland Police Officers Benevolent Association. To let
everybody know that they knew this was a car belonging to a cop, and
the woman was a cop's wife.

For maybe four weeks now, we've been campaigning a "War on Drug Gangs" in Oakland, because of all the drug-related killings, so now, it's figured, their retaliation has begun. Two weeks ago Butch arrested a projects gangster for breaking into a car, and maybe the perp fingered Butch for the target. Who knows, that smalltime dirtbag could be related to some big crack gangster. So maybe the gang-bangers start following Butch and decide to hit him where it's easier for them and for a bigger psychological effect on the department . . . We can get you right in your homes, cops. You can run but you can't hide.

"Thing is, they know the spray-paint could be a fake, Butch," I tell him. "Planted to throw them off. Could be some fucking lunatic who's been watching her for a while, got obsessed with her, maybe somebody she knows."

"I hope so," Butch says, "because then maybe we could nail him. And I could kill him myself." With a catch in his voice.

IT'S WHILE I'M watching "Jeopardy!", Jilian's favorite show. All of a sudden, right at the start of Double Jeopardy, I think: He's a suspect. After "Jeopardy!", I'm watching "Wheel of Fortune". The phrase letters the contestant has, are: _A_ _ _D PE_C_ Something makes me squirm in the La-Z-Boy while I'm watching this. The contestant starts to fill in the letters. My wife, who's the brainy one, figures it out first. "War and Peace," she says. There's more to the phrase but that's the main part.

"Yeah, that's . . ." I don't finish what I started saying, and she looks at me.

"You okay?"

"Yeah." I'm feeling sick, though.

"I feel weird too," Jilian says. "God, Della was just over here taking care of Ashley and Ben. It was hard explaining it to them, Hank." She starts to sniffle, and I go to the couch and put my arm around her.

"I know. But they're a cop's kids. They know the world a little better than their friends."

She shakes her head, her face getting swollen from crying, nose going red on the end, the way it does. "That's maybe the worst part of being a cop's kids."

Another time, I might get a little put off. *The worst part,* like it was all bad one way or another. But I'm thinking about War and Peace, and Jilian's attitude is low on the priorities.

I remember Butch, when we were young. He was the older kid across the street, helping with football, soccer, basketball. I was twelve and thirteen, the nerdiest kid with a ball, the Jerry Lewis character, Butch was like my surrogate big brother. Dean Martin. Or almost like my dad. He liked to talk about sex with me, looking at those *Playboys,* that was some heavy duty intimacy for a thirteen-year-old when it came to hanging with a senior. There was circle-jerk feeling about it, though he never touched me. Makes me embarrassed now.

He took me to the drive-in with him sometimes too, and he'd leave me in the car to watch one of those sixties movies where hippie girls in paisley miniskirts get involved with Hell's Angels and paint flowers on their chests and do a lot of making out to psychedelic music but never quite screw while Butch went to drink some beer with his football friends in Andy's van. But he always came back and snuck me a can of beer, and told me some incredibly dirty joke and asked me how I liked the sex scenes in the movie and what did I think about who did what to who. He could turn back to thirteen with me, just like that, though he was about to go into community college.

I know for sure he strangled Della.

THERE'S NO DETECTIVE work about it. I just know him, and the "War" thing is like some bullshit from a Mel Gibson movie, and Butch loves that crap: Mel Gibson, Clint Eastwood, Bruce Willis's *Diehard.* He makes fun of it, like all cops do, because it's such fantasy, but he loves it anyway. Like all cops do. And thinking about that "War" spray-painted on the car . . . how Jilian got a skeptical look when I told her about that. And I remember Butch, oh, six months before Della was murdered saying he thought about divorcing her, but he'd still never be rid of her, there would be alimony fights, and fights over the house and she knew all his friends and it'd be awkward going out with people and he finished up by saying, "So I *still* wouldn't get any peace from her. Just no—peace."

People talk about divorcing all the time. It's no big deal. They fought a fair amount. That's no big deal either. Me and Jilian fight our share.

War and Peace.

HERE'S THE THING: Butch and I stole some money from the department. Well really, it was from the bugs. It was money confiscated from drug dealers and it was a *lot of fucking money,* see. It was about four hundred eighty grand. We took it from an evidence locker and covered our tracks clean, but they could still find out. So, we were sitting on it. We weren't going to spend it for five years. That was our deal, a blood oath. No calling attention to yourself. Save it for later. No matter how broke we got in the meantime. *Don't touch it.*

But suppose Butch is about to go down for killing Della. *If* he killed her for sure. Suppose he wants to bargain with the department. Suppose he shafts me. *Hey Captain, remember that half a mil that took a hike?*

BY ABOUT TWO PM the next day I am almost sort of nearly pretty sure I was wrong. He didn't kill her. You can do that; it's like one of those rides at Great America where you go in a loop, completely upside down. That's how I feel while I'm following Butch over the bridge into Oakland. Like the bridge is going into a loopdeloop.

And it's the worst thing in the world, somebody you knew all your life turns out to be something *else.* I mean—what's real, then? Nothing. Not a fucking thing. So it can't be right, what I'm thinking about Butch.

I'm officially supposed to be on a Drug Task Force detail in the unmarked car, which basically means watching the basketball court next door to the high school to see if anyone buys or sells, and then I buzz the detectives who get the glory of the collar. But I coop it off. I am following Butch.

Why is he driving into Oakland?

He's on special leave, and he might be going to see a therapist or something, and then I'll feel like a jerk.

He didn't fucking kill her, you asshole.

And the whole time I am mumbling this I am keeping my car back in traffic so Butch doesn't see me follow him.

He drives to San Pablo Avenue, and he cruises a whore. She makes eye contact and points down the road, not knowing he's a cop, and he picks her up. *What the fuck.*

She's a black girl, or maybe what they call a high yellow, wearing an elastic tube-top thing that shows her stretchmarked middle, and a short fake-leather skirt. Probably no underwear: if they can't do it all giving head, you cough up a little extra money and they hike up their skirt.

They like to do it in the car. It's easier than keeping a room some-where—those Pakis who run the weekly-rate hotels wring money out of the whores same as pimps. And it's faster just to do it in the car. They're always thinking ahead to the next trick; to the time they got enough money to go kick it. And the faster they fuck, the faster they get it over with.

They all have their choice spots picked out getting it done in a car: back parking lots of warehouses; certain kinds of dead end streets; dirt tracks along deserted railroad yards; out next to the dumpster behind Safeway; oh, and parking lots under freeways. The butt-end of the city.

That's where Butch has the pavement princess. They're under a freeway, in a county equipment storage lot. Dull yellow road graders, defunct street cleaning trucks, stuff like that. Butch has some county keys, and he's unlocked the gate.

I watch from across the street, with a piece of fence and a parked truck between; I'm peering around the truck, through the fence, be-tween a couple of road graders. I can make them out in there. Butch is showing her his badge and she looks royally pissed off. I can read her lips. "Oh, man you *motherfucker.*" But it's not a bust. I watch as he makes her bend over his car, spreads her legs, her hands flat and far apart on the trunk, while he checks out her pussy, grinning the whole time, slap-ping her thighs wider apart with a nightstick he's taken out of the car.

Then he starts shoving the nightstick in her, slapping her ass, pinching her titties, and playing with himself. I can make out what he's saying. "You a *ho* aren'tcha, huh? You a *ho,* right?"

He's having a *good* time. The son of a bitch strangled Della.

I can't watch this.

JILIAN SAYS, "YOU shouldn't go, you're not supposed to bother people with too much attention and giving them all kinds of stuff, you're supposed to leave them to feel their grief." She went to a grief workshop when her mom died. She's like that: going to workshops.

"It wasn't my idea!" I tell her. "The fucking fishing trip is his idea! He wants to go!"

So we go, me and Butch. Driving up in his Bronco, he's really pissed off that Stinson made him get permission from the captain to leave town. "Eighteen years on the force and they're treating me like a dirtbag!"

"Hey and you'd be with me the whole time anyway," I say. That was the wrong thing to say somehow. He gave me this *look*.

I don't say anything about how a few days after they found his wife dead he's gleefully rousting prostitutes and playing with their asses. I don't say anything, but I'm thinking about it. How I could tell, watching him play sick games with the whore, he's done this a lot. You hear people talk about how you know somebody for years but you don't really know them. This case, it's like he's almost not even the sex I thought he was. I mean I don't know shit about this guy. And now I'm driving up to a remote mountain lake with him. This is great.

We go to Robins Lake. It's one of those reservoir lakes, a sweetheart arrangement between developers and some senator who swung the dam. Except for a little bit of gas slick around the edges from the outboards and the jet-skis, it's pretty clean, and they stock it with fish. If you go to the north end, the jet-skis they keep at the south end scare the fish up to you.

It's the kind of sunny day that looks friendly and waits till its gets you out in the open and then it pulls out the glare. HAVE A HEADACHE, BUDDY. We rent an aluminum outboard, and since it's the middle of the week we're almost the only guys out on the lake. We both got sailor hats on, folded down like bowls on our heads, and Ray-Bans. Butch's brought a Styrofoam cooler full of Miller Lite. I'm wishing I brought sunscreen for the back of my neck, after just a half hour it's already rasping. I'm asking myself why I'm out on the lake with a murderer.

Because I have to talk to him. Because he's been my more-or-less best friend for, what, fifteen years or so. Because it's inertia, and he asked me.

We fish, either end of the boat, and he doesn't say much. Until finally, "I guess you could see the idea of a fishing trip as kind of weird, now. But I had to get away." I can see sundogs off the lake in his dark glasses.

It's like my lower jaw got real heavy, as I say what I'm supposed to. "People adjust in their own ways. If this keeps you sane, hey, go for it."

He doesn't say anything for a minute. "You think there's anything weird about how the gold badges came back last night, askin' me questions?"

I feel some hope, then. Maybe it wasn't up to me.

"Buddy, when they don't have a *name*—I mean, okay, they got the gang-bangers lead. But when they don't have a name, or even a description . . . they fall back on the family. Doesn't mean anything."

"You mean, the 24/24 rule."

"Yeah." The 24/24 rule is that the most important time in a murder investigation are the last twenty-four hours in the victim's life and the first twenty-four hours after the body is found. "So it's been longer than the twenty-four, and they feel like it's getting cold. They're clutching at straws."

My lower jaw's *really* heavy now. I can barely force myself to say this horseshit. I'm thinking about his small hands, and figuring he didn't do it with his hands, he did it with a cord or a scarf or something. Thinking he's cute for choosing strangulation so she doesn't bleed all over the place. Only, the gang-bangers pretty much never strangle people. They love guns and knives. Just fucking love them.

I decide I can't sit here like this anymore. It's too quiet out here and I just keep seeing him go through the laundry for just the right scarf and then I see him with the ho.

You have to think things through. That's a rule. You're sorry if you don't think things through.

I come at it from left field. "I mean, shit, even if . . . if a cop flipped out and killed his wife, the department'd be stupid to push too hard on it."

He stares at me. My mouth goes dry. I open a beer.

I make myself go on, not sure what I'm trying to accomplish, and thinking it might be good to leave the lake early in the afternoon. "I'm just thinking about ol' Detective Stinson's point of view. Or anyway, the captain's." He opens his mouth to say something like *What are you getting at?* and I put in real quick, "See, they could *talk themselves into* thinking you did it." (He did it.) "And the DA could get wind of it and then they got to go through with it. I mean, we know you didn't do it." (He did it. By now he knows I know he did it.) "But you know, if they haven't got a suspect they'll keep turning to look at you and you know how people can kid themselves into shit." (He killed her. We have a picture of Della feeding Ashley with a baby bottle.)

"So what's the point?"

The smell of gas from the outboard is making me ill. "Well is there anything that could give them the wrong idea? Something they could misunderstand and think it was physical evidence."

He's almost smiling. I'm wishing I could see his eyes behind the Ray-Bans.

"Naw. No I don't think so. I mean, I'm not . . ."

He doesn't actually say it. *I'm not stupid.*

"You know what?" I stretch, and rub my neck. "This sun is, like, too much for me. Maybe we oughta get back a little early."

He shrugs. He's still not quite smiling. "Hey Hank—there's the money we took."

"We're not even supposed to talk about that, man."

"We're out in the middle of a fucking lake, Hank. Just keep that money in mind. You wouldn't want to lose that. And who knows what."

I just nod.

My stomach feels like it's got a bag of sand in it. But I just keep thinking, *You got to think things through.* That's the bottom line, right there.

STINSON'S HAPPY. WHICH is fucked up.

Stinson thinks he's going to make his first detective collar. We're sitting in captain's office. Butch and the captain and Stinson and Mann, the heavyset black guy from Internal Affairs, and me for Butch's moral support.

Stinson disarms Butch, first thing, which freaks everyone out, even the captain, who looks like he's going to object, and then doesn't.

Butch tries to be cool. "You want my Beretta, keep it oiled. I don't want a fucking dust speck in it when I get it back."

I'm groaning inside and thinking, shut the fuck up, Butch.

"Whatdya think of Omnichrome, Butch?" asks Stinson, putting Butch's gun on the captain's desk, way out of Butch's reach. Like Butch is going to start busting caps around the office.

"Stinson, you watched too many movies-of-the-week," Mann says. "Butch, you know what Omnichrome is?"

Butch shakes his head. He manages not to swallow.

Mann goes on, "It's this new thing, alternate light source device, picks up stuff you can't see with the naked eye. Foreign matter. The Omnichrome shows up stuff under special wavelengths . . ."

Stinson can't contain himself. "Like paint specks."

Mann gives him a tired glare. "Like paint specks, yeah. Same color and chemical composition as the ones on the car. Forensics found them on a pair of your shoes."

"Like you get," Stinson says, actually grinning now, "when there's a real fine cloud of spray-paint, and you think you're being real careful not to get any on you, but the stuff is so fine you can't see it settle."

Butch's voice is almost a monotone, carefully flat, as he says, "Spray-paint's mostly all the same composition. And I helped Hank here spray-paint his kid's bike-frame. I think it was red or orange or something."

Everyone turns their heads to look at me.

JILIAN DOESN'T SAY anything about it till we're halfway to Yosemite in our RV. About two months later. No charges against Butch. The kids are playing with Gameboys far enough in the back they can't hear us talk over the noise of the engine and the tires, and there's been a silence for about sixty miles before she said it.

"He never was there, helping spray-paint Ashley's bike."

I'm wondering how come what she said makes me feel like I'm the one who killed Della. I say, "You remember that for sure?"

"I thought about it a lot, Hank. I mean, *a lot*. He came over the next day after the bike was dry and she was showing it off, the new paint you put on so drivers could see it better, and she was telling Butch all about it when he and Della . . ." her voice catches ". . . when they came over."

Is she, I wonder, going to come out and flat out accuse me of perjuring myself, which I sure as hell did, to protect Butch?

If she does, I'll have to tell her about the money. And I haven't figured out how to tell her about the money yet.

Should I lie to her, and pretend I remember him coming over earlier, some time when she wasn't there, standing there with me when I was using the paint? It sounded too forced. Jilian's smart. I elect to go around it.

"He just figured that's where he got the stuff on his shoes, maybe from some dust that got stirred up or something."

"Oh." She decides to believe it.

I don't say, *You don't really think that Butch could have . . . !* or some such shit, because I couldn't do that believably.

I just change the subject. Only, it's not really a different subject. I tell her I'm thinking of joining the Sheriff's Department, maybe around Santa Cruz, so we could get the kids away from the Oakland area, all the crime and drugs and stuff. But I'd never do it if she didn't want to.

She says she'll think about it. It's a big step.

It's a step the fuck away from Butch.

I TRY TO see him enough so he doesn't get nervous, but not so much it'll make me nervous. It's not that I think he'd kill me. It's just like spiders. I'm not really scared they're going to hurt me. I just don't like them crawling around me.

At least spiders are what they're supposed to be.

It's easy to be self-righteous. But you got to look at the whole picture. The kids and Jilian and the money and covering my ass and the department. No, fuck the department. It's the fucking money. It's me in the joint with a bunch of dirtbags.

Because, you know, Butch thought it through, himself. He collected her life insurance, too. It was way premeditated. He'd get the gas chamber like some dirtbag. But his getting away with it is hard to stand. I hear him say, "You a *ho*, right?"

ONE NIGHT I go over to his house, after he's been drinking heavy, and I go up to his bedroom, same room where he slept next to Della for years and years. He's sacked out, fully clothed on the bed, his head deep in those blue satin pillowcases Della picked out. I know him, he won't wake up after all the beer. I'm standing over Butch, who's snoring these long contented snores, and I've got his gun in my gloved hand, and I think maybe I'm going to blow his brains out. And slip away. Because otherwise the guy'll always have something over my head. The money. And I just can't fucking stomach him walking around.

I put the gun muzzle up to the back of his head. But then, at the last moment, I think it through: if I do it, it might look like suicide. Which would imply that yeah, he killed Della and so I must've perjured myself. And making it look like a gang-banger did it would be a big mess to step into.

Sweat's sticking the gunbutt to my palm. So finally, I take his gun and I put it back in its holster, and I go downstairs.

I'll put in my app at the Santa Cruz SD. They got a great benefits package. That's what I'm half thinking about as I walk out to my car.

You got to think things through. That's the bottom line.

Hey. They're not going to say shit about perjury.

I go back upstairs, get the gun and I blow his fucking brains across that satin pillowcase.

ONE STICK: BOTH ENDS SHARPENED

WHEN SIMA CAME home to the apartment building in South Central L.A., Old Gypsum was as usual in that half-sleep of his on the first flight of steps, his gray head leaning on the paint-flaking wall. His half gallon of Gallo family size, most the way empty, was on the steps between his feet.

"Ya'll got some holes in your socks, Ol' Gypsum," Sima said. "You toes stickin out."

He slitted his hooded eyes and lizard-looked at her, then down at his feet. "See that, child, somebody done stole my motherfuckin shoes. You steal my shoes, child?"

Then he made that *Hooo!* coughing sound, with lots of phlegm, that he did when he was trying to clear his breathing tubes.

"Nobody stole yo shoes, Ol' Gypsum, they're up there on the landing, I can see' em up there."

She pointed at the shoes. She was just nine years old but she didn't miss much.

"Look at that! What them motherfuckers doin' up there?"

"You left em up there."

"Lord, look at that. I'm gettin' old and forgetful."

"You gettin' drunk too much."

"Well I know that." He smiled at her; his remaining teeth were yellow and spotted, but it was a sweet smile anyway. Last smiling face she was like to get tonight if Mama didn't get that hubba. And if Mama did her crack, the smile wouldn't last long; she'd get all down inside herself and hard, hard if she was interrupted. Old Gypsum dug a finger in one hairy ear and said, "I didn't see your sister, three days now. Where your sister at, girl? She go see Granma?"

"Marinda gone to stay with my Aunt Pitty for a while. She gone a week already."

"When she come back? Your sister give me sticky rolls from school, some days. Ya'll get your lunch for free, that school program, you could bring me sticky rolls. You bring me a sticky rolls?"

"Sticky rolls is only at the middle school cafeteria, I'm third grade, Ol' Gypsum. Marinda don't like 'em, she don't like cinammon . . . "

She thought for a moment about Marinda, who could say such mean things but who she missed hard, and about how Marinda could have sold her cafeteria sticky rolls to some other kid who wanted a second dessert for fifty cents, a dollar, but she brought them back for Old Gypsum and his sweet tooth. She thought about how when Mama had sold the television, Marinda had taken her to a big store to watch TV there, till they were chased out, and how they'd had fun picking the one they would get when they had their own money.

Old Gypsum rubbed his forehead, came out with another *Hooo!* and started his story up: "I worked in them gypsum mines, we had a chef and everything, come out there, make us a pastry. Wasn't like those motherfuckin' Dixie coal mines—up that gypsum mine in Illin-noise, Lord they treated us like we was val'able, not like a packa motherfuckin' yellow hounds."

She knew he could talk about when he worked in the gypsum mines for an hour and then reach the end of it—and start over again. So she said, "I heard that too," and ran past him up the stairs, praying that Mama had gotten her shit.

IT WAS TWO weeks before sweeps when Brenda told him she wasn't sure about the marriage. She was going to Europe to think it over.

Durritt was sitting in a folding chair on the set, talking to Brenda on his cell phone, and watching their second-female-lead, Tanya Rennock, as she paced out the action sequence for scene seventeen: the valiant young nurse fighting the Japanese who were over-running the hospital—courageous Selma Jamison, RN, trying to save her patients. She'd be captured, taken on a sort of death march, then sold into a comfort girl brothel from which the hero would rescue her. The Japanese Americans would protest that one—at least he hoped so. It'd be good for ratings.

Damn she had fine legs.

And Tanya was aware the show's Executive Producer was watching her. Maybe there was just a shade more shimmy in her walk than there would've been if he hadn't been watching. It was good to cover your bets.

"I'm only saying," Brenda was saying, a little voice in a piece of plastic pressed to his ear, "that I want time to think and, you know . . . I mean, you just seem so totally into your work, I just feel like you don't, I don't know, connect with anything else and . . . well it's like that pre-nup, that's so, you know, emotionally empty, that's so unromantic—"

Just then Durritt noticed Tanya turned to look at him—and her eyes lingered on his for just two seconds longer than necessary. Clear enough, when you've been in the business a few years. She wanted her own show, or something else. She was willing to make a trade.

"You know what, Brenda?" Durritt said abruptly, into the pocketfone, when he saw Trombley signaling to him, his face a thundercloud. "Don't do me any favors." Trombley probably had another production crisis. Maybe historically inaccurate props again. "Okay, Brenda? Go to Rome, find yourself a nice Italian fashion designer, if you can find one who isn't gay, and party your little princess ass off. I don't need this bullshit."

Feeling relieved the marriage was off, he broke the connection, and speed-dialed his assistant Wendy on the pocketfone, waving to Trombley, signaling that he'd be right over. Wendy'd done well, in the last six months. He paid her half what he'd paid Medina, which gave him a cryptic satisfaction. But he might have to slip her a small raise to keep her much longer. "Wendy—no more calls from Brenda. Not ever. Tell her I'm in a meeting for all eternity."

"You got it. The guy from the Black Congressional Caucus called about a fund-raiser. He said last year you were—"

"That was last year. I don't do that shit anymore. No time, no way. And hold all my calls for now, I gotta soothe Trombley . . ."

"Okay—oh, do you want to see this *VideoView Magazine*? It's your cover piece."

"Is it flattering? I don't need to process any negative bullshit."

"The photos are good, Alex. The article is and isn't—you know, sort of 'he's so creative, but he's so ruthless.' A lot of trash about what a tough businessman you are or something."

"That's not trash, that's the most flattering fucking part. Yeah, leave it on my desk." He cut the connection without saying goodbye. That was the beauty of an assistant like Wendy. She didn't care if he chummed it up or not.

He got up and skirted the shot set-up, on his way over to Trombley. Tanya lay sprawled patiently on the ground as they set up a shot, after a Jap had knocked her stunned to the floor of the hospital.

Now she lay like an accident victim, her glossy black hair spread out on the area-rug they'd laid down over the set's concrete floor . . .

He felt a kind of interior sagging and he decided it was okay to have a little boost.

HE HAD BEEN trying to stay off the blow, but Trombley loved to share the stuff, one of those druggies who didn't like to use alone.

A little cocaine addiction was good in a director, really, if it didn't consume him. If he kept working, not using so much he got psychotic, he'd make everybody work long hours, get the thing in under budget and on time; he'd be a ruthless autocrat—the stuff made you a vain asshole, of course, if you used it regularly, but that'd never happen to Alex Durritt. He only chipped on it. Now and then.

He hoped to God that bastard Trombley had some today.

Trombley was scowling over the scene-list clipboard as his assistant, a prissy little film student named Fiske Bundt, rather imperiously put Tanya through her paces.

Alex cleared his throat and made that nose-twitch signal that Trombley liked.

Trombley glanced up and smiled cynically. "A bee up there, ay?" (From what part of Britain had come that accent? Who cared). He twitched his nose back at Alex. "Right, Fiske, carry on. Be right back, do be ready to go for a take. Step into the doctor's office, won't you, Alex?"

• • •

OPENING THE DOOR to their assisted-housing apartment was a little bit of anticipation and a lot of scared. Sometimes Mama was rolling along fine and it was alright. Other times she wasn't home at all which was better than when she had a man in the house with her and some other strangers smoking the rock in Mama's bedroom—because times like that, Mama was hitting the pipe and doing her business with the Paying Man in Sima's bedroom.

But today, as Sima came into the small, mostly bare living room, she knew instantly it would be bad, because Mama was alone, and she was using a coat-hanger wire to scratch out the inside of her glass pipe in that frantic way she had, mumbling to herself, and there was a new crop of open tweak-sores on her arms.

Mama was bent over, like a burnt match, that shriveled and used up and bowed, her hands starting movements they didn't finish, darting this way and that, her fingers now and then pinching fresh lesions on her skin as she mumbled about the fucking bugs, the fucking bugs. Looking at her, Sima remembered how she'd been walking with Mama to the Social Security office, for the look-here-I-got-a-child visit, and how Bellesa from school had seen her and said, "That your grandma?" and not cappin' on her either. She really thought Mama was a grandma, though Mama was only twenty-eight, because of how old the crack had made her. She was down to half her teeth . . .

Sima had made up her mind to back out and go down the stairs, carrying that heavy feeling she got in her chest down with her, but then Mama's head snapped up, like a blind person Sima had seen sniffing the air and cocking her head to listen, when people had come around, though Mama's eyes worked. Only she was so sickly-stoned it seemed sometimes to make her eyes go cloudy on her. She rasped, "Sima! Get you ass over here!"

Sima froze . . . .

Then Mama was up, like that striking snake Sima saw in the video at school and, though Sima was halfway out the door by the time Mama crossed the room, she got a firm grip on Sima's shoulder. She dragged Sima back in, with no more than the usual hurt, and kicked the door shut.

"Now, now you gonna help you Mama. You know, and I know, you wouldn't be alive weren't for me. I carried you eight month and I suffered a fourteen hour labor. You going to help Mama."

Sima turned and looked at her, carefully keeping her face expressionless. "What I got to do? Borrow some money from Aunt Pitty? I can try that. I git over there. I'll go over there, you don't even have to give me no bus fare, I can git right on over—"

The slap and the shut up came so much together it was like the slap was speaking: "Shut up!"

Sima knew what to do. Just wait. Just stay stony cool, like her sister told her, and wait for the chance. She didn't even raise a hand to wipe the blood from her nose.

"You want your mama to kill herself, she get so sick?"

"No Mama."

"That what gone to happen I don't get what I need now. Your daddy made me this way, and those people at that vocational school axed me to leave, and you know that it's not Mama's fault, so you gone do what I say?"

"Yes Mama I surely will."

Mama dragged her into the barren kitchen. Refrigerator long since sold, only a dirty square on the crumbling tile remained. The copper pipes on the old gas stove torn out and sold though the useless bulk of the stove sat there still, angled crookedly out from the wall. The cabinets were empty, there was just one thing in the kitchen, besides the roaches: A bottle that said SLEEPEZE on it. It was one of those kind you could get without a doctor's say-so, and Mama had tried to sleep, one time, using them, and it had reacted with the dope and made her real sick. She'd tried to sell the bottle but no one would give her anything for it. So there it sat, mostly full.

"You gone take some these pills, for me, girl," Mama said, grabbing the open bottle with her free hand—the other one still tremblingly clamped on Sima's shoulder. She dumped the pills out on the counter, immediately caught up a handful—making Sima think of a child playing jacks, throw em down and pick em up—and tried to force the pills into Sima's mouth.

Sima instinctively squirmed away. "Why I got to take those?"

"You don't ax your mama why you just do that shit, you little ho, now git onto it!"

Sima didn't look at Mama as they spoke. The closer she got to her physically the more she was afraid to look at her. Afraid, really, of the things she felt when she looked at what her Mama had become, up close.

"You gone to wish you take them if you don't, because we gone to do what we have to do anyway. I caint take care of you no more, and now I got a chance to get what I need and done—"

"You got that girl done yet?" A man's voice.

Sima looked up to see Melvin standing in the doorway, a white man with prematurely gray hair, sunken eyes, a dirty REO Speedwagon T-shirt (What was a "REO Speedwagon" anyway?) that looked ten or twenty years old, jeans; prison tattoos. One of the tattoos, on his forearm, homemade in the cell by some prisoner using blue and red pen-ink and the points of opened safety-pins, was a fading Christian cross with its bottom sharpened, like a sharpened stick, stabbing a man through the heart and underneath that the legend CURSED BY GOD. The top post of the cross was sharpened too and there was blood on that like someone else had been stabbed. She knew Melvin was a dope dealer fallen on bad times, because he'd started doing his own crack, and then got behind with his source, and he was bad in the hole, he was desperate, and his Man was asking him for the money now, right now, yesterday.

"I caint git her done," Mama was saying, in a voice like a crow, "because I don't got nothing but a old steak knife, you said you was going to bring—"

"I bring it, he loan me one of his," Melvin said. Missing most of his teeth in front; Mama was missing hers in gaps like a jack-o-lantern.

He drew something shiny and silver from his backpocket. It looked expensive and new but Sima couldn't tell what it was at first.

"How much that worth?" Mama asked immediately.

"I ain't selling this shit, I need it," Melvin said. "And I'll tell you what, she got to be still when I do this thing, because he show me how to do it and it got to be just right because if it's damaged they don't pay a motherfucking penny—"

"You bring me some rock?"

"I don't bring you shit, you get what you get when you give what you give—and that's when he pays me too."

"I don't get nothing until—what that bullshit about when he pays you? This my daughter here motherfucker—I want that shit as soon I give her shit over!"

"See I got it all worked out," Melvin said. Both of them talking at once, neither one looking at Sima. "I git the money I pay off my Man—"

"—I ain't givin' up this part my life without that motherfucking shit and the money right out in advance motherfucker—"

"—I git a buttload more with the cash, after I pay off the Man, I buy me up a pile, and I got a way to make it into a new market—"

"—because you don't even bring me a motherfuckin' chip, you don't bring me a dime, I'm supposed to trust you with my daughter's—"

"—I'm going to sell a *pound* to this guy who drives for the TV studios, over there in Burbank, *he* steps on the shit, sells it for powder to a movie director guy he knows, who sell it to *all* those motherfuckers got the money in that scene, what, your actors, those motherfuckers—there so much money over there—and I can move on up out of this shit-hole, sell to them cocksuckers over there, be selling shit to movie stars and—"

"—and how you going to get that shit to Tijuana, man wants fresh—"

"—shut the fuck up woman I got an ice chest, I got jars, it's all in there, but I'm going to need this shit from you I only got enough—that girl Marinda move at the last moment, fucking ruin her liver—got to make sure this one is asleep—"

They went on and on . . . and Sima looked at the thing he was waving in his hand . . .

And Sima stopped listening right then; most everything they said after that was all gabbledy-gabbledy in her head, like noises she didn't understand, because she saw what that thing in Melvin's hand was, now, it was a surgery knife, like she'd seen on TV. He had something else hanging from his back pocket like a long handkerchief, she saw now: a plastic sack. Gabbledy-gabble . . .

Then she started working out what they'd been talking about—bits of it, through the roaring sound that filled her head:

Fresh organs. Donors.

A clinic in Tijuana.

. . . only had enough from the other kids for half of his payment. The other kids . . .

That girl Marinda move at the last moment, fucking ruin her liver . . .

Make sure this one is asleep . . .

Sima shouted it just once, that one word holding a world of stunned disbelief and grief and terror: "MAMA!"

"THING IS, WHAT you for real got to understand here is," Durritt was saying, talking too fast, wiping the powder coke off his nose, "every woman is a parasite. I know it's harsh but you got to consider that everything is parasitical sometime. I mean maybe me and you too sometimes."

"Speak for yourself," said Trombley silkily, as she chased his double hit of cocaine with a tall Scotch.

". . . but see women, even if they got their own money, they're *emotional parasites,* because men, check it out, dude, men cannot—"

"Check it out, dude? Here, you turn into *American Pie 3* all of a sudden on me, mate?"

Durritt, who had a lot more difficulty keeping a handle on himself on cocaine than Trembley did, went on obliviously, dipping a little finger into the tiny remaining grains on the glass top of Trombley's desk, next to the storyboards for a TV movie he was planning, and rubbed the coke grains on his gums, between phrases, "—men cannot relate on that kind of emotional level unless they're gay so women have to force emotionality out of them, have to create conflict 'cause they'll get it one way if they can't get it another, they're sucking on you—"

"—now you're back in territory I appreciate."

"—but sucking in all the wrong ways. I mean no matter how much money I make my ex wants more and no way I'm going to be pressured into getting married again—I mean Brenda is acting like she has to think about the marriage but you know what it is, it's the fucking pre-nup, she's claiming it's unromantic but the truth is she's *thinking ahead to the divorce—*"

"Might be right, mate, might be right, or you might be wrong, women is enigmatic creatures, ain't they, but you know if you've got enough money it don't matter what their agenda is, now does it? I've got a little something in mind . . ."

"You going to hit me up for investment you better lay out another couple of lines, dude," Durritt said immediately.

"Now I'm dude again," Trombley said. But he had the bindle out and shook out a little more of the white stuff, onto the glass desk top, began chopping it with the edge of his pocket knife.

Durritt watched his every motion fixedly.

"So what I have in mind," Trombley said, "is that we have a bit of a comeback in Hollywood. Mr. Robert 'I put the gun barrel in my mouth' Downey is clean now but he was just the tip of the iceberg, and most of the iceberg can deal with its dope better than he could. Cocaine is back, and it's our main chance—so long as we know how to get in, and get out. It's people who don't know when to get out of the business who go down with it. You make a million or two, you launder it in a certain overseas casino, you invest it, you live off the interest."

"A million or two . . ." Durritt muttered. "Has a nice ring to it." Would he never finish chopping the stuff?

"There is a man my driver has come into contact with, with the picturesque name 'Melvin', and through him we make certain deals . . . And who gets hurt, really? I ask you," Trombley went on, with great complacency, as he chopped and spread out the lines and then chopped them even finer. "The usual Darwinian refuse like the talented but defective Mr. Downey aside, no one gets hurt."

MELVIN WAS TRYING to force her down into the bathtub, banging her head on the porcelain to stun her—

Sima sank her teeth into his wrist—

And he recoiled, howling.

She vaulted over the rim of the tub, darted past him, saw her mama look up with a birdlike quickness from the small dove of hubba that she was burning in her blackened glass stem—Mama burning her thumb pressing it over the metal-meshed improvised bowl at the end of the glass tube to keep the crack in, as she started after Sima—

Sima with sense enough to go for the open window and the fire escape, not the door, scrambling through the window, pounding down two floors to where the fire escape passed the busted-out hall window, through the window, drop into the hall, down the steps—

But Melvin was thundering down the steps, anticipating her. The scalpel flashing in his hand, the plastic sack in the other. Somewhere he had an ice chest, a big jar in there with parts of Marinda in it, maybe Marinda's pretty brown eyes . . . and maybe parts of that girl Chontel that supposedly run away . . .

Sima taking the steps three, four at a time, leaping right over Ol' Gypsum, who sat up with a startled *Hooo!* as she landed in front of him—

"Child, what now—?"

Sima skidding, falling painfully on her knees.

Picking herself up to bolt for the door. Looking back to see Melvin banging down the steps, his snaggles bared. She wasn't going to make it. He was coming too fast.

Just too fast . . . Marinda . . .

OLD GYPSUM WATCHED him bounding past—saw that perfect blade in his hand—saw the white dope dealer was chasing Sima—

"HEY boy," Old Gypsum said, grabbing Melvin's ankle as he thumped past.

Melvin going down, wham, on his face, the scalpel cracking in half on the tiles.

"HEY motherfucker," Old Gypsum went on, "you the one stole my shoes?"

"Ow, fuck! You old fucking asshole!" Melvin yelled, getting up, one hand to his split lip.

But Sima was gone. She was racing down the street, running for a bus that was just holding its doors opened for her, and he'd never get there first.

Sima's Mama came down the stairs, looking out through the door, and it seemed to Clarence, for that was Old Gypsum's real name, that there was some relief in the woman's eyes: relief that Sima had escaped her. Had escaped the thing that compelled her.

Melvin rounded furiously on the old man . . .

"Fo'get him," Sima's mama said, tugging Melvin back up the stairs. "Come on. We got enough. We gone make that motherfucking deal now . . . you see . . . You call the man that knows the television people . . . We gone make that deal right now . . . "

"AND SO—DO we have a deal?" Trombley was asking.

It all looked good to Durritt now, with his mind racing in the familiar megalomaniacal circles. Hell maybe he'd even marry Brenda on her terms now. With enough money it didn't matter, like Trombley said.

"Sure," Durritt chattered, "I'll help you go in to buy the shit, and we'll move it—discreetly, always discreetly, around the studios, but we have to know when to stop, you're so totally right about that, I've always known that . . . "

"Yes. That way . . . no one gets hurt," Trombley said. "I'll tell my man to call Melvin . . . "

JODY AND ANNIE ON TV

FIRST TIME HE has the feeling, he's doing seventy-five on 134. Sun glaring the color off the cars, smog filming the North Hollywood hills. Just past the place where the 134 snakes into the Ventura freeway, he's driving Annie's dad's fucked-up '78 Buick Skylark convertible, one hand on the wheel the other on the radio dial, trying to find a tune, and nothing sounds good. But *nothing.* Everything sounds stupid, even metal. You think it's the music but it's not, you know? It's you.

Usually, it's just a weird mood. But this time it shifts a gear. He looks up from the radio and realizes: You're not driving this car. It's automatic in traffic like this: only moderately heavy traffic, moving fluidly, sweeping around the curves like they are all part of one long thing. Most of your mind is thinking about what's on TV tonight and if you could stand working at that telephone sales place again . . .

It hits him that he is two people, the programmed-Jody who drives and fiddles with the radio and the real-Jody who thinks about getting work . . . Makes him feel funny, detached.

The feeling closes in on him like a jar coming down over a wasp. Glassy like that. He's pressed between the back window and the windshield, the two sheets of glass coming together, compressing him like something under one of those biology-class microscope slides. Everything goes two-dimensional. The cars like the ones in that Roadmaster video game, animated cars made out of pixels.

A buzz of panic, a roaring, and then someone laughs as he jams the Buick's steering wheel over hard to the right, jumps into the VW Bug's lane, forcing it out; the Bug reacts, jerks away from him, sudden and scared, like it's going, "Shit!" Cutting off a Toyota four-by-four with tractor-sized tires, lot of good those do the Toyota, because it spins out and smacks sideways into the grill of a rusty old semitruck pulling an open trailer full of palm trees . . .

They get all tangled up back there. He glances back and thinks, *I did that.* He's grinning and shaking his head and laughing. He's not sorry and he likes the fact that he's not sorry. *I did that.* It's so amazing, so totally rad.

Jody has to pull off at the next exit. His heart is banging like a fire alarm as he pulls into a Texaco. Goes to get a Coke.

It comes to him on the way to the Coke machine that he's stoked. He feels connected and in control and pumped up. The gas fumes smell good; the asphalt under the thin rubber of his sneakers feels good. *Huh.* The Coke tastes good. He thinks he can taste the cola berries. He should call Annie. She should be in the car next to him.

He goes back to the car, heads down the boulevard a mile past the accident, swings on to the freeway, gets up to speed—which is only about thirty miles an hour because the accident's crammed everyone into the three left lanes. Sipping Coca-Cola, he looks the accident over. Highway cops aren't there yet, just the Toyota four-by-four, the rusty semi with its hood wired down, and a Yugo. The VW got away, but the little caramel-colored Yugo is like an accordion against the back of the truck. The Toyota is bent into a short boomarang shape around the snout of the semi, which is jackknifed onto the road shoulder. The Mexican driver is nowhere around. Probably didn't have his green card, ducked out before the cops show up. The palm trees kinked up in the back of the semi are whole, grown-up palm trees, with the roots and some soil tied up in big plastic bags, going to some rebuilt place in Bel Air. One of the palm trees droops almost completely off the back of the trailer.

Jody checks out the dude sitting on the Toyota's hood. The guy's sitting there, rocking with pain, waiting. A kind of ski mask of blood on his face.

I did that, three of 'em, bingo, just like that. Maybe it'll get on the TV news.

Jody cruised on by and went to find Annie.

IT'S ON TV because of the palm trees. Jody and Annie, at home, drink Coronas, watch the crane lifting the palm trees off the freeway. The TV anchor-dude is saying someone is in stable condition, nobody killed; so that's why, Jody figures it is, like, okay for the newsmen to joke about the palm trees on the freeway. Annie has this little Toshiba portable with a twelve-inch screen, on three long extension cords, up in the kitchen window so they can see it on the back porch, because it is too hot to watch it in the living room. If Jody leans forward a little he can see the sun between the houses off to the west. In the smog the sun is a smooth red ball just easing to the horizon and you can look right at it.

Jodie glances at Annie, wondering if he made a mistake telling her what he did.

He can feel her watching him as he opens the third Corona. Pretty soon she'll say, "You going to drink more than three you better pay for the next round." Something she'd never say if he had a job, even if she'd paid for it then too. It's a way to get at the job thing.

She's looking at him, but she doesn't say anything. Maybe it's the wreck on TV. "Guy's not dead," he says, "too fucking bad." Making a macho thing about it.

"You're an asshole." But the tone of her voice says something else. What, exactly? Not admiration. Enjoyment, maybe.

Annie has her hair tossed out; the red parts of her hair look redder in this light; the blond parts look almost real. Her eyes are the glassy green-blue the waves get to be in the afternoon up at Point Mugu with the light coming through the water. Deep tan, white lipstick. He'd never liked that white-lipstick look—white eyeliner and pale-pink fingernail polish that went with it—but he never told her. "Girls who wear that shit are usually airheads," he'd have to say. And she wouldn't believe him when he told her he didn't mean her. She's sitting on the edge of her rickety kitchen chair in that old white shirt of his she wears for a shorty dress, leaning forward so he can see her cleavage, the arcs of her tan lines, her small feet flat on the stucco backporch, her feet planted wide apart but with her knees together, like the feet are saying one thing and the knees another.

His segment is gone from TV but he gets that right-there feeling again as he takes her by the wrist and she says, "Guy, Jody, what do you think I am?"

JOHN SHIRLEY

He leads her to the bedroom and, standing beside the bed, puts his hand between her legs and he can feel he doesn't have to get her any readier, he can get right to the good part. Everything just sort of slips right into place. She locks her legs around his back and they're still standing up, but it's like she hardly weighs anything at all. She tilts her head back, opens her mouth; he can see her broken tooth, a guillotine shape.

THEY'RE DOING FORTY-FIVE on the 101. It's a hot, windy night. They're listening to Mötley Crüe on a Sony ghetto-blaster that stands on end between Annie's feet. The music makes him feel good but it hurts too because now he's thinking about Iron Dream. The band kicking him out because he couldn't get the solo parts to go fast enough. And because he missed some rehearsals. They should have let him play rhythm and sing backup, but the fuckers kicked him out. That's something he and Annie have. Both feeling like they were shoved out of line somewhere. Annie wants to be an actress, but she can't get a part, except once she was an extra for a TV show with a bogus rock club scene. Didn't even get her Guild card from that.

Annie is going on about something, always talking, it's like she can't stand the air to be empty. He really doesn't mind it. She's saying, "So I go, 'I'm *sure* I'm gonna fill in for that bitch when she accuses me of stealing her tips.' And he goes, 'Oh you know how Felicia is, she doesn't mean anything.' I mean—*guy*—he's always saying poor Felicia, you know how Felicia is, cutting her slack, and I've got two more tables to wait, so I'm all, 'Oh right poor Felicia—' and he goes—" Jody nods every so often, and even listens closely for a minute when she talks about the customers who treat her like a waitress. "I mean, what do they think, I'll always be a waitress? I'm sure I'm, like, totally a Felicia who's always, you know, going to be a waitress—" He knows what she means. You're pumping gas and people treat you like you're a born pump jockey and you'll never do anything else. He feels like he's really *with* her, then. It's things like that, and things they don't say; it's like they're looking out the same window together all the time. She sees things the way he does: how people don't understand. Maybe he'll write a song about it. Record it, hit big, Iron Dream'll shit their pants. Wouldn't they, though?

146

"My dad wants this car back, for his girlfriend," Annie says.

"Oh fuck her," Jody says. "She's too fucking drunk to drive, *any*time."

Almost eleven-thirty but she isn't saying anything about having to work tomorrow, she's jacked up same as he is. They haven't taken anything, but they both feel like they have. Maybe it's the Santa Anas blowing weird shit into the valley.

"This car's a piece of junk anyway," Annie says. "It knocks, radiator boils over. Linkage is going out."

"It's better than no car."

"You had it together, you wouldn't have to settle for this car."

She means getting a job, but he still feels like she's saying, "If you were a better guitar player . . ." Someone's taking a turn on a big fucking screw that goes through his chest. That's the second time the feeling comes. Everything going all flat again and he can't tell his hands from the steering wheel.

There is a rush of panic, almost like when Annie's dad took him up in the Piper to go skydiving; like the moment when he pulled the cord and nothing happened. He had to pull it twice. Before the parachute opened, he was spinning around like a dust mote. What difference would it make if he did hit the ground?

It's like that now, he's just hurtling along, sitting back and watching himself, that weird detachment thing . . . Not sure he is in control of the car. What difference would it make if he wasn't in control?

And then he pulls off the freeway, and picks up a wrench from the backseat.

"You're really good at getting it on TV," she says. "It's a talent, like being a director." They are indoors this time sitting up in bed, watching it in the bedroom, with the fan on. It was too risky talking out on the back porch.

"Maybe I should be a director. Make *Nightmare On Elm Street* better than that last one. That last one sucked."

They are watching the news coverage for the third time on the VCR. You could get these hot VCRs for like sixty bucks from a guy on Hollywood Boulevard, if you saw him walking around at the right time. They'd gotten a couple of discount tapes at Federated and they'd recorded the newscast.

". . . We're not sure it's a gang-related incident," the detective on TV was saying. "The use of a wrench—throwing a wrench from the car at someone—uh, that's not the usual gang methodology."

"Methodology," Jody says. "Christ."

There's a clumsy camera zoom on a puddle of blood the ground. Not very good color on this TV, Jody thinks; the blood is more purple than red.

The camera lingers on the blood as the cop says, "They usually use guns. Uzis, weapons along those lines. Of course, the victim was killed just the same. At those speeds a wrench thrown from a car is a deadly weapon. We have no definite leads . . ."

"They usually use guns," Jody says. "I'll use a gun on your balls, shit-head."

Annie snorts happily, and playfully kicks him in the side with her bare foot. "You're such an asshole. You're gonna get in trouble. Shouldn't be using my dad's car, for one thing." But saying it teasingly, chewing her lip to keep from smiling too much.

"You fucking love it," he says, rolling onto her.

"Wait." She wriggles free, rewinds the tape, starts it over. It plays in the background. "Come here, asshole."

JODY'S BROTHER CAL says, "What's going on with you, huh? How come everything I say pisses you off? It's, like, anything. I mean, you're only two years younger than me but you act like you're fourteen sometimes."

"Oh hey Cal," Jody says, snorting, "you're, like, Mr. Mature."

They're in the parking lot of the mall, way off in the corner. Cal in his Pasadena School of Art & Design T-shirt, his yuppie haircut, yellow-tinted John Lennon sunglasses. They're standing by Cal's '81 Subaru, that Mom bought him "because he went to school." They're blinking in the metallic sunlight, at the corner of the parking lot by the boulevard. The only place there's any parking. A couple of acres of cars between them and the main structure of the mall. They're supposed to have lunch with Mom, who keeps busy with her gift shop in the mall, with coffee grinders and dried eucalyptus and silk flowers. But Jody's decided he doesn't want to go.

"I just don't want you to say anymore of this shit to me, Cal," Jody says. "Telling me about *being* somebody." Jody's slouching against the car, his hands slashing the air like a karate move as he talks. He keeps his face down, half-hidden by his long purple-streaked hair, because he's too mad at Cal to look right at him: Cal hassled and wheedled him into coming here. Jody is kicking Cal's tires with the back of a lizardskin boot and every so often he kicks the hubcap, trying to dent it. "I don't need the same from you as I get from Mom."

"Just because she's a bitch doesn't mean she's wrong all the time," Cal says. "Anyway what's the big deal? You used to go along peacefully and listen to Mom's one-way heart-to-hearts and say what she expects and—" He shrugs.

Jody knows what he means: The forty bucks or so she'd hand him afterward "to get him started."

"It's not worth it anymore," Jody says.

"You don't have any other source of money but Annie and she won't put up with it much longer. It's time to get real, Jody, to get a job and—"

"Don't tell me I need a job to get real." Jody slashes the air with the edge of his hand. "Real is where your ass is when you shit," he adds savagely. "Now fucking shut up about it."

Jody looks at the mall, trying to picture meeting Mom in there. It makes him feel heavy and tired. Except for the fiberglass letters— *Northridge Galleria*—styled to imitate handwriting across its off-white pebbly surface, the outside of the mall could be a military building, an enormous bunker. Just a great windowless . . . *block*. "I hate that place, Cal. That mall and that busywork shop. Dad gave her the shop to keep her off the Valium. Fuck. Like fingerpainting for retards."

He stares at the mall, thinking: That cutesy sign, I hate that. Cutesy handwriting but the sign is big enough to crush you dead if it fell on you. *Northridge Galleria*. You could almost hear a radio ad voice saying it over and over again, "Northridge Galleria! . . . Northridge Galleria! . . . Northridge Galleria! . . ."

To their right is a Jack-in-the-Box order-taking intercom. Jody smells the hot plastic of the sun-baked clown-face and the dogfoody hamburger smell of the drive-through mixed in. To their left is a Pioneer Chicken with its cartoon covered wagon sign.

Cal sees him looking at it. Maybe trying to pry Jody loose from obsessing about Mom, Cal says, "You know how many Pioneer Chicken places there are in L.A.? You think you're driving in circles because every few blocks one comes up . . . It's like the ugliest fucking wallpaper pattern in the world."

"Shut up about that shit too."

"What put you in this mood? You break up with Annie?"

"No. We're fine. I just don't want to have lunch with Mom."

"Well goddamn Jody, you shouldn't have said you would, then."

Jody shrugs. He's trapped in the reflective oven of the parking lot, sun blazing from countless windshields and shiny metalflake hoods and from the plastic clownface. Eyes burning from the lancing reflections. Never forget your sunglasses. But no way is he going in.

Cal says, "Look, Jody, I'm dehydrating out here. I mean, fuck this parking lot. There's a couple of palm trees around the edges, but look at this place—it's the surface of the moon."

"Stop being so fucking arty," Jody says. "You're going to art and design school, oh wow awesome I'm impressed."

"I'm just—" Cal shakes his head. "How come you're mad at Mom?"

"She wants me to come over, it's just so she can tell me her latest scam for getting me to do some shit, go to community college, study haircutting or something. Like she's really on top of my life. Fuck, when I was a teenager I told her I was going to hitchhike to New York; she didn't even look up from her card game."

"What'd you expect her to do?"

"I don't know."

"Hey that was when she was on her Self-Dependence kick. She was into Lifespring and Est and Amway and all that. They keep telling her she's not responsible for other people, not responsible, not responsible—"

"She went for it like a fucking fish to water, man." He gives Cal a look that means, *no bullshit*. "What is it she wants *now?*"

"Um—I think she wants you to go to some vocational school."

Jody makes a snorting sound up in his sinuses. "Fuck that. Open up your car, Cal, I ain't going."

"Look, she's just trying to help. What the hell's wrong with having a skill? It doesn't mean you can't do something else too—"

"Cal. She gave you the Subaru, it ain't mine. But you're gonna open the fucking thing up." He hopes Cal knows how serious he is. Because that two-dimensional feeling might come on him if he doesn't get out of here. Words just spill out of him. "Cal, look at this fucking place. Look at this place and tell me about vocational skills. It's shit, Cal. There's two things in the world, dude. There's making it like Bon Jovi, like Eddie Murphy— that's one thing. You're on a screen, you're videos and CDs. Or there's shit. That's the other thing. There's *no fucking thing in between.* There's being *Huge* and there's being nothing." His voice breaking. "We're shit, Cal. Open up the fucking car or I'll kick your headlights in."

Cal stares at him. Then he unlocks the car, his movements short and angry. Jody gets in, looking at a sign on the other side of the parking lot, one of those electronic signs with the lights spelling things out with moving words. The sign says, *You want it, we got it . . . you want it, we got it . . . you want it, we got it . . .*

HE WANTED A Luger. They look rad in war movies. Jody said was James Coburn, Annie said it was Lee Marvin, but whoever it was, he was using a Luger in that Peckinpah movie *Iron Cross.*

But what Jody ends up with is a Smith-Wesson .32, the magazine carrying eight rounds. It's smaller than he'd thought it would be, a scratched gray-metal weight in his palm. They buy four boxes of bullets, drive out to the country, out past Topanga Canyon. They find a fire road of rutted salmon-colored dirt lined with pine trees on one side; the other side has a margin of grass that looks like soggy Shredded Wheat and a barbed wire fence edging an empty horse pasture.

They take turns with the gun, Annie and Jody, shooting Bud Light bottles from a splintery gray fence post. A lot of the time they miss the bottles. Jody said, "This piece's pulling to left." He isn't sure if it really is, but Annie seems to like when he talks as if he knows about it.

It's nice out there, he likes the scent of gunsmoke mixed with the pine-tree smell. Birds were singing for awhile, too, but they stopped after the shooting, scared off. His hand hurts from the gun's recoil, but he doesn't say anything about that to Annie.

"What we got to do," she says, taking a potshot at a squirrel, "is try shooting from the car."

He shakes his head. "You think you'll aim better from in a car?"

"I mean from a moving car, stupid." She gives him a look of exasperation. "To get used to it."

"Hey yeah."

They get the old Buick bouncing down the rutted fire road, about thirty feet from the fence post when they pass it, and Annie fires twice, and misses. "The stupid car bounces too much on this road," she says.

"Let me try it."

"No wait—make it more like a city street, drive in the grass off the road. No ruts."

"Uh . . . Okay." So he backs up, they try it again from the grass verge. She misses again, but they keep on because she insists, and about the fourth time she starts hitting the post, and the sixth time she hits the bottle.

"WELL WHY NOT?" She asks again.

Jody doesn't like backing off from this in front of Annie, but it feels like it is too soon or something. "Because now we're just gone and nobody knows who it is. If we hold up a store it'll take time, they might have silent alarms, we might get caught." They are driving with the top up, to give them some cover in case they decide to try the gun here, but the windows are rolled down because the old Buick's air conditioning is busted.

"Oh right I'm sure some 7-11 store is going to have a silent alarm."

"Just wait, that's all. Let's do this first. We got to get more used to the gun."

"And get another one. So we can both have one."

For some reason that scares him. But he says: "Yeah. Okay."

It is late afternoon. They are doing sixty on the 405. Jody not wanting to get stopped by the CHP when he has a gun in his car. Besides, they are a little drunk because shooting out at Topanga Canyon in the sun made them thirsty, and this hippie on this gnarly old tractor had come along, some pot farmer maybe, telling them to get off his land, and that pissed them off. So they drank too much beer.

They get off the 405 at Burbank Boulevard, looking at the other cars, the people on the sidewalk, trying to pick someone out. Some asshole.

But no one looks right. Or maybe it doesn't feel right. He doesn't have that feeling on him.

"Let's wait," he suggests.

"Why?"

"Because it just seems like we oughta, that's why."

She makes a clucking sound but doesn't say anything else for awhile. They drive past a patch of adult bookstores and a video arcade and a liquor store. They come to a park. The trash cans in the park have overflowed; wasps are haunting some melon rinds on the ground. In the basketball court four Chicanos are playing two-on-two, wearing those shiny, pointy black shoes they wear. "You ever notice how Mexican guys, they play basketball and football in dress shoes?" Jody asks. "It's like they never heard of sneakers—"

He hears a crack and a thudding echo and a greasy chill goes through him as he realizes that she's fired the gun. He glimpses a Chicano falling, shouting in pain, the others flattening on the tennis court, looking around for the shooter as he stomps the accelerator, lays rubber, squealing through a red light, cars bitching their horns at him, his heart going in time with the pistons, fear vising his stomach. He's weaving through the cars, looking for the freeway entrance. Listening for sirens.

They are on the freeway, before he can talk. The rush hour traffic only doing about forty-five, but he feels better here. Hidden.

"What the *fuck* you doing?!" he yells at her.

She gives him a look accusing him of something. He isn't sure what. Betrayal maybe. Betraying the thing they had made between them.

"Look—" he says, softer, "it was a *red light*. People almost hit me coming down the cross street. You know? You got to think a little first. And don't do it when I don't *know*."

She looks at him like she is going to spit. Then she laughs, and he has to laugh too. She says, "Did you see those dweebs dive?"

Mouths dry, palms damp, they watch the five o'clock news and the six o'clock news. Nothing. Not a word about it. They sit up in the bed, drinking Coronas. Not believing it. "I mean, what kind of fucking society *is* this?" Jody says. Like something Cal would say. "When you shoot somebody and they don't even say a damn word about it on TV?"

"It's sick," Annie says.

They try to make love but it just isn't there. It's like trying to start a gas stove when the pilot light is out.

So they watch *Hunter* on TV. Hunter is after a psychokiller. The psycho guy is a real creep. Set a house on fire with some kids in it, they almost got burnt up, except Hunter gets there in time. Finally Hunter corners the psychokiller and shoots him. Annie says, "l like TV better than movies because you know how it's gonna turn out. But in movies it might have a happy ending or it might not."

"It usually does," Jody points out.

"Oh yeah? Did you see *Terms of Endearment?* And they got Bambi out again now. When I was a kid I cried for two days when his mom got shot. They should always have happy endings in a little kid movie."

"That part, that wasn't the end of that movie. It was happy in the end."

"It was still a sad movie."

Finally at eleven o'clock they're on. About thirty seconds worth. A man "shot in the leg on Burbank Boulevard today in a drive-by shooting believed to be gang-related." On to the next story. No pictures, nothing. That was it.

What a rip off. "It's racist, is what it is," he says. "Just because they were Mexicans no one gives a shit."

"You know what it is, it's because of all the gang stuff. Gang drive-bys happen every day, everybody's used to it."

He nods. She's right She has a real feel for these things. He puts his arm around her; she nestles against him. "Okay. We're gonna do it right, so they really pay attention."

"What if we get caught?"

Something in him freezes when she says that. She isn't supposed to talk like that. Because of the *thing* they have together. It isn't something they ever talk about, but they know its rules.

When he withdraws a little, she says, "But we'll never get caught because we just *do it* and cruise before anyone gets it together."

He relaxes, and pulls her closer. It feels good just to lay there and hug her.

THE NEXT DAY he's in line for his unemployment insurance check. They have stopped his checks, temporarily, and he'd had to hassle them. They said he could pick this one up. He had maybe two more coming.

Thinking about that, he feels a bad mood coming on him. There's no air conditioning in this place and the fat guy in front of him smells like he's fermenting and the room's so hot and close Jody can hardly breathe.

He looks around and can almost see the feeling—like an effect of a camera lens, a zoom or maybe a fish-eye lens: Things going two dimensional, flattening out. Annie says something and he just shrugs. She doesn't say anything else till after he's got his check and he's practically running for the door.

"Where you going?"

He shakes his head, standing outside, looking around. It's not much better outside. It's overcast but still hot. "Sucks in there."

"Yeah," she says. "For sure. Oh shit."

"What?"

She points at the car. Someone has slashed the canvas top of the Buick. "My dad is going to kill us."

He looks at the canvas and can't believe it. "Mu-ther-*fuck!*-er!"

"Fucking assholes," she says, nodding gravely. "I mean you know how much that costs to fix? You wouldn't believe it."

"Maybe we can find him."

"How?"

"I don't know."

He still feels bad but there's a hum of anticipation too. They get in the car, he tears out of the parking lot, making gravel spray, whips onto the street.

They drive around the block, just checking people out, the feeling in him spiraling up and up. Then he sees a guy in front of a Carl's Jr., the guy grinning at him, nudging his friend. Couple of jock college students, looks like, in tank tops. Maybe the guy who did the roof of the car, maybe not.

They pull around the corner, coming back around for another look. Jody can feel the good part of the feeling coming on now but there's something bothering him too: the jocks in tank tops looked right at him.

"You see those two guys?" he hears himself ask, as he pulls around the comer, cruises up next to the Carl's Jr. "The ones—"

"Those jock guys, I know, I picked them out too."

He glances at her, feeling close to her then. They are one person in two parts. The right and the left hand. It feels like music.

He makes sure there's a green light ahead of him, then he says, "Get 'em both," he hears himself say. "Don't miss or—"

By then she's aiming the .32, both hands wrapped around it. The jock guys, one of them with a huge coke and the other with a milkshake, are standing by the driveway to the restaurant's parking lot, talking, one of them playing with his car keys. Laughing. The bigger one with the dark hair looks up and sees Annie and the laughing fades from his face. Seeing that, Jody feels better than he ever felt before. *Crack, crack.* She fires twice, the guys go down. *Crack, crack, crack.* Three times more, making sure it gets on the news: shooting into the windows of the Carl's Jr., webs instantly snapping into the window glass, some fat lady goes spinning, her tray of burgers tilting, flying. Jody's already laying rubber, fishtailing around the corner, heading for the freeway.

THEY DON'T MAKE it home, they're so excited. She tells him to stop at a gas station on the other side of the hills, in Hollywood. The Men's is unlocked, he feels really right there as she looks around then leads him into the bathroom, locks the door from the inside. Bathroom's an almost clean one, he notices, as she hikes up her skirt and he undoes his pants, both of them with shaking fingers, in a real hurry, and she pulls him into her with no preliminaries, right there with her sitting on the edge of the sink. There's no mirror but he sees a cloudy reflection in the shiny chrome side of the towel dispenser; the two of them blurred into one thing sort of pulsing . . .

He looks straight at her, then; she's staring past him, not at anything in particular, just at the sensation, the good sensation they are grinding out between them, like it's something she can see on the dust-streaked wall. He can almost see it in her eyes. And in the way she traps the end of her tongue between her front teeth. Now he can see it himself, in his mind's eye, the sensation flashing like sun in a mirror; ringing like a power chord through a fuzz box . . .

When he comes he doesn't hold anything back, he can't, and it escapes from him with a sob. She holds him tight and he says, "Wow you are just so awesome you make me feel so good . . ."

He's never said anything like that to her before, and they know they've arrived somewhere special. "I love you, Jody," she says.

"I love you."

"It's just us, Jody. Just us. Just us."

He knows what she means. And they feel like little kids cuddling together, even though they're fucking standing up in a Union 76 men's restroom, in the smell of pee and disinfectant.

Afterwards they're really hungry so they go to a Jack-in-the-Box, get drive-through food, ordering a whole big shitload. They eat it on the way home, Jody trying not to speed, trying to be careful again about being stopped, but hurrying in case they have a special news flash on TV about the Carl's Jr. Not wanting to miss it.

The Fajita Pita from Jack-in-the-Box tastes really great.

WHILE HE'S EATING, Jody scribbles some song lyrics into his song notebook with one hand. "The Ballad of Jody and Annie."

They came smokin' down the road
like a bat out of hell

they hardly even slowed
or they'd choke from the smell

Chorus: Holdin' hands in the Valley of Death
(repeat 3X)

Jody and Annie bustin' out of bullshit
Bustin' onto TV
better hope you aren't the one hit
killed disonnerably

Nobody understands 'em
nobody ever will
but Jody knows she loves 'im
They never get their fill

They will love forever
in history and they'll live together
in femmy

Holdin' hands in the Valley of Death

He runs out of inspiration there. He hints heavily to Annie about
the lyrics and pretends he doesn't want her to read them, makes her
ask three times. With tears in her eyes, she asks, as she reads the lyrics,
"What's a 'femmy'?"

"You know, like 'Living In femmy'."

"Oh, infamy. It's so beautiful . . . You got guacamole on it, you
asshole." She's crying with happiness and using a napkin to reverently
wipe the guacamole from the notebook paper.

THERE'S NO SPECIAL news flash but since three people died and two are
in intensive care, they are the top story on the five o'clock news. And at
seven o'clock they get mentioned on CNN, which is *national.* Another
one, and they'll be on the *NBC Nightly News,* Jody says.

"I'd rather be on *World News Tonight,*" Annie says. "I like that Peter
Jennings dude. He's cute."

About ten, they watch the videotapes of the news stories again. Jody guesses he should be bothered that the cops have descriptions of them but somehow it just makes him feel more psyched, and he gets down with Annie again. They almost never do it twice in one day, but this makes three times. "I'm getting sore," she says, when he enters her. But she gets off.

They're just finishing, he's coming, vaguely aware he sees lights flashing at the windows, when he hears Cal's voice coming out of the walls. He thinks he's gone schizophrenic or something, he's hearing voices, booming like the voice of God. *"Jody, come on outside and talk to us. This is Cal, you guys. Come on out."*

Then Jody understands, when Cal says, *"They want you to throw the gun out first."*

Jody pulls out of her, puts his hand over her mouth, and shakes his head. He pulls his pants on, then goes into the front room, looks through a corner of the window. There's Cal, and a lot of cops.

Cal's standing behind the police barrier, the cruiser lights flashing around him; beside him is a heavyset Chicano cop who's watching the S.W.A.T. team gearing up behind the big gray van. They're scary-looking in all that armor and with those helmets and shotguns and sniper rifles.

Jody spots Annie's dad. He's tubby, with a droopy mustache, long hair going bald at the crown, some old hippie, sitting in the back of the cruiser. Jody figures someone got their license number, took them awhile to locate Annie's dad. He wasn't home at first. They waited till he came home, since he owns the car, and after they talked to him they decided it was his daughter and her boyfriend they were looking for. Got the address from him. Drag Cal over here to talk to Jody because Mom wouldn't come. Yeah.

Cal speaks into the bullhorn again, same crap, sounding like someone else echoing off the houses. Jody sees people looking out their windows. Some being evacuated from the nearest houses. Now an *Action News* truck pulls up, cameramen pile out, set up incredibly fast, get right to work with the newscaster. Lots of activity just for Jody and Annie. Jody has to grin, seeing the news cameras, the guy he recognizes from TV waiting for his cue. He feels high, looking at all this. Cal says something else, but Jody isn't listening. He goes to get the gun.

"It's just us, Jody," Annie says, her face flushed, her eyes dilated as she helps him push the sofa in front of the door. "We can do anything together."

She is there, not scared at all, her voice all around him soft and warm. "It's just us," she says again, as he runs to get another piece of furniture.

He is running around like a speedfreak, pushing the desk, leaning bookshelves to block off the tear gas. Leaving enough room for him to shoot through. He sees the guys start to come up the walk with the tear gas and the shotguns. Guys in helmets and some kind of bulky bulletproof shit. But maybe he can hit their necks, or their knees. He aims carefully and fires again. Someone stumbles and the others carry the wounded dude back behind the cars.

Five minutes after Jody starts shooting, he notices that Annie isn't there. At almost the same moment a couple of rifle rounds knock the bookshelves down, and something smashes through a window. In the middle of the floor, white mist gushes out of a tear gas shell.

Jody runs from the tear gas, into the kitchen, coughing. "Annie!" His voice sounding like a kid's.

He looks through the kitchen window. Has she gone outside, turned traitor?

But then she appears at his elbow, like somebody switched on a screen and Annie is what's on it.

"Hey," she says, her eyes really bright and beautiful. "Guess what." She has the little TV by the handle; it's plugged in on the extension cord. In the next room, someone is breaking through the front door.

"l give up," he says, eyes tearing. "What?"

She sits the TV on the counter for him to see. "We're on TV. Right now. We're on TV. . . ".

BRITTANY? OH: SHE'S IN TRANSLUCENT BLUE

Some people go to bed with Lucifer
and they cry, cry, cry when they don't greet
the day with God . . .
        —Monster Magnet

MARISSA DIDN'T SEE why she should get a sitter when Donny was there, he'd watched Brittany before, one time before, and it was right before Brittany's nap anyway. She was telling Henny something like that when they went down into the basement, Doc's "rec room to my neighbors, dungeon to you", and Jill was smiling triumphantly at them from the little built-in bar. "I told you they'd come," Jill said, to Doc, as he came in with that old, masking-taped cigar box of his. Jill, Doc and Marissa's husband Henny were all in their early forties. Marissa was "the baby", at thirty-five.

Marissa and Henny joined Jill at the bar, side by side.

"Gosh it's so nice and cool down here," Marissa said. "It must be eighty-five or ninety outside already and it'll get hotter. August in L.A. The smog makes it worse, too."

"You're not going to diss the valley again, are you Marissa honey?" Jill said, her fingers jabbing the blender buttons.

"No, it's that way all over L.A."

"You need a new stash box, there, Doc," Henny said, his eyes on the box as Doc laid it down on the little bar, Henny probably wondering what it'd be this time. He was a bigger dope pig than Marissa was: she was just as happy with cocktails but she'd try anything—which is what she'd seriously, very seriously, told her sister she wanted on her gravestone, SHE'D TRY ANYTHING and her sister Lizzy had said something like, That's what'll kill you, too, so it *oughta* be on there fuh Chris'sakes, and Marissa had said she didn't need those negative impressions. When he'd taken Marissa's monthly psychic impressions, her psychic, Damtha, had said, "You're definitely getting too many negative resonations from somewhere, there's a lot for me to remove, here." And, you know, they might've been from Lizzy, she could be so negative. So judgmental.

There was just the two couples that afternoon. Their kids playing in the back yard as they got into the party. After Brittany got tired playing with Donny, Henny could take her upstairs for a nap. She'd had her lunch, she'd be sleepy soon. Thank God at four-and-a-half the kid still needed an afternoon nap. It was a mother's little island of sanity.

Jill wore a puce tank top; she starved so she'd look good in it, though her tits didn't have the lift they used to. Her hips were still too wide, no matter what she did, a little "saddle baggy", and the zebra-patterned spandex leggings didn't help. Her luminous-orange hair was teased like a windy fire around her head. Doc's head was a little too big for his body, mustache too small for his face, so it seemed to Marissa, but he was still "a good-lookin' galoot"—that's what she'd called him when they'd first met him and Jill at Harry's "Social Club". He wore blue jeans and sandals and a Jimmy Page/Robert Plant T-shirt.

"Where'd you get that antique Led Zep shirt, it looks almost new," Marissa asked. "You find it in the garage in a box?"

"No, it *is* new. It's not Led Zep. Page and Plant are doing a solo tour now."

"Really? I didn't know that." She took a cocktail from Jill. It was one of those overly-sweet cherry-tasting things with vodka that Doc liked. She decided not to complain about it.

Henny was wearing Gap khakis, a matching shirt, untucked to hide his paunch. He had a hatchet face, flat blue eyes, thinning blond hair tied back into a little pony tail, and a soul patch. Marissa was the chunky one; her arms and legs were a little short but she had those heavy breasts that Doc liked; that he stared at now. She wore a gold satin top that clung to them and dropped off straight below the nipples to hide her own sloppy middle.

"So where's the Mondersons?" Marissa asked, thinking of that big ropy thing Judge Monderson had in his pants.

"Not coming," Jill said. "They're, like, 'swung out' for awhile after the convention in Las Vegas. I guess Judge did a little too much X or something and freaked out the next morning."

"A little is good, a lot is toxic," Doc said, sitting at the bar.

"A lot of what, that's the question," Henny said. Henny was still looking expectantly at the cigar box, maybe hoping it was cocaine.

Marissa hoped it wasn't cocaine: that made Henny impotent fast, it was embarrassing. You're going to swing, you're supposed to do your part.

"Marrisa—where's the..." Henny'd started to say 'Where's the kid?' but he remembered not to. She got mad when he said it like that. It wasn't his kid, it was Luis' kid, but still he didn't need to talk about Brittany like she was some stranger's child. ". . . where's our little one?" He'd been in the bathroom, maybe checking out Doc's medicine cabinet, when she'd put Brittany out back.

"Playing out back. Donny's watching her."

"So—how about some music? I like my action with a beat," Henny said.

This made Marissa think of the ad at that Internet personals club site. How they'd met Doc and Jill.

> ## LOOKING FOR MR'N'MRS RIGHT!
> Tired of no-swap swingers? We're believers in action too, and we like our action with the big rock beat, wherever it'll take us.
>
> Role playing, light B&D, four-ways, six-ways and everyone gets some.
>
> If you're into it, so are we. Will we try anything? Maybe not—but definitely, make the suggestion! Doc and Jill, seeking couples between 30 and 45. N/S. Must exchange photos, email, before meeting. Mailbox 455895

Jill switched on the six-CD-cycle boombox Doc kept by the kingsized blue-silk bed on the concrete floor beyond the rec-room bar. In that half of the room the concrete floor was painted black, and dusted with glitter, in places, to be like starry space. Above the bed—a big futon, really—was an old black-light poster of people fucking in an exotic Kama Sutra position, with op-art lines radiating from their joined genitals. On the walls to either side were posters; one side was Mel Gibson, without his shirt on—that was for Jill—and the other side was Doc's life-size Xena Warrior Princess poster. "I'd love to get that Lucy Lawless in the sack," Doc had said, more than once, gazing goatishly at Xena.

Yeah, Marissa always thought, like that could happen. Like she'd sleep with you if you had a gold plated introduction, a bottle of Dom Perignon and a Plaza suite. Dream on.

Under Xena were two metal rings in the wall, that Doc tied the girls to, when the mood was on them, and sometimes himself. There was a ring in the ceiling, too.

The first CD on the cycler was Doc's new Plant/Page album, which sounded like Led Zep to Marissa. Jill made another pitcher of cocktails. Doc bobbed his head in time to the music as he rolled joints.

Henny frowned at the makings Doc was working with. "I dunno, maybe I should stick with cocktails, pot makes me paranoid, sometimes, man."

Doc grinned. "Jill—this pot going to make him paranoid?"

Jill was dancing, pulling off her tube top. Henny watched her small, pointed breasts jump. "Not going to make him paranoid," she said. "Going to get him high as a motherfucker."

"Those kids going to be okay?" Marissa said, glancing at the back door at the top of the stairs. Asking because she felt like she should, though she didn't want to think about it. "Usually we got a sitter."

"Check on 'em, you want. They're fine," Henny said. "What kind of pot is it?"

"It's *pot plus*," Doc said. His eyes were always a little too deeply-shadowed and to Marissa it seemed like the shadows got deeper when he was about to get loaded.

"Pot plus what?"

"Special formula, dude."

DONNY WAS TIGHTENING the strap on Brittany, blinking in the bright sunlight.

"Ow," she said. "That hurt, some." She shaded her eyes to see his face. It looked like the palm tree behind him was growing out of the top of his head.

"Oh shit it does."

"Don't say shit," Brittany said, glancing toward the house. Mama didn't care if they said shit but Dad Henny didn't like it. There was no sign of the adults. They were alone out here.

"Shit, why, shit, not, shit, huh shit?"

He gave out a long pealing sort of laugh. Brittany watched his belly button jump when he laughed. "Boinkaboinka," she said. He tightened the strap on the plastic carapace a little more. "Not that much, that's some hurt."

He stood back and looked at his handiwork—he'd simply strapped her into the laser target vest but it had taken some doing to get it so it wouldn't fall off, she was so small.

"Okay," Donny said, "you run around and hide, and I chase you and try to shoot that target, that thing here." He touched the panel in the middle of her chest that looked like a bicycle reflector. "And if I shoot it, it'll buzz and light up and I win."

He stood back and pointed the little lazer-laser pistol from point blank range and pulled the trigger. The panel lit up with a blue flash, faint in the bright sunlight, and it made an unpleasant buzz feeling against her stomach.

"Gross. I don't think I want to play that. We could play Spice Girls."

"Oh shit you bet Spice Girls. No arfin' way, okay?"

She stood with one bare foot on the other, and shifted in the stiff plastic vest, squinting at the swimming pool. A bug with shiny green wings dimpled the water, uselessly paddling its legs. As she watched, it was sucked toward a filter.

"You going to play or not?"

There was a wriggling chain of light in the blue pool water…the bug went into the filter . . . the light shook itself . . .

"Brittany? You going to play?"

Her foot was hurting on the hot concrete. She turned and hopped, twice, to get into the shade of the house. "How come there isn't grass?"

"What?"

She pointed. The ground all the way around the house was green concrete with stuff stuck in it. The green paint on the concrete was faded, worn away in places. There were a lot of abalone shells, some of them broken now, some pieces of lava glass, some shiny round rocks, a couple of half-broken statues of little men with beards and pointed hats and wrinkled up faces, the broken base of a bird feeder and, embedded face up in the concrete: a silvery frisbee with a lot of names signed on it in magic marker and the numbers *1 9 8 3*. It was like that all the way around the house—concrete with things trapped in it, an arm's length between each little pushed-in thing. There was a blue crystal doorknob in one spot; she liked to look at it. See her reflection in it, tiny and blue.

"It's Jill, she did that." For some reason, Donny called his mom "Jill" instead of "Mom". "I mean, she doesn't like weeds but she doesn't like to work on weeds so she said it was an art project and they took out all the grass and put in this concrete and put this stuff in it and painted it between the stuff. It was before I was born. Watch out, too, you can cut your feet on those shells, they got broke."

"Okay."

"You going to play? It took a long time to put that target on you."

She squinted at him. There were two palm trees growing out of his head now because she and Donny were standing in a different spot.

"You're pissing me off now," he said. She couldn't see his eyes, hardly, because of the way the sun was.

She didn't want to admit she didn't know what that meant so she just said, "Okay. I'll hide."

Doc bought and restored and sold classic cars. The men were talking about cars, something about blown hemis. "Shit next they'll be talking about fucking football and here we are with our tits hanging out in front of them," Jill said.

"I know, they take us for granted."

"I take you for very, very good *heart-breakin' good* pussy, that's what I take you for," said Doc, who sometimes talked that way. He used to read Hunter Thompson and it had something to do with that. Pretty soon he'd start with the comedy.

Jill looked at Marissa narrowly and blew her a kiss. "*I* take you seriously honey."

Marissa made a kissy at her. "Me too, you."

But she was always uncomfortable when Jill was sucking on her tits and playing with her pussy. Jill had way more dyke in her than she did. But you had to be flexible, and not get hung up.

"You still working out at the airport?" Jill asked.

"No, I fucking quit," Marissa said. "It was making me crazy, those announcements. Selling magazines and candy and listening to those announcements all day. Blahbuhdahbuhdah all day."

"God I guess. Henny still selling software?"

"Yeah, he just sold a whole line to . . . I don't know, some big company . . ."

Doc was just firing up the doobies. The specials. One for each couple. The music was—what *was* that, the guy with the high pitched voice and as soon as they made up their mind what the song was going to be it changed like they thought that was real heavy.

"What band is that, Doc?" Marissa asked, taking the joint from Henny.

"Rush, that's fuckin' Rush, are you kidding?"

"Mahogany Rush?"

"No, shit, that's another band, this is Rush, rush rush rush-rush ruuuuush, oh-*kay.*" Doc had slipped into some *Saturday Night Live* character, though she wasn't sure which one. He fantasized about being a stand up comic. Next would come a lame joke.

She drew on the joint and coughed. It was sour, chemical tasting. "God, what is that?"

"Okay so God called Bill Gates, Boris Yeltsin, and Clinton—" Doc was saying. "Here's the deal, boys, God said . . . um . . ."

"Did you sign that letter from the Swingers Coalition to Clinton?" Jill whispered.

Marissa nodded and took another hit.

"—and said the World is going to end in twenty-four hours and so Clinton went to the American people and said I got some good news and some bad news, folks . . ." He was trying to do an Arkansas good ol' boy accent over that part of the joke, she could tell by his expression, but she couldn't hear the accent because of the music. ". . . good news is God is real after all, bad news is that the world's gonna end. So then Yeltsin he goes to the Russian people and uh . . ." The music was getting louder and louder, on its own. She could feel the weight of it in the air. She could feel the music on her skin. She watched as Jill unzipped Henny's pants, right there at the bar, and took his dick out, and started playing with it, and he wet the tip of his thumb and started rotating it on one of her nipples; he had an exaggerated idea of how much she liked that.

"And Bill Gates said, the good news is the Y2K thing is not gonna be a problem but . . ." Without anyone touching the boombox the music rose to such volume that she couldn't hear the punchline but it was a pain in the butt when Doc sulked so she watched him for the right moment and laughed on cue and he bent over, laughing, pushed his head between her breasts, butted them around. "You think it's funny too, boys?" he asked her breasts and he bounced them to make them nod. "Yes we do!" He did it in a high pitched voice, mimicking her breasts talking back to him, making Henny bark with laughter. The laughter broke off abruptly as Jill bent and took Henny into her mouth. She was bent over from the waist, legs straight, her butt jutting out behind, holding herself up with her hands on the sides of his stool, maybe hoping Doc would come around and pull her tights down and slip into her from behind, because that's what she liked best from the guys, one in her from either end, and one of the things Marissa liked best was watching someone suck her husband, which her sister thought was weird. But her sister didn't understand swingers, said they were sex addicts, and all Marissa knew was that it got her off, the ripples of—she didn't know *what* the feeling was—ripples of *that feeling* going through her, and now she could *see* the feeling, when she looked down at herself—never before could she actually see it but now she saw it in rings moving up through her body, shining gold-green rings . . .

Somehow she was standing, though she didn't remember getting up, and Doc had his head under her blouse and Henny was shouting over the music about hell let's get in bed . . . That's what the good Lord made beds for . . .

THE CONCRETE HURT Brittany's feet, where it was rough, and she'd broken a toenail on the lavaglass, but right then she was having fun staying away from Donny. One of his feet was smaller than the other so one of his shoes had extra rubber on the bottom and he didn't move very well so it wasn't hard for her to stay away from his laser shooter-thing. "You're cheating," he yelled, from the back, when she went into the front yard and ducked under the bird-of-paradise plant. She could smell corn and beef cooking from the Mexican house across the street and a Mexican boy was watching her, sitting on his bike and watching her; he was a little older than her, he might be in first grade, or almost, and he was watching but he didn't have a look on his face like he wanted to be asked to play. She wanted to ask him, to have someone else there, because Donny's eyes were like that cartoon she'd seen, where the cartoon had holes instead of eyes—

She heard Donny's tennis shoes' uneven slapping coming along the side of the house and she got out from under the bird-of-paradise and dodged between the little islands of things in the concrete front yard, around the other side of the house and away from him. This was easy, she could just keep the house between her and him.

"You're cheating!" he yelled, which is what he yelled when he wasn't winning, "you are supposed to stay in the back shitbutt!"

ANOTHER TIME IT would have bothered Marissa when Henny threw up, but this time it didn't seem to bother anyone, it made them all laugh, Henny too, as he threw up into the little aluminum sink behind the bar. He gargled with vodka as another CD came on, it was the Moody Blues, "Knights in White Satin", and Marissa, lying on her back, could see the Knights in White Satin riding horses across the ceiling as Doc slapped against her, his half-erect dick just making it in, getting a little harder as he worked at it, and Jill gave her another hit of the sour tasting dope, holding the joint between Marissa's lips, and then sat on her tits, which is one of the things Jill did to her that Marissa sort of liked, when she kind of rode her big tits with her naked ass like that, and Marissa could see Jill's buttocks looking like tits now themselves, nipples growing on them—

"What was that dope?" she asked, absently. Skin felt rubbery, plasticky, distant to her now.

The slender man in white sitting next to her—was he the Knight? He looked like that boy she'd liked when she was in high school, Lenny—he said, "It was PCP, angel dust, dear lady." Or maybe Doc said that because Henny came back to the bed, asking about it.

"Oh Christ, dust joints," Henny was saying, "Jeez, Doc." But of course he took another hit. Anytime: Whatever it was, Henny always took another hit.

She suddenly remembered the time Henny had taken speed. The one and only time; she'd never let him do it after that, or not that she knew about. He'd gone down on a black girl that Jill had brought over and the girl was on some other drug, 'ludes maybe, and was watching TV at the time, Dennis Rodman on some talk show, and laughing at him, but at the same time the woman was playing with her clit while she talked about the TV, and more than an hour passed that way until Marissa saw that Henny's knees were bloody . . . bloody from grinding on the concrete floor . . .

Marissa looked for the man in white sitting next to the bed, and he was there, pointing at the wall. There was a buzzing in her head, like a smoke alarm inside her, so loud she couldn't hear what he was saying, but he was pointing at her and Judy Chula, who was Luis' little sister, and they were in high school, way back in high school, senior prom night, they were walking to the prom because they didn't have dates but they decided to go anyway, because there would be guys without dates there too, supposedly, and they could dance, and you never knew, and then a Trans Am pulled up beside them. In the car were two guys she didn't really know but she thought one of them was named Charles something, and the other one was either Rafe or Rufus, both of them blond, cousins, big good-looking guys major in football at school, but not in her scene, and they asked if they wanted a ride to the prom. She and Judy looked at each other and got in that car *fast*. The guys were wearing football jackets and jeans, though; they weren't dressed for the prom. "If you're going to the prom, you're dressed kind of weird for it," Judy said, which made Marissa cringe, and the cringing made her feel her tampon inside her, she felt it trickle a little when she squeezed her thighs, and she was afraid the trickle would get out, she'd been having these really full periods, and that, if it happened, would be the ultimate humiliation for sure, but the guys were saying something . . .

"Do you remember what they said?" the man with the shining white face and the long, long hair asked her, as she turned her head to look at Jill's churning buttocks as Doc ground at her pussy. Jill was sucking Henny at the same time.

"Yes . . . they said they were going to change pretty soon for the prom, but did we want to smoke a joint with them first. We said okay."

"Who's she talkin' to?" Doc asked, laughing. "Whoa, she's high. Come on, girl..."

She felt Jill climb off her, a sudden coolness, then Henny taking her by the wrist, agreeing with Doc about something she couldn't hear because the smoke alarm sound was up again, and they were leading her to the ceiling hook, making her wobble through a gelatinous air . . .

They chained her with mink-lined leather cuffs to the chain that ran from the ceiling.

I'm a Christmas tree ornament, she thought.

This was one of her favorite things, when people did this to her. They were completely paying attention to her when they did that. Spanking her, while Jill sucked on her tits. After awhile Doc would lengthen the chain so she could kneel and get him hard again—

The smoke alarm sound in her head rose and fell.

"That's it, learn what you're here for, to make us feel good, little bitchy love," Jill was saying. "Now you're going to . . ."

The sound rose again and she couldn't hear the rest. She couldn't feel her wrists. She could barely feel Doc screwing her from behind.

She was looking over Jill's shoulder at the pictures on the walls—no, the pictures were in the walls, like holograms, and mixed up with the poster: part of the image of Mel Gibson. Mel was now wearing a high school football jacket, and was making Judy kneel down and give him head, forcing her mouth onto him by pushing the back of her head; while beside him, on the grass of the park the other, shorter jock was trying to force Marissa's legs apart, and succeeded though she tried to squirm away, and she was saying, no, no, I'll give you a blowjob, I'll give you a blowjob, but he wanted to be able to say he'd gone all the way with someone, and he forced her legs open and the blood gushed…

At the same moment the jock standing gushed in Judy's mouth, making her choke and whimper angrily and she pulled herself away and spat—

Then they saw the lights of the cop car coming down the road into the parking lot of the park, and they ran, zipping up and pulling up their pants respectively, sprinting through the brush of the park toward the street where they'd left the Trans Am, and both Judy and Marissa were crying, their prom dresses ruined with cum and grass stains and blood and the two cops came and stood over them and one of them made an involuntary disgust-sound when he saw the blood running down her thigh and the blood tampon with its little string that had come out when she was struggling away from the shorter jock—

Marissa was weeping so Jill said, "Oh *gawd*. Well, hell, let her down."

And they undid the cuffs and she sank down and saw their disappointed faces and said, "I'm sorry. Let's do something. What do you want to do?"

"I DON'T WANT to *do* that," Brittany was saying, as Donny pushed her against the fence. Her foot was bleeding now from the broken shell she'd stepped on. That's the only reason he'd caught her.

"Just for a few minutes more," he said. "I didn't get the target but one time."

"I don't care, my head hurts, I want to lay down, my foot's bleeding, I'm tired, I don't care, I don't like it, I want to lay down."

She was hungry too. She wanted to see her mom.

"Go—run!"

"I don't want to play that anymore."

"You'd better."

"Okay—I'll run." But she ran through the fence gate, where he didn't want her to go, leaving little red blotches on the walk, and hid under the bird-of-paradise plant and wriggled out of the plastic vest. It scratched her as she struggled with it. It was hard to get off. Finally she got it off and she'd just thrown it aside when he found her, and he yelled something. She couldn't make out what he was yelling.

She ran around the side, limping a little now, and through the other fence gate, and into the back yard, looking for the door into the house where her mom had gone.

"Mom?" she yelled. "Mom!"

Donny came into the back yard, his mouth all flattened out, pinched looking, his eyes like the hole-eye cartoon guy's. He got between her and the back door.

He pushed her toward the pool.

MARISSA THOUGHT SHE heard her daughter calling, from somewhere far away.

It was hard to tell, with the music, and the noises that Jill was making, and the rising, falling buzzing sound. Jill was face down in the blue silk pillow, on the blue silk sheets, with both Doc and Henny holding her down, her hands cuffed behind her. It was the erotic smothering she liked—they were careful not to go too far with it. But she liked to get at least dizzy, blurry, before they let her up. The boombox was playing an oldies CD, the song "Crystal Blue Persuasion".

And then she saw Henny split in two, another Henny stepping out of him looking like an inaccurate copy, with a long strip of bristly brown fur down its back, running into a long wolflike tail; with eyes like holes thumbed into the putty of its almost-Henny head. It rose humming, buzzing and growling, to turn, to swim through the air itself, the shining blue air, moving in slow motion up the stairs and out the door and out to backyard, to the pool—the pushing motions of the original Henny's shoulders and hips as he drove himself into her, seemed to translate into the movements of the thing that rose from him, the bristle-tailed thing with holes for eyes and a slit for a mouth, that went out the basement door without touching the floor.

Two of her husband, one down here, one up there, the same and yet not the same, the second created from the first, moving into the back yard—

"Mama . . ."

But the voice wasn't a distant shout, it was a whisper right into her ear. The air whispering.

Marissa rose from watching Jill being pressed down into the sheets, Jill drowning in silk, and found herself drifting up the stairs, to the back door. She opened the back door—it was hard to turn the knob, it felt wrong in her fingers, but she got the door opened.

Marissa looked out the back door into the blazing afternoon. The sky was so blue. . .

The water in the pool so blue . . .

One somehow bled into the other, the sky part of the pool, the pool part of the sky, melted together by the sunlight . . .

She remembered Lenny Baer, the big love of her teenage years, though she'd only gone out with him four times. He'd recited poetry to her. He wrote for the high school paper, and sometimes he wrote poetry for extra credit in English. A skinny, bignosed kid with long brown hair, down to his waist almost, and soft grey eyes and an easy smile. He'd taught her things. He'd made her understand that poem by Robert Frost about choosing the two roads, and she'd gotten her first B in English, writing about it. First time over a C. Man, she'd loved him.

He'd written a poem about how he'd seen one of his dreams caught "in the translucent crystal of a raw piece of quartz" he found on the beach, and he'd had to explain to her what translucent meant, and she never forgot it.

But he'd stopped seeing her because his best friend had told him she was a skank. Judy, jealous of her going out with Lenny, had enjoyed telling her when she'd found out. "He heard you were a skank. Fucking all kinds of guys. His dad heard it too, I guess, said he was disappointed or something. Said 'I'm disappointed in you but go out with whom you choose, son.' His dad teaches polyscience. So he just . . . that's why he's not calling you and stuff."

Skank. Slut. Dreams caught in a piece of quartz. Translucent quartz...

Like the sky; like the pool. How beautiful: Brittany, her baby, was flying, arms outspread, face-down in translucent blue, part of the sky, part of the water, all one great piece of translucent crystal beauty. Crystal blue persuasion. The song still playing. How beautiful, her little girl so free, flying, swimming through the sky, it was a miracle . . . The Henny demon with the bristling tail and thumb-hole eyes—he was crawling around the edges of the translucent blue, yelling something, but he couldn't get into it, she was safe from him there . . . Brittany had gone flying there to get away from him . . .

She heard Jill shouting angrily at Doc, and there was suddenly a banging in her head, each thump an individual sharply defined ache, and with Jill yelling like that downstairs the aches were sharper, harder, and she needed to tell Jill please be quiet, so she went down the stairs, back into the basement...

"Shhh . . . Jill . . . my head . . ."

"You fuck he almost killed me . . ."

"You're all right, what'd you think, you like it that far, you told me anyway, you were groaning up a storm—"

"You shit I was yelling to stop—You just get me a fucking drink, Doc, shit . . . The stuff you gave us is makin' me sick—fucking angel dust—"

"Some other stuff too, dust and something else he told me, I forget what, and of course the . . . the . . . "

"You don't even fucking know? Ow, shit, my head hurts..."

"Jill be quiet . . ." Marissa heard her own voice saying it. "My head hurts too . . ."

"Marissa . . ." Henny was squatting on the floor, his head dipping a little, then jerking up, then dipping. "Where's . . . the kid?"

"Brittany? Oh: she's . . ." She sank onto the bed, wanting her head to stop thunking, banging.

"Drink some of this honey . . ."

Drinking, sucking smoke; they were arguing, the other three; she threw up. Other sounds from the ceiling . . .

The police sirens hurt her head, too, and Marissa went outside to tell them to be quiet, and the policemen put a blanket on her, they insisted on it, though it was rough material, because she was naked. Then she saw the little girl, same size as Brittany, same clothes and hair, the little girl on a gurney, as someone pulled a sheet over her face, an institutional-blue sheet, and they asked if Marissa knew what had happened to her daughter, did she see anything. They said that the little boy said he didn't push her into the pool but there were bruises on her fingers like he'd stepped on them when she'd tried to get out and they wondered if anyone had seen anything.

"Who? What girl?"

"Your little girl's named Brittany, right? That's what the boy says. Just sit down . . . sit down in the back of the car . . . the blanket's falling off . . ."

"Brittany? Oh: she's in translucent blue . . ."

THE WORD "RANDOM", DELIBERATELY REPEATED

He was tired of the library. The faint, echoing words of the librarian were shaped like the books they passed through.

Lingering in the scant poetry section, he thought: No one reads poetry at this whitebread university. Lots of dust on the book covers. They haven't been checked out in ages. Except for an occasional harried coed, maybe, looking for an ode to roses.

He leaned his large athlete's frame against the lonely shelves and remembered the canyons of eastern Oregon.

He closed his eyes.

He and Maria were drunk—they were drunk together. Being drunk together wasn't the same, somehow, as two people together who were both drunk. They lay balmed in the smell of sage and sequoia. They rolled off the blankets in search of new touchings and caked their bare sweaty skin with dust, dust still warm from the sun that was igniting the horizon.

He remembered the desert and Maria often because of one peculiarity in the incident: afterward, they had not regretted it, not even secretly, not at all.

They washed and sobered themselves in a canyon stream. But neither made a move to dress, though the air grew chill. With most, it was quickly over and followed by an embarrassed silence and a scuffle to get dressed. But not with Maria. They had sat together, close for warmth, watching the desert sunset burn the outline of the hill in the sky. He thought about school, about the team-letters ceremonies and the smiling principal and the smile managed by his star athlete. He tried not to think about the cheerleaders that he had pretended to like. No one had understood when he had refused to go out for football that last time. They had berated him for trying to start a poetry club—that was for women. Had Haggart become a faggot?

But he loved The Game and the feel of muscles that were so much part of his responses that they jumped as his thoughts did. He loved to feel the pain of pushing a little beyond the limit and the feeling of growth afterward. And as Maria pulled him again on top of her, he thought of the sexual elasticity of contact sports; the catharsis of Scoring.

The desert evening draped them, pressed them closer together. They moved against each other like clapping hands at a pep rally. He came, and as he reared and shuddered over her, his vision seemed to coalesce, then sharpen. The randomly placed boulders of the hillside were scattered seemingly without pattern, edged and shaped without purpose. He had never noticed any organization in the morose shapes of the desert or the crumbling wind-swept canyons. But now, they seemed to shift, falling into an astonishing coherence. Each boulder, each stone and gnarled bush became an elaboration of a central theme. They had relationship, and in that fragmented orgasmic second, they came together as though in an order codified to an alien intent. The image was burned into his mind as the desert sun burns stark its landscape.

He opened his eyes.

The image of the broken layers of rock and shale, of torn igneous lumps and gouged ravines was still strong. He looked at the directly purposeful arrangement of the books in the library, and suddenly felt the desert image transposed over them.

They were the same.

He looked at the objects lining the shelves and allowed himself briefly to forget that they were books. And he laid aside, for the moment, the knowledge that this was a library, ordered according to the Dewey Decimal System. He saw the books stripped of anthropomorphic associations. They were alien objects, new and unidentifiable, bound together on the shelf apparently at random. Some were tall, reaching almost to the next shelf; others were short and thin. He could see no pattern in their visual arrangement. They progressed with three high and thin ones, went to four low and thick ones, shifted to pamphlets. They were colored at random, with random tint and texture.

He laughed loudly. A scuffle of feet. Something on two spindly limbs swathed in green cones of cloth waved a gangly wrinkled upper limb at him and flapped its lips. It said something he chose not to hear. He looked away from the thing and back to the wild chaos of straight ravines filled with rectangles. He stopped playing the game.

They were ordered again. Dewey Decimal System. You can look up anything you want in the card catalog.

He ignored the librarian who was whispering angrily at him for ignoring her.

He caught a glimpse of himself in a window as he left the building: tall, broad chest and shoulders, short parted black hair, blue eyes that looked back from the reflection like a separate person would. His face was distinctly anglo and his chin always stubbled. He wore a blue shirt, jeans, and tennis shoes. Big deal, he thought. I wonder if something that'd never seen a human being before would see a purpose in the way I was put together?

THE CAMPUS WAS emptier than the desert. All the buildings were cast in the same ugly gray concrete mold, mottled by little holes where the metal supports for the forms had been. The long naked windows that stretched uninterrupted from top to bottom concentrated thin transparency on him as though he were an ant burning under a magnifying glass. There were a few stunted trees set in pots on the concrete like tiny patches of healthy skin remaining on a leper.

There was so little life in the passing, self-involved faces. There was no ambition in the cement. Haggart debated with himself as to whether he should go to class. Sociology. Where they tried to make the fluid movements of societies as concrete as their campus.

Forget it, he decided. He startled, hearing a feminine voice call after him. He turned, half expecting to see a smooth dark Chicano face, dark-eyed Maria. But it was Leslie. Blonde, hot pants, trite questions in philosophy.

"Where you going?" she asked.

"Home. Where you going?"

"I was going to find someone to skip class with. Need a ride somewhere?"

"Why not someone to skip a beat with? You could skip me, I've been reading Corso."

She laughed, though she probably didn't know who Corso was. "Come on, I'll give you a ride."

He followed. He looked at the doll-like symmetry of her profile. She's really pretty. Uses make-up well. Big tits. So how come I'm not attracted to her? All the beautiful women at this goddam university, I should be—

"Here it is," she said interrupting his thoughts. She unlocked a red Grand Torino and got in. Her parents bought the car, he thought. And they paid for her tuition and room. They'd like the looks of me; they wouldn't like me if I talked to them.

She drove easily from the parking lot and into the street, steering with one hand. Very casual. Very cool.

"How do you like the philosophy class?" she asked, trying to spark the conversation. He didn't have an answer. He didn't give a damn. Finally, out of habitual politeness, he answered.

"She proselytizes. Everybody swallows it. She pushes her Zen on everybody, tries to make Plato sound like a narrow-minded ass."

"You're right," she said. She *would* say that. "Zen is fun to play with, but it doesn't have any pragmatic value. I mean, the philosophy has to serve the people; otherwise you've just got an excuse for an autocrat to . . ."

He stopped listening. Pieces of a poem began to fall together in his mind as he watched the autumn-yellow trees flash by. Some of them had lost part of their leaves already and they bared limbs as if they wore short-sleeved shirts. He interrupted her and asked for a pencil. She gave him a puzzled sideways look, then indicated the glove compartment and fell silent. He found a scrap of paper to write on.

> At this speed, not really *auto*,
> trees revolve
> like children on a carousel;
> arms, branches, outstretched.

> Bleached-white teeth
> Break the edges of
> bloated clouds
> into film-negative faces.
> The faces would continue laughing
> even if we had an accident.

"What's that?" Leslie asked when he finished.

"Just some notes. Reminding myself of something."

She pulled up in front of his apartment house. "Well," she said with a mock sigh, "here we are." She looked at him, obviously expecting to be asked in "to smoke a little something."

He almost asked her, then realized he really didn't want to see her, that if he asked her in it would only be because one is always careful not to waste an opportunity that might be unavailable later. But he only said, "See ya." And climbed quickly out of the car and walked up the steps.

He stopped at the top step and remembered the desert in the library. He heard Leslie drive off.

He walked back down the steps, and along the road a block to a small park where he began to pick up odds and ends of litter that lay in grass. In a few minutes he had enough. He walked home, but just before he reached his apartment the irritatingly familiar voice of Benny Chummworth rumbled from behind.

Benny was a serious athlete. He had no other real interests. He had come from the same high school that Haggart had, and he lived a few doors down. He was one of the jocks who had given Haggart a hard time for "going with a Mex." Haggart had ignored him. No one got why he didn't challenge Benny to a fight. Just as no one got why he had to drop out of the team. Benny's being there made Haggart think of Maria again. And he wondered if he'd broken up with her for her sake, like he'd told her, or to make the jeering stop.

"Whatcha doing?" Benny asked, as though he were building up to a monumental witticism. "Picking up litter for the sanitation department?"

Haggart looked at him blandly.

"Come on," Benny persisted. "Whatcha gonna do with that shit? Cans and beer bottles and sticks and stuff—"

"Make a mobile," Haggart lied. "Or a sculpture of something." That was closer to the truth. He shook his arm loose from Benny's tightening grasp. The jock laughed.

"A copy of the Venus de Milo?"

Haggart turned his back on him and walked to his apartment, careful not to drop anything. It was a three-room flat: bedroom, kitchenette, bathroom. The walls were bare but the floor was a litter of books and papers. He went into the bedroom, dropped the things he had carried in, and sat heavily on the bed. He expelled great gust of air and lay back, covering his eyes with his arms.

Maria had been like the desert, straightforward and potent. She had little education, but always understood what he meant when he said it without dressing it up. Calm, she'd been calm and resilient like the desert. He tried to shake memories of her out of his head. He stood and stretched, felt young muscles complain with the need for exercise. With a last puzzled glance at the odd array of artifacts on the floor he grabbed his swimming suit and towel and walked swiftly out of the building and four blocks to the YMCA.

Forty-five minutes later, exhilarated by a brisk swim, he sat at the edge of the pool, staring at chlorinated ripples. The shouts of other swimmers came to him across the water, vibrating slightly, as loud as if they shouted in his ear—HEY IF YOU DIVE ON ME I'M GONNA—and—IF YOU SPLASH ME AGAIN BOY—

A random splash covered Haggart's face with water. A mask of water. Something tugged at the edge of his understanding. He got up, walked carefully over the slick wet tile to the diving board. He waited his turn, but when it came, he hesitated, still thinking of the library and splashing water. Randomly splashing water. Someone yelled in his ear:

"Hey, let's *go!*"

Startled, Haggart ran out on the board and jumped, coming down sloppily on the end and springing out and up in poor form. He might hit the water wrong and slap it with his face. The first part of the dive had been clumsy. But at the last moment he snapped his legs straight and arched his back, cutting the surface cleanly.

It came to him underwater, as he was yet a knife sheathed in frothing bubbles. He had started awkwardly, diving askew, righted himself—making purpose out of aimlessness.

He surfaced quickly and swam to the side.

A HALF-HOUR LATER Haggart came back to his apartment, almost running up the stairs. He unlocked the door and entered hurriedly, kicking books aside. What the hell, he thought, they're just random rectangles. He laughed at that. He thought of the term paper abandoned last night and of the overwhelming feeling of purposelessness that possessed him whenever he entered the college. I'm going to find out what it is, he thought. Where purpose comes from. I'll be wearing nothing but a mask of water.

He went to the things he'd left on the bedroom floor and took inventory. Four or five sticks, some string, pipecleaners, some cardboard, some sandpaper, a fingernail clipper, a tin can, a small block of wood, two beer bottles and a spoon. He went to the bathroom to get tissue, came back tearing it into small strips. He put the tissue in an open can after winding sandpaper around the can, and let the paper ribbons spill out like hair. He put the sticks in the beer bottles and used them to support two others to make a small gate of wood that arched over the other things protectively. He hung a string from the ceiling light, attached pipecleaners to that, and wound up a spoon in them. He hung a Styrofoam cup from the string and a length of steel wool that hung like Spanish moss from the cup. He was putting things together at random, but thinking all the time of the desert and the ragged, weather-carved cliffs that were somehow linked together. In a half-hour, he had an anomalous shape that at the same time carried an odd affinity with something unknown, something waiting in the wings. He was sweating with the deliberate effort to randomness. He had caught himself several times making a recognizable symmetry with seemingly unrelated shapes. Random. *Got to be random. No pattern.* He decided it was done as he put the bottle caps in as a finishing touch.

He sat back and *closed his eyes:* Tried to forget having ever seen the shape he'd made. He felt his mind blank, opened his eyes. Random impressions: A gate. A gate under a rocket (the cup) that had just run out of fuel and was spewing a trail of smoke (the tail of steel wool). A paper-fountain (the can with strips of tissue emerging) spilling over granite facing (the sandpaper). The fingernail clippers that stretched from the upper edge of the sponge to paper looked like a jackknifing diver in midleap. The beveled block with the paper and the bottle caps looked like a car. A car passing under an arch by a waterfall that flowed into a pool into which someone dived.

Maria died in a car accident in a place like that.

Run off the side of a cliff by a drunk under an arch of wind-shaped desert stone. The car had crashed into the water, and she had died from impact before she could drown. Maria masked in water.

He shut his eyes and cried out.

A feeling like an icy hand on his face made him look up again. His attention was drawn to the outlines made by random twisted shapes; they seemed to delineate the space between the objects in the random construct into the features of a face.

"Maria," he said.

"Thank you, Ronny," her calm voice said. "Thank you for the mirror." Her voice resonated with hollow reassurance. "I needed a mirror so badly in this place. Nothing here reflects. I couldn't see myself . . ."

Her voice faded into the lines of jagged sticks and cups and blocks. Random lines. A mirror.

THE SEA WAS WET AS WET COULD BE

MARY DID NOT expect to survive so long after the airplane began to break up. But she did survive as she was pitched through the crack in the bulkhead, as the fuselage split in the screaming air and people clung wailing to each other. She survived to fall; first spinning, but then—by some serendipity of her flailing—to fall spread eagled, like a skydiver with no parachute.

She was falling toward the sea. She could breathe. She was conscious. They hadn't been so very high, had been only a mile from the airport, reducing elevation in preparation for landing, but they were still over the sea. Then the bang, the crack, the screaming of air and children.

Somehow the bigness of what was happening overwhelmed fear; there was nothing left but to drink in these last few seconds alive— thinking: How alive I am, I've never been this alive, this awake! Is it always possible to be so awake? Now she saw the sea rushing up at her, waves taking on definition. And she thought she might survive if she went into a diving posture and aimed her fingers, with the hands together as if in prayer, down at the water; if she cleaved the water sharply enough, she thought, she might survive. She tried to angle herself that way. She put her hands together and aimed herself straight down and thought: I might—

That was her last thought before she struck, the word *might*.

Then she struck the water. There was a flash of sensation so powerful it could not be identified as pain. There was a white light. Then she was shooting down through the water, down and out, thinking without words that it had worked, she had somehow cleaved it so fine that she had survived, even though she'd always heard that from that high up water would feel as hard as concrete when you hit it.

It was true that her body was behind her, was spread out over the top of the waves, liquid to liquid, parts already nourishing ambitious seagulls, but she had kept going—like her clothes had been pulled off by the impact. Only it was her body that had been pulled off, wasn't it?

But no—she could feel her body now. She could feel it quite clearly. It was vast and shifting. It lapped on the shore nearby; it supported birds, on its surface, and a million million fish within it; she could feel each and every one as well as bigger things moving in her depths. She felt oil slicks on her body, and ships cleaving her back, and she knew that she had a new name, a name that was pronounced over and over again with waves and currents, a long name with an infinite number of syllables, and the speaking of it was never finished.

2: THROUGH A LASER-SCANNER DARKLY

BLIND EYE

———

with Edgar Allan Poe

Jan. 1—1796. THIS DAY—my first on the light-house—I make this entry in my Diary, as agreed on with De Grät. As regularly as I *can* keep the journal, I will—but there is no telling what may happen to a man all alone as I am—I may get sick, or worse . . . . So far well! The cutter had a narrow escape—but why dwell on that, since I am *here,* all safe? My spirits are beginning to revive already, at the mere thought of being—for once in my life at least—thoroughly *alone* . . . . What most surprises me, is the difficulty De Grät had in getting me the appointment—and I a noble of the realm! It could not be that the Consistory had any doubt of my ability to manage the light. *One* man had attended it before now—and got on quite as well as the three that are usually put in. The duty is a mere nothing; and the printed instructions are as plain as possible. It never would have done to let Orndoff accompany me. I never should have made any way with my book as long as he was within reach of me, with his intolerable gossip—not to mention that everlasting mëerschaum. Besides, I wish to be *alone* . . . . It is strange that I never observed, until this moment, how dreary a sound that word has—"alone"! I could half fancy there was some peculiarity in the echo of these cylindrical walls—but oh, no!—this is all nonsense. I do believe I am going to get nervous about my insulation. *That* will never do. I have not forgotten De Grät's prophecy. Now for a scramble to the lantern and a good look around to "see what I can see" . . . . To see what I can see indeed !—not very much. The swell is subsiding a little, I think—but the cutter will have a rough passage home, nevertheless. She will hardly get within sight of the Norland before noon to-morrow—and yet it can hardly be more than 190 or 200 miles.

• • •

Jan. 2. I HAVE PASSED this day in a species of ecstasy that I find impossible to describe. My passion for solitude could scarcely have been more thoroughly gratified. I do not say *satisfied*; for I believe I should never be satiated with such delight as I have experienced to-day . . . . The wind lulled about day-break, and by the afternoon the sea had gone down materially . . . . Nothing to be seen, with the telescope even, but ocean and sky, with an occasional gull.

Jan. 3. A DEAD CALM all day. Towards evening, the sea looked very much like glass. A few sea-weeds came in sight; but besides them absolutely *nothing* all day—not even the slightest speck of cloud . . . . Occupied myself in exploring the light-house . . . . It is a very lofty one—as I find to my cost when I have to ascend its interminable stairs—not quite 160 feet, I should say, from the low-water mark to the top of the lantern. From the bottom *inside* the shaft, however, the distance to the summit is 180 feet at least:—thus the floor is twenty feet below the surface of the sea, even at low-tide . . . . It seems to me that the hollow interior at the bottom should have been filled in with solid masonry. Undoubtedly the whole would have been thus rendered more safe:—but what am I thinking about? A structure such as this is safe enough under any circumstances. I should feel myself secure in it during the fiercest hurricane that ever raged—and yet I have heard seamen say occasionally, with a wind at South-West, the sea has been known to run higher here than any where with the single exception of the Western opening of the Straits of Magellan. No mere sea, though, could accomplish anything with this solid iron-riveted wall—which, at 50 feet from high-water mark, is four feet thick, if one inch . . . . The basis on which the structure rests seems to me to be chalk . . . .

Jan 4. TODAY I WAS drawn to the lamp at the zenith of the light-house, with a sense of summoning so clearly defined that I half expected to find someone waiting for me beside the lamp. The lamp itself—a dozen brass lanterns, in fact, symmetrically arrayed in an iron framework before the mirror—were all that awaited me. But I lie! There was my own distorted reflection awaiting me, in that reflective silver concavity behind the lamps. A seagull, too, hung almost motionless, itself a lantern in the sky beyond the glass, balancing in the stream of air, poised and waiting for me to throw scraps, as perhaps the last keeper had done . . . On the night before my embarking to the island I sat late at the Watcher Inn with Orndoff, an acquaintance in the village closest to the light-house; he and I had gone to the same university.

Very different, were Orndoff and I. At university he had drifted through the instruction with a kind of amused indifference, scarcely attending. But my mania for history had kept eye and ear so fixed upon the professors that I seemed to make them nervous. This is hard to parcel out from the remainder of my intercourse with humanity, however: perhaps because I was an orphaned child, raised without siblings by an uncle who seemed aggrieved by the responsibility, I have never felt that other people warmed to me; have always felt a vague, undefined hostility from them. Oh there was Elena, of course—would I be here skulking alone upon a rock in the midst of the sea if not for Elena? She alone looked past my dark countenance; saw more than my scowl. And that one died when her ship caught fire. She died in the midst of the sea; I have chosen to live there. Where is this lighthouse but the midst of the sea?

As for Orndoff—who will palaver at anyone with the patience to listen—he told me his gossip of the former keeper. I knew nothing of the erstwhile light-house watchman, having come to this comparatively prosperous, snug little village near the light-house only a fortnight earlier, at De Grät's suggestion. Hendershaw, an expatriate from England, had been a queer antiquarian, liked by people who knew him a little, feared by those who knew him well. "Oh!" said Orndoff importantly, puffing his pipe and sloshing his ale, "many leatherbound folios, and even a scroll or two, came to him on this very island by cutter, in protective chests from such places as Paris and Moscow and Rome and Mount Athos; one, indeed, hailed all the way from Bombay, and was said to be writ in Sanskrit; and how came he to read that?—One day," so Orndoff went on, "Hendershaw was heard to shout at people in the village, as if from high above, and to implore them to 'Stop it, stop it!' . . . Or, he would shine the light! said he."

"So," said I to Orndoff, "Hendershaw was back in the village, shirking his duty and drinking and making fools of you, when he should have been at the light-house?"

"Why no," said Orndoff. "He was at the light-house when he spoke! He must have been, for he had no boat out there of his own, and when someone went to the island the next day, they found him dead, at the foot of the light-house—he had fallen through a window close beside the lamp; stumbled, we supposed. Fallen all that long way down!"

"You know as well as I, Orndoff, that if he was heard in the village then someone was mocking his voice. This, or else he had come here. This village may be the closest to the light-house,"—for the cutter returns to distant Norland only because there is no good harbor hereabouts—"but the lighthouse is miles distant, out in the sea, and he could not have been heard. Unless perhaps some meteorological peculiarity reigned that night—that is not beyond the limits of possibility."

"Not only was he heard," Orndoff insisted, indignantly tapping the dottle from his pipe, "he was heard clear as like to yonder church bell! Clearer, for a bell is usually heard from a steeple, and to everyone who heard him it was as if he were standing right beside them!"

. . . I remember the conversation now with a dim smile. There is not a remote parish in this land—or any other!—which has not its share of ghosts, quite often said to be the shades of witches who'd cursed the place on their burning. What hamlet is without one, or two—or three? Just as every village has a wit like Orndoff who practices on the credulous. I am not to be taken in . . . But today, standing at the curved mirror, blinking in the reflected light from the sea, the near cloudless sky, and listening to the sough of the wind against the stone tower, I thought I saw a second likeness in the reflector mingled with my own . . . . De Grät was right! Isolation acts on the imagination . . . and I am glad of it! This journal is just a sort of morning walk for the mind, to get the blood moving in the limbs of imagination. My book calls to me . . . Perhaps I'll change the subject matter and write of the rustics in the village. But I've never thought for a moment of writing anything else but my account of mad royalty! What turns of mind one takes in abject solitude—and I will now take a turn on the rocky beach.

Jan. 9. Has it really been four days since I wrote the last entry in this journal? I have come to spend most of my days sleeping, since my duties are to be carried out at night. The inspection of the lamps is a lighthouse keeper's sacred duty: the renewing of their oil, the rekindling of their flames should the wind push its nose through some errant crack—and the wind here does show a certain mischievousness. It's true that every couple of days I polish the mirror during the day, but it is at night that I must check and re-check the light, to see that all of the lamps are lit. No diminution of the illumination is to be permitted. My own glow has diminished, somewhat—the shift to activity in all the hours of darkness has perplexed me somehow, and my body resents the change. The days have blurred together, so. And thus it is that I work late afternoon, wearing toward dusk, laboring feverishly on my book—squinting in the candle light, for the sun is on the other side of the tower, affording little light for this chilly cabin attached to the light-house. I scratch away with the wind's buffeting threatening to overturn the stone tower onto my little lodging—but I am indifferent to nature's vain threats. I write, uncaring: I write what seems to have welled up from my dreams. I find myself writing not on the madness of kings in history, as I had planned, but instead on the madness that accompanies quotidian life in an ordinary village—the very village I quitted to come here! The lines pour out of me with a species of self-determination—as determined as the Republicists in the American colonies. I find myself describing the lanky red-nosed village Mayor, who plays the sad widower by day, but at night, I watch, in my mind's eye, as he drinks his laudanum and then beds the wife of the snoring tax collector. I discover I have written four and a half pages on the stout, ham-fisted Constable, a record of his robbery of the men in his jail; I find that I have scrivened two pages with glee on the sodomy of a choirboy by the grave and sallow Minister; I am astonished to see that I have written seven close pages on the Schoolmaster's beating of his wife, and have related how that same Schoolmaster then repairs to the back room of the chandler's shop, where he offers himself to be beaten by the drunken candlemaker himself . . . Sometimes I seem to see them in the glimmering reflections of the concave mirror behind the lanterns, after they are all lit. I seem to see the village, the little houses opened up and laid bare . . . Then the image fades but in some wise it has crept into my mind, like a lean wolf creeping into a den, only to emerge in my dreams. It was thus when I saw the stableman locking himself in his attic to pray for the courage to not—oh yes! the courage to not murder his hateful snaggletoothed wife . . . I laughed aloud, at times as I scribbled these fantasies—and later felt ashamed of my facetiousness. How could I wheeze away like that over such tragic doings? How could I indeed, ever have written anything so perverse!

But this has to end! I must assume that this indulgence arises from fancies provoked by the last society I had enjoyed, if enjoyed is the word to describe my interview with De Grät—as if in recoiling from my solitude (which has gone from delight to burden) I people my world instead with figures from a kind of fever dream.

I can see De Grät's supercilious smile even now. I can hear his oily voice. "I told you so! A gentleman whose head thus teems is not suited for such isolation! Did I not warn you? But you would insist on taking the post!" Perhaps he was right—But how am I to extricate myself without a loss of face that would preclude anyone offering me another post? I must remain . . . I must remain alone. Just me and the god of the sea whose great grey body surges in the swells without ceasing, shifting and murmuring, endlessly grumbling to himself . . .

Jan. 14? (Is this date correct?) WHAT DAY OF the week is this? Is it Sunday? I had intended to pray on Sunday; to read from the Old Testament aloud; to give myself a bit of a church service. There will be no one here for another week and I needed some rhythm in my life. So I told myself yesterday.

To think of praying now! After what I've seen! Somehow it seems a mock of the idea of prayer . . . No—let me be honest—I have not ceased praying, since the Eye of the Light-house showed itself to me. A silent prayer without words—a prayer incessantly calling out help me . . . *help me . . . help me . . .* while in fact I'm saying nothing at all.

Shall I tell you? Someone must read this, surely. *You!*

. . . .Can you hear me, climbing the stairs, breathing like a horse at the end of a race? No—*see* me! See me as I carried a lantern up the spiral staircase, just at sunset. Here and there a bent square of dying sunlight bled scarlet through the occasional window, only to be blotted by my circle of light as I ascended. (You do see? That's exactly what must be done—you must see! To see as I have!)

As always there was the sharp feeling of vulnerability when I reached the top—for here the wind invariably batters at the windows, threatening that this night, *this* time, it will at last shake the glass from its frames . . . I was well aware that one of these panes of glass was new, having been replaced after Hendershaw fell through it to his death. I knew which pane it was too—a cheaper glass than the others, blurred by poor glazing so it distorted the moon, making it into a bent countenance, a leering yellow face, like a figure of wax in the heat.

I set about lighting the lanterns before the reflector, and this time tried to keep myself from looking into the curved mirror—to prevent its practicing upon my imagination—

My task done, I stood . . . and heard a rattling from the back of the mirror.

I had only once looked behind the mirror—there was only dust there, cobwebs, the curved inner wall of the light-house. But beyond that formidable stone wall was the windy air above the rocky verge of the island, and beyond that verge the sea—and beyond that curving stretch of sea, the shore, a little distance beyond which stood the village. That dusty dim place—barely room for a man to pass—had seemed repugnant to me, and I had never questioned my intuition . . . The stability of the mirror was my job, my duty, and if it seemed to rattle, why, I must needs reinforce it. So with the tool box in one hand and the lantern in the other I sidled behind the mirror . . . I saw nothing amiss. The bolts holding the curved reflector to its frame seemed quite sound. Then the mirror trembled once more—it shook off some of its dust from exactly marked places, from a shape scratched on the dull, convex metal of its back. I lifted the lantern to more closely look. A diagram was scratched into the surface there . . . I shall not try to reproduce it here . . . I hope no one ever reproduces it again! . . . An intricate diagram of geometrical forms, but a geometry I did not recognize, none of them quite Euclidean, though some might have alchemical significance—I might have glimpsed something of the sort in the margins of some half-remembered illuminated manuscript perused while studying Greek. There were letters too, unintelligibly cryptic words in a script I had never seen . . . I had a terrible desire to wipe it away—indeed, to break the mirror itself, on seeing these marks. I felt distinctly as if someone was urging me to do just that . . . But I could not. I would be not only discharged from my sinecure, but arrested, perhaps sent to a madhouse.

I returned to the front of the mirror, with that diagram still fixed in my mind. I gazed into the mirror behind the lanterns, then, forgetting my earlier resolve, and the diagram seemed to float before my eyes, like the image haunting the vision when one has stared into the sun, and some incomprehensible completion took place then: I felt it like a key turning in a lock.

So it was that the mirror became a great eye. For me, staring into it, at just that instant, the light-house mirror did not reflect; it showed nothing of me, as it usually did, it gathered light but seemed to push it all to the sides so that I could see the window it had become . . .

Was it indeed like a window? Nay, a telescope lens, looking out the back of the light-house, right through the stone wall, through the intervening sky, across the arm of sea, across the strand and into the village . . . I could see into the village, exactly as if I was staring into the eyepiece of a giant telescope, though nothing so powerful and precise in its magnification exists. I talk as if I'm trying to find some rational description of what I experienced—but I was looking not only through the solid mirror, but *through a stone wall!*—and oh! I could see every house in the village clearly and distinctly. If I looked at any one house, in particular, the house would swell to fill the mirror . . . My eyes burned, of course, with the light of the lanterns prodigiously reflected. At the same time, I couldn't quite see that light. The pain I felt from gazing at it seemed distant, like the pricking of a benumbed limb. My eyes ran with tears, but I could not look away . . . But come here, reader, gaze over my shoulder as I write this, see it with me: when I looked at any one house, it opened itself up to me, as if a cabinet was flung open from within—First, the Mayor's house, twice as big as the others. Two storeys, with balconies and its own courtyard and stables, it drew my eye—and as I looked at it, seeing every cornice, every crack, every shingle and gutter with an etched clarity, suddenly all this minute marking fell away, as if a page was turned in a picture book, and the interior of the house was revealed. It looked exactly like a doll's house, seen from the open back, everything miniature, each furnishing exquisitely reproduced . . . but here the dolls moved about on their own, requiring no childish hands to put them through their paces. I watched as the Mayor sent his housekeeper away, turned the portrait of his departed wife to the wall, unlocked a leaded glass cabinet and drew out a bottle of laudanum. I recognized that manner of bottle, having had too much recourse to it myself—one of the reasons I came to this light-house—and saw him decant a thousand drops or so, drink them down, and then go to the back door, where the fat and tittering tax collector's wife awaited . . . what they did then, not in the bedroom but in the kitchen, I did not propose to observe—past satisfying myself what they were about—and looked away, thinking that I had observed all this before in a dream, and written about it too, only in that instance they had trysted in the parlor...When I looked back at the mirror, the Mayor's house shrank and another filled the lens, and here the Dressmaker's Widow was whipping her small daughter with a horse-crop—I could bear to look only a moment. Still, a kind of heated hunger had me, a voyeur's passion stoked by a sense of godlike power, as I looked at another house, and another: Behold the Fisherman at prayers—the only good and honest man in the village. Yet his son was creeping out a window to meet another young rogue, the two of them donning masks, carrying cudgels to the back door of the inn, where they skulked, awaiting the first moneyed drunk to step out into the night . . . Here was the Minister's house, and here he caressed a new boy, who shrank from him. But leering, the minister forced the boy into a corner . . . . Here was the Usurer, keeping accounts late with a candle—and I saw no sin in him. But who was this creeping up behind him? The son of the pious fisherman, the corrupted youth too impatient to wait at the inn.

I watched as he struck the Usurer over the head from behind and scooped up his gold. The Fisherman's son quarreled with his partner about the gold . . . and then he struck him dead!

I could watch no more . . . and the pain in my eyes no longer seemed distant. I turned away . . . And beheld only darkness! My eyes had gone blind, for a time, staring into the lanterns, the reflected light of the mirror. I had been staring, I told myself, into the glare of my own imagination.

But I know it was not imagination. Had I not met most of these people in the village? Had I not sensed this very venality, this viciousness, this familiar brutishness, behind their formal bows, their countrified manners? I'm in the habit of ignoring such disquieting perceptions—as I believe we all are—and blanketed them away immediately they were shewn. But now my recollection of that disquiet returned and insisted on remembering itself to me Even as their dissimulating faces returned to me, so also sight seeped back into my burning eyes. I beheld the moon rising over the sea, daubing the streak of restless waves beneath it with silver light even as the rest of the sea dimmed. I fled down the stairs, my eyes throbbing . . . burning! My conscience burned far worse.

Jan 17. I AM ALMOST sure it is January 17. I managed to see the calendar, though the numbers of the days rippled in the swimming shadows. I am near completely blind now, and though it is daylight I write these lines with three candles set about the page, to ease the permanent night that has settled over my vision. Only in bright sunlight can I see well enough to walk freely about, and I do not think I will have another day of bright sunlight.

For they are coming for me. I hear them coming. I have ignored their shouted demands. Now they are at the door—let them thunder upon it! I have bolted and barred the door. It will take them time to break it down, since the fools have come ill prepared. Someone, I gather, has been sent back to the cutter for tools. I hear the imprecations of those left waiting.

I should not have looked through the Eye again. How long was it? Three, perhaps, four days? Is this how long I managed, without looking again into the Eye of the Light-house? Every intervening dusk, when

I lit the beacon, I was careful to look only at the lanterns themselves, never at the mirror. But still I caught movement in the concave surface, and it was not my own movement. Yet I did not turn to look. I heard voices from the village coming from the mirror—yes I could hear them as well as see! . . . I forced myself not to listen . . .

Three, perhaps four days I did not look in the Eye. I drank the whiskey I had brought with me, jeering at my earlier resolve to limit myself to a single glass on retiring. I tried to work on my book. But the giddiness would seize me, and I would find myself writing of the Schoolmaster's wife locking herself in a root cellar while he raged drunkenly outside, reciting Ovid between pulls on his jug . . . So I put the writing aside and attempted to read. But the words shifted on the page, and an account of Henry the Eighth transmuted itself in mid-sentence. *Thus Henry took for himself a wife without choosing at all, his counselors having selected this wide eyed Hollander lady . . .* This becoming, *Thus the Mayor took for himself the milkmaid over the tax collector's wife . . .* I clapped the book shut at that!

I told myself that soon the cutter would come with supplies. I resolved to refuse the supplies and demand of the coxswain a return to the mainland . . .

Once this resolution was made, it was suggested to me—perhaps something within me suggested it, perhaps not—that one last look would not run amiss, since after all I was leaving . . . so it was that I succumbed to temptation. When I'd finished lighting the—

—O how they howl out there! How much time remains to me? My eyesight fails—!

—so it was, I say, that I finished lighting the lamps, and turned to look into the mirror, envisioning that obscure diagram, and immediately the reflector became like the widening iris of an eye, a dilating that revealed again the village, every house in every detail. My eyes burned with the fogged pain, and still I gazed into the eye of the light-house, looking with utter and entire impossibility through the mirror itself and the stone wall behind it, through the intervening spaces, seeing—I cannot think how to convince you of this, but it is true!—seeing what was happening at exactly that moment in the village . . . .

I saw Orndoff's house, then, for the first time—opening itself to me like a magician's cabinet. He was at the back door, with a wooden crate, paying the groom of the Inn and from their whispered discourse I understood that the groom had stolen goods, rum and beer and vodka from the Inn, which Orndoff proposed to sell at a profit in the hamlet that lay further south along the coast.

"Thief!" I shouted, in a kind of giggling hysteria. "Cease your theft, Orndoff! And tell the Minister to cease his predation!"

And Orndoff heard me! I saw him whirl, looking for the source of the sound.

"Who?" he sputtered.

The horse-groom ran away—and I turned to look at another house. Here the Fisherman argued with his son, demanding to know where he came upon the gold that had fallen from his coat. Was it he who had robbed the usurer? The son refused to answer and made for the door—his father tried to stop him. The boy turned and struck at him with a length of wood from the pile by the fireplace. His father fell, stunned—

"Do not kill that old man, you fool, you'll regret it the whole of your life!" I shouted.

The boy turned this way and that to see who was speaking and I laughed . . . though my eyes streamed with the blazing light of the mirror, I laughed . . .

I looked at another house, and more—saw the Mayor at his peccadilloes, the Minister at his fondling, the Mistress of the Inn plotting to run away with a coachman—

Thereupon I was struck with a terrible revulsion. I could no longer bear to see these people scuttling and capering about in the shadows. I felt like a man who has awakened in a noisome inn and hears what may be the feet of rats on the floor beside him. Wishing to know if he's to be invaded by vermin, he strikes a lantern alight, vowing that he will catch them in the light, and call the innkeeper and demand an explanation.

That's what I felt must be done . . . I must bring the vermin out of the shadows and demand an explanation!

And so I seized a handle to one side of the beacon, used before-times only for the light's repair. This I heaved on, against the rust, till at last the creaking mirror turned and shone against the back wall. The enchantment of the mirror did not fail me; it behaved as the whispering in my mind had suggested it would: it shone its light right through the wall, making a window where none had been—the light streamed in a concerted shaft through intervening miles, in a magnification no oculist could explain, and struck full upon the house of the Fisherman . . . And the house was laid bare! The opacity of its walls vanished, it became as of a house of glass, each room all lit up with the beam of the beacon—so that not only I, but *everyone in the village* could see the Fisherman's son standing over the fallen form of his parent. The Fisherman's son turned and shouted—seeing that his own walls had become as glass, and everyone was staring at him . . . Then I shifted the beacon again, so that it fell upon the Mayor's house. And this too became a house of glass, and he was caught *en flagrante* with the daughter of the tanner. I shifted the light again so that it shone upon the Inn, where the Mistress of the Inn—her husband busy with the horses—was creeping out the back with the Coachman, her bag in hand. The Innkeeper turned and saw, through the new transparency of the walls, his wife's departure— her horrified face to see him gawping at her! And how I laughed!

I shifted the light again and again, revealing each house's secrets— so that they could be seen by everyone else in the village. "Now you see," I shouted, "how the all-seeing eye of the light-house has revealed you all for the crawling vermin you are!"

Then the darkness closed over my eyes—darkness like shutters slammed by pain. The agony in my eyes was unspeakable as I turned the light back to the sea . . . but I could not see the sea, or the moon, or the steps I stumbled down. I nearly fell, having to feel my way along. The lantern in my hand seemed dim as a candle a hundred strides away in a heavy fog . . . Ravaged by emotions that passed so quickly I could scarce distinguish them—revulsion, shame, anger, a desire to return to the great Eye, terror—I felt my way down and down, spiraling down in darkness, till at last I felt the cold air of the night on my face . . . I returned to my cabin to drink the last of my whisky. I slept—and the voices of my tormentors woke me. I heard them coming, shouting for me, howling like animals in their rage. I barred the door . . . And now . . . .

Now I hear them worrying that door with some great tool. It sounds as if they might be angling away with a bar of iron. I hear it from time to time, squeaking at the door, like the teeth of rats on wood. They pause in their gnawing to accuse me of sorcery, of trying to destroy them all with lies—with magic, a magic lantern of some kind, creating a puppet theater with the innocent, Godfearing villagers as the Punch and Judys. Lies, they say—you tell lies about us! They say they'll burn me out if they have to and more than one agrees that burning is peculiarly appropriate for me . . . The dregs of my sight evaporate as I write these lines, and I must secrete this away in some niche of the wall where it will be preserved. I know just the place . . . They're breaking in! I must hurry! I will not live out this night. Oh God preserve me from the workings of their black, black hearts . . .

AM PERPLEXED AS to what to do with this hasty and typically deranged piece by Poe, found in his papers—there is a shorter version, an unfinished fragment, that some have seen. They have not seen this longer one and my impulse is to suppress it for its references to depravity, a disgrace to include in the works of a man of letters. Poe was all too aware of such depravity, just as he knew the bottle and pipe, but never had he written of licentiousness so boldly, and he must have reckoned his own mistake and decided not to publish the piece—it was writ about a year before his death—but there is also the note in the margins to wit: "True story, if the Danish coxswain is to be believed—though some say the light-house keeper was killed because in his drunkenness he turned the beacon and allowed a ship to founder . . . but the coxswain had seen the manuscript and was insistent—material here would have to be cut and disguised . . . EAP" Not sure what I shall do with this. Hide it as I have hidden so much, perhaps—best to turn a blind eye.
—Rufus Wilmot Griswold 1851

SLEEPWALKERS

. . . the environment that Man creates becomes his medium
for defining his role in it.— Marshall McLuhan

"ANYTHING FOR A BUCK," Ace said.

"A man's gotta live, a man's gotta eat, a man's gotta have shoes to walk down the street," Bernie said.

"Another day, another dollar,'" Jules chimed in.

"Five'll get you ten and ten'll get you a fuckin' twenty," Ace added. "And all that shit."

"Fucking beggars can't be fuckin' choosers," Bernie said. "And all that shit too."

"When the motherfuckin' wolf's at the door you gotta pay the goddamn piper, or some fucking thing like that," Ace muttered, getting bored with it. They'd begun the recitation game when Jules had told them he was going to rent himself to the Sleepwalker Agency.

They were silent then, and listened to Mick Jagger on the oldie station explain that although it was only rocknroll, he liked it. The song ended, another began, a lovesong styled like a dirge, and that started Jules thinking about Zimm and the money he needed before he could see her again. "Neither a dumbshit borrower nor a fucking lender be," be murmured. *Well, I've got the lender part sewed up, he thought. I wish I didn't owe her anything. Money. Or anything.*

That's when Barb came in, and since she had her swagger on they knew she had the shit; the fake-platinum grill on her teeth shining like a needle in the afternoon light slanting through the only unbroken window. It was impure meth, kinda yellowy, so it had to be cooked. Seeing her cook up the meth, Bernie danced around her in a circle, clapping his hands and growling. Bernie had downslanted brown eyes and curly black hair bowed from the weight of six washless weeks. He'd been nineteen and Jewish before he'd started shooting crystal. That's the way Jules thought of it. That Bernie was no longer Jewish, he was no longer young; he was a speedfreak. Made you a whole new species of person.

Jules watched with a slight smile, tapping his fingers to the music against the plywood nailed over the side window. On a bygone giddy summer night Ace had a kind of meltdown and had broken out all the windows but one and now the small stucco house glared like a one-eyed man at the rest of East Hollywood. Jules felt left out, times like this, because he'd given up on drugs. A little peyote here and there, maybe some 'shrooms now and again; next to being straight, almost, with these guys. He was tempted every damned time it came around, too. He'd had a Narcotics Anonymous sponsor—before the guy blew him off for taking 'shrooms—who'd said the desire to use would go away. But it never did completely. It just backed up a little and yelled at you from across the street, instead of yelling in your ear.

Ace was half Chicano, or had been before he made the agreement with methedrine. The pockmarks in his gaunt cheeks seemed to glow like tiny fumaroles as he watched Barb, his old lady, preparing the syringe with clinical detachment. His eyes were black: sharp, pointed black.

Ace went to his room and returned with a can of lighter fluid. Skipping in a circle around Bernie, Ace sprayed the lighter fluid on the floor. Bernie danced. "Hey, HEY!" Bernie growled as the guitar player on the stereo went into an incendiary solo. It was the band Witch with that guy from Dinosaur Jr. Ace tossed a match at the ring of lighter fluid and gossamer flames darted up, encircling Bernie like footlights, tickling at his ankles. Laughing, he danced them dead. They died quickly and with little smoke, like starved infants dying easy.

"Wuh-ooo!" Jules shouted obligatorily, clapping his hands. Not feeling it much.

Barb, her black skin shining with sweat, leaned over the candle so the light glinting off the spoon was reflected in her inky eyes.

Jules hadn't been molded into a functional component of the Overmind Amplifier, as Bernie called it, the Speed Machine, as Barb called it, because he had not made the agreement. He combed slender fingers through his long, straight brown hair and pouted. He swiped at his eyes, making a black smudge on his hand. His makeup was smeared. He could give a shit. Yeah, he definitely felt left out, when his roommates fixed. He loved a woman who was only desultorily interested in him; he played bass but had no band; he'd played with drugs . . . but he had not come to terms with them; and he could no longer bear to peddle his ass—he was a cog without its clockworks.

He drooped back against the wall, slumped to the floor, stretched out his legs and reflected that the machine-and-petroleum scent from the combusted lighter fluid would be appropriate perfume for Zimm. He ran his thumb along the shiny inner thigh of his skintight dungarees, staring at the worn, pointed toe of his black boots.

The record ended. Jules watched as Bernie and Barb fixed, rubber bands tight around their biceps, their foreheads beaded with sweat. They drove the spikes home at precisely the same instant.

Ace was still filling his spike, chewing his lower lips, head tilted downward, eyes fixed on the almost transparent liquid. He was loading up more this time, and the last time he'd used more than the time before. Jules looked harder at the lineaments of Ace's skull pressing out through his sallow skin, and knew; knew that Ace was sure to overdose. Dust himself. It was like the speed was inside him pushing, pushing, pushing his skull out through the skin. Jules sagged inwardly—nothing he could do.

The hell with it—it's what he wants.

Jules turned off the radio, put on a CD, smirked, knowing what Bernie's reaction would be to this particular song, and put it on: The Velvet Underground, "White Light, White Heat."

"Take that motherfucker OFF!" Bernie snarled, shivering from the first influx of rush. His pupils shrank like coffee going down a drain; they expanded all of a sudden like the coffee had hit an obstruction and was welling back up: his eyes dilating.

Barb laughed as Bernie shrieked, "Take it off before I step on the fucking stereo!"

Snickering, feigning surprise, Jules put something on that Bernie could accept because it was absurd: A scratchy copy of Judy Garland singing "Somewhere Over the Rainbow." "'At's better," Bernie said, sinking into an already sunken velour easychair. He was shaking like a wet dog, breathing quickly, tongue snapping between his teeth. In the storm-eye of the rush, Bernie's face, muscles tight, was flushed so white it was like the chrome grill of an onrushing Cadillac. Jules liked seeing Bernie this way just as he had once enjoyed watching his father at work—both of them doing something that defined their lives. Bernie had made a career of being a speedfreak. "You put on that speedfreak song on purpose, Jules, you sucker. You know I can't stand music if it's appropriate. I hate things that are appropriate and obvious, like people coming out of the Betty Boop film festival all giggling and goin' *Oohboopeedoo* and you KNOW you KNOW you know I hate that shit Jules-you-ugly-mother. Oh you KNOW it grinds on me like a giant pitbull in heat, a big giant pitbull with a big, giant—"

And Bernie was well launched into his speedfreak rap which everyone knew better than to listen to and which he had to get out of his system for the next two-and-a-half hours.

"That Judy Garland song's appropriate," Jules ventured. "She was a speedfreak too."

"'At right," Ace said, teeth chattering, head bouncing like a violently dribbled basketball; he'd intended a slight nod.

Barb and Ace went into the next room to get passionate. The speed had done its work—Ace had been unable to get it up for months, but he did her with his fingers and that was fine because she only liked sex as an excuse to be held and rocked.

Naturally, this turned Jules's thoughts to Zimm. How he had to get some money to her. So she'd look at him with respect.

Some liberated woman, he thought. She pretends she's above it all, but she lives for money. Maybe he would go to the club and watch her shake 'em, and laugh at her, loudly, see how liberated she felt with someone besides a TV-snowed middle-ager watching for the sake of The Big Machine.

I'm onto her, Jules thought. She plays feminist but she gets off dancing nude for those whip-offs, it's a sick throwback to her fixation on her father .... *Maybe I can get in good with her by kidnapping her old man and bringing him to her on a chain and making him crawl for her. Maybe that would be enough.*

Nope. No way that would be enough.

Even then, she'd want the money "for the role-playing."

But he had to see Zimm tomorrow. He needed her. That much was established. He couldn't wait any longer. He had to get five hundred dollars to pay back the money he owed her. Five hundred dollars and maybe enough extra cake for a down payment on a car so she'd stop calling him a deadbeat. And he could get that kind of money quick only one of two ways. He could steal. Or he could go to the Sleepwalkers Agency.

"It's nothin' you ain't done before," said Bernie suddenly, as if he'd read Jules's mind. Which maybe he had. Speed gave him access to normally inaccessible channels. "You ought to know the scene. I'd figure it for a step up. I mean, you don't remember it, afterwards. Except for twelve lost hours it's like free money. For sleeping. If they wanna fuck you, they gotta use condoms. I don't know anybody who was ever hurt by it," he said like a car salesman, tapping his fingers, licking his lips, tapping his feet and shrugging—all simultaneously. Bernie wanted Jules to take the job because he knew Jules would donate some of his earnings to the house kitty. "Nobody gets hurt, much. A few bruises. A few people went nuts. But there's a hazard to every profession. Just as bad being a cop as it is being a bum, sometimes, an' it's just as lonesome being a burglar as a priest or a mom as a dad or an embryo as a dyin' old man it all has its compensations and its reversals and the dues to pay you gotta pay your dues if you wanna sing the blues and *everything* but everything has a slot for you to put in your quarter—"

Jules screened out Bernie's rap. But he thought: *You gotta pay your dues if—*

So he got up and went to pay his dues.

He left Bernie talking to the walls of the dingy stucco house with the boards over the windows and the house was soon wrapped up in the city as he walked on, consumed and gift-wrapped behind him in the Hollywood downer district. Houses of plaster, houses of pine, one storey, one story at a time, he thought. Palm trees nodded in agreement in the faint breeze, a violet twilight settled over the dirty skyline and the bite of lemons graced the reek of car exhaust.

He felt the wind ruffling his hair, felt it very distantly, as a junkie feels a kiss.

He thought about Zimm standing for hours outside the theatre, in the cold, from four AM to ten PM just to get a thirty-second audition for a ten minute bit in a minor play. She hadn't got the part but she had paid her dues.

He pictured her there, standing in the gunmetal early morning light, full lips pursed, snapping blue eyes limned with shards of bitterness, high cheekbones standing out with the determination of her set jaw, her platinum hair tossed by the chill wind . . . and he wished he could go to her and put his arms around her then and say: you don't have to be so hard and relentless, there's a soft place where we can go where you can be a performer and I can play my bass and we'll be audience enough for one another.

But she'd only laugh bitterly, if he had said that, and call him a jerk.

Long ago she'd settled on the hardcore role and it was too late to change her like it was too late for Ace. "Oooooh, isn't it nice, when you find your heart is made out of ice . . . " Another Lou Reed number Jules sang to himself as the bus rumbled up.

He glanced at the plate on the brow of the bus, verified the destination —yeah, Hollywood and Vine—and climbed aboard.

He tossed seven quarters into the slot, as a snob contributes to a beggar. He ignored the wooden faces of the passengers the way a squirrel never looks right at the trees of its own forest, and found a seat.

IN THE VESTIBULE to the Sleepwalkers Agency he reread the pamphlet, wished he had the nerve to ask for another look at the contract he'd signed and hardly read. He noted that the sweat on his fingers was making the pamphlet's print smear and that reminded him of his makeup. He went to the restroom, imitation-black-marble stalls, imitation-wood wallpaneling, imitation-mother-of-pearl toilet seat—where he shakily voided himself. Then he washed the makeup off his eyes.

He came into the lounge, sat down, and the tall white girl with the blue Afro-wig and the smile that was like a smile an embalmer might put on a corpse, softly called his name. He was the only one in the waiting room.

He followed her, taking deep breaths to calm himself. Passing through a very clean, very white door, they came into a room with battleship-gray walls, empty except for a padded diagnostic table.

The girl turned to him and repeated words she'd repeated many times before, not hearing herself say them: "Remove your clothes, take a shower in that room there, wash *thoroughly,* then come back in here and lay down on your back, relax, close your eyes, take deep breaths and dream about how you will spend your money. You won't feel a thing." Jules was certain she could repeat the same speech verbatim while watching her favorite reality show and playing solitaire. She left him alone.

Fingers shaking, glancing nervously around the spare, gray room, he removed his clothes, folded them neatly, left them in a pile at the foot of the table in a yellow plastic box stenciled: YOUR CLOTHES.

He took a shower, used the liquid soap dispenser liberally, dried off with a towel that was way too small, then came back into the room with the couch. There was a thin sheet of clean white paper on the couch. He stretched, and lay down, listening to the paper rustle beneath his weight. He could hear the sleep-gas hissing through the ventilator. It smelled like lemons and car exhaust and musk. He shut his eyes, breathed in deep, thinking: *Nothing you haven't done before. Only you won't be aware of it this time and the pay is better. And with an ordinary trick you wouldn't know for sure if the dude wasn't planning to beat you up afterwards. This way you've got the agency's written guarantee you won't be hurt or infected. And five hundred dollars when you wake up tomorrow. A sure thing . . .*

He said these things to himself, an inward litany, and he thought it was working to make him feel better because soon he was relaxing and humming. But an instant before dropping off, he realized it was only the gas.

IT WAS OVER like nothing. Just like that. He woke up, saw the young woman with the funereal smile bending over him. He looked down at himself, discovered with surprise that he was dressed. He smiled in momentary embarrassment, but then the detached urbanity he'd labored nineteen years to perfect (his mother claimed he'd begun to act cool and distant at two years old) took the wheel.

He shrugged.

"How do you feel?" she asked disinterestedly.

"Fine," he said, though the gas had left him with a dull qualm, like seasickness in his gut. He sat up, and the feeling quickly passed.

"When you're thoroughly awake you can come out to the front desk for payment," she said, and went through the door.

At the mention of money he stood bolt upright and stretched. Well. That was a snap. He looked himself over. His body didn't seem the worse for wear. A distant ache between his legs. Maybe a bruise on his left thigh. Better than hustling on the Boulevard. Whoever had played with him had been careful.

With a shiver he tried to remember—and came up with nothing. Yet his eyes had been open, his ears had heard, parts of his brain had followed someone's spoken directions. But he couldn't remember a damn thing. He straightened his collar, tightened his scarf, regarded his chipped silver-painted fingernails ruefully and went to get his money. The secretary handed him an envelope. He left immediately, but outside the office he stopped and tore open the envelope. Five hundred cash, as promised.

It was eight AM and the traffic was beginning to work itself into a frenzy. He grinned at the scowling copper sun, the smog-burnished sky, and set off for Zimm's apartment.

SHE WAS IN the tub when he arrived. He knocked and called, "Zimm!"

"Jules?" There was no welcome in her, "Come on in."

He pushed through the green paint-peeling bathroom door and managed not to stare at her as he sat on a rickety unpainted wooden chair beside the tub. It was an old-fashioned bathtub; its legs rusty eagle's claws clutching globes. She toyed languidly with a pulpy bar of soap. The bubblebath made a lace gown beneath her breasts and about her upraised knees. The ends of her hair dangled in the water, the platinum dye showed where the black roots were growing out. She still wore silvery lipstick and false eyelashes and chrome-tinted contact lenses; her head lolled a little to the left as if its weight was too much for her neck.

"Doing Quaaludes again?" he asked, trying to sound indifferent.

"None of your business."

That answered his question.

"You can buy some more with this . . ." he withdrew the fold of bills from his shirt pocket and laid it on the soap shelf. "What I owe you."

After counting the money, she said, "Thank you very much, sir." Pretending to bat her eyelashes.

His eyes wandered. Her breasts bobbed in the water like the slick backs of jellyfish. Her pubic hair—he frowned. "Christ! You've still got your underwear on."

She giggled and admitted, "I'm stoned."

She tucked the money into the pocket of the white pants lying rumpled beside the tub. "Wanta get in?" she inquired politely. "Water's still warm."

He was undressed in seconds, sliding into the water; the first of a variety of damp penetrations.

Her kisses were more ardent than the last time, when he'd still owed her money.

ACE WAS THE only one home when Jules got there at two in the afternoon.

Ace was lying on his back on the floor amidst a scattering of discs like autumn leaves: he was into vinyl recordings; his head was clamped into earphones, eyes closed, toes making jerky figure-eights to the music. Jules frowned at the bare walls, the sunken, splintered furniture, mostly wicker foraged from trash heaps. They could get some decent furnishings if he made some more money.

. . . it was then that he was sure he would go back to Sleepwalkers. But it wasn't because of the furnishings. It was only because of Zimm and the change in her voice that came when she'd seen the money. She hadn't asked where he got it. Ace opened his eyes, squinted up at him. He took off the earphones which leaked a howl of thrash. "We gotta get some new tunes," Jules said, hoping to distract Ace from the pitch that must come. "Most recent stuff we have is four years old."

"Yeah," Ace agreed, his pinpoint eyes flickering, not seeing much. "Yeah we gotta keep up, we live inna world of the future after all." He laughed. "*You* know: Magnetic rocket cars and telepathy booths." He rubbed his nose. "I been reading my uncle's 1938 *Popular Science* magazines with a special feature about "The Marvelous World of The Future". And we're in it because guess what, the time they're talking about is right now! They say we got telepathy booths and people go to work in jet-propelled rollerskates."

Jules laughed.

But then Ace asked what he must inevitably ask: "Hey, can you let me have some'a the squeeze you got sleepwalkin'? You must have some left and my connection won't take—"

"Gave it all to Zimm, man. Owed her. I'm going back tonight. Get you some dollars tomorrow, for why, I don't know, you never give it back. But I'll give you some—"

Ace was content. "Hey, it's better than street hustling, huh? Like, you look okay—used to come home all crumpled-up and forlorn lookin' and complaining you only got sixty bucks and what a total ripoff it was—"

"Shut up, Ace."

"You feel nothin' later, with Sleepwalkers, huh?" Ace continued doggedly.

Suddenly feeling odd, tingling all over, Jules said, "No, not a goddamn thing." He didn't want to talk about it. He realized he was rubbing the palms of his hands, again and again, on his shirt sleeves. He trapped his hands in his armpits. But now he was suddenly feeling grievously annoyed, seeing the deltas of built-up filth in the corners of the room. "Place needs a good cleaning." He said.

"They just gas you like Gary said and that's it? And then they rent your body out to people and it walks around like a zombie and does what it's told and you don't feel a thing? You don't even ache in your asshole?"

Jules shot him a look. Ace made an elaborate shrug and replaced the earphones, lay back.

Jules got up and went to his room and threw himself on the air mattress, the cushions billowing up around him. He turned onto his back and thought of getting stoned. No.

It was there. In there, somewhere. Whatever they'd used him for was stored up in the back of his head somewhere, locked in with their electrical repressors, but intact, in there all the same. In a cell in his brain. In a little room somewhere in his brain re-enacting endlessly what they'd made him do. And maybe Methedrine would unlock the door. No. Don't get started again, and especially not now. He decided that next time he did the sleepwalk he'd take the money to a bank and deposit half of it into a new account so that Ace and Bernie couldn't talk him out of that much, anyway. He'd say he'd given it to Zimm. They'd been his best friends for years. He couldn't say no to them. He'd been there himself. He fixed his eyes on the fierce and empty heart of the naked bulb shining white light overhead. He stared, unblinking, till the pain of staring at the bright bulb made him close his eyes.

Pictures came. It wasn't dreaming, really. And not daydreaming either. They weren't hallucinations. It was re-living. He could see it so clearly, there under his eyelids, almost cinematically. Yet none of it was familiar. A dark room, a fire at one end in a huge gray-stone fireplace throwing tongues of light on the hooded congregation. People in black robes, faces in shadow. On a table of polished mahogany he dimly made out a huge oyster shell on its back, open and empty but for an enormous blue pearl which seemed to emanate its own black-light. On the ornate rug, woven in red and black gargoyle visages, a silver casket like an infant's coffin faced him. "This the young man from the agency?" came a reedy voice from the right. He was unable to move, he couldn't turn his head to see who had spoken.

"Yes," replied another voice, business-like. One of the hooded figures stepped forward, tilted back the milky lid of the casket and said, "Come forward." Distantly, Jules felt himself striding forward. "Stop. Stand where you are, look into the casket." Jules looked.

JOHN SHIRLEY

It took time for his eyes to adjust. He saw the iridescent gleam of multifaceted eyes. "Bend you over and open wide your mouth," the hooded figure commanded. Jules bent toward the casket, looked closer, opened his mouth, his head near the edge of the casket, he looked closer . . .

He sat up, struggling to escape the clinging air mattress, and heard the echoes of his own scream. Slippery with sweat, he floundered off the bed and crawled over the wooden frame, across the floor. He lay face down, breathing heavily, drained. Then he got slowly to his feet, went to the refrigerator, got the vodka and drank what remained, nearly half the bottle.

That seemed to help.

THE NEXT EVENING he plugged in his bass and played simple, aggressive riffs, building up his courage to return to Sleepwalkers.

In the next room Ace and Bernie were loudly arguing:

"Com'on, Ace. Wha'sit to you?"

"I just don't like to do that stuff when Barb's around."

"She ain't here."

"Man she'll be here in half an hour."

"So it won't take that long. Twenty minutes. I'm on my knees, Ace. I'm down—"

"Okay—okay, go get it for me then."

Jules heard Bernie run obediently down the hall to his room to get the handcuffs and flog.

Minutes later Bernie breathlessly pleaded, "Now say the things."

"You half-assed slimy PUNK!" Ace shrieked and there was the counterpoint wet sound of the flog tasting Bernie's buttocks, and Bernie's grateful moan like a liturgical reply.

Annoyed, Jules turned the volume up and played loud and brutally through the fuzz-tone, until it was over and Ace came out, looking exhausted and wired. Ace looked out the single intact window. He let the curtains drop and turned away. "No sign of Barb," Jules said, without looking up.

"Keep playing that thing, man. Don't stop. Sounds good."

214

Jules dipped his fingers into the guts of the bass and savaged the steel-string nerve-ends and made it groan for Ace. Speeding again, Ace walked back and forth slapping his thighs, a martinet parading too fast for the music, twitching his shoulders and bobbing his head.

When Barb arrived they tied off together, Jules playing for them as they rushed, thinking that Ace didn't look quite satisfied and that next time he'd probably double the dose and that would be it. Involuntarily grinning, Ace moved to the music like a striking cobra. Jules looked at him and could see the agreement Ace had made with the speed, signed and sealed in the noiseless workings of his mouth. He knew that Ace was connected, in that instant, that he was one with the cars hurtling over the freeways and the buses rumbling through the avenues and the electricity whining in the powerlines; that he was synched with the rhythms and pistons and jackhammers. That was the contract: *Take my body and make me one with the world's machines.*

Ace knew what he was doing. To live, you must deal. You must deal with someone of the big machine's agents. Speed or heroin or lonely old breadwinners on the prowl or guns or editors or music managers. You had to make an agreement somewhere, and modify yourself, mutilate yourself to fit, like the Amazons removing a breast for the quiver-strap.

Trying not to think of the Sleepwalkers in those terms, Jules wondered if he should join a band. If he could.

He turned the volume up full.

THIS TIME, THE girl with the Afro-wig and the fixed smile didn't bother with the directions. She simply opened the door for him and he went in and lay down.

The gas seeped in. He could hear the faint susurration.

Drifting off, he thought about Zimm and wondered, if ever he took the trouble to scrutinize the fine print in the Sleepwalker contract, if he'd see her name there, as part of the exchange.

Loan us your body, we pay you back in your lover's respect.

He tried hard not to wonder what they were going to do with him. This time.

The gas was getting to him. Experimentally, he tried to get up. He couldn't move a muscle. There was a moment of panic when a large blue-black fly lit on his right chuck and walked up toward his eye. He tried to move to shake it off, but couldn't do more than blink. It came onward, growing to a bristling huge black blur. His only escape was in closing his eyes.

And the gas took him down.

He deposited half the money in a new account, took seventy-five home to Ace and Bernie and simply handed it to them, to save them the trouble of having to ask.

Now he walked down Sunset Boulevard to the apartment building where Zimm lived. It was six, the sky melting like candle wax, tangerine-lemon at the horizon. The balmy June air slid velvet past his fingers as he hurried.

It was getting rapidly darker. He smiled. Thank God it gets dark this time of evening, thank God for that. That's fine and it's getting darker.

Suddenly lonely, Jules continued down the street, toward Zimm's. He was in a gay hustler district now, and there were others, slowly drifting down the street like blossoms on the wind. He nodded to those he recognized and shook his head at a customer who approached him. He lit another cigarette, though his throat felt raw.

But he was feeling left out again, and sinking. It called back the vision of the casket and the pearl and the cowls.

And that was something he wanted very much to forget.

His clothes clung to him. He was sweating excessively. Nerves. There was electricity sparking between his teeth and the air was so charged with tension that the streetlight poles were straining to keep their upright shape against it and the buildings were squatting with secret muscles flexed. What were they afraid of?

No. He didn't want to remember. He didn't want to find out that way what the Sleepwalker Agency did with him while he was under. But he knew then that he would have to find out another way. He needed to know what the full terms of the agreement were, in detail. Otherwise this fucked-up feeling, this tripping on uncertainty would never leave him.

A long dusty navy-blue air-turbine Cadillac pulled up beside him, honking. Unthinking, acting on reflex, Jules accepted the ride. He climbed into the car, grateful for the air-conditioned coolness. Beside him was a squat man with rubbery florid skin, a wide blocked-out nose and a collie's entreating tiny brown eyes. The man pulled the car back into the light traffic. Jules noticed the guy's hands on the steering wheel—noticed what small hands they were. "Come and sit closer by me," he ordered.

Jules came alert. *Christ, I should have known.* "I'm not into it, man," he said. "I don't work that way anymore. Don't need it." He assumed the man was one of his old tricks from when he'd hustled. "I just wanted a ride. I'll get out here."

The john smiled, thinking that Jules was playing games, and reached a tubby hand for his crotch.

Jules backhanded the guy across his flaccid right cheek.

More startled than hurt, the stranger gave him a long look. "You didn't mind last night. I guess they don't let you remember . . . but kid, last night you performed." Was that a grin? Or a grimace?

The man grabbed for him again and, spasmodically, Jules kicked the steering wheel. The car nosed far left, began to slide sideways. Jules braced himself. A small import sedan hit the right front fender, which had crossed into oncoming traffic. The Cadillac's driver was jolted forward and his forehead cracked viciously on the steering wheel; he slumped over.

Jules was only wrenched. When the car stopped sliding he hopped out, dodging traffic, and ran to the curb, down the sidewalk. He looked back only once. The import was almost totaled, crumpled in supplication against the dominant, glistening block of the Cadillac. The fat man was alive, he stumbled out of the car, leaning on the import's crushed hood, the lines of his face defined in blood streaming from a head wound.

Jules turned away and ran around the corner.

When he arrived at Zimm's he was glad she wasn't home. He was going to be sick and he wanted to get it over alone. Vision swimming, he let himself in and ran to the bathroom. He vomited, flushed the toilet, watched the piebald churn swirl down into the city's gut. Then he washed out his mouth, several times, and undressed. He ran a bath and got in before it had filled. He washed himself thoroughly, seeing everywhere unaccountable gray smudges on his limbs. Scrubbing violently, he rubbed them off, but they reappeared seconds later. It looked like mold.

He emptied the tub, cleaned it completely with ammonia and Ajax, rinsed it and filled it again. Again he cleansed himself. Emptied the tub, refilled it, scrubbed.

Finally, he stopped seeing the spots of mold.

But after he had toweled himself dry he saw in the mirror something dark red on the inner side of his left buttock. A handprint. Not the handprint of the man in the blue Caddy. Much bigger, and with long fingers which must have ended in sharp nails.

It wouldn't go away.

HE GOT THE nose filters from Ace, who had worked briefly in a paint factory the year before. They were something new, two thimble-like wire meshes, guaranteed for eight hours. Ace had only used them for a few hours. Jules hoped no one could see them. He pressed them deeply into his nostrils.

He lay back on the couch. He could hear the lisp of the gas coming through the grate, but he couldn't smell it. Good.

He was wide awake when the man in white came into the room ten minutes later. "Stand up," the man told him.

Jules stood up, moving slowly, gracefully, trying not to think. He had heard a friend of Ace's who knew an attendant at Sleepwalkers describe how the tranced moved, how they responded to orders. Slowly but not jerkily. *Look alert, but don't focus your eyes on anything, don't move unless you're told.*

"Follow me." He followed the man out through the rear door and into a dressing room. The stranger was tall and brawny, with blond hair cut into a shag. He wore a white suit with a black tie, a patch sewn on one shoulder of the suit said only: SWA.

"Get dressed," said the attendant, and left him. Jules went to one of the racks and selected a black robe. He began to frown, then instantly repressed it. There was no one else in the room, but they might be watching. From somewhere.

The robe, with its soft black cloth and black cowl, was the same sort of robe he'd seen in his vision. The vision of the fly.

Probably the visions weren't literal, he thought, pulling the gown over his head. Probably the pictures were symbols, dream interpretations, with a few real-life components, like the robe.

There was no getting around it. He was getting scared.

He almost jerked around when he heard the door slam behind, but he caught himself. "Follow me," the attendant intoned, sounding bored.

Jules turned slowly and trailed after the attendant out the back door, down three concrete steps and into the Los Angeles night. They got into a van, all-white except for the agency's symbol in red with their motto: YOUR PLEASURE IS OUR BUSINESS.

The attendant opened the back door for him. Jules waited for the order. "Climb in, sit down."

Jules obeyed.

Like a trained dog, Jules thought. He talks to me like I'm a trained dog.

The attendant started the van and drove down the alley.

Jules sat on a metal bench staring at a metal wall and listening to the creak and grind of metal machinery around him. He sat upright with hands folded in his lap, staring straight ahead, braced against the inertia of the van's turning.

The van turned into a driveway and pulled up in another alley.

Jules was ordered out of the van and through the back door of an old tin-roofed warehouse.

He was led to stand on the lowest of five wooden steps rising to a stage, behind two other people. The curtains were drawn, backstage was twilight. Jules could hear the unseen audience murmuring. Two other hooded figures stood before him, one after the other, waiting: immobile, backs straight.

He heard, slightly muffled through the curtain, a voice addressing the audience through a microphone. "Please remember to keep your requests within the limitations prescribed by the contract. Only those with red cards will be permitted the private use of these bodies, after the performance is over. Red cardholders interested in particular bodies should see the attendant for schedules and user-fee rates."

Then the curtains rolled back, but from the wings the audience was still invisible. An attendant came up from behind and whispered to the first shrouded figure. "Go up on the stage, get undressed, turn to face the audience."

The figure obeyed and, leaning very slightly to the right, Jules could see that the sleepwalker was a young woman. With platinum hair. He looked closer. No, it wasn't Zimm. For ten seconds he had been sure it was her. He realized that he was not particularly relieved. He would not have been surprised or dismayed if it had been Zimm.

The woman was shorter, plumper than Zimm, with full breasts and rings glittering on her fingers. Her profile was all curves and puckers.

"First call," the attendant told the hidden audience.

Jules heard someone shout, "Dance like a monkey." The woman leapt clumsily up and down, knees bent, until the voice added, "Monkey in heat." Face bestially contorted, the woman postured obscenely.

An attendant sent the second tranced onto the stage. He tossed off his robe and even from behind Jules knew it was Bernie.

Bernie needed a fix and couldn't wait on Jules.

"Monkeys mating," came the command. Bernie did a mock-apish dance around the woman, then grasped her by the buttocks. She bent over. They simulated copulation, making bestial faces, and the crowd roared in satisfaction.

Jules heard the attendant behind him. "That long-haired kid up there, got track marks on his arms. Plenty."

"Goddamnit!" the other man said. "They're supposed to inspect 'em before signing. Shit, this could be bad."

"How 'zat?" the first attendant said.

"These fuckhead dopers—any stuff in their bloodstream, it reacts with the sleep-gas, see—they can come out of it. Doesn't matter what shit they're shootin'."

Bernie was facing toward Jules, ten feet away. Looking into Bernie's eyes, Jules realized it had already happened. Bernie had thrown off the effects of the gas. His eyes wandered, he looked scared. His lips twitched. But he did as he was told and Jules could see the inward litany in his eyes: *Make me one with the world's machines.* It worked. It fit. No one noticed that he was out of the trance. And maybe he wasn't, some kind of way.

Jules almost nodded to himself. This was home.

"Where's this guy go to?"

"Lemme see, what time is it? Oh—just take him up to Mr. Carmody now. He should have gone on stage first, I guess."

"Follow me," the blond attendant whispered to Jules. Jules turned and followed, leaving Bernie behind as he'd left him twitching on the floor at home many times before.

Jules was escorted to a door, down a passage into another building. He was taken up an elevator, along a carpeted hallway. The dun carpet was spongy beneath his bare feet. The attendant took him into a bathroom, made him shower yet again, dry off, then left him sitting nude on the edge of a wide round white bed in the bedroom of a luxurious apartment decorated Victorian; lace curtains, ancient yellowed oil paintings, quaint, elaborately carved furniture. Dust. Jules sat still, staring ahead, feeling a hot wire stretching tighter, tighter within him. It took him nearly two minutes to recognize this sensation: rage.

It had been a long time since he'd been angry at anyone but himself. And he could always hurt himself without outside retribution. But now—it was a rush to feel the anger, made all the hotter by his immobility. Coiling up inside.

And if he was taken to a place where there was a huge black pearl and a white casket containing something hideously outsized with shiny wings and faceted eyes—then he would do his best to kill someone.

Out of the corner of his eye he saw a door open. A withered little man, almost completely bald, entered and shuffled toward him.

Age spots dappled the old man's lumpy scalp and trembling hands, and he walked with the aid of a fiberglass cane. He wore a red terry cloth robe and red satin slippers. His eyes were sunken, watery gray-blue.

He was toothless. He was a very old man. He faced Jules, looked him impishly up and down and smiled wistfully, showing withered gums. He was bent, hardly came up to Jules's biceps. *I could strangle him with one hand,* Jules thought. The fury mounted. *Just let him touch me. I'll choke him for Bernie and Ace and me and Connie and Barb and for the child Zimm must have been.*

The old man, Carmody, giggled and rasped, "Com'on—com'on, ol' buddybuddy!" He turned and Jules followed him into the next room.

It was a wealthy child's nursery and playroom. A prodigious room painted in gaudy colors with a sprawling electric train set at the far end, a miniature two-rider carousel nearer, a sand box, and a huge wooden crate of toys, five feet to a side.

Humming, the old man went to the chest of toys. A hysterical orange orangutan was painted on the facing side of the chest.

Carmody fumbled through the toys till he found a small wooden broom and a battered red wig. "I'll be the mommy and you'll be the daddy and you can mow the lawn." He nodded again and again. His hands shook with excitement, the gray skin on them so loose and vitreously wrinkled they looked like rubber gloves.

Once more digging into the box he found a small plastic lawnmower and handed it to Jules.

Gazing in wonder at the toy, Jules accepted it. All semblance of the trance was now discarded. Carmody either didn't notice or didn't care. He had put the red wig crookedly on his head and was busily sweeping the floor of an imaginary kitchen. Humming in an unnaturally high-pitched voice.

Jules felt duped. The fury drained from him, the beautiful transparent rush of long-suppressed hostility like the rush of meth, fading away. The acceptance returning.

No, he told himself. Uh-uh. *Don't fall for it. This is the same as if you'd performed sexually. You're still following orders, he's still using you, you're just a toy.*

Jules dropped the plastic lawnmower and turned away. He went to the light switch. He would turn out the light and strangle the old man. He put his fingers on the switch.

He turned at a tap on his shoulder. The old man was smiling, holding out the scarlet wig. "You don't wanna be the daddy? You can be the mommy if you want."

Once more, for an instant, Jules felt cheated.

Then, for Bernie and Ace and Barb and Connie but not for Zimm, he went back to the lawnmower, picked it up, began pushing it cheerfully back and forth, saying to the old man: "No, you can be the mommy."

BURIED IN THE SKY

Imagination called up the shocking form of fabulous Yog-Sothoth—only a congeries of iridescent globes, yet stupendous in its malign suggestiveness . . .
                                        —H.P. Lovecraft

"IF HE DIDN'T kill mom, then why are we moving away?" Deede asked.

"We're *moving* because I have a better job offer in L.A.," Dad said, barely audible as usual, as he looked vaguely out the living room window at the tree-lined street. Early evening on a Portland June. "I'll be working for a good magazine—very high profile. See those clouds? Going to rain again. We won't have all this rain in L.A., anyhow . . . Hanging Gardens will be a nice change . . . You'll like L.A. high schools, the kids are very . . . uh . . . *hip.*" Wearing his perpetual work shirts, jeans, and a dully stoic expression, he was a paunchy, pale, gray-eyed man with shaggy blond hair just starting to go gray. He stood with his hands in his pockets, gazing outward from the house. In a lower voice he said, "They said it was an accident or . . ." He didn't like to say suicide. "So— we have to assume that's right and . . . we can't harass an innocent man. Better to leave it all behind us."

Deede Bergstrom—waist-length sandy-blond hair, neohippie look— was half watching MTV, the sound turned off; on the screen a woman wearing something like a bikini crossed with a dress was posturing and pumping her hips. Deede's hips were a shade too wide and she'd never call attention to them like that.

Deede knew Dad didn't want the travel writer job in L.A. that much—he liked Portland, he didn't like Los Angeles, except as a subject for journalism, and the travel editor job with the Portland newspaper paid their bills. He was just trying to get them away from the place where mom had died because everything they saw here was a reminder. And they had to get over it.

Didn't you have to get over it, when someone murdered your mother?

Sure. Sure you do. You just have to get over it.

"You think he killed her too, Dad," said Lenny matter-of-factly, as he came in. He'd been in the kitchen, listening. The peanut butter and jelly sandwich dripped in his hand as he looked at his Dad, and took an enormous bite.

"You're spilling blueberry jelly on the carpet," Deede pointed out. She was curled up in the easy chair with her feet tucked under her skirt to keep them warm. The heat was already turned off, in preparation for the move, and it wasn't as warm out as it should've been, this time of year.

"Shut up, mantis-girl," Lenny said, the food making his voice indistinct. He was referring to her long legs and long neck. He was a year older than Deede, had just graduated high school. His hair was buzz-cut, and he wore a muscle shirt—he had the muscles to go with it—and a quizzical expression. His chin was a little weak, but his features otherwise were almost TV-star good looking. The girls at school had liked him.

"Lenny I've asked you not to call your sister that, and go and get a paper towel and clean up your mess," Dad said, without much conviction. "Deana, where's your little sister?"

They called her Deede because her name was Deana Diane. Deede shrugged. "Jean just leaves when she wants to..." And then she remembered. "Oh yeah, she went rollerblading with that Buzzy kid..."

Lenny snorted. "That little stoner."

Dad started to ask if he Lenny a good reason to think his youngest sister was hanging with stoners—Deede could see the question was about to come out of him—but then his lips pinched shut. Decided not to ask. "Yeah, well... Buzzy won't be coming with us to L.A., so..." He shrugged.

Dad was still looking out the window, Deede mostly watching the soundless TV.

And Lenny was looking at the floor while he listlessly ate his sandwich, Deede noticed, looking over from the TV. *Dad out the window, me at TV, Lenny at the floor.*

Mom at the interior of her coffin lid.

"I think we should stay and push them to reopen it," Deede said, doggedly.

Dad sighed. "We don't know that Gunnar Johansen killed anyone. We know that mom was jogging and Johansen was seen on the same jogging trail and later on she was found dead. There wasn't even agreement at the coroner's on whether she'd been . . ."

He didn't want to say *raped*.

"He was almost bragging about it," Lenny said tonelessly, staring at the rug, his jaws working on the sandwich. "'Prove it!' he said." Deede could see the anger in his eyes but you had to look for it. He was like Dad, all internal.

"It was two years ago," Deede said. "I don't think the police are going to do anything else. But we could hire a private detective." Two years. She felt like it was two weeks. It'd taken almost six months for Deede to be able to function in school again after they found mom dead. "Anyway—I saw it . . . in a way."

"Dreams." Dad shook his head. "Recurrent dreams aren't proof. You're going to like L.A."

She wanted to leave Portland—and she also wanted to stay here and make someone put Johansen in jail. But she couldn't stay here alone. Even if she did, what could she do about him, herself? She was afraid of him. She saw him sometimes in the neighborhood—he lived a block and a half down—and every time he looked right at her. And every time, too, it was like he was saying, *I killed your mom and I liked it and I want to kill you too and pretty soon I will.* It didn't make sense, her seeing all that, when he had no particular expression on his face. But she was sure of it, completely sure of it. He had killed her mom. And he'd liked it. And he had killed some other people and he'd liked that too.

She had no proof at all. Recurrent dreams aren't proof.

" . . . the movers are coming in about an hour," Dad was saying. "We're going to have a really good new life." He said it while looking out the window and he said it tonelessly. He didn't even bother to make it sound as if he really believed the part about a really good new life.

• • •

Two days later, they were ready to go to Los Angeles—and it had finally started to warm up in Oregon, like it was grudgingly admitting it was the beginning of summer. "Now that we're leaving, it's nice out," Jean said bitterly, from the back seat of the Explorer. The sky was showing through the clouds, and purple irises edging the neighbor's lawn were waving in the breeze and then, as Deede just sat in the front seat of the car, waiting for her Dad to drive her and her brother and Jean to the I-5 freeway, she saw Johansen walking down the street toward them, walking by those same irises. Dad was looking around one last time, to see if he'd forgotten to do anything, making sure the doors to the house were locked. He would leave the keys for the realtor, in some pre-arranged place . . . The house where Deede had grown up with her mother was sold and in a few minutes would be gone from her life forever . . .

Jean and Lenny didn't see Johansen, Lenny was in back beside Jean, his whole attention on playing with the PSP and Jean was looking at the little TV screen over the back seat of the SUV. Fourteen years old, starting to get fat; her short-clipped hair was reddish brown, her face heart-shaped like mom's had been, the same little dimples in her cheeks. She was chewing gum and fixedly watching a Nickelodeon show she probably didn't like.

Deede wasn't going to point Johansen out to her. She didn't much relate to her little sister—Jean seemed to blame Deede for not having the same problems. Jean had dyslexia, and Deede didn't; Jean had attention deficit, and Deede didn't. Jean had gotten only more bitter and withdrawn since Mom had died. She didn't want anyone acting protective. Deede felt she had to try to protect her anyway.

Johansen was getting closer.

"This building we're moving into, it's, like, lame, living in a stupid-ass building after living in a house," Jean said, snapping her gum every few syllables, her eyes on the SUV's television.

"It's not just any stupid-ass building," Lenny said, his thumbs working the controllers, destroying mordo-bots with preternatural skill as he went on, "it's Skytown. It's like some famous architectural big deal, a building with everything in it . . . It has the Skymall and the, whatsit, uh, Hanging Gardens in it. That's where we live, Hanging Gardens Apartments, name's from some ancient thing I forget . . ."

"From *Babylon*," Deede mumbled, watching Johansen get closer. Starting to wonder if, after all, she should point him out. But she grew more afraid with every step he took, each bringing him closer, though he was just sauntering innocently along, a tall tanned athletic man in light blue Lacrosse shirt and Dockers; short flaxen hair, pale blue eyes, much more lower lip than upper, a forehead that seemed bonily square. Very innocently walking along. Just the hint of a smirk on his face.

Where was Dad? Why didn't he come back to the car?

Don't say anything to Jean or Lenny. Jean would go back to not sleeping at night again, if she saw Johansen so close. They all knew he'd killed mom. Everyone knew but the police. Maybe they knew too but they couldn't prove it. The coroner had ruled "accidental death".

Johansen walked up abreast of Deede. She wanted to look him in the eye, and say, with that look, *I know what you did and you won't get away with it . . .*

Their gazes met. His pale blue eyes dilated in response. His lips parted. He caught the tip of his tongue between his teeth. He looked at her—

Crumbling inside, the fear going through her like an electric shock, she looked away.

He chuckled—she heard it softly but clearly—as he walked on by.

Her mouth was dry, very dry, but her eyes spilled tears. Everything was hazy. Maybe a minute passed, maybe not so much. She was looking hard at the dashboard . . .

"Hanging Gardens," Lenny said, finally, oblivious to his sister's terror. "Stupid name. Makes you think they're gonna hang somebody there."

"That's why you're going to live there," Jean said, eyes glued to the TV. "Cause they going to hang you."

"So, *you're* gonna live there too, shrimpy."

"Little as possible," Jean responded, with a chillingly adult decisiveness.

229

Deede wanted to ask her what she meant by that—but Jean resented Deede's protectiveness. She'd called her, "Miss Protective three-point-eight." She resented Deede's good grades—implied she was a real kiss-ass or something, to get them. Though in fact they were pretty effortless for her. But it was true, she was too protective.

"Deede?" Dad's voice. "You okay?"

Deede blinked, wiped her eyes, looked at her Dad, opening the driver's side door, bending to squint in at her. "I'm okay," she said.

He never pushed it, hadn't since mom died. If you said you were "okay", crying or not, that was as good as could be expected. They'd all had therapy—Lenny had stopped going after a month—and it'd helped a little. And Dad probably figured it was all that could be done.

He got in and started the car and they started off. Deede looked in the mirror and she saw Johansen, way down the street, his back to them. Stopping. Turning to look after them . . .

As they drove away from their home.

"THIS PLACE IS so huge . . . so high up . . . " Deede, Lenny and Jean were in the observation deck of the Skytown building, up above Skytown Mall and the apartment complex, looking out at the clouds just above, the pillars and spikes of downtown L.A. below them. They were in the highest and newest skyscraper in Los Angeles.

"It's a hundred-twenty-five stories, fifteen more than the World Trade Center buildings were," Lenny said, reading from the guide pamphlet. "Supposed to be 'super hardened' to resist terrorist attacks . . ."

Deede remembered what she'd read about the Titanic, how it was supposed to be unsinkable, too. Skytown, it occurred to her, was almost a magnet for terrorists.But she wouldn't say that with Jean here, and anyway Lenny had been calling her *Deana Downer" for her frequent dour pronouncements. "Just an inch the wrong way on that steering wheel and Dad could drive us under the wheels of a semitruck," she'd told Lenny, when they were halfway to L.A. Jean had been asleep—but Dad had frowned at her anyway.

"When's Dad coming back?" Deede asked, trying to see the street directly below. She couldn't see it—the "hanging gardens" were in the way: a ribbony spilling of green vines and lavender wisteria over the edges of the balconies encompassing the building under the observation deck. Closer to the building's superstructure were rose bushes too, but the building was new and so were the rose bushes, there were no blossoms on them yet. The building had a square base—filling a square city block—and rose to a ziggurat peak, a step pyramid, the lowest step of the pyramid containing the garden, the penultimate step the observation deck.

"Not till after dinner," Lenny said. "He has a meeting."

"Is this part of, what, Hanging Gardens Apartments?" Jean asked, sucking noisily on a smoothie.

"No, that's actually down," Lenny said. "This is the observation deck above Skymall. Whole thing is actually called Skytown. The apartments are under the gardens but they're called the Hanging Gardens apartments anyway, just to be more confusing."

Feeling isolated, lonely, gazing down on the tiny specks that were people, the cars looking smaller than Hot Wheels toys, Deede turned away from the window. "Let's go back to the apartment and wait for Dad."

"No way!" Jean said, talking around the straw. "The apartment smells too much like paint! I want to see the Skymall! We're supposed to have dinner there!" She sucked up the dregs of her smoothie. "And I'm still hungry."

AT FIRST IT was like any mall anywhere, though it was so high up they felt a little tired and light headed. Deede heard a security guard talking about it to the man who ran the frozen yogurt shop—the young black guard had a peculiar uniform, dark gray, almost black, with silver epaulettes, and the shapes of snakes going around his cuffs. "Yeah man, we're so high up, the air's a little thin. They try to equalize it but it don't always go. They're working out the bugs. Like that groaning in the elevators . . ."

Windows at the end of the mall's long corridors showed the hazy dull blue sky and planes going by, not that far above, and the tops of high buildings—seeing just the tops from here made them look to Deede like images she'd seen of buildings in Egypt and other ancient places.

There were only a few other customers; they were among the first to move into the building and the mall wasn't officially open to the public, except for the apartment owners. Walking along the empty walkway between rows of glassy storefronts, Deede felt like a burglar. She had to look close to see shopkeepers inside—the ones who noticed them looked at Deede and her siblings almost plaintively. *Please give me some business so I feel like this new investment isn't hopeless and doomed to failure.* "Sorry, Mister," she muttered, "I don't want to buy any NFL Official Logo gym bags."

"What?" Jean said. "Lenny she's mumbling to herself again."

He sniggered. "That's our Deede. Hey what's that thing?"

He pointed at a window containing a rack of objects resembling bicycle helmets crossed with sea urchins. The transparent spikes on the helmets seemed to feel them looking and reacted, retracting.

"Eww!" Jean said. "It's like critter antenna things!"

The store was called INTER-REACTIVES INC. There was a man in the back, in a green jump suit, a man shaped roughly like a bowling pin, who seemed to have a bright orange face. It must be some kind of colored light back there, Deede decided, making his face look orange. The man turned to look at them. His eyes were green—even the parts that should be "whites" were green.

"Is that guy wearing a mask?" Jean asked.

The man looked at her and a rictus-like grin jerked across his face—split it in half—and was gone. From expressionless to grin to expressionless in half a second.

Deede backed away, and turned hastily to the next store.

"That guy was all . . ." Jean murmured. But she didn't say anything more about it.

You got weird impressions sometimes in strange places, Deede decided. That's all it was.

The next shop was a Nike store. Then came a Disney store, closed. Then a store called BLENDER. Jean stopped, interested: It seemed to sell things to eat. Behind the window glass, transparent chutes curved down into blenders; dropping through the chutes, into the intermittently grinding blenders, came indeterminate pieces of organic material

Deede had never seen before, bits and pieces of things: they weren't definitely flesh and they weren't recognizably fruit but they made you think of flesh and fruit—only, the colors were all wrong, the surface textures alien. Some of them seemed to be parts of brightly colored faces—which, when you didn't look at them directly, squirmed in the blender, and when you looked closer you saw the apparent eye was now lined up properly with a nose, above lips, the disjointed face looking out at them for a moment before being whirred away into bits. But the parts of the faces, when she looked closer, weren't noses or eyes or lips at all. "What *is* that stuff?" Deede asked.

Lenny and Jean shook their heads at once, staring in puzzlement—and the blenders started whirring all at once, making the kids jump a bit. In the back of the store was a counter and someone was on the other side of the counter, which was only about four and a half feet high, but you could just see the top of the person's head on the other side of the counter—a lemon-colored head. Someone very short. The top of the head moved nervously back and forth.

"Some kid back there," Jean said. "Walkin' back and forth."

"Or some dwarf," Lenny said. "You want to go in and see?" But he didn't move toward the shop. The other two shook their heads.

They moved on, passing an ordinary shop that sold fancy color photo portraits, a store that sold clothing for teenage girls that neither Jean nor Deede would be interested in—it was for cheerleader types—and then a store . . .

It was filled with bird cages and in the cages were birds that didn't seem to have any eyes and they seemed to have beaks covered with fur, from which issued spiral tongues. They moved around in their crowded cages so fast it was hard to tell if the impression Deede had of their appearance was right. A woman in the back of the shop had a fantastic piled-up hair style, an elaborate coif with little spheres woven into it, reminding Deede of eyes, randomly arranged into the high hairdo; she turned around . . .

She must have turned all the way around, really quickly, so quickly they didn't see the turn, because they saw only the elaborate coif and the back of her head again.

"This place is making me feel all sick to my stomach," Jean said.

"I think it's like . . . not enough oxygen . . . or something . . ." Lenny said. Sounding like Dad in his tentative way of speaking, just then. Then more decisively: "Yo look, there's an arcade!"

They crossed into the more familiar confines of an arcade, its doorway open into a dark room, illuminated mostly by light from the various machines. "Lenny, give me a dollar!" Jean demanded.

"Stop ordering me around!" But he gave her a dollar, mashing it up in her palm, and she got a videogame machine to accept it. Deede had never seen the game before: it was called KILLER GIRL and it appeared to show a girl—so low-rez she had no clear-cut features—shooting fiery red bullets from her eyes and the tips of her fingers and her navel—was it her navel?—toward dozens of murkily defined enemies who cropped up in the windows of a suburban neighborhood, enemies with odd looking weapons in their pixilated hands. The neighborhood was rather like the one they'd left in Portland. As Jean played, Deede and Lenny watching, the video figure that Jean controlled changed shape, becoming more definite, more high resolution—looking more and more like Jean herself. Then a videogame "boss" loomed up over a building in the game, a giant, somewhat but not quite resembling Gunnar Johansen . . .

"What are you kids doing in here?"

All three of them twitched around to face him at once, as if they'd rehearsed it. A security guard was scowling at them. A man with small eyes, a flattened nose in a chunky grayish face that looked almost made of putty. He wore a peculiar, tight-fitting helmet of translucent blue, that pressed his hair down so it looked like meat in a supermarket package. There was a smell off him like smashed ants. He wore the almost-black and silver uniform with the snake cuffs.

"What you mean, what're we doing?" Lenny snorted. "Dude, it's an arcade. Work it out."

"But the mall's closed. Five minutes ago. Closes early till full public opening next month."

"So we didn't know that, okay? Now back the fuck off. Come on, Deede, Jean . . ."

"My game!"

"Forget it. Come on, Deede—you too Jean, now."

The guard followed a few steps behind them as they headed for the elevators leading out of the mall—Deede thought Lenny was going to turn and hit the guy for following them, his fists clenching on rigid arms, like he did before he hit that Garcia kid—but he just muttered "Fuck this guy" and walked faster till they were in the elevator. The guard made as if to get in the elevator with them but Lenny said, "No fucking way, asshole," and stabbed the elevator "close doors" button. It shut in the guard's face, on a frozen, minatory expression that hadn't changed since he'd first spoken to them.

Jean laughed. "What a loser."

The elevator groaned as it took them down to the apartments—like it was old, not almost brand new. It groaned and shivered and moaned, the sound very human, heart wrenching. Deede wanted to comfort it. The moans actually seemed to come from above it, as if someone was standing on the elevator, wailing, like a man waiting to be executed.

IT WAS A relief to be back in the apartment, the doors locked, in the midst of thirty floors of housing about half way up the building: a comfortable, well organized three-bedroom place—the bedrooms small but well ventilated. No balcony but with a view out over the city. They had cable TV, cable modems, a DVD player, big LCD screen, an Xbox and a refrigerator stocked with snacks and sodas . . . and Dad finally came home with pizza. Life was pretty good that evening.

A few days later, though, Dad announced he was leaving for five days. He had an assignment for the magazine, had to fly to Vancouver, and they'd spent too much money getting here, he couldn't afford to bring the kids with him, though school was out for the summer. Jean refused to respond to the announcement with anything but a shrug; Deede found herself almost whining, asking whether this was going to be a regular thing. As a travel editor in Portland Dad hadn't left town all that much, mostly he just edited other people's pieces. Standing at the window, a can of Diet Coke in one hand, he admitted he was going to be gone a lot in the new job.

"Yeah well that's just *great*," Lenny said, his mouth going slack with disgust, his whole frame radiating resentment—and he stuck his fists in his pockets, the way he always did when he was mad at his father, so that the seams started to pop. "I need to get my own place. I can't be babysitting all the time, Dad."

"Well until you do, you've gotta do your part, Lenny," Dad said, gazing out the window at downtown L.A. "Just . . . just help me out this summer, while you figure out what community college you want, get a day job, and all . . . all like that . . . And, and you're responsible, while I'm gone, for your sisters, you have to be, I just . . . don't have time to find anyone reliable . . ."

"Like we need him to take care of us," Jean said. "Like Mom would leave us this way."

They all looked at her and she stared defiantly back. Finally Dad said, "This building is very safe, really safe . . . I mean, it's high security as all hell. You have your door cards. But you shouldn't even leave the place while I'm gone if you can help it. Everything you need's here. Supermarket, clinic, it's all in the building . . . There's even a movie theater."

"It doesn't open till next week," Lenny said bitterly.

Dad cleared his throat, looked out the window again. "There are kids to meet here . . ."

"Hardly anyone's moved in," Jean pointed out, rolling her eyes.

"Well . . ." Dad hesitated, taking a pull on his Diet Coke. ". . . only go out in the day and . . . and don't run around in downtown L.A. Downtown L.A. is dangerous. You can go to Hollywood Boulevard and go to a movie. Lenny can drive the car, I guess. But . . . just . . . try to stay . . . to stay here . . ."

His voice trailed off. He gazed out the picture window, watching a plane fly over . . .

SHE MET JORNY in the Skymall when they got their iPods mixed up in the frozen yogurt shop. "Yo, girl, that's my iPod," Jorny said, as Deede picked it up from the counter. He had blue eyes that glimmered with irony in a V-shaped face, dark eyebrows that contrasted with his long, corn-rowed sun-bleached brown hair, a tan that was partly burn. He was slender, not quite as tall as her; he wore pants raggedly cut off just above the knees, with *Anarchy? Who the fuck knows?* written on the left pants leg in blue ballpoint pen, and a way-oversized T-shirt with a picture of Nicolas Cage on it hoisting a booze bottle, from *Leaving Las Vegas.* He had various odd items twined around his wrists as improvised bracelets—twist-its worked together, individual rings of plastic cut from six-packs. He wore high topped red tennis shoes, falling apart—probably stressed from skateboarding: a well worn skateboard was jammed under his left arm.

"No it's not your iPod," Deede said, mildly. "—look, it's playing The Hives' 'Die All Right', the song I was listening to—"

"That's the song I was listening to. I just set it down for a second to get my money out."

"No it's—oh, you're right, my iPod's in my purse. I paused it on 'Die All Right'. I thought I . . . sorry. But that really is the same song I was listening to—look! Same one—at the same time!"

"Whoa, that's weird. You're, like, stalking me and shit."

"I guess. You live in the building?"

"You kids want these frozen yogurts or what?" asked the man at the counter.

They bought their frozen yogurts, and one for Jean, who was in the Mall walkway looking in store windows. It turned out that Jorny lived downstairs from them, almost right below. He was three weeks younger than Deede and he mostly lived to do skateboard tricks. His Dad had "gone off to live in New York, we don't see him around much." When she said her mom was dead he said, "Between us we almost got one set of parents."

Jean told him she did rollerblading—he managed not to seem scornful at that—and he and Deede talked about music and the odd things they'd seen in the mall shops and how they didn't seem to be the same shops the next day. "One place seemed like it was selling faces," Jorny said. "'Latest Face'."

"I didn't see that one. They must mean masks . . . or make-up."

He shook his head but didn't argue and tried to show her some new skateboard ollies right there in the mall but the putty faced guard began jogging toward them from the other end of the walkway, bellowing. "You—hold it right there, don't you move!"

"Security guards everywhere hate skateboarders," Jorny declared proudly, grinning. "Fucking hate us. Come on!" He started toward a stairwell.

"Jean—come on!" Deede shouted, starting after him. Sticking her tongue out at the security guard, Jean came giggling after them as they banged through the doors into the stairwell and the smell of newly-dried paint and concrete, and descended, pounding down the stairs, laughing.

"Hey you kids!" came the shout from above.

They kept going, Jorny at the next level down jumping a flight of stairs on his skateboard, and landing it with a joint-jarring clack. "You actually landed that!" Deede shouted, impressed—and privately a little dismayed. It was a big jump, though skateboarders did that sort of thing a lot. She was also pleased that he was evidently showing off for her.

"Yeah, huh, that was tight, I landed it!" Jorny called, clacking down the next group of stairs, ollying from one stair to the next. Jean squealed, "Agggghhh! Run! He's coming! That blue helmet weirdo's coming!"

They pounded down the stairs, easily outdistancing the security guard, and ran into the mid-level observation court and community center. They took the elevator to the Hanging Gardens, where they went to check out Jorny's place, an apartment almost identical with their own. Deede didn't want Jean to come but couldn't think of any way for her not to.

Jorny's mom was there for lunch. She was a lawyer, the director of the county Public Defender's office, a plump woman in a dress suit with a white streak in her wooly black hair, and a pleasantly Semitic face. She seemed happy to see Deede, maybe as opposed to some of the rougher people she'd seen her son with—all that was in her face, when she looked at Deede. She smiled at Deede, then glanced at Jean, looked away from her, then looked back at her, a kind of double-take, as if trying to identify what it was about the girl that worried her . . .

It had only just recently occurred to Deede that what she saw in other people wasn't visible to everyone. It wasn't exactly psychic—it was just what Deede thought of as "looking faster." She'd always been able to look faster.

"Come on," Jorny said, as his mom went to make them sandwiches. "I want to play you the new Wolfmother single. It's not out yet—it's a ripped download a friend of mine sent me . . . "

THE NOTICE WAS there on Saturday morning, when Deede got up. Dad had left at six that morning, not saying goodbye—they all knew he was going to be gone several days—and he wouldn't have seen the notice, she thought. Someone had slipped it under the door from the hall. It read:

NOTICE

DUE TO SECURITY CONCERNS ONLY AUTHORIZED PERSON-
NEL WILL BE ALLOWED TO LEAVE THE BUILDING THIS WEEK-
END, AS OF 8 AM, SATURDAY MORNING EXCEPT FOR DESIG-
NATED EMERGENCIES. (SEE SKYTOWN MANUAL, PAGE 39
FOR DESIGNATED EMERGENCY GUIDELINES.) RESTRICTIONS
WILL BE LIFTED IN A FEW DAYS—PLEASE BE PATIENT.

THANK YOU FOR YOUR COOPERATION
SKYTOWN OFFICE OF SECURITY

"What the fuck!" Lenny burst out, when Deede showed it to him. "That is totally illegal! Hey—call that kid you met, with the lawyer mom."

"Jorny?" It would be a good excuse to call him

Jorny answered sleepily. "Whuh? My mom? She left for . . . go see my aunt for breakfast or something . . . s'pose-a be back later . . . why whussup?"

"Um check if you got a notice under your front door . . ."

He came back to the phone under a minute seconds later. "Yeah! Same notice! My mom left after eight, though and she hasn't come back. So it must be bullshit, they must've let her go. Maybe it's a hoax. Or . . ."

"We're gonna go to the bargain matinee over on Hollywood Boulevard . . . You wanta go? I mean—then we can see if they really are making people stay . . . "

A little over an hour later they were all dressed, meeting Jorny downstairs outside the elevators at the front lobby. They walked by potted plants toward the tinted glass of the front doors . . . and found the doors locked from inside.

"You kids didn't get the notice?"

They turned to see a smiling, personable, middle-aged man standing about thirty feet away. He wore a green suit-and-tie—maybe that was why his face had a vague greenish cast to it. Just a reflection off the green cloth. Behind him were two security guards in the peculiar uniforms.

"That notice is bullshit," Lenny said flatly. "Not legal."

"You look a little young to be a lawyer," said the man in the green suit mildly.

"Your face is sort of green," Jean said, staring at him.

But as she said it, his face seemed to shift to a more normal color. As if he'd just noticed and changed it somehow.

"Or not . . . " Jean mumbled.

The man ignored her. "My name is Arthur Koenig—I'm the building Supervisor. I'm pretty sure of the laws and rules and I assure you kids, you cannot leave the building except under designated emergency conditions . . ."

"And I'm pretty sure," Jorny said, snapping his skateboard up with his foot to catch it in his hand, "that's what they call 'false imprisonment'—it's a form of kidnap."

The security guards both had the odd translucent-blue helmets. They stood behind and to either side of Koenig—one of them, who might've been Filipino, stepped frowning toward Jorny. "That's the boy who was doing the skateboarding in the Mall—I saw him on the cameras. Boy—you give me that skateboard, that's contraband here!"

"Not a fucking chance, a-hole," Jorny said, making Jean squeal with laughter. "Come on," he said to Lenny, "—we'll go to my place and call around about this . . ."

"Building phone line's being worked on," said Koenig pleasantly. "Be down for a while. Building cable too."

"We've got cell phones, man," Lenny said, turning toward the elevators. "Come on you guys . . . "

As they went back to the elevators, Deede glanced over her shoulder, saw that Koenig was following, at a respectful distance—and while they were walking at an angle, the shortest way to the elevator, he seemed to be following a straight line—then he turned right, and she realized he was following the lines of the square sections of floor. And she saw something coming off his right heel—a thin red cord, or string, like a finely stretched out piece of flesh, that came from a hole in his shoe and went into the groove between the floor tiles . . .

A thread, stuck to his shoe, is all, she told herself. *It's not really a connection to something inside the floor.*

"That skateboard!" The blue-helmeted security guard yelled, following Jorny. "Leave it here! I'm confiscating it!"

But Koenig reached out, put his hand on the guard's arm. "Let him go. It doesn't matter now. Let him keep it for the moment."

Deede followed the others into the elevator. She didn't mention the red cord to them.

"Yes this is 911 emergency. May I have your name and address . . ."

Lenny gave his name and address and then said, "I'm calling because we're being held against our will by the weirdos in this building we live in. The manager, all these people—no one's allowed to leave the building! It's totally illegal!"

"Slow down, please," said the dispatcher, her voice crackling in the cell phone, phasing in and out of clarity. *"Who exactly is 'restraining' you?"*

The skepticism was rank in her voice.

"The building security people say we can't leave, no one can leave, there're hundreds of people who live here and we can't—"

"Was there a bomb scare?"

"I don't know, they didn't say so, they just said 'security concerns' . . ."

"The security at that building interfaces with the police department, if they're asking people not to leave it's probably so they can investigate something. Have they been . . . oh, violent or . . . ."

"No, not yet, but they . . . look, it's false imprisonment, it's . . . "

"They are security, we'll have someone call them—but they're probably doing this for your protection. It could be a Homeland Security drill—"

"Oh Jesus, forget it." He broke the connection and threw the cell phone so it bounced on the sofa cushion. "I can't believe it. They just assumed I was full of crap."

Jorny was on his own cell phone, listening. He frowned and hung up. "I can't get my mom to answer, or my aunt."

"Jorny . . ." said Deede thoughtfully, looking out the apartment's picture window at the smog-hazy sky. "You think maybe they stopped your mom—took her into custody 'cause she tried to leave?"

Jorny stared at her. "No way." He shot to his feet. "Come on, if you're coming. I'm gonna ask if she's at the security office . . ."

Deede looked at Lenny to see if he was coming but he was on the cell phone again, trying to call Dad. "I'm gonna call Dad . . . he's not picking up though . . . "

"Lenny—where's Jean?" Deede asked, looking around. It wasn't like Jean to be so quiet.

"Hm? She left. She said she's going to that coffee lounge where those kids hang out . . ."

"What kids?"

"I don't know. She started hanging with them yesterday sometime. She came back at three in the morning. I think she was, like, stoned . . ."

"What? I'm gonna go get her. And help Jorny . . ." She called this to Lenny as she followed Jorny out the door. Lenny waved her on.

ANOTHER NOTICE HAD been taped up on the wall next to the elevator call buttons.

NOTICE

ELEVATOR MOVEMENT HAS BEEN RESTRICTED TO THE UPPER SEVENTY FLOORS UNTIL FURTHER NOTICE. ELEVATOR WILL NOT DESCEND FROM THIS LEVEL.

THANK YOU FOR YOUR COOPERATION . . .

"What the fuck!" Jorny said, gaping at the notice.

"I wouldn't have put it that way," said a white haired older woman standing a few steps away; she had thick, horn rimmed glasses and a long blue dress. "But that's generally my feeling too . . ." She had her purse over her shoulder, as if she had planned to go out. "I was going to Farmers Market but . . . I guess not now . . . " The woman went back toward the doors to the apartment complex, shaking her head.

Jorny shook his head as the woman walked away. "Everyone just accepts it . . . "

"Security office is downstairs," Deede said. "We can't get to it on the elevators. But we could take the stairs . . . Only, I want to find my sister. But then she could be down there too . . ."

He was already starting toward the door to the stairwell, skateboard under his arm—you can't skateboard on carpet.

But the stairwell door was locked. "What about the fire laws and all that?" Jorny said, wondering aloud. He looked toward a fire alarm, as if thinking of tripping it. Deede hoped he wouldn't.

"Okay," he said, "let's go upstairs on the elevators to that lounge, see if we can find some way from there to go down. There must be a way—the security guards must be able to do it."

"I wanta get my brother to go with us . . ."

They went back to the apartment . . . and found the apartment door standing open.

Inside there was a lamp knocked over. And Lenny was gone. He'd left his cell phone where he'd thrown it and he was just . . . gone. She looked through all the rooms and called up and down the halls. No response except a Filipino man looked out a door briefly—then hastily shut it when Deede tried to ask him a question. They heard him lock it.

"I'm sure he's okay," Jorny said.

Deede looked reproachfully at him. "I didn't say he wasn't."

"You looked worried."

"I . . . I'm worried about Jean and . . . this whole weird thing. That's all. Lenny gets in a snit sometimes and goes off and says 'Screw everybody' and wanders away . . . gets somebody to buy him beer somewhere and he gets a little smashed and then he comes home. But leaving the door open that way . . . "

Jorny was on his cell again, trying to call his mom. He called his aunt, spoke to her for less than a minute in low tones—and hung up. "She never showed up. She was supposed to meet my aunt—and she never got there."

"It's too soon to call it a 'missing persons' thing . . . We could look for your mom in the building. And Jean."

"You want to try the lounge?" Jorny asked. She nodded and they went to the elevators and rode up toward the lounge. On the way he tried to call his mom on the cell phone again—and gave up. "Doesn't work at all now. Just static."

"There are places in the elevators for keys," Deede said, pointing at the key fixture under the floor tabs. "The security guards must have keys that let them go to restricted floors . . ."

That's when the moaning started up again, in the elevators above them—and below them too. As if the one down below were answering the one above. A moan from above, the ceiling shivering; an answering moan from below the elevator, the floor resonating.

Jorny looked at her quizzically, but saying nothing.

They got out at the coffee lounge, a big, comfortable cafeteria space spanning most of one side of the floor, with a coffee shop and a magazine stand. Both were closed. But there were kids there, about nine of them, five boys and four girls, middle-school like Jean, in a far corner, crowded together in a circle near the rest rooms. Deede hurried closer and found they were standing in a tight circle around Jean, circling, and each one pointing an index finger at her, one after the other, like they were doing "the wave", the fingers rippling out and pointing and dropping in the circle, and each one pointing said, "Take a hit."

"Take a hit . . ."

"Take a hit . . ."

"Take a hit . . ."

Like that, on and on around the circle, and when Deede and Jorny got there, Deede looked to see what Jean was taking a hit of, what drug or drink, but there was nothing there, no smoke, no smell, no pipe, no bottle, only the pointing fingers from the rapt, feral faces of the other kids, their eyes dilated, their lips parted, saying, "Take a hit, take a hit, take a hit . . ." And Jean was swaying in place, rocking back, staggering in reaction from each pointed finger, each 'take a hit', her eyes droopy, her mouth droopier, looking decidedly stoned. Was she play-acting?

"What're you guys hitting on?" Jorny said, laughing nervously.

All nine of them turned their heads at once to look at them. "You can't join," the tallest of the boy's said. An acned face, a spiky hair cut. "You can't. You're not trustworthy."

"We don't want to," Deede said. She waved urgently at her sister. "Come on, Jean—let's go. There's some weird stuff going on . . . We've gotta find Lenny."

Jean shook her head. She was swaying there, hyperventilating. "I'm not feeling any pain at all and I'm between the suns . . . I'm not going with you, I'm going to stay here . . ."

"Jean—come on!" Deede tried to push through the circle—and someone, she wasn't sure who, shoved her back, hard, so she fell painfully on her back. "Ow!"

"This way," said the big kid with the acned face, leading the group around Jean into the men's room, taking Jean with them. Both males and females filed, without a word or hesitation, into the men's bathroom.

Jorny helped Deede up. "That was fucked up," he said, shaking his head in disgust. "I'm going in there."

"I'm going too. I don't care if it's the men's room . . . They took my sister in there."

"She went on her own. But fuck it, let's go."

He led the way into the men's room—which was empty.

Not a soul in it. Jorny even opened the toilet booths. No one. There was only one entrance. There was no way out of the bathroom except the one door. There were no ventilation shafts. There was just the big, over-lit, blue-tiled and stainless steel bathroom and their own reflections in the mirrors over the metal sinks.

Jorny gaped around. "Okay, what uh . . ." His voice seemed emptied of life in the hard space of the room. "We were right in front of that door. They didn't get out past us . . ."

"Look!" She pointed at the mirrors. They were reflected in a continuum of mirrors, as when mirrors are turned to mirrors. Only, there was only one set of mirrors on one wall. There were no mirrors opposite—yet the reflection was the mirror-images-within-mirror-images telescoping that happened only if you turned mirrors to mirrors . . . And Deede saw hundreds of Deedes and Jornys stretched into infinity, each face looking lost and shocked and scared.

Lost and shocked and scared endlessly repeated, amplified . . .

And then she saw Jean in the mirrors, about thirty reflections down the glassy corridor, passing from one side to the other, glancing at her as she went past.

"Jean!" She turned from the mirror, looked the other way as if she might see Jean throwing the reflection there—but saw nothing but a row of toilet booths and urinals. She looked back at the mirrors. "Jorny—did you see someone in the mirrors beside us?"

Jorny's endlessly repeated reflections nodded to her. "Thought I saw your sister."

Feeling dizzily sick, Deede turned away. "It's like there's another room in this room . . ."

She noticed an outline, about the size of a door, on the farther wall between the urinals and the corner, etched with what looked like red putty along the joins in the tiles. She walked over to it. "There's a door-shaped mark here . . . but . . ." She touched the puttied areas. "This gunk is hard, here, like it's been this way a long time . . . It couldn't be where they got out . . ." Jorny came over and battered at the marked section of wall with his skateboard; they pushed at tiles but could find no way of opening the door, if it was a door. And when they touched it there was a sensation like a very weak electric shock—not enough to make them jump but just enough to give a feeling of discomfort. Electrical discomfort—and the hairs rising on the back of their necks. And chills too, sick chills like you get with the flu. "It's like a warning," she whispered. "Come on—I want out of here . . ."

Jorny nodded, seeming relieved, and they hurried out of the men's room, back into the lounge area—where they were entirely alone. "I've been thinking about some of the shops we saw," Deede said, as they walked over to the elevators and the door to the stairwell. The stairway door was locked. "And—it was like something was influencing stuff around here, something changing the way things . . . just the way they are." Should she tell him about the cord connecting Koenig's foot to the floor tiles?

"I know what you mean," Jorny said absently, as he fiddled with the door to the stairway. " Locked. But yo—*that* door's open . . ."

The door he was pointing at, between the stairs and elevator, was marked MAINTENANCE 47-17. It looked like it hadn't quite closed—like the doorframe was slightly crooked and it had stuck with the door just slightly ajar. You had to look close to see it was open.

She went to it and put her hand on the knob.

Jorny whispered, "Be careful . . . you could end up locking it."

She nodded and turned the knob while pulling hard on the door—and it swung open.

Inside, it was an ordinary closet, containing a new vacuum cleaner with the price tag still on it, and bottles of cleaning fluid, all of them full, and a push broom . . . and another smaller door, in the wall of the closet to the right. She bent over and turned the little chrome handle it had in place of a knob—and it opened onto the stairway. "Cool! Come on!"

Hunching down to fit, they went through—and found themselves in the main stairway. It was dimly lit, echoing with their every movement, a smell of rot overlaying the smell of new concrete and paint.

"Smells like road kill," Jorny said. He turned to look at the door they'd come through—which shut behind them into the wall, hardly showing a seam."Weird that they put that door there . . ."

"It's for *them,* to use—in case of emergency," Deede said. "And don't ask who *they* are—I don't know."

"Deede—there's something moving down there . . . and it doesn't seem like people."

She leaned over the balcony and looked. Something slipped across the space between flights about four stories down—a transparent dull-red flipper . . . feeler . . . tentacle? She couldn't get a clear visual picture of it from where she stood. But it was big—maybe three feet across and very long. Slipping by, like a giant boa constrictor. She could just make out that it was connected to something bigger, something that stretched down the open space between the descending flights of stairs . . .

And as it moved she heard the familiar moaning. That sobbing despair.

She stepped back and said, "Jorny—punch me in the shoulder."

"Really?"

"Yeah. I'm pretty sure I'm not dreaming. But only pretty sure. So go ahead and—ow!"

"You said to! Okay—do me now. Right there. Stick out your knuckle so it—shit!"

"So what do you think?" he asked, rubbing his shoulder, wincing. "Damn you hit hard for a girl."

"That's sexist. And I think we're awake. We have to decide."

He surprised her by suddenly sitting down on the steps, and taking a cigarette out of his shirt pocket. "I've been trying not to smoke . . . Promised my mom I'd give it up . . ." He took a wooden match out with the cigarette and flicked it alight on his skateboard— Deede thought it was an admirably cool thing to do. He lit the cigarette, and puffed. "But right now I don't care what my mom thinks about cigarettes."

"So what're we gonna *do?*" She was thinking of going back to the apartment again and seeing if Lenny had come home. She'd made excuses for him but under the circumstances she thought he'd have left her a note or something if he'd left . . . voluntarily.

Don't think about Lenny, too, she thought, sitting on a step a little below Jorny. *One person at a time. Get Jean. She's younger. He's older and he can take care of himself.*

Jorny was blowing smoke rings, and poking at them with his finger, at the same time absentmindedly running his skateboard back and forth on its wheels with one foot. "One time two or three years ago," he said, his voice a dreamy monotone, "when my Dad was still living with us, I was worried about where he was all day. See, he was a photographer, and he worked at home. So he was usually there. But one summer he just started being gone all day and there was a lot of . . . I dunno, him and my mom were arguing all the time about little things. About bullshit. Like there was something else . . . but they weren't saying. I was feeling like he was doing something—and it was gonna make them break up. So anyway I followed him. I didn't even think about why. I borrowed my sister's car—she's moved out now—and I followed him . . . and he didn't notice I was following. He was really into where he was going, man. And he went to a motel. I should've left it there but I saw which room he went to and after awhile I went up and they had the windows curtained but there was a place where if you bent over and looked, at the corner, you could see in . . ."

"Oh Christ, Jorny."

"Yeah. And he was doin' it with some woman I never saw before. They had champagne and stuff. Later on he left my mom for her . . ."

"That must've been . . ." She couldn't keep from making a face.

"It was. I wished I hadn't gone, wished I hadn't looked. It's different, really seeing it. Worse. He was still married to my mom, and . . . Anyway, since then, I figure there's things I don't want to find out about. And if we go looking down there, we'll see things we don't want to know about." He flicked his cigarette away half smoked. "And—I'm not scared. Not that much. I just . . . don't want to see anything else that I don't want to know about . . . especially since my mom might be any one of a million places."

"But . . ." Deede heard the moaning again from below. She just wanted to go back to the apartment, and wait there with the doors locked. But that hadn't helped Lenny . . .

"You okay?" Jorny asked, looking at her closely.

"I'm just worried about my brother. And Jean. I'd like to go back to the apartment but . . . " She sighed. "No one did anything about my Mom being killed. No one . . . no one *pursued it*." Deede felt her hands fisting—and she couldn't prevent it. "They said it was suicide or an accident. But there was a man who scares people—he was following some girls in the neighborhood, and there's rumors about him—and he was there that day, he was seen on the same trails, and then there was the dream. The dream seemed almost as real as . . . as today is."

"What dream?"

"It was one of those dreams you get over and over—but the first time I got it was the morning my mom was killed. She was out jogging early and I was still asleep. Our house was out on the edge of town, by this sorta woodsy area with an old quarry. And in my dream I saw her jogging along the edge of the old quarry, where there's this little pond, jogging like she always does on the trails there, and I saw Gunnar Johansen watching her and he looks like he's been up all night, he's sort of swaying there, and then he starts following her and then starts running and she turns and sees him and stumbles and falls on the trail and then he throws himself on her and she struggles and hits him, and he laughs and he knocks her out and then he . . . plays with her body kind of, with one hand on her throat, squeezing and the other hand in his pants, and then she kicks him in the groin and he gives a yell and picks her up and throws her down in the quarry, and she falls face down and she hits hard in that shallow water down there. And . . . bubbles come up . . . *And that's exactly how they found her.*"

"They found her like that, in that exact place? And you hadn't heard about it yet?"

Deede nodded. "I tried to tell them but they said dreams don't count in court. And I had that dream again, I had it a lot . . . I was afraid to go to sleep for a long time . . ."

She put her face in her hands and he came and sat close beside her, not touching her, just being there with her. She appreciated that—the sensitivity of it. Him not trying to put his arm around her. But coming to be right there with her.

A few seconds more, and then a moan and a long, drawn-out scraping sound came from below. Deede decided she had to make up her mind. "I have to go down there. No one found out about my mom— I'm going to find out about Jean. You can go back."

He cleared his throat. Then muttered, "Fuck it." Nodded to himself. He stood up and offered his hand to help her up. "Okay. Come on."

They descended. Jorny carried his skateboard for two turns, and then decided to do a jump, as if some kind of oblique statement of defiance of whatever waited below, and he jumped a whole flight—and the skateboard splintered under him when he came down, snapped in half, and he ended up sliding on his ass. "Shit god*damn*it!"

She helped him up this time. "Sorry about your skateboard. You going to save the trucks?"

"I don't know. I guess . . . ." Disgustedly carrying half a skateboard in each hand, he led the way downward—and they stopped another floor lower, to peer over the concrete rail . . .

Something slipped scrapily by thirtyfive feet below, something rubbery and transparently pinkish-red . . . it made her think of the really big pieces of kelp you saw at the shore, thickly transparent like that, but redder, bigger—and this one had someone swallowed up in it: one of the kids, a young boy she'd seen in the lounge. The boy was trapped inside the supple tree-trunk-thick flexible tube, trapped alive, squeezed but living, slightly moving, eyes darting this way and that, hands pressed by the constriction against his chest . . . and moaning, making the despairing moan they'd been hearing, somehow louder than it should be, as if the thing that held him was triumphantly amplifying his moan.

"You *see* that?" Jorny whispered.

She nodded. "One of those kids . . . who was with Jean . . . in a . . . I don't know what it is . . . " And then it moaned again, so loudly the cry echoed up the shaft of the stairway.

It's calling to us, she thought. *It's luring us . . . Saying "Come and save him, come and save them all . . . Come down and see . . ."*

And the slithering thing, connected to something below, itself descended—or, more rightly, was pulled down—ahead of her and Jorny, themselves going down and down, the light diminishing ever so subtly toward the lower floors. The transparent red tubule drew itself down, like an eel drawing itself into a hole, pulling the boy— and others, too, squirming trapped human figures glimpsed for a moment enveloped in other thick tendrils, moaning, down and down. Did she see Jean, caught down there? Deede wasn't sure. But she felt that sick flu-chills feeling again and she wanted to turn and run up the stairs and—

"I saw my mom down there," Jorny said, his voice cracking. Inside that thing. "Now I've really got to go."

Deede wanted to run. *Don't let them scare you into not going.* She almost thought she heard her mom's voice saying it. Almost. *He needs someone to go with him. And Jean . . . don't forget Jean . . .*

"Okay," Deede made herself say. She started down, following the slithering descender . . . following the moans and the moaners, following the trapped squirmers . . .

Down and down . . . till they got to the dimly lit bottom floor. And to the basement door.

Deede had expected to find the squirming thing at the bottom but it wasn't there, though there was a thin coating of slushy red material on the floor, like something you'd squeeze from kelp but the color of diluted blood . . . surrounding the closed basement door. The thing had gone through the door—and closed it behind . . .

She half hoped the door was locked. Jorny tried it—and it opened. He stood in the doorway, outlined in green light. She looked over his shoulder . . .

About forty feet by thirty, the basement room contained elevator machinery— humming hump shaped units to the right—and cryptic pipes along the ceiling. But what drew their eyes was a jagged hole in the floor, right in front of the door, about seven feet across, edged with red slush—the green light came from down there. From within the hole.

She followed Jorny into the room, and—Deede taking a deep breath—they both bent over to look . . .

Below was a chamber that could never have been made by the builders of Skytown. It was a good-sized chamber, very old. Its stones were rough-carved, great blocks set by some ancient hand in primeval times, way pre-Columbian. Grooves had been carved in the stone floor by someone with malign and fixed intentions. They were flecked with a red-brown crust that had taken many years to accumulate.

"It looks to me like they dug this building in real deep," Jorny said, in a raw whisper. "I heard they dug the foundation down deeper than any other building in Los Angeles. And . . . I guess there was something down there, buried way down, they didn't know about . . ."

She nodded. He looked at the fragments of skateboard in his hand and tossed them aside, with a clatter, then got down on his knees, and lowered himself . . .

"Jorny!"

. . . through the hole in the floor; into the green light; into the ancient chamber.

"Oh fuck," she groaned. But she lowered herself and dropped too, about eight feet to a stinging impact on the balls of her feet.

Jorny caught and steadied her as she was about to tip over and they looked around. "Some kind of temple!" he whispered. "And that *thing . . .*"

The grooves cut into the naked bedrock of the floor, each about an inch deep, were part of a spiral pattern that filled the floor of the entire room—and the gouged pattern was reproduced on the ceiling, as was the dais, the spirals, above and below, converging on the circular dais and the translucent thing that dwelt at the room's center. Spiral patterns on ceiling, spiral patterns on floor; while between them a thing hung suspended in space—suspended between the space of the room and the space between worlds: an enormous, gelatinous, transparent sphere containing a restless collection of smaller iridescent spheres, like a clutch of giant fish eggs—were they smaller than the encompassing sphere, or were they of indefinite size, both as small as bushels and as big as planets? The iridescent spheres shifted restlessly inside the enveloping globe, changing position, as if each sphere was jostling to get closer to the outside of the container, the whole emanating a murky-green light that tinted the stone walls to jade; the light was a radiance of intelligence, a malign intelligence—malevolent relative to the needs and hopes of human beings—and somehow Deede knew that it was aware of her and wanted to consume her mind with its own. She could feel its mind pressing on the edges of her consciousness, pushing, leaning, feeling like a glacier that might become an avalanche.

And then as her eyes adjusted she saw what the green glow had hidden, till now its extensions, green but filled with diluted blood, stolen blood, the tentacles stretching from the sphere-of-spheres like stems and leaves from a tuber, but prehensile, mobile, stretching out from thick tubules to gradually narrow, to thin, very thin tubes that stretched out red cords, thin as fishing line and thinner yet, stretching up into the grooves on the ceiling, and from there into minute cracks, and, she knew—with an intuitive certainty—up high into the building, where they reached into people, taking control of them one by one, starting with those who'd been here longest, Skytown's employees. And some of the tentacular extensions had swallowed up whole people, drawn them down and into itself, so that they squirmed in the tubes, dozens of them, shifting in and out of visibility . . . She saw Koenig, drawn down in one of the transparent tentacles—impossible for him to fit in it, but he did, because the suctioning thing shaped space as it chose to. And he was sucked through it, his face contorted with a terrible realization . . . blood squeezing in little spurts from his eyes, his mouth, his nose . . . And then he was jetted back up the tentacle, becoming smaller as he went, transformed into transmissible form that could be reconstituted up above . . . And all this she glimpsed in less than two seconds.

Visibility was a paradox, a conundrum—the tentacles were visible as a whole but not individually, when you tried to look at one it shifted out of view, and you just glimpsed the people trapped inside it before it was gone . . . And the moaning filled the room, only she and Jorny heard it more in their minds than in their ears . . .

"It's like this thing is here but it's not *completely* here," Jorny said, wonderingly. "But it's like it's getting to be more and *more* here as it . . . as it . . . I don't know . . . "

"The people look pale, some of them like they're dying or dead," Deede said, feeling dreamlike and sick at once. "I can't see them clear enough to be sure but it's like they're being drained real slow . . . "

Jorny said, "It's not coming at us . . . Why?"

"It's waiting," she said. It was more than guessing—it felt right. The answers were in the air itself, somehow; they throbbed within the murky green light. Her fast-seeing drew them quickly into her. "It wants us to come to it. It's lured the others in some way—we saw how it lured Jean. Everyone's been lured. It wants you to submit to it . . ."

"Look—there's something on the other side . . ."

"Jorny? How are we going to get out of here? There's no way back up . . ."

"There has to be another entrance."

"Okay—fine." She felt increasingly reckless—she felt so hopeless now that it felt like little was left to lose. She led the way herself—she was tired of following males from one place to the next—and edged around the boiling, suspended sphere-of-spheres, getting closer to it and learning more about it with proximity . . .

It was only partly in their space; it was in many spaces at once. There was only one being: each sphere they were seeing was another manifestation of that same being, one for each world it stretched into. It slowly twisted things in those worlds to fit its liking. And they were only seeing the outside of it, like the dorsal fin of a shark on the surface of the water. It had many names, in many places; many varieties of appearance, many approaches to getting what it wanted. Its true form—

"Look!" Jorny said, pointing past her at a jagged hole in the floor—a hole that was the *exact duplicate* of the one in the ceiling they'd dropped through on the other side of the room. Its edges were shaped precisely the same . . .

The tentacular probes of the sphere-of-spheres teased at them as they passed, almost caressing them, offering visions of glory, preludes of unimaginable pleasure . . .

But the creature frightened her, more than it attracted her—it was somehow scarier for its enticements. It was as malevolent to her as a wolf spider would be to a crawling fly. Or as a Venus fly trap would be . . .

"Jesus!" Jorny blurted, hastening away from the thing. "I almost . . . never mind, just get over here!"

She wanted to follow him. But it was hard to move—she was caught up in its whispering, its radiance of promise, and the undertone of warning. *Run from me and I'll be forced to grab you!* Jorny ran to her and grabbed her wrist, pulled her away from it. She felt weak, for a moment, drained, staggering . . .

He knelt by the hole in the floor and dropped through. "Come on, Deede!"

After a moment she followed—almost falling through the hole in her weariness. He half caught her, as before—and she felt her strength returning, away from the sphere-within-spheres.

"Look—we're on the ceiling!" Jorny burst out. "Aren't we?"

They were on a floor—with pipes snaking around their knees—but above them was the machinery of the elevators, affixed upside down on . . . the ceiling. Or—on the floor that was now their ceiling. There was a door, identical to the one they'd come through to find the hole into the temple room above—but it went from a couple feet above the floor to the ceiling. The knob seemed in the wrong place. The door was related to the ceiling the way any other door would be related to the floor—it was upside down. Jorny went to it and jumped to the knob, twisted it, pulled the door open, and scrambled through, turned to help her climb up . . . and then he yelped as he floated upward . . . They both floated up, tumbling in the air . . .

They were floating in space for a moment, turning end over end, in the bottom level of the stairway they'd come down. It was the very same stairway, with the occasional cabinet with fire extinguishers and floor-numbers painted on the walls—only, it stretched down below them, instead of up above them. They instinctively reached for a railing, Jorny caught it . . .

A nauseating twist, a feeling of turning inside-out and back right-side out again, and then they were standing on the stairway, which once more was zig-zagging upward, above them. Only—it couldn't be. It had been below the temple room. Or had they been somehow transported back above?

"What the fuck . . ." Jorny said, pale, fumbling for a cigarette with shaking hands. "Damn, out of smokes . . ."

Deede stared. Someone was up above—crawling down the walls toward them. Two someones. A man and woman. Coming down the walls that contained the stairs, crawling like bugs, upside down relative to Deede . . .

"Jorny—look!"

"I see 'em."

"Jorny I don't know how much more I can . . ."

"I'm not feeling so good either. But you know what? We're surviving. Maybe for a reason, right? Hey—they look . . . familiar."

They were about thirty-five, a man and woman dressed in what Deede could only describe, to herself, as dark, clinging rags. The man had a backpack of some kind tightly fixed to his shoulders. They approached, crawling down the wall, and Deede and Jorny backed away, trying to decide where to run to—up the stairs past them? And then the strangers stopped, looking at them upside down, the woman's hair drooping down toward them . . .

And the woman spoke. "Jorny—it's us, me and you as kids!"

"What—from earlier, somehow? But we never discovered the temple as kids!" said the man. "We just found out about it last year!"

"They're us in one of the other worlds—younger versions . . . and they found their way here! Just like in my dream, Jorny! I told you, there was something here—something that would help us!"

Jorny—the younger Jorny standing at the younger Deede's side— shook his head, stunned. "It's us—in, like, the future or . . ."

Deede nodded. "Would you guys come down and . . . stand on the level we're on? Or can you?"

"We can," the older Deede said. "The rules shifted when Yog-Sothoth altered the world, and gravity moves eccentrically."

She crept toward the floor, put one foot on it, then sidled around on the wall like a gecko, finally getting both feet on the floor and standing to face them; the older Jorny did the same. His blond hair was cut short and beginning to recede, his face a trifle lined, but he was still recognizably Jorny.

Deede found she was staring at the older version of herself in fascination. She seemed more proportional, more confident, if a bit grim—there were lines around her eyes, but it looked good on her. But the whole thing was disorienting—was something she didn't really want to see. It made her want to hide, seeing herself, just as much as seeing the thing in the temple.

"Don't look so scared, kid," the older Jorny said, smiling sadly at her.

Deede scowled defiantly at him. "Just—explain what the hell you are. I don't think you're us."

"We're *another* you," the older Deede said. "And we're connected with you. We all extend from the ideal you, in the world of ideas. But this sure isn't that world . . . Time is a bit in advance in our world, I guess, from yours, for one thing . . ."

"Come on with us," the older Jorny said. "We'll show you. Then we can figure out if there's a way we can work together . . . against *him*."

They turned and climbed the stairs—after a moment's hesitation, Jorny and Deede followed. They went up eleven flights, past battered, rusting doors. "Your building," the older Deede said, "extends downward from ours—but to you it will seem upward. Ours is downward from yours. They're mirrored, but not opposites—just variants at opposite poles from one another. Me and Jorny found out that the primary impulses were coming from the basement of our building so we cut the hole in the sub-basement floor—that's the ceiling of the other room."

"I think it's the other way around," said the older Jorny.

"I don't know, it depends. Anyway the Great Appetite—that's what we call it, though some call it Yog-Sothoth—he reaches out through the many worlds through that same temple . . . and he changes what he comes to, so the beings on that world become all appetite, all desire, and nothing else—so he can feed on low desires, through beings on those worlds."

"You say *he?*" the younger Jorny asked. "Not *it?*"

"Right—he has gender. But little else we can comprehend . . . Once he's changed a world enough, he can eat what you eat, feel what you feel. Some he will already have changed, in your world—the rest he will change later. He changed our world about eighteen years ago. We've resisted—but most people don't. They get changed—the Great Appetite removes whatever there is in them that checks appetites and desires and impulses. Any kind of strong controlling intelligence, he takes it out. Makes psychopaths of some people, and zombies of just *feeding,* of different kinds, of others—"

"Like Gunnar Johansen!" Deede burst out.

The older Deede stopped on a landing and turned to look at her. "Yes," she said gravely. "He killed my mother too—before the Great Appetite took over. Like him. He was already under Yog-Sothoth's control . . . without knowing it."

She looked like she wanted to embrace the younger Deede—but Deede was afraid of her, and took a step back.

The older Deede shrugged and turned to follow the older Jorny through a doorway—the door at this landing had been wrenched aside, was leaning, crumpled against the wall, hinges snapped. They passed through and found themselves in the lower mezzanine lounge, exactly like the one they'd left—sterile in its furnishings and design.

They walked over to the window and stared out at the world—the transformed world.

There was no sky. Instead there was a ceiling, high up, just above the tallest building, that stretched to the horizon. And the ceiling was covered with images, enticing objects and enticing bodies flashing by and intermingling and overlapping. She saw an advertisement for BLENDER—and the indeterminate segments of fleshy material that she'd seen in the Skymall shop window; she saw an ad for something called BRAIN BLANKER, "for really changing your child—remake it exactly as you please!"; she saw an ad for INTER-REACTIVES, INC., the sea urchin helmets she'd seen in Skymall; she saw an ad that said simply, WE ELIMINATE PROBLEM NEIGHBORS—GOVERNMENT CERTIFIED AGAINST RETALIATION; another ad asked, WANT A PET THAT REALLY SCREAMS? ORDER 'LITTLE PEOPLE'! and there was an image of a frightened, dwarf sized semi-human figure lifted by its neck from a "home-grow vat"—by a grinning man holding a two by four with nails sticking out of it, in his other hand; there was an ad for LATEST FACE—THE TOP TEN FACES, WITH NEAR-INSTANTANEOUS TRANSFER GUARANTEED, AT REDUCED PRICES. The images were sometimes blurred by great gray clouds of smog—clouds pierced by people who flew through them, people mechanically enhanced to fly, their bodies pierced by pistons and wires, shrieking as they went; other people crawled up and down the sides of buildings like bugs; clusters of junk material floated by, clouds of metal with people clinging to them, wailing and tittering and fornicating; unspeakably fat people drifted by on flying cushions tricked out with pincers and mechanical hands; emaciated people drifted by too: their heads penetrated by wires, their faces twitching with pleasures they no longer really felt, their vehicles suddenly spurting with speed to deliberately crash headlong into other vehicles, going down in spinning, flaming wreckage to join the accumulation of twisted metal and weather-beaten trash that filled the streets hundreds of feet deep, black with insects . . .

"That's pretty much the way the whole world looks," the older Jorny said, his voice cracking. "There are attempts at changing it, in places—

but the influence of the Great Appetite is too strong . . . unless you have with you . . ." He turned to his younger self. "What you are supposed to have?"

"What? What do you mean?"

"You have something I need . . ." The older Jorny took off his backpack, and took out a boxy device that had speakers at both ends, like a boombox, but no place to put in CDs or an iPod—only a small recess at one end. "You see? It goes here . . ."

"You're expecting something from us?" Deede asked, confused.

The older Deede looked out the window. "When we found the locus of the Great Appetite, in the temple, we found I had a kind of . . . a sensitivity to it. I could pick up information from it. By something I think of as 'looking fast'."

Deede nodded. "I'm like that too."

"I saw you, then—saw that you were coming and that you carried something the Great Appetite is afraid of. A many-voiced note of refusal."

"A what?"

"Do you have a recording device with you?"

Jorny stared at them . . . then slowly reached into his pocket and drew out his iPod.

The older Deede frowned. "That's not what I saw . . ."

"It's inside it!" the older Jorny said. He snatched the iPod from Jorny's hand and—ignoring Jorny's protests—smashed it again and again on the metal window frame till it burst open.

"There it is!" The older Deede shouted, pointing at the wrecked device. "That thing!"

"It's a microdrive!" the older Jorny said excitedly. "We use them to make sounds too—but we put them directly in our sound machines. We have only sounds that have been appropriated, co-opted by the Great Appetite. Now . . ."

"This better work," Jorny grumbled.

The older Jorny plucked the microdrive from the wreckage and pressed it in the recess of the alternate boombox. It fit neatly in place. He hit a switch and the box boomed out—with a roaring cacophony.

"Shit!" the younger Jorny yelled, reaching over to snap the boombox off again. "It's not picking out any one song—it sounds like it's playing all of them at once! There's more than a thousand songs in there!"

"So that's it . . ." the older Deede murmured. She looked at the older Jorny. "Remember? 'A thousand voices will silence his roar!' That's what I heard from the green light—it tried to cover it up but I saw it! *It's supposed to play them all at once!*"

A vast moaning shook the floor then, and the ceiling shed bits of plaster. It was coming from the elevator banks . . .

"We've frightened *him* with the sound—for just that one second!" the older Jorny said. "He's coming for us!" He handed the younger Jorny the boombox. "Play it as loud as possible in the temple! Go on! It'll make everything possible! We'll draw it off!"

They he looked at the older Deede—and, to Deede's exquisite discomfort, the two adults kissed, kissed hugely and wetly. She looked away—so did Jorny. Then the older Jorny and Deede turned and ran past the elevator. The elevator doors opened and something red and green and endlessly hungry reached from it, stretching after them . . .

"Oh no . . ." Deede said.

"We'd better try this . . ." Jorny whispered. And they turned and pounded down the stairs.

In minutes they'd reached the upside down basement room, and dropped through the ceiling, coming up, spinning in space with momentary weightlessness, in the temple room . . .

Deede found herself on the floor, with the sphere-within-spheres, the Great Appetite, Yog-Sothoth looming over her, reaching for her, making its unspeakable offering . . . .

And then Jorny reached to switch on the boombox, at full volume . . . .

"Jorny!" His hand hesitated over the boombox and he looked up to see his mother, trapped in one of the transparent tentacles, compressed and terrified. *"Jorny—wait! I don't know what you're doing but it'll punish me if you do it! Stop!"*

He drew his hand back. Deede knew she had to trigger the box—but she was afraid of what she'd see if she reached for it. This thing had the power to hurt, to punish, beyond time. It could reach into your soul. It was evil times evil. It was the dark side of pleasure and it was the green light of pain. It wasn't something to defy . . .

But she remembered what the world looked like, after the Great Appetite was done . . .

"I don't know what to do," Jorny said, covering his eyes with his hands.

Deede knew what to do. She reached for the box . . .

"Deede—don't!" Jean's voice.

"Deede, wait!" Lenny's voice. "Look—we're here—you can't—"

Deede refused to look. In defiance, she stabbed her fingers down on the PLAY button . . .

The sound that came out of the box was the joined booming of a thousand songs at once, the sort that Jorny would choose—a thousand songs of angst, rebellion, uncertainty, insistence, fury. Everything but a certain kind of surrender. They all had one note in common: a sound that was a refusal to be anything untrue.

One great thousand-faceted roaring white noise, black noise, every noise of the sonic spectrum . . . roaring. Roaring refusal—roaring defiance!

And the sphere-of-spheres withdrew into itself, dropping everything it touched in the two worlds connected by the temple, retreating to other planes, where it could find surcease from the amplified, crystalized sound of refusal to surrender to its dominance.

The temple shuddered, and the spiral grooves seemed to spin for a moment, like an old fashioned record—and then the ceiling tumbled down . . . and smashed the boombox. Came tumbling toward Jorny—

Deede pulled Jorny aside, at the last split-second, and the great ceiling stones tumbled down in the center of the room, leaving a crust of chamber, the edges . . . and a pile of stone that blocked off the hole into the other Skytown, and rose in a cluttered knob into the basement room above . . .

"You did it?" Jorny asked, coughing with dust.

"I had to. It couldn't have been worse for anyone . . ."

He nodded and they climbed, together, silently, through the dust cloud, and up into the basement room. They found their way to the stairways . . . where they found dozens of people, clothes soaked and skin wet with blood. They were weak—but most were alive, lying one to a step, up and up and up the stairs, feebly calling for help. Among them, they found Lenny and Jean and Jorny's mother. They couldn't remember where they'd been. No one could quite remember it.

Not all of them were alive. Koenig was there—crushed almost flat.

The elevators were no longer blocked, the security guards were gone—except the ones that were dead. The front doors were wide open. When the ambulances came, no one could completely explain where they'd been or what had happened to them. Some internal disaster was inferred, and explanations were generated. Deede's father returned that night, summoned to deal with the emergency, and they moved out, to a hotel on the other side of town . . . the same one that Jorny and his mother were staying at . . . He asked remarkably few questions.

Lenny and Jean spent most of the second day away from the Skymall in the hospital, getting transfusions, getting tested—they seemed dazed, slowly coming back to themselves.

It was just three days later that Deede set out for Portland, to visit her cousin. "Just need to get away from this town, Dad," she said. "Just for a few days. I want to go to Mom's grave . . . "

He simply nodded, and helped her pack—and he put her on a plane.

DEEDE HAD TO traipse the trail by the old quarry for three days before Johansen showed up. She'd known he was watching, somewhere out of sight; she let him see her go there, every night—but he'd been cautious. Still, since she was wearing as little as she could get away with, finally he couldn't resist.

And that night he followed her along the trail under the moonlight . . .

She went to the precipice, where her mother had taken her fatal plunge. She waited there for Johansen, humming a song to herself. No particular song—bits of many songs, really.

Johansen came up behind her, chuckling to himself.

She turned to face him, feeling like she was made of steel. "No one's here," she said. "I'm sure you checked that out. And you can see I'm not wired. Not wearing enough to cover up a wire. You may as well say it. You killed her. You want to kill me."

"Sure," Johansen said. His hair was a jagged halo in the moonlight; his teeth seemed white in a face gone dark because the light was behind him. His eyes were two dark holes. "Why shouldn't I kill the little slut as well as mama slut?"

"I don't think you can, though," she said calmly. "You know what? I used to be afraid of you. But I'm not now. *I'm not afraid anymore!* You're small time. *I* stopped what made you. I can stop you easily—you're so very small, in comparison, Johansen, to the Great Appetite itself."

"You're babbling, kid."

"Yeah? Then shut me up. If you can. I don't think you can, you limp dicked jerk. You're nothing!"

His face contorted at that, and he rushed her—and she moved easily aside, drawing the razor-sharp buck-knife she'd hidden in her belt, under her blouse in back. Then his ankle struck the fishing line she'd stretched (that made her think of the fine tube stretching from Yog-Sothoth), the line taut and down low between the roots, over the little peninsular jut of the cliff. And he stumbled and plunged, headlong, into the quarry, just as she'd known he would. She wouldn't need the back-up knife, after all, she decided, pleased, as she watched him fall wailing into the shallow water, to break on the jagged rocks she'd arranged down there.

He lay face down in the shallow water on the rough-edged stones, struggling, calling hoarsely for help, his neck broken, unable to lift his head but a few inches . . . finally sagging down into the water. Drowning.

Smiling, she watched him die.

Then she stretched, and waved cheerfully at the moon. She cut the fishing wire, put it in her pocket, tossed the knife into the quarry, and, humming a thousand songs, trotted back along the trail to the street. When she got to the sidewalk, she called first her dad, then Jorny on her cellphone, said she'd be coming back soon.

And then she caught a bus to the cemetery to have a talk with Mom.

SKEETER JUNKIE

———

IT STRUCK HIM, then, and powerfully. How consummate, how exquisite: A mosquito.

Look at the thing. No fraction of it wasted or distracted; more streamlined than any fighter jet, more elegant, for Hector Ansia's taste, than any sports car; in that moment, sexier—and skinnier—than any fashion model. A mosquito.

Hector was happily watching the mosquito penetrate the skin of his right arm.

He was in his El Paso studio apartment, wearing only his threadbare Fruit of the Loom briefs because the autumn night was hot and sticky. The place was empty except for a few books and busted coffee table and sofa, the only things he hadn't been able to sell. But as soon as he'd slammed the heroin, the rat-hole apartment had transformed into a palace bedroom, his dirty sofa into new silk cushions, the heavy, polluted air became the zephyrs of Eden, laced with incense. It wasn't that he hallucinated things that weren't there; but what was there he had recast into a heroin-polished dimension of excellence. As he'd taken his shot, he'd looked out the windows at the refineries that studded the periphery of El Paso, through the lens of heroin transformed into Disney castles, their burn-off flames the torches of some charming medieval festival.

He'd just risen out of his nod, like a balloon released under heavy water, ascending from a zone of sweet weight to a place of delicious buoyancy, and he'd only now opened his eyes, and the first thing he saw was the length of his arm over the side of the old velvet sofa. The veins were distended because of the pressure on the underside of his arm, and halfway between his elbow and his hand was the mosquito, pushing its organic needle through the greasy raiment of his epidermis . . .

It was so fine.

He hoped the mosquito could feel the sun of benevolence that pulsed in him. The china white was good, especially because he'd had a long and cruel sickness before finding it, and he'd been maybe halfway to clean again, so his tolerance was down, and that made it so much better to hit the smack in, to fold it into himself.

Stoned, he could feel his mama's hands on him. He was three years old, and she was washing his back as he sat in a warm bath, and sometimes she would kiss the top of his head. He could feel it now. That's what heroin gave him back.

She hadn't touched him after his fourth birthday, when her new boyfriend had come in fucked up on reds and wine, and the boyfriend had kicked Mama in the head and called her a whore, and the kick broke something in her brain, and after that she just looked at him blank when he cried . . . Just looked at him . . .

Heroin took him back, before his fourth birthday. Sometimes all the way back.

Look at that skeeter, now. Made Hector want to fuck, looking at it.

The mosquito was fucking his arm, wasn't it? Sure it was. Working that thing in. A proboscis, what it was called.

He could feel a thudding from somewhere. After a long moment he was sure the thudding wasn't his pulse; it was the radio downstairs. Lulu, listening to the radio.

Lulu had red-blond hair, cut something like the style of English girls from the old Beatles movies, its points near her cheeks curled to aim at her full lips. She had wide hips and round arms and hazel eyes. He'd talked to her in the hall and she'd been kind of pityingly friendly, enough to pass the time for maybe a minute, but she wouldn't go out with him, or even come in for coffee. Because she knew he was a junkie. Everyone on Selby Avenue knew a junkie when they saw one. He could tell her about his Liberal Arts B.A., but it wouldn't matter: he'd still be just a junkie to her. No use trying to explain a degree didn't get you a life anymore, there wasn't any work anyway. You might as well draw your SSI and sell your food stamps; you might as well be a junkie.

Lulu probably figured if she got involved with Hector, he'd steal her money, and maybe give her AIDS. She was wrong about the AIDS—he never ever shared needles—but she was right he'd steal her money, of course. The only reason he hadn't broken into her place was because he knew she'd never leave any cash there, or anything valuable, not living downstairs from a junkie. He'd never get even a ten dollar bag out of that crappy little radio he'd seen through the open door. Nothing much in there. Posters of Chagall, a framed photo of Sting, succulents overflowing clay pots shaped like burros and turtles.

She was succulent; he wanted her almost as much as her paycheck.

He watched the mosquito.

If he lifted his arm up, would the mosquito stop drinking? He hoped not. He could feel a faint ghost of a pinch, a sensation he saw in his mind's eye as a rose bud opening, and opening, and opening, more than any rose ever had petals.

Careful. He swung his feet on the floor, without moving his arm. The mosquito didn't stir. Then he lifted the arm up, very, very slowly, inch by inch, so as not to disturb the mosquito. It kept right on drinking.

With exquisite languor, Hector stood up straight, keeping the arm motionless except for the slow, slow act of standing. Then—walking very carefully, because the dope made the floor feel like a trampoline— he went to the bookshelf. Easing his right hand onto the edge of a shelf to keep the arm steady, he ran his left over the dusty tops of the old encyclopedia set. He was glad no one had bought it, now.

The lettering on the book-backs oozed one word onto the next. He was pretty loaded. It was good stuff. He forced his eyes to focus, and then pulled the *M* book out.

Moving just as slowly, his right arm ramrod stiff, so as not to disturb his beloved—the communion pinch, his precious guest—he returned to the sofa. He sat down, his right arm propped on the arm of the sofa, his left hand riffling pages.

Mosquito . . .

(There was another shot ready on the coffee table. Not yet, pendajo. Make it last).

. . . the female mosquito punctures the skin with equipment contained in a proboscis, comprised of six elongated stylets. One stylet is an inverted trough; the rest are slender mandibles, maxillae, and a stylet for

the injection of mosquito saliva. These latter close the trough to make a rough tube. After insertion, the tube arches so that the tip can probe for blood about half a millimeter beneath the epidermal surface . . . Two of the stylets are serrated and saw through the tissue for the others. If a pool of blood forms in a pocket of laceration the mosquito ceases movement and sucks the blood with two pumps located in her head . . .

Mosquito saliva injected while probing prevents blood clotting and creates the itching and swelling accompanying a bite . . .

Hector soaked up a pool of words here, a puddle there, and the color pictures—how wonderfully they put together encyclopedias!—and then he let the volume slide off his lap onto the floor, and found the other syringe with his left hand, and, hardly having to look, with the ambidexterity of a needle freak, shot himself up in a vein he was saving in his right thigh. All the time not disturbing the mosquito.

He knew it was too big a load. But he'd had that long, long Jones, like mirrors reflecting into one another. It should be all right. He stretched out on the sofa again as the hit melted through him, and focused on the mosquito.

Hector's eyelids slid almost shut. But that worked like adjusting binoculars. Making the mosquito come in closer, sharper. It was like he was seeing it under a microscope now. Like he was standing—no, floating—floating in front of the mosquito and he was smaller than it was, like a man standing by an oil derrick, watching it pump oil up from the deep places, the zone of sweet weight . . . thirty-weight, ha . . . . An *Anopheles Gambia,* this variety. From this magnified perspective the mosquito's parts were rougher than they appeared from the human level—there were bristles on her head, slicked back like stubby oiled hair, and he could see that the sheath-like covering of the proboscis had fallen in a loop away from the stylets . . . her tapered golden body, resting on the long, translucent, frail-looking legs, cantilevered forward to drink, as if in obeisance . . . her rear lifted, a forty degree angle from the skin, its see-through abdomen glowing red with blood like a little Christmas light . . .

. . . it is the female which bites, her abdomen distends enormously, allowing her to take in as much as four times her weight in blood . . .

He had an intimate relationship with this mosquito. It was entering him. He could feel her tiny, honed mind, like one of those minute paintings obsessed hobbyists put on the head of a pin. He sensed her regard. The mosquito was dimly aware of his own mind hovering over her. He could close in on the tiny gleam of her insect mind—less than the "mind" of an electric watch—and replace it with his own. What a rare and elegant nod that would be: getting into her head so he could feel what it was like to drink his own blood through the slender proboscis . . .

He could do it. He could superimpose himself and fold his own consciousness up into the micro-cellular spaces. Any mind, large or small, could be concentrated in microscopic space; micro-space was as infinite, downwardly, as interstellar space, wasn't it? God experienced every being's consciousness. God's mind could fit into a mosquito. Like all that music on a symphony going through the needle of a record player, or through the tiny laser of a CD. The stylet in the mosquito's proboscis was like the record player's stylus . . .

He could circle, and close in, and participate, and become. He could . . .

. . . see the rising fleshtone of his own arm stretching out in front of him, a soft ridge of topography. He could see the glazing eyes of the man he was drinking from. Himself; perhaps formerly. It was a wonderfully malign miracle: he was inside the mosquito. He was the mosquito. Its senses altered and enhanced by his own more-evolved prescience.

His blood was a syrup. The mosquito didn't taste it, as such; but Hector could taste it—through his psychic extension of the mosquito's senses, he supposed—and there were many confluent tastes in it, mineral and meat and electrically charged waters and honeyed glucose and acids and hemoglobin. And very faintly, heroin. His eggs would be well sustained—

Her eggs. Keep your identity sorted out. Better yet, set your own firmly atop hers. Take control.

Stop drinking blood!

More.

No. Insist, Hector. Who's in charge, here? Stop drinking and fly. Just imagine! To take flight—

Almost before the retraction of her proboscis was completed, he was in the air, making the wings work without having to think about it. When he tried too hard to control the flight, he floundered; so he simply flew.

His flight path was a herky-jerky spiral, each geometric section of it a portion of an equation.

His senses expanded to adjust to the scope of his new possibilities of movement: the great cavern, the massive organism at the bottom of it: himself, Hector's human body, left behind.

Hector sensed a temperature change, a nudge of air: a current from the crack in the window. He pushed himself up the stream, increasing his wing energy, and thought: *I'll crash on the edges of the glass, it's a small crack . . .*

But he let the insect's navigational instincts hold sway, and he was through, and out into the night.

He could go anywhere, anywhere at all . . .

He went downstairs.

Her window was open.

FROM A DISTANCE, the landscape of Lulu was glorious, lying there on the couch in her bikini underpants, and nothing else. Her exposed breasts were great slack mounds of cream and cherry. She'd fallen asleep with the radio on; there were three empty cans of beer on the little end table by her head. One of her legs was drawn up, tilted to lean its knee against the wall, the other out straight, the limbs apart enough trace her open labia against the blue silk panties.

Hector circled near the ceiling. The radio was a distorted boom of taffied words and industrial-sized beat, far away. He thought that, just faintly, he could actually feel radio and TV waves washing over him, passing through the air.

He wanted Lulu. She *looked* asleep. But suppose she felt him, suppose she heard the whine of his coming, and slapped, perhaps just in reflex, and crushed him—

Would he die when the mosquito died?

Maybe that would be all right.

Hector descended to her, following the broken geometries of insect flight-path down, an aerialist's unseen staircase, asymmetrical and yet perfect.

Closer—he could feel her heat. God, she was like a lake of fire! How could the skeeters bear it?

He entered her atmosphere. That's how it seemed: she was almost planetary in her glowing vastness, hot-house and fulsome. He descended through hormone-rich layers of her atmosphere, to deeper and more personal heats, until he'd settled on the skin of her left leg, near the knee.

Jesus! It was revolting: it was ordinary human skin.

But up this close; hugely magnified by his mosquito's perspective . . .

It was a cratered landscape, orange and gold and in places leprous-white; here and there flakes of blue, where dead skin cells were shedding away. In the pores and around the bases of the occasional stiff stalks of hair were puddly masses of pasty stuff he guessed were colonies of bacteria. The skin itself was textured like pillows of meat all sewn together. The smells off it were overwhelming: rot and uric acid and the various compounds in sweat and a chemical smell of something she'd bathed with—and an exudation of the food she'd been eating . . .

Hector was an experienced hand with drugs; he shifted his viewpoint from revulsion to obsession, to delight in the yeasty completeness of this immersion in the biological essence of her. And there was another smell that came to him then, affecting him the way the sight of a woman's cleavage had, in his boyhood. Blood.

Unthinking, he had already allowed the mosquito to unsheath her stylets and drive them into a damp pillow of skin cells. He pushed, rooted, moving the slightly arched piercer in a motion that outlined a cone, breaking tiny capillaries just inside the epidermis, making a pocket for the blood to pool in. And injecting the anti-coagulant saliva.

Her blood was much like his, but he could taste the femaleness of it, the hormonal signature and . . . alcohol.

She swatted him.

He felt the wind of the giant hand, before it struck. She struck at him in her sleep, and the hand wasn't rigid enough to hit him; the palm was slightly cupped. But the hand covered Hector like a lid, for a moment.

The air pressure flattened the mosquito, and Hector feared for his spindly legs, but then light flashed over him again and the lid lifted, and he withdrew and flew, wings whining, up a short distance into the air . . .

She was mostly quiescent now. Looking from here like the rolling, shrub-furred hills you saw in parts of California: one hill blending smoothly into the next, until you got close and saw ant colonies and rattlers and tarantulas between the clumps.

She hadn't awakened. And from up here her thighs looked so sweet and tender . . .

He dipped down, and alighted on Lulu's left inside thigh, not far from the pale blue circus tent billow of her panties. The material was only a little stained; he could see the tracery of her labia like the shadows of sleeping dragons under a silk canopy. The thigh skin was a little smoother, paler. He could see the woods of pubic hair down the slope a little.

Enough. Eggs, outside.

No. He was in control. He was going to get closer . . .

WHEN AT LAST he reached the frontier of Lulu's panties, and stood between two outlying spring-shaped stalks of redbrown pubic hair, gazing under a wrinkle in the elastic at the monumental vertical furrow of her vaginal lips, he was paralyzed by fear. This was a great temple to some subaquatic monster, and would surely punish any intrusion.

With the fear came a sudden perception of his own relative tininess, now, and an unbottling of his resentments. She was forbidden; she was gargantuan in both size and arrogance.

But he had learned that he was the master of his reality: he had found a hatch in his brain, and a set of new controls that fit naturally to his grip, and he could remake his being as he chose.

A sudden darkness, then; a wind—

He sprang up, narrowly escaping the swat. Hearing a sound like a jet breaking the sound barrier—the wind of her hand and the slap on her thigh. Then a murky roaring, a boulder-fall of misshapen words. The goddess coming awake; the goddess speaking.

Something like, *"Fucking skeeter . . . little shit . . . get the fuck out . . ."*

Oh, yes?

The fury swelled in him, and as it grew—Lulu shrank. Or seemed to, as rage pushed his boundaries outward like hot air in a parade balloon, but unthinkably fast. She shrank to woman size, once more in perspective and once more desirable.

She screamed, of course.

He glimpsed them both in her vanity mirror . . .

A man-sized mosquito, poised over her, holding her down with slender but strong front legs; Lulu screaming, thrashing, as he leaned back onto his hind legs and spread her legs with the middle limbs . . .

In her delighted revulsion, she struck at the mosquito's compound eyes. The pain was realer and more personal than he'd expected. He jerked back, withdrawing, floundering off the edge of the bed, feeling a leg shatter against the floor and a wing crack, one of his eyes half blind . . .

The pain and the disorientation unmanned him. Emasculated him, intimidated him. As always when that happened, he shrank.

The boundaries of the room expanded and the bed grew, around him, into a dirty white plain; Lulu grew, again becoming a small world to herself . . . Her hand sliced down at him—

He threw himself frantically into the air, his damaged wings ascending stochastically; the wings' keening sound not quite right now, his trajectory uncertain.

The ceiling loomed; the window crack beckoned.

In seconds he had swum upstream against the night air, and managed to aim himself between the edges of the crack in the glass; the lips of the break like a crystalline take on her vagina. Then he was out into the night, and regaining some greater control over his wings . . .

That's not how it was, he realized: *she,* the mosquito had control. That's how they'd gotten through the crack and out into the night.

Let the mosquito mind take control, for now, while he rested his psyche and pondered. That great yellow egg, green around the edges with refinery toxins, must be the moon; this jumble of what seemed skyscraper-sized structures must be the pipes and chimneys and discarded tar buckets of the apartment building's roof.

Something washed over him, rebounding, making him shudder in the air. Only after it departed did it register in his hearing: a single high note, from somewhere above.

There, it came again, more defined and pulsingly closer, as if growing in an alien certainty about its purpose.

The mosquito redoubled its wing beats in reaction, and there was an urgency that was too neurologically primitive to be actual fear. *Enemy. Go.*

Hector circled down between the old brick apartment buildings, toward the streetlight . . .

Another, slightly higher, even more purposeful note hit Hector, resonating him, and then a shadow draped him, and wing beats thudded tympanically on the air. He saw the bat for one snapshot-clear moment, superimposed against the dirty indigo sky. Hector knew he should detach from the mosquito, but the outspread wings of the bat, its pointed ears and wet snout, caught him with its heraldic perfection—it was as perfect, poised against the sky, as the mosquito had seemed, poised on his arm. It trapped him with fascination.

Sending out a final sonar note to pinpoint the mosquito, the bat struck its head forward—

But Hector was diving now, under it, swirling in the air, letting himself fall for a ways just to get the most distance.

He glimpsed the hangarlike opening of a window and flew for it. He sensed a body inside and newly flowing female blood. An even bigger woman.

He had to rest first. He found a spot on a wall near the ceiling. Sometime later there was the sound of a radio alarm coming on to wake the sleeper below him, the radio in mid-monologue . . .

And this is the KRED crack-of-dawn-news, all the news that's fit to transmit. Lookout for your hamburgers, folks, that's the story that comes to KRED radio from Lubbock where a woman was shot by a burger. It seems that some twisted soul has been putting .22 calibre bullets into ground meat sold at a Lubbock supermarket. The bullet exploded while the burger was cooking last night, and the woman suffered a minor facial wound from a bullet fragment . . . . Chrysler has announced two new plant closures and plans to lay off some 35,000 people . . . . Give us about, oh, about an hour and we'll give you the first KRED morning traffic report . . .

WHEN LULU WOKE, she had cramps. But it was the aftertaste of the dream that bothered her. There was a taintedness lingering in her skin, as if the nightmare of the giant mosquito had left a sort of mephitic insect pheromone on her. She took two showers, and ate her breakfast, and listened to the radio, and, by comforting degrees, forgot about the dream. When she went downstairs the building manager was letting the ambulance attendants in. They were in a hurry. It was the guy upstairs, the manager said. He was dead.

No one was surprised. He was a junkie. Everybody knew that.

Next day Lulu was scratching the skeeter bites, whenever she thought no one was looking.

ISOLATION POINT, CALIFORNIA

GAGE PUSHED THE door of his cabin open with his booted foot, as he always did, peering inside, right and left, without going in, to make sure no one was hiding there waiting for him. He looked around, saw only his single bunk, neatly made up, with the solar-powered lamp on a small stand beside it, glowing faintly in the overcast, late afternoon gloom. Faces did stare back at him: the old magazine photos of smiling people, mostly girls, on the wall over his bunk. The wooden chair stood just where he'd left it, pulled back slightly from the metal table with its two coffee cups, long bereft of coffee, and his collection of pens, stacks of spiral notebooks, the radio. Above the table were the shelves of random books, many of them blackened at the edges, foraged from a burned library in Sweetbite. The ax leaned on the stack of firewood beside the river-stone fireplace, opposite the old woodstove, with its two pots.

It was tedious, having to stop and look around in the cabin and the out-house, before going in, day after day. But as he went inside, he told himself that the first time he neglected to do it, someone would be there to brain him with his own ax.

He closed and barred the door behind him, saw that the fire was out, but went immediately to the desk and stood there, looking out the window. It was nailed shut and curtained—a risk having a window at all—but he could see the light was dimming, the clouds shrugging together for rain. The charge on the lamp was low, so he plugged it into the socket that connected to the solar-collection panel on the roof, and the lamp's charge meter bobbed to near full. He dialed up the light, and looked at the radio but decided not to try it. He was usually depressed for a while after listening to the radio and didn't want to ruin his hopeful mood.

He leaned his shotgun against the wall, within reach, put the binoculars on a stack of notebooks, and sat down at the table. He

277

adjusted the shim under the short table leg to minimize the wobbling, picked up a pen, and wrote his newest journal entry. His fingers were stiff with the chill but he wanted to tell his journal what had happened more than he wanted to stoke up the fire.

NOVEMBER 1ST, 2023

I saw her again this afternoon, about forty-five minutes ago. She was standing on what was left of the old marina, coming out from all those burned-out buildings along San Andreas Spit, across the river's mouth from me. She was standing right where the river meets the tidal push from the ocean. That always seemed suggestive to me, the river flowing into the ocean; the ocean pushing back, the two kind of mingling. "Here's some silt" and "Here's some salt back at you." Silt and salt, never noticed how close the words were before now.

I looked at her in the binoculars, and when she saw I was doing that, she spread her arms and smiled as if to say, "Check me out!" Not that I could see much of her under all those clothes. It's pretty brisk out now, Northern coast this time of year, wind off the sea, and she was wearing a big bulky green ski jacket, and a watch cap, and jeans and boots. She had a 30.06 bolt-action deer rifle leaned against a rock. She never went far from it. She's got long wavy chestnut hair, and her face, what I could make out, seemed kind of pleasant. She's not tall. Taking into account the silhouette of her legs, she seems slim. Not that there's anyone obese left, not on this continent, anyway. She seemed energetic, confident. I wonder if she found a new supply drop somewhere? If she found it first, she could be doing well. Another reason to make contact.

But who knows what she's up to? She could be talking to men at a safe distance all over the county. Getting them to leave her gifts or something. But that'd be risky. They'll kill her eventually. Unless someone finds a cure for the AggFac soon. Not very goddamn likely.

Anyway it felt good talking to her. Shouting back and forth, really. I got pretty hoarse, since of course she was several hundred feet from me. Said she was from San Francisco. Got out just in time. Told her I was from Sacramento. She laughed when I told her this little peninsula of mine is called "Isolation Point." Had to swear and cross my heart it was

always called that. She said she used to be a high school English teacher.
Told her, "Hey that's amazing, I used to be a high school student!" She
laughed. I can just barely hear her laugh across the river.

She asked what did I used to do. Said I managed some restaurants.
Wanted to be a journalist, write about America. Big story came, no one to
tell it to. She said I could still write. I said for who? She said for people—
you leave the writing in places and other people find it. "I'd read it!" she
said. I said okay. Thinking that writing for one person at a time wasn't
what I had in mind, but you scale down your dreams now. Way down.

I was running out of breath and my voice was going with all the yelling
back and forth so I asked her name. Told her mine. Our ages too, me 43,
she 34. I tried to think of some way to ask her to come closer, maybe at
the fence. To ask her without scaring her. But I couldn't think of any way
and then she waved and picked up her rifle and walked off.

Her name's Brenda.

I was hiking back to the cabin going, "Brennnn-da! Brennnn-da!" over
and over like an idiot. Like I'm twelve. Not surprising after two years alone
here, I guess. It was good just to see someone who isn't trying to kill me.

Wish the dog would come back. Someone probably ate him, though.
I need to check the fence again. Going to do it now. It might rain. Might
get dark before I'm back. Might be someone there. I've got the shotgun.
Not that I can afford to use the shells. The sight of the gun keeps people
back, though, if they stay beyond The Nineteen. Going now. Should stay
here . . . Too antsy . . .

Gage put the pen down and picked up his shotgun. "That's right,"
he said aloud. "Put down the pen, pick up the gun." He had to talk
aloud, fairly often, just to hear a human voice. Brenda's was the first
he'd heard, except for the warning noise, for three months. "That's
how it is," he said, hearing the hoarseness in his voice from all that
shouting. Bad time to get laryngitis. Bad time to get anything—he'd
almost died of pneumonia that once. No pharmacies anymore. You ran
into a doctor, he'd try to kill you. He'd be sorry afterwards but that
didn't do you any good.

Gage unbarred the door, and went out, closing the door carefully
behind him. There was still some light. He walked out to the edge of

the trees to take a quick look out at the Pacific, beyond the edge of the cliff, fifty yards away. It was steely under the clouds. He was looking for boats and hoping he wouldn't see one. Nothing out there, except maybe that slick black oblong, appearing and disappearing—a whale. At least the animals were doing better now.

He'd chosen this little finger of land, with its single intact cabin, partly because there was no easy way to land a boat. Mostly the sea was too rough around it. You could maybe come in from the sea up into the mouth of the river, clamber onto the big slippery wet crab-twitchy rocks that edged the river bank, if you could secure your boat so it didn't float away, but the current was strong there and no one had tried it that he knew of. His cabin was pretty well hidden in the trees, after all, and it didn't look like much was here. And of course, they were as scared of him as he was of them. But then, that's what his father had told him about rattlesnakes.

He turned and tramped through the pine trees toward the fence, a quarter mile back, noticing, for the first time in a year or more, the smell of the pine needles mingling with the living scent of the sea. Funny how you see a girl, you start to wake up and notice things around you again. To care about how things smell and look and feel.

The wind off the sea keened between the trees and made the hackles rise on the back of his neck. He buttoned the collar of his thick, blue REI snowline jacket with his left hand, the other keeping the Remington twelve-gauge tucked up under his right armpit, pressed against him, the breach-block cupped in his palm. He was good at getting the Remington popped fast to his shoulder for firing. So far nobody had noticed what a lame shot he was. The two guys he'd killed since coming to the area—killed four months apart—had both got it at close to point-blank range. That was the AggFac for you. If people sniped at you, it was out of desperation, not because of the AggFac.

He felt the wind tugging at his streaked beard, his long sandy hair. "I must be getting pretty shaggy," he said to a red squirrel, looking beadily down from a low branch. "But the only thing I've got left to cut it with is a knife and it's so dull . . . I'm down to my last cake of soap. Half a cake really . . ." For two years, cognizant that no one on the continent was making soap anymore, he'd only washed when he could no longer bear his own smell.

The squirrel clicked its claws up the tree, looking for a place to curl up out of the wind, and Gage continued, five minutes later cutting the old deer path he took to the fence. Another ten minutes and he was there: a twenty-five foot hurricane fence with antipersonnel wire across the top in a Y-frame. The fence and the place at the river where he got the fish and the crabs were two of the main reasons he'd chosen this spot. There was no gate in the fence—they'd used a chopper landing pad of cracked asphalt, near the edge of the cliff on the south side of the cape. There'd been some kind of military satellite monitoring station, here, once, and the fence, he figured, had been put up to keep people away from it. It kept bears and wolves out too. The post building had crumbled into the sea after a bad storm—you could see the satellite dish sticking up out of the water at low tide, all rusty; the cabin was all that was left. There was forage, if you knew where to look; there was river water to filter; there was a way he knew to get around the fence, underneath its southern end, when he was willing to try his luck checking the crossroads at Sweetbite Point for supply drops. But he hadn't been out to the crossroads in seven months. Previous time, someone had almost gotten him. So he stayed out here as long as he could. It was a great spot to survive in, if you wanted to survive. He'd almost stopped wanting to.

The fence looked perfectly upright, unbreached, so far as he could see from here, no more rusted than last time. Of course, a determined man could get over it—or around it, if you didn't mind clambering over a sheer drop—but it was rare for anyone to come out onto the cape. There weren't many left to come.

He walked along the fence a ways south, wondering what'd brought him here. He had a sort of instinct, especially sharp post-AggFac, that kept him alive—and usually it had its reasons for things.

There it was. The sound of a dog barking. He hoped it was Gassie.

"Hey Gassie!" he shouted, beginning to trot along the fence. "Yo, dog!" Be a great day, meeting a woman . . . sort of . . . and getting his dog back too. "Gassie!"

Then it occurred to him to wonder who the dog was barking at. Maybe a raccoon. Maybe not.

He bit off another shout, annoyed with himself for getting carried away. Shouting. Letting people know where he was.

He circled a lichen-yellowed boulder that hulked up to his own height, and came upon Gassie and the stranger—who was just a few steps beyond The Nineteen. Gassie was this side of the fence, the man on the other side, staring, mouth agape, at the hole the dog had dug under the fence to get in . . .

Despite the dangerous presence of the stranger, Gage shook his head in admiration at the dog's handiwork. It was the same spot he'd gotten out at—some critter, raccoon or skunk, had dug a hole under the fence where the ground was soft, and the dog had widened it and gotten out and wandered off, more than a month ago. Gage had waited a week, then decided he had to fill the hole in. Here he was, Gassie, his ribs sticking out, limping a little, but scarcely the worse for wear—a brown-speckled tongue-drooping mix of pit bull, with his wedge-shaped head, and some other breed Gage had never been sure of.

The stranger—a gawky, emaciated man in the tatters of an Army uniform, who'd let his hair fall into accidental dreadlocks—goggled stupidly at the hole, then jerked his head up as Gage approached the dog.

Gage reckoned the stranger, carrying an altered ax handle, at twentyone paces away, with the fence between them. Not at The Nineteen yet. Everyone alive on this continent was good at judging distances instantly. Nineteen paces, for most people, was the AggFac warning distance. It was possible to remain this side of psychotic—like this side of the fence—beyond nineteen paces from another human being. Nineteen paces or less, you'd go for them, with everything you had, to kill them; and they'd go at you just the same. Which was why most people in North America had died over the past few years. A couple of phrases from one of the first—and last—newspaper articles came into his mind: *The very wiring of the brain altered from within . . . That portion of the brain so different victims become another species . . . .*

"You're outside the margin, dude," Gage said. "You can still back up."

He knew he should probably kill the guy whether he backed up or not, on general principle. For one thing, the guy was probably planning to kill and eat his dog. For another, now that the son of a bitch knew there was someone camped on the other side of the fence, he'd come over to forage and kill—or rather, to kill and forage.

But you clung to what dignity you could. Gage did, anyway. Killing people when you didn't absolutely have to lacked dignity, in Gage's view.

"Don't come no closer," the man said. He hefted the ax-handle warningly. It was missing its ax blade but he'd found a stiff blade from a kitchen knife somewhere and he'd pushed it into a crack at one end of the handle and wrapped it in place with black electric tape.

"You were a soldier," Gage observed. "Where's your weapon?"

"I got it, real close," the man said. After thinking laboriously a moment, he said, "My partner's got it trained on your ass right now."

Gage laughed. "No one's got a partner. I saw some people try it, before I came here—watched from a roof for two days. They tried partnering by staying twenty feet away from each other. But eventually they would fuck that up, get too close—and you know what happened. Every time. You haven't got a partner—or a gun."

The man shrugged. He wasn't going to waste his breath on any more lies. He looked at the dog, licking his lips. Finally he said, "You knock that dog in the head, push it where I can get it, I'll go away for good."

"That dog's worth ten like you," Gage said. He made up his mind. It'd be pretty ironic if the AggFac had worn off, finally, and he and Brenda were staying out of reach for no reason. Of course, there was no reason to think it ever wore off. But everyone, as far as he knew, hoped it would, eventually. They didn't know what caused it, exactly—there were lots of theories— so maybe it'd wear off as mysteriously as it came. For no good reason, the brain would revert to normal.

Yeah right. But for Brenda's sake he stepped closer to the stranger, within The Nineteen, to see if the AggFac was still there in him.

He felt it immediately. The clutching up feeling, the hot geysering from the back of his skull, the heat spreading to his face, his arms. The tightening of his hands, his jaws, the background humming; the tight focus on His Enemy. And the change in the way things look—going almost colorless. Not black and white, but sickly sepia and gray, with shadows all deep and inky.

Since Gage had come within The Nineteen, the stranger was seized by the AggFac too, and his face went beet red, the veins at his temples popping up. As if propelled from behind he came rushing at Gage, stopped only by the fence, hammering at the chain links with his ax handle, making that *Eeeeee* sound in the back of his throat they all made—the sound Gage might've been making himself, he could never tell somehow. Hammering the ax handle to splinters as Gage shoved the barrel of the shotgun through a fence link and pulled the trigger at point blank range . . .

The stranger fell away, gasping and dying. The AggFac ebbed. Color seeped back into the world.

Gage heard the dog barking, and saw it start for the hole in the fence. Wanting to get at the stranger's body.

"No, Gassie," Gage said, feeling tired and empty and half-dead himself. He grabbed the dog by its short tail, pulled it back before it was quite through the hole. It snarled at him but let him do it. He blocked up the hole with rocks, then started toward the end of the fence, where it projected over the cliff. He'd have to go down by the rocks, about fifty feet south of the fence's end, thread the path, climb the other cliff, to get the body, drag it to the sea. A lot of work.

But he didn't want to leave the bloody corpse there for Brenda to find. He wanted her to come to the fence . . .

So he trudged off toward the cliffs.

NOVEMBER 2ND, 2023

My face hurts from scraping at it with that knife. Used up a lot of soap in place of shaving cream. Hope the contusions go down before she sees me up close. Not too close, of course.

Will she come? She'd be foolish to come. She doesn't know me. She can see the fence from across the river but she doesn't know if it'll keep her safe from me. I might have a gate for all she knows. She's never been out to the point.

She says she's coming. We agreed on high noon. She's got a longer-range weapon than me. She doesn't seem stupid. She'll be smart about it. She'll get close enough to take stock of the situation, with that gun right up against her shoulder, but not so close I could rush her.

I think she does understand that outside the AggFac I'm not some thug, some rapist. But she may decide not to take the chance. Or someone may kill her before she gets here. I think it's almost noon . . .

"Hi! Can you see me okay?" Gage called, spreading his hands so she could see he didn't have the shotgun. She was still about a hundred feet off, on the other side of the fence, assessing the situation from cover, like he'd figured she would, the rifle propped on the top of a big tree stump and pointed right at him.

Dangerous, not to bring the shotgun. But it was meaningful. They both knew that. Not carrying your gun was like, in the old days, bringing a bouquet of flowers.

Still, this could be a set up. She could be after his goods. She could want his cabin, maybe. She could shoot him, and Gassie, if she had the ammo. Shoot him from safety where she was. Nothing to stop her. A couple of rounds, one'd get through that fence. Down he'd go . . .

He kept his arms spread. Standing in the open, a little clearing with just rock-strewn dirt on the ground, so she could see he didn't have the shotgun anywhere near—like, hidden behind a rock close to him. His gun could be somewhere in the brush, of course. But at least it wasn't in easy reach.

Slowly, she got out from behind the stump and walked toward him. She glanced right and left now and then. Looked at the dog, sitting there wagging its tail, beside him. She smiled.

"Hi Brenda," he said, when she got to about twenty-one paces, and stopped. Slowly, she lowered the gun, holding it cradled in her arms.

Then she sat down, her legs crossed, deciding to trust him that much. He sat down too, on his side of the fence. The dog put his head on Gage's lap.

"I'm embarrassed to tell you his name," Gage said, patting the dog. "It's Gassie."

"Gassie!" She laughed. "After Lassie, right?" She had all of her teeth, which was unusual in itself. Her face had lots of roundness to it, but she wasn't pie-faced. Her eyes were dark brown, he saw, and the shape of them suggested she had some American Indian blood. She'd put her hair up, in a simple kind of way, and she seemed clean.

"What now?" he asked, as mildly, as casually, as much without pressure as he could.

"I don't know," she said. "I just needed to see someone up close as I could, and you seemed nice." She shrugged. "As much as anyone can be, with the—you know."

He nodded, deciding he needed to be as completely honest with her as possible. "I tried it, yesterday, when a stranger came up to the fence. I deliberately stepped closer, just to see. I always hope it might go away some time."

· "I've never heard of it going away."

"No. Reports on the radio say it never has for anyone. Kids don't outgrow it, old people don't get over it. It hit me the same as always."

She nodded, not having to ask what'd happened.

"I don't feel too bad," he added. "Guy was trying to eat my dog."

She nodded again. That she understood too, both sides. "You fish?"

"Sure." They talked a long time about practical things like that. He told her about his water filter, the crabs, the fish, the wild plants he knew—she knew them too—and about the forays to the food drops.

"They'll drop food to us sometimes, the foreign people," she said, "but they seem to have just . . . given up on curing it. Unless—you said you had a radio? You heard anything?"

He shook his head. "Nothing new. One guy—hard to get the signal, I think it was from the Virgin Islands, I had to move the radio around—he said the Japanese thought it was some kind of nanotech-creation that got out of hand, like an artificial virus, supposed to alter your brain wiring in a good way, does it in a bad way instead, jumps from person to person. Then there's the biowarfare theory, the mutated virus theory . . . "

"The one I liked was about the schizophrenia virus. Back in the twentieth century some people thought a lot of mental illness is caused by a virus that gets in the brain. They think this is a mutation of the schizophrenia virus. They thought schizophrenia was something you could get from cat-shit, once."

"I always knew there was some reason I didn't like cats."

She laughed.

"Whatever it is," he went on, venting, "you'd think someone would make some damn progress by now. No vaccines, nothing. It is like they're just waiting for us to die. Won't let anybody come to their perfect little countries. That blockade in Panama, shoot down our planes . . ."

"Can you blame them?" she asked.

He knew what she meant. The world had watched, as the "Aggression Factor" rolled over a hemisphere; as millions of people had killed one another: people in North America and Mexico, all the way to the geo-quarantine at the Panama Canal; the world had watched as millions of longtime neighbors had killed one another; watched as an unthinkable number of husbands had killed their wives, and wives their husbands; as unspeakable quantities of children were murdered by parents, by siblings, by friends; as others murdered their parents. As women throttled babies freshly plucked from the womb—and then wept in utter bafflement. He remembered a boy walking through the ruins of Sacramento, weeping, "Why did I kill my mom? Why did I kill my mom?" And then the boy had come within nineteen steps and . . . without meaning to, Gage had put him out of his misery.

"Nah. I don't blame them. I just . . ." He didn't have to say it. She smiled sadly and they understood one another.

"Nice not to have to shout."

"Yeah. I . . . have some dried fish for you, if you need it. I'll leave it at the fence. I thought maybe I'd loan you my solar radio, too, if you wanted. The dog dug a hole under the fence a ways down. I could push it under there . . . leave it for you to get later. You can see me walking a good quarter mile off from there."

"That's so sweet. You look like you carved your face up a bit . . ."

"Best I could do with what I had."

"You're still a nice looking guy."

Probably not when the AggFac hits, he thought. But he said only, "Thanks."

"I'll borrow the radio, I promise to bring it back . . . "

NOVEMBER 6, 2023

I've seen her every day but yesterday—I was really worried yesterday when she didn't come but she had to duck a guy who had gotten wind of her. He was stalking her. She finally managed to lure him up to a hill she knew real well and she shot him from cover. Smart, cool-headed girl. I'm crazy about her. Of course, I can't get within nineteen steps of her but . . . I'm still crazy about her.

She told me about a girl who'd lived down the street from her, they talked from rooftops, sometimes. The girl would trade a look at her naked body to guys who'd come around, look at her naked up on a second floor balcony. She had a gun up there in case they started up. They'd leave her food and stuff and they'd look at her naked and masturbate. It worked for awhile but of course some predator got wind of it, some guy who was always more or less AggFac, even before it came along, and he busted in and jumped her. Killed her, of course, the AggFac won't be denied, but I figure her body was still warm afterwards. Lot of bodies get raped now.

Why did Brenda tell me this story? Maybe suggesting we trusted each other enough to get naked, if only from a distance? I'm too embarrassed to masturbate even if she's doing it too. That desperate I'm not.

I wrote her some poetry I'm going to leave for her. She might blow me off for good after she reads it, if she's got any taste . . .

"FEELS LIKE IT might snow," Brenda said, hugging herself against the morning mist, the occasional gusts of cold wind.

"Kind of cold. I could go back, get you a blanket, toss it over." They were sitting in their usual spot, fence between them.

"Oh, it'd probably get stuck on the wire," she said.

"I could send Gassie over again to keep you warm."

"Last time he came over he humped my leg."

"He did? I didn't see that." He was only momentarily tempted to say, I don't blame him. Even now he could be slicker than that.

"There's something I wanted to talk to you about," she said. She chewed her lip for a moment, then went on, "Look—you ever hear about someone being cured of, like, a phobia, before the AggFac, by getting used to whatever they were scared of, little by little? Scared of flying, they made you go to airports, sit in a plane, but then get off the plane before it flies, look at pictures taken out a plane window, till you're ready to fly . . . all that kind of thing. You know?"

"Yeah, I forget what they call that. But . . . you don't think the AggFac would work that way. It's not a phobia."

"No it isn't. But it's a kind of compulsive aversion for people . . . when they get physically close. Right? What if a person could sort of inure themselves to the presence of another person within nineteen steps— by slow degrees? Make the brain accustomed to the other person . . . the wiring of the brain itself acclimated to them."

"How? It's so powerful that even if your eyes are shut and you can't see the person, soon as you know they're close, the AggFac hits and you kill them. Whatever you do, the murder reflex comes out. I mean—I could probably find a way to restrain myself, somehow, for awhile, so I couldn't get loose too easily. So you could get close—but then, let's face it, *you'd* kill *me*. I mean, mothers killed children they loved all their lives . . . "

"Sure. But . . . suppose we both restrain ourselves somewhat. With rope, whatever, the weapons off somewhere, we keep the fence between us at first . . . but we're basically within reach. I don't think I could even bite you through those links. But we could have some contact . . ."

The idea made him breathless. His blood raced as he thought about it. But then he shook his head. "Even if we didn't hurt one another— we'd hate one another, within The Nineteen. There'd be no pleasure in it—just rage."

"Our brains would feel that way—at first. But our bodies! Our bodies would . . . I think they'd respond. It'd be a kind of . . . counter force in the brain. Maybe enough, after awhile, to . . . Oh, Gage I can't take this distance from people much longer. I'm . . . I've got skin hunger. It's bad. I have to try something."

"Hey. Me too. And I really, really like you. I'd have liked you before all this stuff, I swear it. But—even if we couldn't hurt each other, how would the encounter ever end? We'd be smashing at each other through the fence!"

"That's the risk. There has to be some risk. There always was some risk. But Gage—I want to try. I think that . . . if I'm starting to hurt myself against the fence, I'll finally manage to back off and the AggFac'll go away. Then we can try again. We can *inure*. We can *accustom*. We can . . . acclimate. Maybe you'll stop seeing me as . . . the other. Maybe I'll be, like, an extension of you, after awhile, so the AggFac won't come any more, at least when it's me."

"You mean . . . you want to get naked, on either side of the fence . . ."

"Yeah. Well, I'll keep my coat on, and some boots. Won't look too elegant but . . . I'm burning to touch you. I want to love you. I want you to love me . . ."

She was crying now. Finally he said yes.

NOVEMBER 11, 2023

The weather cleared up some, and, partly naked, we tried it. We each had our guns put way out of reach but where the other could see it. She had some rope, left some for me—she'd pushed it through the mesh, inch by inch, while she was waiting for me. We took turns, measuring it out carefully. The rope went from a tree behind me to the fence, just enough so I could press against it, but restraining me so I couldn't start to climb over it easily. My arms were tied to my sides. That was tricky. Had to work with our teeth, use a fork in a tree to pull a knot taut, stuff like that. Laughing a lot back and forth as we worked out how to do it, all alone, each on their side of the fence. Of course we knew it was still possible to get out of the rope but it would take time and the other could get away or get their gun . . . We thought maybe we'd be too frenzied with kill lust or the other kind to do really work out how to attack the other person with all that stuff in the way. The AggFac isn't about thinking or planning, god knows.

I used up the last of my soap, getting ready for this. She had cleaned herself up too . . .

We came close, the fence between us, the rope restraining us. The AggFac hit and there was no remembering how we'd said we'd loved each other, there was no remembering how we wanted to trust . . .

• • •

He tried to snap at her nose through the mesh, envisioned tearing it off in his teeth, but couldn't reach her. She tried to bite into his chin, couldn't reach it.

But their skin touched, through the links, *and he did get a hard-on under the rope*—it was roped to his belly, no way it was going to be free to go through that fence, she'd bite it off for sure. They writhed and snapped and snarled and then she managed to back away . . .

Still, I swear something did get through the AggFac, some other feeling—it really did get through. Just enough.

We both got bloody on the fence but we're going to try again. We have a plan, a way to try it in the cabin.

His heart was slamming in his chest, so loud he could hear it in the quiet of the cabin. He just lay there on his bunk listening to his heart thudding, trying the ropes, hoping the self-restraint system he'd worked up was going to hold him long enough. He could get out of the ropes, afterward, but it'd take time. The dog was tied up in the woods. He was ready for her to come. Maybe she wouldn't show up. He'd lie here like an idiot and some son of a bitch would climb over the fence and find him here, before he got loose, and he'd be helpless. Then dead.

Big risk, trying it in the cabin this way. Risk from her too. She said she was getting some control over the AggFac, but how long would it last, in close proximity?

He knew he couldn't bear it if he killed her. If she killed him, well, it wouldn't matter.

The door opened and he looked up and saw her there, inside The Nineteen, almost naked. Her hands were all muffled, tied together and smothered in big thick home-made boxing gloves, and her mouth was gagged, she'd gagged it herself, to try to keep her from biting him.

The color drained from the room. The *Eeeee* was building up in the back of his throat; was trying to get out of her too. He could see her struggling to keep it back. But the other thing, the distance from the

AggFac, that they'd worked on, built up through the fence, that was there too. He was able to look at her, like a man close to the sheet of flames in a forest fire—feeling the heat painfully but not quite so close he was burned yet.

She waited there for a moment, looking at his ropes. Then she started toward him. He tried to hold onto the memory of her touch, through the fence, the desire he felt for her, but the AggFac rose up. He writhed against the ropes.

She rushed him, her face reddening with AggFac, leaped on him, straddled him . . .

IT WAS FUNNY *how the two feelings were there, right close, so distinct. Kill. Love. Almost intertwined. But not combined. Like, alternating. I just kept trying to drag my mind back to the love feeling. I looked in her eyes, saw her doing the same thing. Whole moments of close, intimate sanity, each one of those moments—impossible to explain how precious they were. Impossible.*

THE AGGFAC WAS still there but somehow, for a few moments, they were in a kind of blessed state of betweenness. She was there, so close, her breath on his cheek, the feeling of her closeness like a hot meal after a week of hunger.

Something in him, something that went to sleep during the Aggression Factor, quivered awake and brought color back to the room . . . Their eyes locked . . . hers cleared . . . She stopped shaking . . . .

She stopped pounding at him . . . and slipped him into her, pumped her hips, working the gag out of her mouth, chewing the gloves off her hands so she could touch him.

There was intimacy; after so much privation, there was rapid mutual orgasm. Then he drew away from her, instinctively, as he came, and the AggFac returned, and he started thrashing against the ropes, trying to kill her, and her own Aggression broke free in response, and she started clawing at his eyes, snapping at his throat. She bit hard, she tore, his blood began to flow . . .

Some of his rope gave way. Enough.

He seized her by the throat and—just to get her hands from his eyes—threw her off him, to the floor. He tore loose as she scrambled to her feet, turned snarling to face him. He reached out with one hand, scooped up the chair, threw it at her—it felt light as cardboard to him in that moment. It struck her on the side of the head and she fell backwards, crying out. He still had ropes around his ankles and jerked them loose, looking for another weapon to kill her with. Stunned, confused, she crawled to the door . . .

She turned and stared dazedly at him. He hunkered, ready to spring at her. Panting, they stared at one another. She was within Nineteen. He wanted to kill her. But a second passed and he didn't spring. Neither did she. The betweenness was in her eyes. But it wouldn't last, not now.

"Run!" he managed, huskily.

But she hesitated . . .

And then the moment passed.

FEBRUARY 2, 2024.

I've met someone else. Her name is Elise. Pretty soon I'm going to tell her about the fence and the process. I'm going to try again. I have to try again.

There was that one second, when I was free, and didn't attack. Seeing the humanness in her eyes, too, for a moment. It gave me hope. That one second could telescope out to a lifetime of forbearance . . .

Some day I'll get control of it, and then I can be honest with Elise. And show her Brenda's grave.

MISS SINGULARITY

She'd mentioned suicide to the therapist, but not in any real serious kind of way. The only time Lani told anyone she was seriously thinking of killing herself was at school, in detention, in a text message to her friend Bron.

Outside, the spring was prissily insistent. The Northern California sunlight, Lani thought, was adamant about its detestable cheeriness. Through the classroom window she could see yellow flowers on the hill above San Jose Hills High School. Butter colored daffodils, green green grass, spotless blue sky, sunlight like a little kid who'd just thought of being sunlight: Lani found it all quite sinister and deceptive.

Thnk gonna kill mself soon 4 real, she messaged to Bron, on the little coffin-shaped cell phone. (Why do you think she'd picked this phone?)

Detent ovr n 14 min then freedom Bron replied, thumbing away on his own.

Mr. Gornblatt, supervising afterschool detention, didn't seem to notice or care about the cell phones, though theoretically they could be confiscated. He wasn't one of those teachers who got off on confiscating things—it was too much trouble. A chunky math teacher with a slightly crooked toupee, Gornblatt was sitting at his desk leafing through a *National Geographic*. He stopped on a photo page and stared, swallowing. It was hard to be sure at this angle but Lani suspected Gornblatt was looking at the topless aborigine women like some breathless sixth grader—and it was truly gross.

No serious not kddng maybe fri day 2 die, she messaged. She had to send and go to a new screen pretty often. *Maybe not see u . . . yer dad pick u up rt after schl.*

She glanced at Bron. Felt some satisfaction seeing he was staring at her; she'd managed to shock him. Then she felt kind of bad about making him worry.

He scratched at the soul patch under his lip, giving her that owlish look that meant, *What the fuck?* He was proud of that tenuous black soul patch against his doughy skin; he'd had to fight to convince the school to let him have that and the shaved head. His thick lips—not too thick, really, kind of cute—were pierced on the right side by two studs, top and bottom. They clacked, very softly, when his lips came together: he liked that. Like her, he wore all black; hers was fringed with blood-red lace. They were two of four Unapologetic Goths at the school, as Bron called them. UGs—he relished pronouncing it *ughs*. The school had nurtured various pseudo-Goths and semi-Goths but only four UGs.

U cant he messaged.

Y?

Tell u after schl my dad can just wait

But it was her dad who came after school, which was a surprise; Bron's dad didn't show, which was not a surprise. Bron's dad, a sometime-Harley salesman, was maybe on a drinking binge again, in which case his family's weekend camping trip to Lake Tahoe would be put off because his dad was "feeling under the weather". Bron wouldn't mind, or wouldn't admit minding; he professed to hate the idea of vacation with his family. Probably both did hate it and didn't. She knew that feeling.

So they were blinking in the sunlight in front of the school and Bron only got as far as, "Lani, you're so full of shit, and you're not going to do that. Abjectly true: you will not do it." *Abjectly true* was a phrase he'd coined, and frequently traded in. "Your friends are, like, going to be fucked without you, and there's a Death Club concert in three weeks and I have a ticket for you, a free fucking ticket, hello—?"

She looked at him with studied pity. "Concerts . . ." She shook her head. She was beginning to be sorry she'd told him. But then again maybe she wanted him to talk her out of it? She wasn't sure.

That's when her dad showed up. He was a tall, tanned man, with a small sharp nose contrasting a firm jaw, amused blue eyes. He was quite fit, dressed in a golf shirt and jeans and tasseled loafers with no socks. He was not the usual picture of a physicist; he didn't need glasses and his graying brown hair was only a little tousled. He played golf, pretty badly, and he jogged, and he liked to swim in the sun. But he was a physicist, all right: sometimes, at the pool, he talked about Einstein's insight on the sailboat watching light in the water.

"Hiya kid," he said, as he always did.

"What're you doing here? I don't need a ride, Dad."

"That's so touching, the way you greet your old man." But he didn't say it like he was really hurt. She'd never seen him show he was really hurt. She'd never seen him show much but a kind of surfacey joviality, and mild irritation. Sometimes he'd show her a little affection, sort of like the affection her older brother had given his gerbil. Her brother Albert hadn't wanted the gerbil but his therapist said he should have a pet. Albert was in college now and they pretty much never heard from him.

Her dad looked at Bron. "Hey Bron, what's up?"

"Not a whole lot, Mr. Burnside."

He smiled thinly. "Just chillin' at the skizzy?"

Lani winced. Bron said, "Yeah. The skizzy. Chillin, at."

Her dad considered the two of them. She cringed at what he might say next. She wasn't wrong. "You're kind of the odd couple, you two— except for the matching clothes. Lani, tall and skinny . . ." He looked at Bron who was short and chunky.

"We're not 'a couple', Dad," she said. "You're hurting Bron's reputation."

"We're a couple of *somethings*," Bron said. He looked like he was a long ways away, in his mind; she was afraid he was trying to think of a way to talk to her dad about what she'd text messaged. Maybe he'd just blurt out, *Your daughter's threatening suicide, dude.* That wouldn't be like Bron—but he might think it was an emergency.

"So are we going somewhere?" she asked her dad, to get away from Bron before he could say anything.

Dad nodded, taking his car keys out of his pants pocket. "Yeah. Let's go. You're coming to the lab with me. Your . . . We'll talk about it on the way."

She waggled her fingers in an ironic goodbye at Bron; he stuck his thumb and little finger out from his fist by his ear in a "call me" handsign and she nodded as she followed her dad to the BMW.

Her dad looked at a butcher-paper sign under the school windows that the pep squad had made up. It said VOTE FOR MISTER AND MISS POPULARITY MAY 1!!!

Dad looked at her. She knew he was thinking about making a joke and she knew pretty much what it was. Something about how she should run for Miss Popularity. She saw it in his face when he thought better of it.

"IT'S SUCH BULLSHIT to do it just because 'oh, the therapist recommends it'," Lani said.

"But if we don't try it and you, I don't know, run off with the circus or something because you're depressed," Dad said, driving up the hill to the lab, "then we'll say 'Hell, we shoulda tried something, anything, and now she's marrying Boffo the clown'."

"That's funny."

"You used to think my sense of humor was funny. But now you're a teenager. When I was a teenager I thought my dad was, I don't know, Hitler's long lost son. We got to be pretty good friends later, after I realized that Republicans aren't actually fascists."

She remembered the way Granddad had looked at Dad when he made excuses about not going to see Grandma in the hospice, and she didn't think they ever got to be "pretty good friends".

"I miss Granddad," she said.

You never knew, Granddad might be listening, if that afterlife stuff was true. She'd seen a show about Near Death Experiences. She doubted if it was real. It was probably all oxygen starvation. But maybe.

"I miss him too," he said. She could tell it was work for him to say that.

The road wound up, around the highest hill of the San Jose Hills district, on one of the ragged outer fringes of Silicon Valley.

Lani and her Mom and Dad lived in the two-year-old Hillview Hideaway gated tract home complex, which was just now below and behind the car. She didn't turn to look at it when they spiraled around the hill again, the tract laid out under them. When she was a little girl, if she'd seen her neighborhood from above she'd have wanted to pick out her own house from the others: Hard to do in a housing tract. Now she was reluctant to look at the development at all, especially from up here: depression had levels of discomfort, and some things made it an ache. But she could see the walled tract in her mind anyway: a rat's maze of identical houses; now and then a tiny stunted little tree planted in barkdust. No wonder Mom was into that Shiatsu massage guy—you'd have to have an affair just so you knew you were alive, down there. She wondered, for about the fiftieth time, if Dad knew.

She felt the pit open up in her—it was just like a trap door opening—and felt the suction from it, the vacuum drawing her downward. She'd been teetering on the edge of it all day. She felt the inner plunge, and her stomach recoiled in nausea when they took a hairpin turn. Staring at the snaky road seemed to make it worse, so she looked out over the valley, beyond the Hideaway tracts.

Blue-gray smog blurred the vineyards to the west and the sun flared from the tangled Silicon Valley freeways to the south—freeways ribboning between endless Wal-Marts and Costcos and malls; patches of green residential areas.

It was like a great stovetop, to her then. It wasn't a very hot day but somehow every place she looked at was something being cooked, and people were the main recipe ingredient. Something, somewhere, was cooking up their souls for consumption. The Something used Time as its heating element, and when people finally gave up and became a kind of suburban zombie, they were finished being cooked, and the Something consumed their souls. Sometimes the Something aged them first before it ate them; sometimes it heated them up too fast and burned them. She thought of her friend Justin who was drooling on himself in a long-term care place.

Justin had been on the down side of manic depression for a long, long time, before the pill salad, and his dad kicking him out for hitting his sister—half an hour later his dad, regretting it, had gone out driving to find him but Justin had gone to San Francisco and somebody had given him some methedrine and the needle. He'd gotten HIV from that one shot and when it was diagnosed ten months later he took that double handful of random stuff from the bathroom cabinet . . . and it fried his brain.

She wasn't going to *try* to kill herself, like Justin; she was going to do it right. She was going to be smart about it like the Romans. Like the Hemlock Society. Justin panicked. That was stupid. You had to ease your way out . . .

But sometimes she just wanted it all to stop—quick. Trying to tell people how she felt seemed so hopeless—like now, her dad was rattling away next to her. She could try—she could break in, yell at him, *You're so all up in your own self, you're all about playing the game really well and you only get excited by science and I remember when you said that when people like Justin die it's just "natural selection in action" well fuck you, he was my friend and no matter if you say you love me I never believe it, you're always so distant about it and why do you think my brother never comes around and why do you think Mom is like making moo-cow eyes at that Shiatsu guy because you abandoned her emotionally and—*

But if she did say that out loud everything would just get even worse; he'd get all chilly and analytical and defensive and he'd double her trips to the therapist—that nodding, smiling, puppetlike therapist Mary who made Lani's blood run cold—and make her go on medication or something, like it was all in her imagination. And she'd tried Prozac, it made her feel like she was in a bottle, in no pain but all distant from things. Maybe it'd turned her into what Dad was.

If she tried to really honestly talk to the therapist, the woman just tried to convince her that she was wrong, that her view of the world was unfair—but that was so *irrelevant*. It didn't *matter* if she was mistaken, if it was all she could see.

And if she tried to talk to her mom, if she told her how she really felt, Mom'd get mad, like Lani was blaming her parents, like she was saying they'd fucked up the world. But she didn't blame them—not really. They were clueless, is all. Everybody got to a point where they realized their parents were clueless and so were they. But you couldn't make them understand that—"Mom, it's like we're all so clueless, it's all meaningless. People pretend they know what they're alive for and what the point is but they don't. They're just trying to keep from screaming." And Mom would say that was "just drama," she'd refuse to get that— refuse to even try to understand it.

Lani wanted to say: You don't have to agree but if you could *just feel it* too, feel what she felt . . . even for a moment . . .

That was the point: you couldn't make anyone understand, really, except a few friends like Bron and Lucinda. They'd kept her going this far. But even they would say there were reasons to live. The world had adventure, it had friends, it had art . . .

She shook her head. The world? Look closer. It was like the world was this vain sickly old woman who didn't realize she was about to die, insisted she was still twenty-five, and you just wanted to hold up a mirror and say *Look at what you are, accept it and let go! Just die!*

Only the world wouldn't die. So the people in it had to die to get away from it.

She wanted to show her Mom and Dad and that educated idiot Mary the therapist what it really looked like, in Lani's World. Somehow that was the only way to communicate: get them into your world. And that was impossible. You can't put two worlds in one space. That was the whole point: everyone was isolated. They had some indirect contact with other people, but really they lived and died alone.

She looked at the traffic down below her on the freeway under the hill and saw hundreds, thousands of vehicles, each with a driver in their own personal daydream, their own impenetrable personal world, not thinking about being just another little metal box moving on an asphalt ribbon. They were all looking for some kind of comfortable equilibrium, which was the best you could hope for in the long run. And it was so . . . meaningless. It just went on and on and then you dribbled your life away like Grandma in the hospice, some sullen stranger cleaning the poop off you every day as you tried to remember your husband's name. Maybe that's when this feeling had started— when she'd gone to visit Grandma towards the end. How could you look Alzheimer's in the eye and think that life was meaningful?

She looked at the sky and its blue seemed to part for her, revealing itself as but a thin veil over the black aching emptiness between the planets; the remote stars. Matter spinning out there, burning, cooling, seeking its own state of dull equilibrium, as her dad had told her. Just a lot of empty process in the midst of infinitely empty space, headed for the fulfillment of the steady state theory or the heat-death theory, or . . . what difference did it make how the universe ended? What was one human life in all this—or even on the Earth? One human life was a single bubble in a cauldron on that stovetop. The bubble rose from the bottom of the heated pot, made a brief journey to the surface; there was a moment of seething and then it popped, was sucked away by the Something, and was gone to be replaced by another bubble. No two exactly alike—yet they were all alike. Meaningless. Like Ernest Hemingway had said in that story she'd done the report on for English: *Nada, nada . . . and nada.*

And what'd Hemingway done, in the end? Blown his brains out. Had the good sense to be efficient about it. No time to think, just a clicking sound and then . . .

"We're here," Dad said, driving into the parking lot of Silicon Quanta Labs, at the very top of the hill. "Anyway, your therapist, that Mary what's-her-name, says you need to spend more time with me, says maybe if you understand my work more you'll relate to me, maybe even stop with the suicidal imagery . . . And I have to work late today, so . . ."

She looked at him. What was he talking about? How did he know? "Stop with what . . . imagery?"

"From your poetry," he said, as they got out of the car. The sun was so bright up here, on top of the hill; heat thudding in waves from the asphalt. "On that website." Looking at his watch. "Your mom showed me—well, actually, Justin's mom sent it to your mom. Justin's sister saw it. I told your mom you're too smart for . . . to try what Justin did. You're just letting off some steam, but you know Mom—she's pretty dramatic."

"You guys read my poetry?"

"What are you being so outraged for? You put it up online! That never seemed like a public space to you? And you put your name to it!" He smiled crookedly at her and recited, *"Death come, death numb, numb me like the bite of an arachnid so I cannot feel being eaten alive . . .* Vivid stuff! Imaginative! Melodramatic yes— but hey, I was a teenager too. I remember when I was taken with *Stranger in a Strange Land* and your granddad thought Heinlein was a cult leader or something . . ."

"My poem was at a site that only a few people are supposed to know about and it's . . . not *really* public, I mean . . ."

God, he could make her feel stupid sometimes . . .

The little Filipino security guard, steeped in boredom, waved them through the double glass doors and then they were in the coolness of the building. Too hot outside, but too chilly indoors, in these air conditioned, immaculate spaces; this lobby where the abstract art was selected to color coordinate with the furnishings. The elderly secretary at the big horseshoe-shaped desk looked up from a laptop—which she snapped shut as they came in, probably watching a movie on it—and beamed at them. "Oh, Lani . . . hi! How are ya?" Her smile, as she gave Lani a visitor's pass, seemed completely unreal, disconnected with the bleakness in her eyes. And Lani saw the old woman in her coffin. It wasn't precognition, it wasn't hallucination—it just happened to Lani a lot that she imagined people she met in their coffins. The old woman in her coffin at the funeral home with one or two mourners. An impatient son looking at his watch. Later the coffin slammed shut. Darkness inside . . .

"Hi . . . " Lani managed.

Dad just waved at the receptionist and led the way across the lobby; swiped his card through the scanner, and the door to Research opened for them. She followed him past offices and cubicles, past locked doors reeking of obscure chemicals used in experimental computer chips, to a special elevator that needed to scan the card again before it would take them down to the primary Quanta labs: the ones the stockholders were supposed to get excited about, though the techs hadn't yet produced anything practical in quantum-computing.

Dad's lab—she'd been there only once before—reminded her of a big industrial laundry room because it was dominated by a bulky circular machine with a round window in its center. Ranged clunkily around the circular centerpiece were angular solid-state machines, completely arcane to Lani, bright with chrome surfaces, restless with digital readouts ticking over.

Her Dad went muttering to one of the computer work stations set up in the cramped space near the door. "Where the hell is Dinwiddy? He's supposed to be here. If he's smoking pot at work again I'll kick his ass. He fu . . . he screws up and wanders off every time he does that stuff. I hope you don't get into pot, you won't get a goddamn thing done."

"Stoners are retards." She said it automatically but she believed it.

"He's left a program running, too . . ." Dad muttered, bending over a keyboard.

She approached the wire-clustered machine dominating the room, feeling like Dorothy walking toward the Wizard of Oz: she felt like she was being watched from behind a curtain. The device was some kind of experimental new particle accelerator, for Dad's quantum physics project—a new kind of collider, supposed to be able to do within its tightly wound coils what the big ones did over miles of tunnels.

Light glittered, multicolored sparks fountaining and sinking back on the other side of the round window. The collider clicked and muttered to itself in a language without words or grammar.

"What the hell's he been up to?" her dad said, squinting at a Dinwiddy's notes on a monitor. "He's not supposed to be running the damn thing when I'm not here . . . Says he thinks there might be a singularity. Right. He *has* been smoking something."

"What's a 'singularity'?" she asked. Almost interested.

"Uh . . . well usually it's something in astrophysics." He was barely audible over the chirring, the hissing from the accelerator. "Theoretical point where physical laws break down . . . supposed to exist in a black hole . . . Anything you can think can be real there . . ."

"That's tight. Break down the laws of physics. Like to do that myself."

"That's my girl," he muttered, poking through a sheaf of papers on Dinwiddy's desk. ". . . never mind Miss Popularity—she's Miss Singularity . . ."

"You can't, like, make your own singularity?" She was trying to work out the glimmering shapes forming in the oval, metal and glass spaces within the accelerator. As soon as she thought they were this or that shape, they were some other. "I mean, in a lab?"

"Maybe for a few seconds . . . Where'd he put that equation? Uh, some people say a singularity could be created with an accelerator if you can get the right balance of matter and antimatter and . . . "

His voice trailed off as he tapped at a keyboard. She wasn't really listening to him anyway. She was staring into the circular window. Putting her hand on the glass. Something inside seemed to be looking back . . .

She saw a baby inside. A familiar baby: she'd seen it in old, color Kodaks in Mom's photo album. Then she glimpsed herself as a toddler, on the other side of the glass. Then a two-headed child; one head was herself as a melancholy ten-year-old; the other was herself too, only it was a different ten-year-old Lani—smiling. The two Lanis vanished one into the other and . . .

"Dad?" she heard herself say.

And there was her dad, inside: a teen in the sixties, with long hair, a headband; Dad as a US Marine in Vietnam, later on. Only he'd never been a US Marine, never been to Vietnam. He'd gotten some kind of college research exemption. But there he was in uniform, carrying an M16, looking scared and alone—and then he was gone and instead of toddlers and dads, there was an eye, just a black eye looking back at her. But it wasn't an eye, exactly—that was just the description that came to mind because it looked at you, you knew it was aware of you, and it was elliptical, but in fact it was a kind of squeezed tornado of space itself, spinning this way and that: whatever way she wanted. She felt sure of it, at that moment: it was responsive to her.

Oh, she told it, answering a question she never quite heard asked, *if only people could see the world I live in. If only two people really could share the same world . . . then maybe we could find some meaning.*

The eye seemed to blink . . .

"Lani!" Her Dad dragging her back from the accelerator. "Get the hell away from that thing . . . It's not shielded for whatever it's putting out . . . Dim-witty is what he oughta be called . . . Come on . . . "

He took her by the wrist, drew her out of the lab. She glanced at him. He looked pale, shaken. "There was an eye looking at me from in there," she said. "Thought I saw pictures, too . . . of me, and you and . . ."

"Yeah, you get a lot of Rorschach inkblot effect with all those third-level energetic responses . . ."

"No, it . . . never mind." He wouldn't believe her. And she was, she had to admit, pretty prone to imagining things. She saw faces in tree trunks, imagined sasquatches in the brush.

"Come on, I'm gonna have to shut down the lab." Suddenly he stopped at the intersection of two hallways and looked at her. "You feel okay, kid?" She thought she saw real concern in his face. But no—probably not. How likely was that?

"Yeah. I'm fine."

"No nausea, or, uh . . . dizziness?"

"No."

"Uh—okay. Well let's get something to eat. Screw the lab. I missed my lunch. I need a beer and a burger." He dug out his cell phone, and speed-dialed Dinwiddy, but couldn't get him on the line.

And dad never did get his assistant on the line. Nor did Dinwiddy ever return to his apartment. No one found Dinwiddy, anywhere. Not ever.

LANI PICKED AT a shrimp salad, trying to decide if she'd imagined what she'd seemed to see in the collider. Dad ate a cheeseburger, every third bite or so speed-dialing to try to reach Dinwiddy on his cell phone. Finally he shook his head, tucked the cell phone away and looked at her as if trying to remember why they were in a restaurant together at this time of day. He seemed to realize he was supposed to talk to her, Dad to daughter here, so he brought up exactly what she wasn't interested in talking about: how she was doing in school; told her that her sinking grades might not matter to her now but they would later. After that oh-so-surprising comment they had nothing much to say and they got home early . . . and when they were just getting out of the car, Dad saw Bergman, that longhaired muscular Shiatsu massage guy, rushing out the side garage door, clutching his Birkenstocks in his hand, giving them a whitefaced glance as he jumped onto his Zapbike. Rode off pretty fast.

Dad went into the house and found Mom half undressed, her hair mussed, and she was saying it was just massage and he said then *why's he running out of here and goddamn it, this is a condom, a used condom, the dumbshit's too damn stupid to take his condom with him, and Mom was bursting into tears, saying Dad hadn't touched her in so long, and—*

An hour later they were talking soberly, quietly, in the kitchen, of divorce. There was no glimmer of reconciliation in their talk. It was all excuses, bitterness, and dismissive finality.

They usually made Lani eat dinner with them but Mom just nodded when Lani asked if she could eat a sandwich in her room—Mom with her frosted golden-brown, spiky-top hair, thatch-hut straight at the sides: a look she'd seen in *Cosmo* that the movie stars had given up a year or two before; her eyes looked pouchy, her makeup runny. Mom tried to look young, tried too hard, even getting a little nose-stud in one nostril—but now for the first time, looking at her, Lani noticed that faint cheek fuzz that women get after menopause.

Shrugging, Lani went to her room, ate only a couple of bites of the peanut butter sandwich as she booted up her computer. Bron was online too, got a prompt that she was online and Instant-Messaged her.

U OK? Concert?

Still here, she responded. *No concert. Dad caught Mom boffing Shiatsu. Divorce now. Not joking.*

That's fucked up, he typed back. *Want me 2 come over?*

No. Feel like being alone.

Maybe not a good time 2 b alone. Go to concert w/me. Death Club & Desktop Junkies.

Can't stand 2 b around people. Fucking depressed.

I don't know if I should tell u this now but somebody will. Justin finally died. 4 real.

Shit. Really?

Really. Today.

But—and she decided it as she typed it—*that's a good thing, that's what he wanted, it's finally over 4 him.*

Not a good thing 4 his mom. She doted on that dude. U going 2 b OK? Serious! Answer serious. You have friends. Stuff 2 do. You were talking about —

I'm not going 2 commit—

—suicide. You're not?

She wanted to scare him by saying maybe, maybe not. But she knew that was just to get a reaction, it was selfish, so she typed *No.*

K i'm going 2 concert. u promise? No suicide 2nite?
I promise.
Concert? concert concert concert! Yeah: concert. Come.
No. g2g. bye.

THE DEPRESSION RAN like crude oil over everything she did, everything she saw and heard and said the rest of the evening—making her think of the old Sisters of Mercy song "Black Planet". Looking at the news window on the Comcast site—nothing but morbid curiosity, to take in the news—she read about a group of children blown to pieces by American landmines; read about birth defects caused by mercury in fish and about a woman who'd punished her child by making him kill his beloved dog; read about the lives of refugees in Chad. The journalist quoted a young woman as saying, "Why do we live, if we live like this?"

She went to the bathroom and heard her mom in the bedroom next door shout at her dad that he had discouraged her from being an actress, from doing all she ever really wanted to do, and that dream was dead now . . . *dead.*

Lani thinking: All she ever really wanted to do? Like raising Albert and me hadn't meant anything to her . . .

And Dad shouted back that Mom was just a selfish, stupid woman, and "That sums it up and I'm not going to say anything more to you except through a goddamn lawyer."

The divorce, her parents' argument, it was all just part of the same evaluation typing out in Lani's mind like the print-out from an imaginary computer program: *You come from a family of hopelessly selfish people. Projected probability: you're going to be just like them. Unless you die.*

Tucked away in her bedroom, she went to that Goth poetry website and read her poetry and now it seemed so lame, childish as her dad had implied. She went to the forms, highlighted her stuff, hit *delete,* thinking: If only deleting myself was that simple and painless. And then she looked over at the mirror on her dresser; saw herself hunched like a questionmark over the keyboard, a dreary, wearily angry expression on her face. Her hair looking stringy, hands long and thin and ugly. And she'd thought:

Look at me. God I'm just a fucking human worm.

She looked out the window. The moon was almost full and you could see the face on it—a face so well etched, to her, so definite. But its usual arch expression was shifting now because there were black clouds blowing by, like twisted thin black-silk cloth drawn over the moon so that its expression shifted in the murk: angry, bitter, sadly amused. Nice of the moon to keep her company. When she turned off the desk lamp she saw the moonlight was falling across her bed; the moon would go to bed with her, too.

So she went to bed, lay in moonlight listening on earphones to Monster Magnet's song "There's No Way Out of Here", downloaded from the Internet, and then an album by Nick Cave. The music seemed to create a space that she could bear to be in, a dimension where tragedy was given meaning and perspective and form by art, and it eased her a little. But then she thought about the news, and her parents, and the look Grandma had given her, the last time she'd seen her in the hospice, like she wanted to say *Save me!*, but she didn't know, anymore, how to ask for help; a look from the far side of a void.

And Lani made up her mind. It was not Nick Cave's doing—this was a decision that had been growing in her for a long time: she would kill herself on the following day, without fail. Then maybe her parents would feel something, experience something besides their own stupid worlds; and she wouldn't have to see people pretend day after day that living was meaningful, and she wouldn't have to end like Grandma after a life like her mother's.

Why do we live, if we live like this?

Yes. Tomorrow.

HER EYES SNAPPED open a little after dawn on Saturday morning—which was something that *never* happened. She usually managed to nestle deep into sleep, to hoard it and mete it out like a miser with pennies, making it last till at least eleven in the morning, or noon, on weekends.

But she was wide awake not long after dawn, convinced that she'd given birth during the night. That's what the dream had been, anyway, a confused dream of missing periods and sudden pregnancies and babies erupting from her, half a dozen of them, wet runny blueskinned babies crawling about the bed, all tangled up in their umbilici . . . Though she had never had that kind of sex, just a little oral sex and some fingering, from that guy Corey with the skateboard he didn't know how to use and breath that smelled like cigarettes and tacos and beer. He'd told everyone, and she hadn't felt like finding a boyfriend after that.

Now she actually sat up and looked at the sheets between her legs for evidence of babies, little bloody footprints or something. She sneered at herself, and lay back down, curled up on her side. Go back to sleep, dumbshit.

Nope. Going back to sleep wasn't going to happen. She was lying there on her side with her knees vibrating together like she had drunk three cups of espresso. She got up and felt a trickle down her thigh; her period had started. She reflected on how death came to a woman's womb regularly, twelve times a year unless she was pregnant: the eggs breaking down in crumbling disappointment.

She had bathed the day before; she didn't feel up to showering now. She wiped her thigh, put in a tampon, put on black jeans, her red high-top tennis shoes, a *Lou Reed: The Raven* T-shirt, and went out back to feed the big koi in the concrete goldfish pond . . . And stared. Stared. Then she shook her foot, briskly—one of the fish had crawled onto it, using its new, copper-colored legs.

MRS WEIRBACHT, a widow of sixty-two who lived a block from Lani, had to get up early to be at the synagogue, the Rabbi needed her there at seven because they had the kids coming for Hebrew school at nine, and as she went to the refrigerator, and opened it, took out a carton of milk, she thought about all she had to do at the temple . . .

The bottom fell out of the carton and milk splashed onto the floor. She had to laugh at that. Have a word with the grocer. But her hands shook as she cleaned up the milk with a great many paper towels, on her hands and knees—as she finished and straightened up she hit her head on a cabinet door that had somehow come open while she was down there. As she looked at it, one hand to her ringing head, the shelves holding the pots up collapsed, and all the pots clattered out. She straightened up, carefully, breathing hard. So, don't panic, a minor earthquake, maybe?

But she closed her eyes, thinking about when Hillel had his nervous breakdown, the bad week when his father and sister were killed in the bombing in Jerusalem and his son had been arrested for a hit and run; Hillel shouting about everything falling apart, you could put it together but everything would just fall apart, and he'd started smashing the kitchen of their house, then, hammering things with a skillet. *Everything would fall apart, no matter what you did . . .*

She felt dizzy, her mouth dry. Decided to get some orange juice. She reached into the fridge, took out a glass quart of orange juice—the bottom fell out of the glass bottle and orange juice splashed all over the floor. Four more containers chose that moment to open in the refrigerator, gushing over the shelves. At exactly the same instant, last night's garbage disposal grindings erupted from the drain of the kitchen sink, spewing onto the window looking out over the back garden. Where all her plants seemed to have turned black . . . and the ornate fountain in the garden that Hillel had built was crumbling, falling into a pile of disconnected, nondescript bones.

DARREN J. KENNECK, gay bachelor of forty-seven, resident of Hillview Hideaway, was sitting on his front porch weeping. His roses had all gotten some kind of strange mold or smut on them and they had turned jet black, from blossoms to leaves to stem: uniformly black. They stood up just as before, but they were jet black. But he was weeping for his mother. She had died a month before and he could hear her voice coming from the moist black earth between the black roses, though she was buried way up the freeway at Colma. It was as if she'd crawled from her coffin, through the soil, never coming to the surface, digging like a mole mile after mile from Colma to here, to come up just under the surface of his rose garden. He could see the outline of her body there in the dirt, just faintly, lying there face up; he could hear her voice distinctly.

"It's . . . lonely, Darrie," his mom said. ". . . it's lonely. It's . . . lonely. It's . . . lonely . . . Darrie . . ."

MR. RAJI JHURAN, a Sikh, postman for Lani's neighborhood, adjusted his turban and stepped out of the boxy blue and white US Mail truck, with his satchel over his shoulder—and came to a dead stop, staring up the walk to 1209 Elm Grove. The two front windows of the house were the gigantic eyes of a pretty girl; the door was gone, replaced by the girl's nose; her lips were where the steps should be; the roof had curved to become her glossy black hair. The woman's head was as big as the house had been; was sunken past the chin into the Earth; a giant living head that seemed to have been built the way you build a house.

Raji turned and looked down the street. The other houses were not what they should be, either; they'd all changed somehow. And a blizzard of black snow began swirling down through the air.

Raji called out to Guru Nanak, in Hindi, and retreated into the truck. The mail, in sacks behind him, shifted and shuffled as everything typed or written on it was spoken aloud, but softly, just audibly. *Dear Mom, I'm not sure when I can come out but if you could send some money, I might be able to pay . . . Dear Mr. Hingeman, we regret to inform you . . . A new Visa card is preapproved for Mrs. Elmer Chasburton . . .*

Raji said, in Hindi: "I dream. Lord Nanak, raise me from this dream." He drove the truck in a careening panic back to the exit at the gates of Hillview Hideaway and the gates were closed and locked in chains that hadn't been there before: chains of hair, glossy black hair. But trying to force the gates open—with his hands and then with the truck—he soon discovered that the long swatches of shiny black hair were hard as steel. He looked for another way out, thinking to climb the cinderblock walls, but he was afraid to go near them: the wall blocks shifted one on another like teeth grinding when he approached them. His cell phone did not work—or more specifically, it would only call people who did not know him, though they seemed to have his last name: they spoke no Hindi, and one of them said "Raji Jhuran? That's my grandfather, dude, guy's dead, stone dead like, what, many years now . . ."

And he crawled under his truck, covering his head, thinking that he was being punished for coming to live in this bloodless place, this place with no understanding of the sacred. He had come from Punjab to California because this was where the world's money was kept, but since coming here he'd lain with a woman other than his wife, and now he saw that he must have died—died a mere *patit,* far short of *Khālsā*—and he'd been cast into one of the worlds to which you were consigned before you reincarnated, where demons mocked you with your karma, your karma falling like black snow from the heavens . . . He wept and called to Gobind Singh, begging for forgiveness . . .

THE KOI WERE crawling out of the pond, on their scaly silver-orange legs, like those ancient fish that walked onto the land, the tetrapods; they were creeping about the edges of the lawn, susurrating and tittering softly, seeming to grin at Lani. Then she noticed the grass itself—jet black. She reached down and plucked at it, thinking it had burned, was ashen and would crumble. But no, it was leathery hard, and it jerked back from her touch.

"Oh shit," she said. Had someone dosed her with something? She decided that wasn't the case. It was harder to decide she wasn't dreaming, especially when she saw that it was snowing flakes of black that vanished on hitting the ground; that the clouds hanging low, nearly low as a ceiling over the neighborhood, were forming very distinctive faces, a crowd of teenage faces looking down at her; she only knew one of them: Justin, who was dead now. She knew somehow that all these other faces were dead kids, too. The cloud faces seemed to be singing something, though she couldn't hear any words. Their misty heads moved back and forth, like people all singing along to the same song at a concert. The black snow plumed from their mouths instead of music.

But eventually Lani decided she wasn't dreaming. Especially when Bron showed up, about three minutes later, rushing in her back gate, his eyes feverish, mouth open in an oval like the shape of the collider in Dad's lab. "My mom was, like, screaming," he said, rushing up, getting it out between gasps, points of red on his cheeks. He must've run all the way here. "She woke me up screaming and she said there were faces in the clouds and the grass was . . . And the phones aren't working, none of them, and you can't get out of the gates, you can't leave the complex . . . I thought somebody'd dosed us but we're all seeing the same fucking stuff!"

They had some discussion about whether or not they could be dreaming the same dream somehow. But finally she said, "No. It's real. I've been sort of expecting something. The singularity didn't blink—it was winking at me."

"The what?"

She told him about the lab, and what her Dad had said, and she thought that somehow she'd made a connection with the singularity, and it was making her world real for everyone, externalizing her inner world, and as she said it they were both grinning, because now there was music rising on the air too—a dark dirge-like but somehow triumphant rock music emanating from the new, startlingly large lilies growing along the mossy fences of her backyard, as if their blossoms were those amplifying trumpets on antique crank-up record players. The music sounded sort of like Switchblade Symphony but then again it was sort of like early Nine Inch Nails or maybe Joy Division but then again it was like Christian Death or Ministry, but on the other hand it was more like London After Midnight . . . or the early Cure . . . or . . . .

"Can you make out the words?" Bron asked her, breathless.

"I . . . no. Well yes . . ." She listened, repeated: "'Have you seen my soul . . . I left it on the subway station . . . someone has taken it and . . .' Uh, I think: 'left it with freebox clutter in their closet . . . some semihuman evasion . . . planning someday to sell it . . . no one will ever get what it's worth . . .'"

"I didn't hear any of that at all!" Bron protested. "I heard 'has the bell finally tolled, has my life measured out its ration . . .'"

She shrugged. Thinking that in a way they were the same lyrics.

She and Bron both put out their hands to catch the black snow; and for .3333 of a second each flake was a distinct geometrical shape on their palms, like snowflakes under a microscope, but in onyx black and made out of an intricacy of interlocking death's heads and skeletal bones—yet no two alike. When you looked close enough you could see the hard, interconnected shapes in the black crystals replicating infinitely, a continuum of the resolutely bleak: infinite cancellation. And then they'd vanish—each going with its own soft sigh. Lani and Bron looked at one another and laughed. All the while the music played, changing from one sonic shape to the next the way colors shifted and overlapped when you turned a prism around and around: there was no one definite song—yet it was all one song.

She and Bron should have been scared, she supposed. But they both felt weightless, as if they'd dropped burdens they hadn't known they'd carried. They teetered near panic, too, especially when shiny anacondas made of volcano-glass oozed—slithering in ripples to the music that played—along the fence tops, jewel-like eyes flashing as they snapped at the great swooping bats: flying foxes. She felt a spasm of fear at two brief flurries of hail when she saw the hailstones were .22 bullets, still in their casings: ready for a gun.

"Those bats are fucking huge," Bron said, blinking up at them.

"That's how big they are in, like, Indonesia," she muttered vaguely, looking up at the flop-flapping leather wings. "I did a report for biology. They're flying foxes, actually, biggest kinda bat . . ."

She was fighting off a wave of panic, as the volcano-glass anacondas all turned to look at her, at once, as if awaiting orders; as a beam of black-light struck down from the clouds and illuminated a coffin shape forming in the ground nearby; taking shape . . . opening invitingly . . .

But the panic and fear were overwhelmed by a rising sense of triumphant belonging. Taking a deep breath, she reflected that this was her creation, and choosing to revel in her new world was a way to survive it; even to thrive in it. Lani only knew that the more she just accepted it, the more it felt increasingly right.

"Yeah—fuck it, it's *mine!*" She danced in place, kicking bullets and creeping crickets made of chrome.

Then she had a sudden thought, and ran to check her folks in the house—careful not to open the chattering closets, deciding not to see what was cooing hugely in the bathroom—and found her parents were still asleep, Mom in the bedroom and Dad on the sofa. They'd probably both taken meds to sleep and their slumber seemed a good thing, in view of the feverishly growing bird-of-paradise plants outside the windows: snapping their orange beaks at the symmetrical filigrees of gray-black mold which spread, in seconds, to cover the window glass . . .

Lani told the snapping flowers outside the window: *Stay out there, don't bother Mom and Dad.* They seemed to draw back a little, at this.

Something took wing in Lani like a joyously hungry flying fox as she returned to the back yard, where the music seemed to boom even louder to greet her return, and the faces in the sky swiveled to gaze with somber affection at her.

"Come on, let's check out the street!" Bron yelled. Laughing—and afraid as he laughed.

They ran to the street out front. Stopped there on the sidewalk, cursing and marveling, gazing at Lani's own, her very own hot-house world. They noticed the cars first—or what they'd become.

"The cars are all changed," Bron said, with approval. He'd done an essay for English on how he disliked cars. In their places were black mariahs and hearses, only they all seemed full of water, and swimming things:

Through the windows of the funereal vehicles they could see dark green and red fish, thin and transparent like scarves woven with eyes and gills, and octopi whose upper parts were human skulls, and detached but delicate human hands with black fingernails that pumped along like jellyfish. "You made them into aquariums! And the whole street . . ."

"It's like that painting I tried to do," she said, at last, her voice almost lost in the pounding of her heart, "when I took art from Mr. Yee, and he said it was so, like, muddled, you couldn't make out a composition."

"I remember," Bron said, looking at the intricate vista of eagerly shifting darkness that the street, the whole neighborhood had become. Bron adding in an undertone: "You could tell Mr. Yee wanted to say it was depressing but he didn't want to be that personal . . ." He looked at her. "So—even, like, right now—you're doing this somehow?"

She nodded. "I think . . . yeah. I am."

The composition had been poorly formed in her mind, even more muddy on her canvas; but here it was as composed as a Goya, dark yet clearly etched:

The sun was a dead white disk through the heavy, low clouds draped only a few hundred feet above the houses —the pallid teen faces overhead still sulkily blowing out the black blizzard. The lampposts, the telephone poles, the eaves of houses, the little trees, the fences, the cars: everything was fringed, edged with living pennants, thousands of them blowing toward Bron and Lani in the black blizzard wind. It was like the street was deep under water, and the streamers were seaweed clinging thickly to sunken ships. But there: instead of the black crepe was a woman's hair blowing thickly from a round roof; no, Lani saw, not a roof, it was a woman's head—some idealization of Lani herself— growing up out of the ground instead of a house, but then again it was a house too, the nose could open, swing back like a door. It did open, showing a red triangle, damp filling like the interior of a gourd. The eyes that were windows turned to look right at them.

"Fuck! Those giant eyes are looking at us!" Bron blurted, sounding scared for the first time.

And all the time the music played, its rhythms interlaced with the living motion of the street: the movement of black streamers, colored-ink fish, translucent anacondas, flitting bats, dimly seen forms chasing one another, littering, in the quivering shrubs along the mold-laced house-fronts.

She was looking at the house across the street from her parents; an owl big as a Bron perched in the Boltons' living room, looked out the picture window, turning its head to regard them gravely with big golden eyes; on the television set to one side of the owl was an image that looked like a home movie Dad had taken of Lani at the beach as a child, playing in the sand; she knew somehow it was playing on all the television sets in the neighborhood.

"You see that fucking owl?" Bron said, swaying to the music. He was looking even paler than usual; she could see him vacillating between being scared and exultant. "And Justin in the sky . . ."

She was past being scared—she had been stoned only a couple of times, and it was like that, you were in the grip of something in your bloodstream just sweeping you along with it.

She saw in her mind's eye a hillside opening up to show a great cavern with a stream emerging from it, a red stream of her own blood, and she saw herself carried on the stream in a white, carven boat, completely naked, hands uplifted like a priestess—just a picture in her imagination—

Bron pointed the other way down the street, behind her, bursting out: "You're over there . . . naked, in a fucking boat!"

She turned and there was the hill that loomed over the housing complex, but now the hillside was literally riven by the cavern; now it spilled rusty fluid on which she rode naked in a boat made of intricately carved ivory . . . hands lifted in hieratic gesticulation . . .

She turned to see Bron gaping at the naked Lani priestess in the boat. "Stop looking at that!" Glaring at Bron. He looked hastily away. She turned back in time to see the figure on the boat disappear behind one of the houses—going where, she wondered. What would that version of herself say to her?

She found she was clinging to Bron's arm as they moved a little farther out into the street, peering down the street toward the woman's head; taking in the pallid, evil-eyed imps wrestling and burrowing in a garden of black irises, daffodils slowly oozing blood, tulips turned to brass: turned to green-stained metal; seeing a middle aged man she didn't know, weeping on his porch beside a rose garden gone jet. Across the street from the weeping man a few huddled figures, a family she knew vaguely, peered from behind curtains that opened and closed, opened and closed in slow modulation as if the house were respiring. The faces in the clouds were boiling in and out of clarity; the volcano-glass anacondas snapping up fox-bats only to sprout their wings and take flight like dragons, anacondas with big bat wings . . . And somehow it all continued to fit together into one deliberately articulated picture . . .

It seemed to her then that the street's transmutation was moving in a kind of direction, as leaves and debris are caught up in hurricane wind and blown one way, one way only; it was going somewhere in time, too. It was going to come to a decision of some kind . . . even as the stunted little trees the contractors had planted began to grow up higher, higher, thicker, extruding Spanish moss, the trees groaning like women in labor as their damp limbs spontaneously populated with screeching, improbable tropical birds, the long ribbons of moss streaming out to follow the crepe fringe. The crepe, the black snow, the purling mist rising from the black lawns, all of it winding together into a kind of tunnel, an oval whirlpool in the air; the shapes on the street twisted one into the next, an owl becoming a raven becoming a burst of black butterflies, swirling into the vortex rotating around the eye in the distance: the eye of the singularity, winking at Lani. And she felt she was going to enter into it with a kind of glorious immolation, a joyfulness like the crash of a dark storm-driven wave bursting into pearls before falling away into the fatal anonymity of the sea . . .

"Lani—" Bron looked down the street toward his family's house. "What's gonna happen to the people here?"

"Oh . . ." She felt like she was falling asleep, into a dream of glory, some ancient palace, Nefertiti riding a flying sphinx through the night sky. Smoke rising from the temple below—they were greeting her with a sacrifice, which was only right and proper . . .

"*Lani?*" Bron's voice was squeakily urgent now.

She twitched, shivering, coming partway back to herself. "Oh, what'll happen? The people here—probably end up in another world, have to adjust. New rules. Gone from this place. Some will die . . . Couldn't be worse than this place was before, Bron."

"You kids!" Her dad's voice, shouting over the music. "Lani, please, oh Christ—come here! You too, Bron! Get over here!"

Lani turned to see her dad, in his bathrobe and T-shirt, gesturing distraughtly from the front door of the house. Lani shook her head. She didn't want to go to her dad—she wanted him to come to her.

Wobbly and hugging herself, Mom came out on the porch in her nightgown, face stricken—frozen in a silent moan. A translucent anaconda dripped from the roof of the porch, wound itself around her mom, and Mom just stared at it, trembling, as hypnotized as a lamb about to be swallowed. Her dad tugged at the snake, cursing to himself, trying to pull it away from her . . .

Lani glared at the anaconda. "Let her go!" Obedient to her, it slithered away from Mom, into the shrugging junipers.

Dad looked at Lani, then at the snake's receding tail, back at Lani, realizing. "It's Lani . . . Dinwiddy . . . she stood too close . . ."

"Our Lani did this?" Lani's mother asked, chewing a knuckle, her face squeezed in fear, a struggle to comprehend.

"I think so," Dad told her. "She was at my lab—I told you about the way the mind can shape things, if . . ." He shook his head. Too much to explain when he only barely understood himself.

Lani looked at the vortex—a black-hearted celebration calling for its guest of honor . . .

"What we gonna do now, Lani?" Bron asked, his voice hoarse, almost lost in the growing roar of the increasingly discordant music, the seething of the wind, the cries of frightened people huddled in their houses.

"Lani!" her Mom called, with surprising firmness. "Please baby . . . stop this thing . . . stop it . . . Come back to us."

But Lani took a step toward the vortex . . . swaying with the music, though its rhythm was almost lost in its increasing thunder.

"Hey kid . . ." She turned to see her dad walking up to her. His trembling hands going to her face. "Baby . . . " His voice breaking. His eyes wet.

Lani looked at him, and her mom in amazement—and really saw them for the first time in years. Her father and mother both, disclosed, paradoxically, by the darkness of Lani's world. Somehow it made their inner lives shine out against its backdrop. Its darkness opened theirs to her: she saw their fears, their dilemmas, for a moment laid bare. They were trapped too . . .

She saw that her father felt things as much as anybody. She could see it in his eyes now, as if those shutters had been thrown open: worry, loneliness, fear . . . longing. Love.

He just didn't know how to show it. He was like a man whose limbs had gone numb, called to dance. But he heard the music.

And her mother, at the porch— her arms open now to Lani. Wanting her daughter in her arms, her husband beside her. Really wanting Lani alive and with them. Behind the shutters of her Mom's eyes there was a light that was more than selfish disappointment—normally nearly impossible to see, but quite real.

Lani let her dad, his gentle hand on her arm, guide her over to Mom. The music seemed to get quieter; some of the restless motion of the street slowed, as if the trees, the streams of black thoughts, the flying anacondas, all waited for Lani; Justin and the other faces in the clouds looking right down at Lani's house, right at this porch. Waiting for her decision.

"Is this how it is for you, Lani?" her mom asked, voice breaking, looking back at those faces; at the dark life on the street, as Lani came to the porch. Hesitating on the flagstone walk. "It's really like a . . . dark storm all the time?"

Lani nodded, and began to sob. "Like this—but worse. This is the way I make it okay. *This way it's a world I can live in.*"

Her dad nodded. Voice hoarse, he said: "I see, kid."

She looked hard at him—and she could see that he really did see. He wasn't judging her anymore, he wasn't hiding from her—he was just there, in her world, with her. Lani's world surrounded him, and he could feel it like weather on his skin. She had captured them both, her mom and dad—captured them and carried them off into the hidden recesses of her life. And for once, they really did see; for long enough, they shared the same world with Lani.

Dad looked down the street. "Dinwiddy was right after all . . . And you . . ." He looked at her. "We're at the wrong end of the scale for this kind of control, sweetheart. Can you let it go?"

Lani closed her eyes. She saw the eye of the singularity behind her closed eyelids staring back at her. It spoke to her somehow, without words or grammar. Telling her that she would never again, in this life, have a chance like the one she was giving up . . .

"Yes—I'm going to let it go. Send it all away," she said.

But Bron, standing a little distance away, simply and quite audibly, barked out one sharp syllable: "No!"

He closed his eyes and Lani could feel Bron reaching out—it was as if the singularity had created a kind of field of sensitivity in the air, and she could feel Bron's life, the energy that shines from every person, and she felt him reaching out and taking control of the singularity . . .

And she saw him lifted up then—a spike of rock was breaking from the lawn and lifting him up, carrying him higher and higher, so that he was higher than the house, going fifty feet up—until at last that spike of granite, shrugging bits of soil from itself, stopped moving. Purple and green lightning—he was always into that kind of melodrama, from playing *Warhammer* and *Dungeons and Dragons*—were issuing from his fingers.

A dog, someone's lost, gray-muzzled cockapoodle, was running down the sidewalk near the house, scared and confused—and Bron pointed his hand at it and purple-green lightning spat and crackled and the dog was a burnt, writhing, furless dying thing on the sidewalk, whimpering to itself and then going silent.

"Oh God, my God," Mom muttered, her hand covering her mouth.

"I'm not going to let go of it!" Bron boomed. His voice amplified just exactly the way it would from a microphone and PA system. *"You make this thing and give me hope and then you act like you're going to make it go away, Lani! Well it's never going away! I feel it now too! I can reach into that thing too! I'm going to build a castle, and take it to another world, and there rule, and anyone who tries to stop me will die—but first I'm going to lay waste to the high school, and anyone who's in it! The throbbing thing in me is gonna come out and take a shape and run around and be free 'cause I'm fucking sick of it being in me and I want it out, out there, right out there!"*

And he opened his hands, held them in front of him, and between them a shape formed, as if partly from his left and partly from his right hand, a sickeningly sticky little homunculus Bron, naked and contorted and clutching itself, like a fetus too long in the womb, twisted by birth defects . . .

And it grew, bigger and bigger, and stretched out its massive arms and looked for something to kill . . .

"Bron—don't—I don't think you can control it!" Lani yelled. "You're too pissed off to control it! You're too—"

But the thing, with its sticky wet leather-crinkled face, hearing Lani, turned toward her, and started down the peak of granite, climbing toward her like King Kong descending a building . . .

"Grunph!" it said. "Grunph ya!"

Her Dad put his arms around her, looked around for some place for them to run to . . .

"Bron it's going to hurt me!" Lani yelled.

Bron's face twitched then—his eyes widened. "No, wait—not Lani! You come back here, you can't—"

"YOU SAY I CAN'T! GRUNPH! I'M TIRED OF 'YOU CAN'T'!" the thing howled, in a scratchy distortion of Bron's voice. And then it turned in a sudden rage and bounded up the peak of rock. And there it clutched Bron to itself, and put his whole head into its mouth . . .

Lani closed her eyes and reached out, to take control back. Felt the singularity looking at her—saw it, in her mind's eye, gazing at her questioningly.

"Yes," she answered. "I know. Take it away from me. And from Bron. And from here."

The eye of the void winked at her, once more.

Then the spike of granite sank back into the ground, and the thing clinging to it—with Bron sucked into its rubbery gizzard—ducked its head under its arm and shrank to something the size of a walnut, and slipped into the soil with the shrinking stone blade, and was gone . . . Bron with it.

Then the street sighed—and surrendered her living daydream. The flying anacondas burst into small flocks of black butterflies, which burst in turn into midges with tiny human faces, which burst into a black mist, which trailed away; the tropical trees shrank back, and melted, their birds taking flight and then becoming blossoms blown on the wind; the faces in the clouds lost definition, and the clouds blew into rags; the color leached back into the plants; the aquarium funeral cars burst open, water gushing out only to instantly evaporate, idiosyncratic fish unthreading, evaporating with it, SUVs and Saturns and Tauruses reasserting their glossy metal shapes; the crepe let go and melted into wisps of fog; the house that was Lani cried out once, a cry of bitter disappointment, then laughed, and crinkled, shriveled like an old gourd, till its rind fell away into dust and the ordinary house was revealed under it: Justin's house, Lani realized. The blizzard ceased, and the lilies fell silent. The music muted. Near silence . . .

Sunlight fell warm over the complex, glanced off car windows, glowed in green lawns. Daffodils perfumed the air. But Hillview

Hideaway looked strangely cold for all the warmth of the sun; it looked like the maze of cookie-cutter sameness it was.

Lani's mom looked at their neighborhood, back to normal, shaking her head, still affected by her daughter's point of view. "It really isn't that much better this way, is it?"

"I know what you mean," Dad said, looking around. He put his arm around his wife. She let him do it.

Lani felt sick, lonely, thinking of Bron . . . But she also thought: I did warn him. I did. Maybe he's where he wanted to be now.

People came out of their houses and looked around. They looked at Lani. They bunched up, muttering, staring at them. They were joined by the Sikh postman, an old widow from down the street. Staring becoming glaring.

"Uh oh," Lani said. They knew—maybe the video of her family at the beach, on the TVs. They guessed who was responsible. No one was hurt—she knew that, could feel it—but they'd all been terrified.

"Okay," Dad said, letting out a long shuddering breath. "I need a lot of time to process this. Let's sell this place. These people are not going to like us being here. Let's all . . . let's go to the coast, hang at a motel. I'll call the real estate people tomorrow . . . So Lani . . . "

He looked at Lani. She could see, now, that he really hoped she wanted to go with them. To stay with them. And that they respected her choice.

And she felt . . . so much lighter now. She'd had a glimpse of possibilities, of the mystery at the heart of the ruthless but energized universe: and the perpetually unfolding heart of that mystery was the very fact of infinite possibilities. After seeing those possibilities, suicide seemed so small and narrow and crabbed a solution to Lani. Suicide was a pitiful little thing: a reeking, cramped broom closet of a choice. So many things could happen . . .

Her dad looked at her. "You give us another chance? Me and Mom? All of us together? What do you say?"

"I say what the hell," Lani said. "Let's see what happens."

MY VICTIM

I'M WATCHING MY victim set up a shot, in the crooked, crosshatch shadow of the Santa Monica beach boardwalk. My victim is Corey Hart, early thirties, lean, nervous movements that suddenly vanish when he says "Action!". Then, during the shooting he becomes still as a lizard relying on its camouflage; he wears a white short-sleeved shirt, khaki pants, Converse high tops that don't quite go with the pants, glasses that would be horn-rim but for transparent plastic frames; there's a clipboard under his arm as he talks to the cameraman.

On this waning September day there are only four people in his crew, a chubby, earnest black cameraman in an alligator shirt; two acned, long-necked college interns, boy and girl, as production assistants, and a bored-looking middle-aged white guy carrying the sound-recording gear, microphone boom in his hand.

A group of bored, sickly teenagers, the runaways this documentary is about, stand in the shadows of the pylons under the boardwalk, waiting to be called for camera interviews. The word is, this guy will pay them twenty dollars each to talk for a few minutes. Other kids are sitting with their back to us on the yellow sand, looking out to sea as they pass a joint, the wavelets sticking dirty foam to their feet.

I'm sitting with my arms around my knees, about twenty yards behind my victim; I'm basking in the late afternoon sun, watching him openly sometimes, other times appearing to let my attention wander; my mouth slack, eyes unfocused, so that I'm just another gawker with nothing else to do. I'm sitting on a faded Universal Studios towel, barefoot, wearing grimy, shapeless clothes I'd never ordinarily wear; got a jug of the cheapest Gallo, half empty. Like I'd ever drink Gallo: I poured half of it out before I came. Normally I'm tailored; normally I drink mostly imported cabernets. Even as an undergrad, last year in the frat, I drank only the best. The frat brothers gave me a lot of crap about it.

My brother Jeremy's first victim is not really as interesting as mine. I'm in the studying phase, following my victim, never letting him know I'm watching him, and it's like studying a Frank Lloyd Wright building, with all its levels and spaces—whereas Jeremy's victim, hell, it's equivalent to studying a mid-western high school gym. I mean, Jeremy's victim has one big ambition: to be the owner of a video arcade. *My* victim? Mine is a guy who makes documentary movies about street poets and all kinds of other stuff. He even won an award for one of his films. Now, *there's* someone worth killing.

The film maker and his crew never even glanced at me, when I first came over and sat down with my towel and jug. It occurs to me now that the disguise might yet be a problem—I might seem colorful enough for them to want to film me, for a quick background shot of other people on the beach: part of the seamy atmosphere these beach-bum kids live in, or something. If they take any notice of me, like they might want to film me, I'll walk away.

It's one of the *Principles of Safe Victimization.* A PSV, my father calls it. He made us memorize the *Principles*—they aren't written down, that'd be bad security. The operating PSV in this case is pretty obvious: don't be seen stalking the victim. If you're going to be visible, blend into the background. Be anonymous, but make that anonymity different every time.

You don't want a detective locating you through what Dad calls "the incremental use of collateral factors," for example non-connected witnesses, like somebody watching from the boardwalk over us, the detective nudging them into remembering "a kind of ordinary looking guy, except he was sort of grimy, with a bottle of wine, watching the documentary people the whole time . . ." And maybe the detective noticing a guy about the same height and weight and race also reported in the vicinity of the victim some other time. From there, the detective starts to put together a picture of a possible stalker: me.

No. Being truly, really anonymous, Dad says, is a great art.

Dad taught me to take mental notes, never to write anything down, or record anything. Never to use videotape. All that stuff can be used as evidence against you. It happened to Granddad: he kept a written journal, and they found it. It was cryptic, but still, it connected him with the victim. His big money connections got him off, but it was a near thing.

So I'm noting everything mentally; taking mental snapshots. Click: My victim has assistants, but no bodyguards. And none of the assistants look to be the physical type. No one is expecting trouble—my victim was chosen, partly, for having no enemies

"There's a trade-off," Dad told me. "If he had no enemies, then his being killed stands out, and that's bad, it makes them look for someone anomalous, like you. If he had enemies then there's a good chance those enemies would be blamed instead of you, should you fall under suspicion. That'd be good. But ... the Principle that applies here is of never letting yourself be *known* to be in the victim's life—so you can't possibly fall under suspicion no matter what. As far as anyone knows, in the context of your victim, you don't exist. They can't suspect someone who doesn't exist. And a guy who has no enemies is not looking around, he has no bodyguards looking around, no paranoid hirelings. And that's worth more than having somebody who can be blamed. It's worth way more, son."

Another mental snapshot. Click: my victim has an easy, comfortable way with strangers. He's now interviewing one of the teenagers, a slack-faced kid whose eyes keep wandering to anything but Corey.

Corey being comfortable with strangers means—if that comfort extends to all strangers and not just interviewees—that I might be able to talk my way into his house, say, on one pretext or another, if I'm sure he's alone. To murder him, of course. To murder him in his home, which is out in the country, in privacy.

Click: he's drinking a can of Coors Lite as he talks to the guy. Drinks *mildly* on the job, three cans a day: obvious poisoning applications. Drinking on the job and from a beer he's packed in a cooler, at home, too, gives me another arena for a possible poisoning.

Dad recommends poisoning. You don't get blood on you; you don't have to be there when your victim dies, which of course means less opportunity for some haphazard, unexpected witness (*Fifth Principle of Safe Victimization: always expect an unexpected witness*) to tie you into the Execution Zone.

Poison sounds good to me too. Jeremy, now, wants to kill his victim with a gun. Dad will allow it, but doesn't advise it. In fact I can see he finds it distasteful. I tried to tell this to Jeremy when we went horseback riding along the beach north of Malibu, the day after his birthday.

"Dude," I said to my brother, "it's not just that he doesn't like the mess and it doesn't matter how careful you are not to get blood on you or to use an untraceable gun or to take care with the fingerprints or whatever. It's about identification with the killing. The whole point is not identifying with the killing. If you want to use a gun, it means you might like killing just for killing. And that's bullshit. It's not about liking or not liking."

"Oh come on," Jeremy said. He's a short, chunky, blue-eyed guy with Mom's curly shiny black hair. He carries himself like a pimp entering a pool-hall, Dad told me once, when he was pissed at Jeremy: High-stepping arrogance. But that's how Jeremy moves through the world. Thinks he's way adult by now but he isn't. "We get all this training so we can destroy people, so we can kill—you're supposed to like what you're good at. Dad even said so. 'Love this art' he said."

"The art is the preparation, the not-getting-caught, the chess game of it—like you're playing chess with all the cops in the world at once. It's not the moment, the actual act of making the victim dead. That's why he doesn't let us kill girls, man. You might . . ."

I broke off. I could tell he didn't like the way this was coming out. "I might what?"

"Not you. I mean anyone. Anyone might get off on that—Dad says there's some kind of sexual thing when you kill any kind of female. It's all subconscious."

"Hey bro, Freud was discredited."

He's proud of getting a 3.8 majoring in psych his sophomore year: Psychology as a preparation for going into marketing later. Behaviorism. We're both heading for the best MBAs we can get, of course. Dad and the family made that part of the Sworn Tradition, in the eighties. Given my choice I'd have been an American Lit major, but Sworn is Sworn.

"It's not Freud, its more like sociobiology or something. Or—I don't know, I just know there's automatically a sexual . . . a sexual part to it."

I'd started to say "sexual component" but said "sexual part" instead because, with Jeremy, if you use a phrase like "sexual component" he'll scowl and come back at you with something like "the elasticity of post-structuralism", some kind of string of ten dollar words that don't mean a whole lot. He's competitive like that. Especially in the context of talking about Dad. He's always worried more about impressing Dad.

"I don't give a goddamn about that," he said. "I kill who I'm assigned to kill. If it's going to be male, fine, whatever. But don't say I'm a fag if I happen to . . . to love the art of it."

"What? No, I wasn't going that way at all—I'm talking about identification with the killing. It's as important to not like the killing *particularly* as it is to not care about the victim."

"Oh come on. Nothing's more important than not identifying with the victim. That's primo, that's tops. Otherwise you blow everything. That's the whole point of doing it in the first place."

I decided to let it drop. He was stating the obvious; he wasn't getting the subtle, and the art of victimization is subtle. "Subtle understanding of setting and situation is what keeps a man from being caught," Dad had told me.

Dad killed three Random Personal Victims, chosen at twenty-year intervals. Sometimes, see, you need more than one. He says you'll know if you need another one; if you need to re-commit. It may be a man only needs one Random Personal Victim. I never asked Dad why he needed three, but I have my suspicions. I figure I'll only need the one—because I'll know I'm killing various other people, routinely, as part of the business, anyway. It's all about not hiding from that knowledge. Having the courage to do *anything* necessary. People use the phrase "moral courage"; there's also such a thing as amoral courage.

But that day, all I said to Jeremy was, "Race you back to the limo, bigshot."

And we did, raced the horses back to the beach parking lot where the limo was waiting. I let him win. The groom put the horses in the trailer behind the truck, and we got in the limo, and played Nintendo 64 in the back, all the way home to the winter house.

NOW, IN SANTA MONICA. The edges of shapes around us grow dull; colors become less colorful: dusk is coming. The shadows are reaching out from the pylons. Another young boy is talking to Corey's camera about how he likes living on the sand under the boardwalk, it's usually warm enough, it's never too warm, "and it don't smell too bad, and there's always some shit happening, somebody's got something, or they can figure out where to get something", and he doesn't mind "renting" himself to some of the guys on the Venice muscle beach strip, sometimes, "because, I mean, people ask me, and I go: Who cares? I mean, shit, whatever."

I wonder how many thousands of years prostitutes have been saying that, in a thousand different languages. I had a really good history prof, Mr. Delany, he really gives you a perspective. He doesn't know about the Sworn Tradition, though. No outsider does. But he knows about P-2, and the Cosa Nostra—

But no—Cosa Nostra—that's so very, very different. We don't involve ourselves in crime, as people understand the word, apart from the Victims. We shear the sheep legally. And, too, the Sworn Tradition is all in one extensive family, or intertwined families, which is never something that can be entered by anyone outside the family, not even by marriage; you have to be a descendant of the original bloodline, which was Northern Italian and Austrian. And still is. *Only* Northern Italian, and Austrian. *Only*. It goes back to just before the Renaissance; to the great Italian conspirators, some of whose names became household words. "Machiavelli was a simpering weakling," my father once said, chuckling.

Anyway, our family doesn't interfere in the broader outline of history, unless it serves us financially. It's all about accruing wealth, of course. "What for others is crass materialism is for us a sacred trust," Uncle Tino once said, after his third Remy. "If we worshipped a god, it would be toothy old Mammon." But of course we worship nothing but "pleasure in survival, survival in pleasure".

I am careful to appear to go to sleep on the sand, with my back to my victim; to be sure he's gone before I leave. *Sixth sub-PSV: Movement calls attention.*

DAD BEGAN ERADICATING my "non-familial empathy" early, very early. Three years old.

"I wish to God my father had started me early," he said, when I asked him about it five, six years later. I was around nine. Asked him, with a sudden and uncharacteristic boldness, why he'd made me kill my Lhasa puppy with the piano wire when I was three. On one level I knew why—he'd explained it to me, he'd been training me all along— but then again I didn't know; in some other way, some deeper way, I didn't understand, not then.

I had expected the question to make him angry. But instead he began, "I wish my father . . ." He broke off and shook his head. He got that odd sort of ghostly look in his eyes, at such moments. I'm only beginning to understand that look.

We were on the back lawn, between the topiaries and the main house of our summer place in Eddington, England; we were watching the trainer work with the hunting dog, in the early morning. The sun was pulling the dew into gossamer streamers. Father was standing there with his hands in his pockets. I had heard one of his hired wives screaming with almost convincing joy from the guest house the night before and thought to see him pleased this morning, but he looked almost in grief.

"You see, my father didn't start me until I was twelve, son, and by then a man has too many opportunities to create the capacity for non-familial bonding. And it was hard when he made me kill my little brother."

I looked at him in real shock: Silent and resonant, I can still feel it, more than a decade later.

He smiled wearily. "Yes. He was only four. Well, you understand: He had spina bifida. He could not have been allowed to reproduce. He . . . was a symbol of family decay—so long as he lived. But once dead, he was, you might say, transformed into a symbol of vitality: to cut away the sickly limb is to renew vitality. However . . ." I remember his hand raised to express something inexpressible; a cryptic gesture, like signing for the deaf, but signing a non-word, something not found in any lexicon. "Somehow I had become identified with him, son . . . though I had been warned that his sickliness made him—we never told him this, of course—it made him non-family. And even within the family we permit only the Higher Bonding. The Higher Bonding is undertaken with a clear vision, and so it is provisional . . ."

So in making me kill the puppy, my father was saving me from what he'd suffered when he'd had to kill his brother by smothering him with a pillow, his father supervising. He was snuffing the candle of empathy for anything outside the Sworn, because that candle grew, over the years, unless you snuffed it early, snuffed it small. The pain was less, after that, and the forgetting, the annihilation of caring came easier.

Dad and I, that day, watched the trainer yank the dog up short on a choke chain. A sense of masculine communion with the trainer, with Dad.

THAT CONVERSATION ON the lawn, more than a decade ago, is on my mind as I get out of a bus a few blocks west of downtown L.A. I can't drive myself here, or take a limo, of course, since I'm here to watch Corey. A cab driver would remember me.

Corey will be on the far side of the old, ragged park, near the reeking duck pond, interviewing runaways. Today I won't be close enough to be noticed. I'll watch through binoculars—

"Son?"

Dad is rolling down the window of his Porsche, at the curb just behind me. I'm surprised to see him so near a stalk-zone. He tilts his head, summoning me into the car. He's wearing a linen Armani sports jacket, collarless off-white shirt, sunglasses. A classical music station plays on the car radio. He closes the windows of the car, as I sit beside him, turns on the air conditioning. "You're going to let him see you again, son?" he asks, looking across the park. Three cholo kids throw broken glass at plastic pop bottles bobbing in the pond.

"He won't see me. I'll use binoculars. Won't get within two hundred yards."

"You might be noticed by someone in the park: a white guy, here, watching another white guy with binoculars."

"Well, I have a way to do it, that . . ."

"Whatever you've got in mind won't work. Strikes me you're taking a long time at this stage. Makes me wonder how serious you are."

My mouth goes dry. "Um . . ."

"We'll talk about it another time. You know, your brother date-raped a girl, last night, at school. He might face charges."

I look at him in real amazement. Why would Jeremy do that? He can have some of the finest women available. He gets laid all the time. And it's so fundamental, not drawing attention to the family by breaking society's laws.

He chuckles dourly. "I was just as surprised. Well, almost. He's growing . . . undisciplined. It happens sometimes. It's usually a genetic defect. We do have to struggle with inbreeding. When it happens, the unruliness has to be weeded out."

I look at him. I made myself ask without a quaver, "Are you sure?"

"No, no I'm not. It could be an aberration. We can arrange for this thing to be smoothed over. A million, two million dollars spread out here and there. And if he reins himself in . . . It might not be necessary for you to prove yourself well and truly Sworn."

I have felt it coming. I try to pretend that I was prepared. I want badly to swallow but I wouldn't let myself. "But—it might be?"

Dad nods, looking at me. "You might have to kill your brother. Say it."

I wet my lips so I could say it. "I might have to kill my brother."

"Good. Sub rosa, all this, of course. You don't even know about the date-rape accusation."

"Yes. Of course."

"And son? I think, today, you will not follow your victim. It may be that your victim will not be this man Corey. It may be your brother instead. If it's Corey—you won't have to kill your brother. But for today—let the stalk-and-study go. Today doesn't feel right for this . . ."

He taps the binocular case on its strap over my shoulder. I nod.

"I'll give you a ride home."

THE CRISIS PASSES. My brother is truly penitent; but in a controlled way. Dad tells me I can go back to choosing The Moment with Corey. Picking the Execution Zone. Today, I'm watching my victim at the mall. And of course I'm looking very different from the way I looked on the beach. I come off young for my age: clean shaven and grunged out, I pass for a teenager who's in the mall because there isn't any other place to go.

My victim is in the sporting goods store, picking up a fresh supply of target arrows. Corey is one of these the Zen and the Art of Archery guys. I've been watching him for about two months—the limit of observation time, if you do it right—and I've seen him here twice before. After he buys the arrows he goes to the tobacconist and gets some Balkan Sobranies, an expensive cigarette he only allows himself when he hits the target near enough to the center. Never smokes except during archery. He's a good archer, and I'm glad the *Principles* are totally opposed to giving the victim a square chance. He'd kill me sure.

At the range I have to be in complete concealment; there aren't enough people here for comfortable camouflage; he might well notice me. But concealment isn't hard, with lots of trees and brush around the range. The oak tree I'm squatting under still has most of its leaves, but the ones that have fallen crackle when I shift my weight from one hunkered leg to the other, adjusting my binoculars. Spiders squat in web tunnels, hundreds of webs like little fishing nets in the tangle of junipers that hides me. A bluejay screams like a British soccer fan overhead. It's getting on my nerves and I'd like to chuck a rock at it but I know better.

Soon I'm engrossed in watching Corey.

We're required to think of our victims by their first names. It's a deliberate invitation to empathy; a sort of test. *The victims are not to be thought of as "it": think of them as three-dimensional, living breathing human beings, with parents and children and feelings. As former children. If this brings up a pang in you, then you're at the secondary stage in your Lifetraining.* And it's all the more reason you must kill the man.

I watch him choose an arrow from the quiver on the rack beside him; I watch him nock it, with the second-nature deftness of long practice; I watch him draw the bow and fire, and somehow it's all one movement even though there are two or three seconds between drawing and firing. The arrow flies to just outside the bullseye. He takes another arrow, nocks it, draws, seems to become very still, as still as the target, and lets fly. To either side of him other archers are cursing, chattering, laughing, muttering, squinting, tensing; in comparison Corey is a study in relaxed self-containment. This time his arrow strikes the bullseye, and he allows himself to light a cigarette, to inhale once, deeply, before nocking, in a way, the cigarette, too, in the ashtray he's brought along.

After four more arrows, three striking the bullseye, the lady next to him— a big-assed, sourfaced woman with short clipped hair and a workshirt—asks him not to smoke anymore. His nod is almost a bow, and he doesn't smoke any more. It doesn't interfere with his shooting, this abstention; it doesn't seem to make him tense, there's not even quiet irritation in his body language.

I let out a long, deep breath and shake my head in admiration. The guy really has something. Talent, skill, grace and imperturbability. Dignity.

I know, of course, that all the victims have noticeable good qualities, or good people dependent on them. Sweet-looking children waiting at home, say. What's the point of trying to burn out empathy where none is likely to be generated? If you aren't instinctively reluctant to kill the victim, then he's probably not challenging enough. Of course, if you've got to the Fixity Point, the aim of our Lifetraining, where you can kill and *genuinely* feel nothing—feel nothing *and without repression*— then your killing is only a necessary ritual, an affirmation of the Sworn Tradition. And something more: it's the Tradition's hold over you. Even if you become infected, diseased by "conscience", you can't report the Tradition without reporting yourself. Not that you'd live long if you tried.

So I let myself feel the admiration for my victim. Repression makes a man "guilty", and that makes him sick. He must kill randomly and consciously and this frees him from repercussions. So it is in theory. But sometimes I see that ghostliness around my father's eyes and wonder.

I think again that a guy like Corey, he's seriously worth killing: it completes him, in a way. This guy, he really is like architecture: you can see the philosophy of the builder in the building's design. This guy blueprints his whole life according to some kind of philosophy. Zen, I think, or something like it. His documentaries are all about raising consciousness of the underprivileged and the lost. I tell myself that uncreation is an art form too.

I saw him with his girlfriend only once—a pretty Asian-American. She's studying film at NYU, back East, and they are being patient and faithful while they wait for her to get through it. They see each other when they can.

She's a feminist but somehow Corey is almost chivalrous around her without seeming to put her down with it. I still haven't figured out how he does it.

I remember feeling a real ache when they kissed. Because you could see him communicating something to her in the kiss. It's something I can't do. I'm allowed to have sex with the best call-girls in the world; at those prices, they'll kiss you, and with passion. You can like them—the expensive ones are educated and pretty and charming—and they can like you. But I'm not allowed to feel *close,* of course. It's against the Sworn Tradition. And when, from the select families, a wife is chosen for me, I am free to feel a passion for her; but to actually fall in love would be foolish. Her life with us is provisional, in so many ways.

I break off surveillance, and trudge through the woods, climb over a barbed wire fence to cross a field where cattle graze. My limbs feel heavy, somehow, and I don't understand why. An old man in a plaid shirt and work-boots, a cranky old rancher, pulls up in his truck and shouts at me to approach with my hands up, he's sick of people wandering over his land, he's going to press charges. I approach him and give him seven one hundred dollar bills, without a word. His mouth hanging open with surprise, he lets me go, just as wordless.

I walk down the gravel road to where the limo is waiting. The driver, of course, is an Initiated Servant. They're all Sworn, on their own level; picked very carefully. They are paid well for their loyalty, and usually retire with at least a million dollars after taxes.

Dad gets out of the limo. He must have come in his own white stretch, and switched over, waited here for me.

We walk down the road together, talking, hands in pockets. The driver is an old man from Corsica; he waits. He'd wait for days if he had to, and not make a sound.

Dad deepens the chill already gathering in my belly when he asks, "Son, why follow him to archery, again, after two months? Are you thinking of arranging an accident there? That'd be tricky. You'd have to be in complicity with someone . . ."

Having anyone help you with the kill is, of course, forbidden; a grievous violation of both the *Principles of Safe Victimization* and the *Basic Articles of Understanding*.

"No, it's just general surveillance."

He looks at me. It's never any use lying to him.

"Well," I add, with an apologetic smile, "I guess I'm feeling pangs, feeling empathy, and I figure I have to *really* feel it before I can 'let the rose wither' . . . I mean, you said don't suppress . . ."

"Yes. But—not at two months. At one month, yes. But son—how long have you been feeling this thing?"

Another lie springs to mind. I dismiss it. "You're right. At least a month."

"So it's gone beyond 'letting the rose wither'. It's stalling, son. You don't want to kill him . . . *because you really like him.*"

I feel the tears coming. My father doesn't chasten me for the tears. He knows they're tears of shame.

COREY IS DRINKING Coors Lite from a silver can as he sits on his redwood deck, out behind his two bedroom place at the end of a long, lonely road east of Thousand Oaks. He's sitting in a wooden deck chair, writing a letter to his girlfriend. He always writes to her in his own handwriting, on stationery: Long letters in flowing freehand. He hasn't looked closely at the can; hasn't seen the needle-hole in it, and after he takes another sip of the beer, he begins to choke. He lurches to his feet and flails toward the back door, trying to get to the bathroom, or the phone, I'll never know which, and then he staggers once more, and he falls.

He is convulsing face-down, the pen gripped in his fist stabbing the redwood planks, his legs jerking, as I climb over the wooden railing and come to stand over him. I flip him over with my foot, so I can look into his face as he dies, as my father has ordered me to do.

There's yellow foam around his lips. His mouth opens and closes soundlessly but it is his eyes that ask the question.

"You'd never understand why I killed you. But I will say I'm not the stranger you think I am."

His head shakes, or maybe it's convulsion, and the ancient, untraceable, traditional poison, which in our family we call only Number 317, moves inexorably into its final stage, and he shivers once, decisively, and stops breathing.

After a moment, tentatively feeling my inner self, I realize the "rose" is withering. I am becoming Fixed. It is a profound relief.

A SUNDAY MORNING in October. Cloudy, damp breeze. I'm riding with my brother on our favorite beach. The family owns it, of course, for miles. He's laughing as he kicks Salmonberry into a gallop, and we race down the beach. He looks a little surprised when I lead him into the rocky area, but then he grins and takes the challenge.

Earlier, I took his groom's place and put the saddle on: While my brother waited in the limo, thinking I was still in the house. Now I ride dangerously close beside him, both of us galloping here; I quickly reach down, and pull the rawhide trip-string.

The saddle comes uncinched, and he falls headlong, as the horse is jumping a rock, as planned. As I feared, he is not killed by the fall. His spine is snapped, but I must get off my horse, kneel beside him, and firmly hold his face in the sand to finish it.

The coroner—our coroner—will rule accidental death.

I'm allowed to explain, as he chokes to death on sand, our land itself killing him. "You were reckless. First you date-raped a girl: endangering the family, the Tradition. Then you didn't control your violence. You shot your assigned victim, shot him yourself with a gun, and tried to tell us you'd arranged for him to commit suicide. Father felt you were a danger, and the danger would grow. And he wasn't sure about me, even after my victim. He needed another test for me. And now it's me, I'm the one who'll take over the company, Jeremy. It's me."

But I think he is dead before I quite finish this.

Father comes out of his place of concealment, on the far side of the rocks. Smiling. "Congratulations, son. Now, and only now, are you fit to run the world's biggest corporation." He embraces me. I feel nothing as he embraces me, except pride of accomplishment. The rose is withered.

SWEET ARMAGEDDON

ALL THAT HAPPENED, really, was that Castle woke up. Woke up a little more . . .

On that day, the sky was smoldering. It was a cool mid-afternoon, yet it smoldered. It seemed to roil with implicit energies, attenuated reds and a livid gas-flame blue; but looking again, ratcheting perception down a notch to something more ordinary, it was simply an ordinary sky leaden with clouds.

It was a perfectly mundane day, made of all the usual elements, fiberboard and polystyrene, monoxides and sulfites, rattling leaves and humming powerlines, high and low pressures, fluctuating influences; the sounds of cars, of trucks; the calls of children playing at being Saturday morning cartoons.

Castle had crystallized a degree of Presence several notes up the Scale from where he'd begun—but those levels had not brought with them this multiworldly prescience. This was something new; an unknown chord.

Castle was walking from Central to Santa Clara, one block, in a small California town near a big California town, and it was taking less than forever but more than a lifetime. It took *absurdly* long to walk that block. But it was not a tiresome length, because he was deeply present, and the resonance that went with that state made it all quite interesting.

Castle made his living as a book buyer, at the moment; he had been a jazz-rock pianist, between office jobs, but he could no longer bear the financial irregularity of the freelance life. That pot-holed road had broken the axle of his marriage and separated him, much of the time, from his little boy. So now, at fifty-four, too late from his former wife's point of view, he had taken a steady job, and ceased to play piano except at home. A friend had told him that freelance artists and producers and the like were predators by nature; were hunters who went seeking into the wilderness of commerce. Job holders, on the other hand, were grazers.

Then I wish to convert to herbivore, Castle had said; I now wish to be a vegetarian of commerce.

Castle paused, now, at a streetlight pole to look at a poster for the Sri Winston rally at the auditorium, its Bombay colors hinting of numinous experience at a reasonable price. Its programmed paper, flashing through holo sequences, was glued to the wall beside the donut shop.

"How you?" asked the man who owned the donut shop, from his fragrant doorway. He was an Iranian fellow, with a very pretty, compact Iranian wife. They had opened the donut shop to indifferent success a couple of months before and quickly learned to include flavored coffee and croissants. It had taken the Iranian a while to get the flavor, as it were, of the community and to notice, for example, that the café next door was also an art gallery.

Now, in the late afternoon, business had slackened, and the Iranian shop owner had time to try again to get to know his neighbors. It wasn't easy—the Americans kept their social functions divided like the parts of their Home Entertainment Centers; and the CD player did not mingle with the DVD player.

"Hello," Castle said. Tasting the word, as he paused to talk. "And how is business?"

Castle felt something in him want to move on. From long and rewarding habit he denied this impulse; he reined it in; he remained to talk to the man from the Donut Shop.

"Business is good," the man said, laboring under his accent. "Not wonderful good but not so bad. Tomorrow I am making the flavored cappuccino. We are putting in a sign for such."

"I'll try it, sounds great. It's smart of you to sell something new from time to time."

The man waved away the compliment. "I come to America, that's the kind I am."

"You're not doing so bad—even at this hour you have two customers."

The man looked into his shop. Blinking a little too much. He shook his head. "No—no one now."

But Castle saw two men sitting in the shop, at a little table. Both had small coffees. Both looked Middle Eastern. Both were old men; one wore a sort of fez made out of black lamb's wool. They were looking out the shop window at the traffic on the street, but Castle had the feeling they were watching him and the shopkeeper.

Perhaps they were the man's relatives, and he didn't regard them as customers. But the shopkeeper's gaze swept right over the two old men, not taking take them in. Castle felt certain the shopkeeper didn't see them.

The older of the two men, in the woolen fez, seemed to tug a smile from his sculpted white beard. He turned, looked at Castle directly, with exactly the sky's own smouldering. There was no harm in him at all.

This old man in the fez shook his head, faintly, so Castle did not tell the shop owner that two of his ancestors were in his shop with him.

A woman with a little girl came to the shop, and the Iranian went to serve them, waving goodbye to Castle.

Next time, Castle resolved, I'll ask his name.

Now and suddenly, the old men were gone from their table. Castle went down the street, glad that what he saw was real; that he was not hallucinating the two old men that only he could see; that he was not a drug user or mentally ill. How terrible it would be, to be subject to hallucinations.

SOMEONE HAD SCRIBED in the beach's sand with a stick: "Sri W! Intuition says Surrender! Surrender and Jump!" above a scratched spiral-and-star symbol. The wind was just beginning to erase the notice.

Fine energies moved in keenly attenuated waves through the hard and soft places of the world. Castle felt the gentle tug of the apocalypse. . .

HE TURNED TO look over San Francisco Bay. There were machinations in the sea. Walking near the lacey fringe of the water, Castle could see machinery just under the surface, DuChamp's pistons and vents and, vaster than that, a subaquatic architecture of chrome, made of vast pipe-organ arrays locked into chromium dynamos, like some flooded Fritz Lang set. Parts of it moved in machine-precise patterns; part was inert, motionless as a mountain of iron.

Several small black children in cut-offs were thrashing through the surf, though the beach was brisk with wind, and they waded right through the machinery, up to their knees in it, making hard machine parts ripple, and yet Castle knew it was there; knew he was not hallucinating the machinery of the sea, either. Hallucinations are often mistaken for visions; but a real vision is not hallucination: a vision is a disclosure.

Why the sea? he wondered. What inexorable function is prefigured here?

Sidewinders of sand skirled the beach, struck at his ankles between his socks and cuffs, with a pleasant stinging of grains; the sky roiled; at the horizon, small angels in dull neon were strung like children's paper dolls, refolding into crystaline orbs.

Gazing at the horizon, Castle thought of time and loss, and of course thought of Jeremy, his small son, who was permitted to see him only one weekend a month. It hurt like a bitch—a particular bitch. He smiled sadly at his own resentment.

Castle thought of the place at the cusp of being, where plus and minus meet; where positive and negative, active and passive neutralize; where the Father and the Son exchange the Holy Ghost. And pinned between these infinitely sharp points is consciousness; the stone dropped in the pond—and here is the unspeakable suffering of God. . .

GRANT YOURSELF MERCY, Lord; give yourself grace.

"The Absolute has no need of grace from you," said the little boy, taking his hand.

The boy was black for a moment, but then Castle blinked, and he was an Asian boy; and then he was Jeremy. Yes! Let him be Jeremy. And so he was, for a while: Jeremy with the stiff straw hair, in his playclothes, jeans and T-shirt.

The boy's touch, more an intuition than a tactile sensation, told Castle that this was one of the dead; he was glad it was not really Jeremy.

This small boy was either one of the dead, or many of the dead in one. Not some walking corpse, but yet one of the dead. Some manifestation of the kind of angel that those who were once human could be.

"Was I in hubris, when I suggested God give itself grace?" Castle asked, his mouth dry. "Are you here to reproach me?"

"No," the boy said. "I only meant: don't worry yourself." For a moment, the wind whisked the sand. "Would you come with me? You can pretend I'm your son Jeremy, if you like."

It was unsettling hearing that from him—since he looked exactly like Jeremy down to the birthmark on his neck.

"How is Jeremy, do you know?" Castle asked.

"I can ask." The boy—the one who was seemingly a boy, just then—paused and looked at the horizon. "Jeremy... is a little distressed because his mother has asked him to clean his room and he imagines that if you were here you would not require it." This sort of diction sounded strange in the little boy's voice.

"He's quite wrong. But I love him."

"Yes. And he loves you."

He should be with his son now. He should go to him. But if he did, his ex wife would threaten to call the police, end his visitation altogether.

The suffering: turn toward it.

"Would you," the boy asked again, "come with me?"

A subtle electricity communicated between Castle's joints. "Yes."

THEY WERE WALKING down a street. The faces in the crowd showed waking dreams. Castle sorted through the people sifting by on the broad sidewalk, beneath the stylish facades of the department stores, and saw quite clearly that they slept. Another kind of REM showed in their open eyes. The daydreams, the fantasies, the anxiety scenarios, played across faces with driven haste, like the shadows of gale-blown clouds.

Some stopped to look in the windows, or chatted, gesturing with almost theatrical animation; but they were asleep.

And so was I for more than forty years, thought Castle. Even now some sphere of potential in Castle slept.

Pulsing from phone poles and the wooden walls around construction sites, were more hologram posters, promoting rap bands, shaped-static bands, television series, self-help cults; particularly enticing were the iridescent colors and warmly beckoning images of the wide eyed curly haired "spiritual leader" Sri Winston and his Open Intuition Foundation. . . holo tape loops showing Sri Winston, with his arms crossed over his chest, smiling with profligate benevolence, then opening his arms, manifesting a spiral of energy that led to a purple star. . .

Now THEY LEFT the broad boulevard, Castle and the Jeremy boy, and turned toward Market and the discount electronics stores.

There were heads on the flat-screen, high-rez televisions in the windows, talking about the Seven Christian States.

The Seven were Oklahoma, Louisiana, Mississippi, Alabama, Georgia, North Carolina, and Tennessee. There was talk of Texas and Missouri and Florida and South Carolina joining, making it eleven states. There were challenges in court, and Congress, as to the legality of declaring, in the Constitutional context of the separation of church and state, that your state was Christian and would uphold Christian values by legislative fiat. The governors were declaring that if their hand was forced they would secede from the United States as a unit. Some people laughed off the possibility, and some people said it could mean real civil war, fueled by ethnic tensions, cultural alienation, religious fundamentalism—whole counties in California were entirely Islamic Fundamentalist, or Winstonite.

There was another window with a miniature videocam hanging on a necklace round the neck of a mannequin; the cam transmitted video of the passersby. Castle was seen by the electronic eye in the mannequin's necklace, his image looking stiff and skewed at odd angles as he walked by the flat screen in the display window. The Jeremy Boy didn't show up in the video screen. It looked like Castle was holding hands with no one. He thought of the movie *Harvey*.

But he felt the boy's hand in his and he was not the only one who saw him. Two others were present enough, as they walked through the city. A black man, wearing an *ifa* charm around his neck; some

Orisha priest. The ifa priest stared at Jeremy, as they passed and the boy smiled at him. Probably the black man saw something other than a little boy, perhaps some large animal. Castle nodded, then glanced over his shoulder at the black man as they passed; the man hunkered to touch the ground, a sign of respect.

The other who saw the Jeremy boy was a woman with silver hair, though only in her forties. She came out of a train station and began to walk along near them, going in the same direction, staring at the boy.

The boy was Jeremy—and wasn't. When Castle chose, he could shift his attention to the boy's hand in his, and through that intensified touch, somehow, he could feel Jeremy out there, in the world. Jeremy was finished cleaning his room. Now his mother came to get him, to take him somewhere; a seminar, she said. What, Jeremy was wondering, was a seminar? Jeremy wondered what his dad was doing now.

Castle felt his eyes sting with tears.

Then things around him began to go transparent.

The walls of the buildings became sheets of fog, diffusing so he could see the shapes of people in chiaroscuro; some going about mundane household business, others going about the mundane business of sexual consummation. He could see them copulating, hunched one over the other, many of them paired like dogs, others kneeling between legs scissored open, people of all preferences. This was happening now— and then *now* fanned out like a deck of cards in a magician's hand, and he saw other times, past and future; he saw himself.

. . . Saw himself thirty-four years before, in one of those rooms, with a woman and a man—the last time he'd taken drugs. . .

He almost laughed. He saw himself then as a kind of trained dog, leaping through hoops for a biscuit. The relief and release didn't last even as long as a dog biscuit. The woman later died of AIDS. Castle had been lucky, and hadn't gotten it.

Then the deck of cards shuffled back together again, and he saw the chambers of the city in its relative Now, tessellated one into the next, becoming a deconstructed nautilus that heaved itself into a contorted iris of living framework, which then disgorged a distilled essence of suffering: the liqueur of pressed misery. People dying of AIDS, dying of cancer, dying of self-mutilation, dying of addiction, dying of abandonment, dying in the smothering toils of paranoid-schizophrenic convolution. This liqueur beaded, exuded, and vaporized, to be sucked into the spaces between the stars. Where something drank.

The drinker was negatively implied, but it was there. It fed off one of the currents, the downward spiral that veered through television sets and boardrooms and Scientology Centers and Open Intuition Centers and Home Shopping Channels and, having taken, moved on, sank into the downturned vacuum; there was another, light-charged immaculate void, that drew a second, parallel but opposite current in another direction; toward the way-station of the sun. This current was more difficult to see, it had to be felt, but Castle knew it intimately. The impression faded and. . .

ONCE MORE, CASTLE was simply walking down the street with the Jeremy boy, and they'd come to an auditorium. What he had just seen, Castle sensed, was a prelude to what was incubating in this big, hangarlike glass and steel building.

UNNOTICED BY THE ticket takers through the opacity emanating from the Jeremy boy, Castle and his companion strolled into the auditorium where Sri Winston worked the stage.

He called himself Sri Winston; his name was in fact Franklin Winston Johnson. He was a thick-bodied man with eyes set widely apart, cherubic, clean-shaven face, lots of curly hair; he wore a charcoal suit jacket and steel blue formal shirt and charcoal tie and fine silk trousers—and he had bare feet. There were flowers, irises and lilies and fully bloomed roses, strewn along the front of the stage.

In the audience, Castle observed that when Winston moved across the stage it was almost diagrammatic, his traverse a kind of Pythagorean exactitude, a moving from one corner to the next in astonishing symmetry, same number of steps from here to there and then from there to there and then from there back to here. Till Sri Winston came to a stop in the center front, and suddenly became a living *idée fixe,* rooted in place just slightly off-center on the stage, left hand on the podium, his right hand gesturing with precision, yes almost Pythagorean precision, fixing the same idea into a vast cabbage field of cerebral soft spots, driving the stake for the scarecrow in, over and over.

"We are what we visualize!" Sri Winston declared to the capacity crowd in the auditorium. He had them, he had them rapt, the thousands here, the millions more watching on the Sri Winston Channel.

Castle looked around; in the crowd he saw the vogueishly lean figure of a well known starlet—the starved look had once more come into fashion—whose right arm was equipped with a permanent intravenous feeding jack, designed to look like jewelry. Probably she'd gone without solid food two or three years; she gazed at Sri Winston hungrily. There were housewives in Ashram drag, and accountants who desperately wanted to believe that Winston was the Avatar but who, with equal desperation, strove hopelessly to maintain their expressions of skepticism, and there were scores of lapsed Seekers, shoppers newly defected from the other aisles of the spiritual supermarket.

On the stage, the cynosure was summoning all eyes, and rhythmically declaiming with effortless verve, "We create our reality, by creating our assumptions! We crystallize the out-there with the in-here! But there is a higher reality, which encompasses all others, and to which you can be granted passage. Yet, yet, there is a price to pay for that leap—and not just the mildly painful price of this seminar!" A grin from Winston, a ripple of audience laughter. "But oh! A price, a glorious price: your life! Only in crossing the abyss of sheer, unsupported faith can you hope to abandon the burden of thinking, thinking, thinking, and begin the transformation that will set you free! Free to make THE JUMP! You will need a lighthouse to guide you across that abyss—something, someone, to act as a beacon, a focal point for the process of Open Intuition that we teach, no, that we unleash—"

"What do you think of him?" Castle asked the angel—the angel who'd adopted the shape of Castle's son.

His tone more dry than fulsome, the Jeremy boy quoted, "Strait is the gate and narrow the way which leadeth unto life, and few there be who find it. Beware of false prophets, which come to you in sheep's clothing, but inwardly they are ravening wolves. . ."

Castle nodded to himself. The usual ironies were at play here. "He mixes in a little suborned truth, so that something is seduced by echoes. The abyss to cross before the transformation. . ."

"Yes. Look at him closer. Then look again into the audience."

Castle felt a shiver, realize that he was about to see why he'd been brought here. Then, Castle was standing on the stage beside Winston. . . quite unseen. Sri Winston could see him but the audience could not.

Looking at Winston up close, seeing the sweat on the man like glass beads, the blood pumping in his temples. . .

CASTLE LOOKED AGAIN with his whole being, and saw that Winston's outer shell was quite hollow. Winston's eyes, from Castle's point of view, were missing. Castle could see through the socket-holes in the living skin of Winston's unoccupied face and could see a smaller man inside, like a particularly small midget, but shriveled, feral and—yet—unmistakably Winston: some miniaturized doppelganger. As the larger, exterior Winston strutted and gestured evocatively and emoted feelingly for the sighing, applauding auditorium crowd and the ghostly television audience, this other, bottled Winston peered fearfully out first one socket, then the next, or squinted out through the open, jabbering mouth. It looked in terror at Castle. *Go away, it hissed, don't see me! Don't look at me you stinking pustule! Fuck you fuck you FUCK YOU!*

It was no "inner child", this thing inside Winston. Instead it was a withered, ancient thing, a ravenous mummy of Sri Franklin Winston Johnson, a kind of parody of another esoteric tradition, the inner being separate from the outer; but this was that tradition's diabolic inversion, like a cross worn upside down.

And did he see another, smaller Winston Johnson inside the agitated inner mummy?

Winston's words came to Castle like a slowed-down tape recording, too taffied to be intelligible, but the flavor was there: something about surrendering mindfulness to Sri Winston, about giving in to Sri Winston, about abandoning critical thinking, about grand promises of enhanced health and sexual glory, of health and immortality; about coming to Papa; the same message over and over, flourished in a thousand permutations, with a prestidigitator's mastery of misdirection. There was a murkiness in the air, too, round about Winston, visible at the most extreme parallax; look at him only peripherally and you could glimpse the web he was caught in, and the thing that crouched in it, practicing its etheric puppetry. . .

Then Castle heard a voice calling him, and it rang in his cells, shimmering in his DNA. His son's true authentic voice. "Daddy. . . Daddy. . . DADDY!"

Castle turned and looked into the audience; past a sea of faces more deeply asleep than those he'd seen on the street; those faces at the same time raptly alert for the waves that struck out from Winston, the waves that struck into their centers of reward, the perversion of Shakti that attuned them to Winston, to his virtual-reality escapism of the personality.

Castle looked past all this and saw, like opalescent stones in the gravel pit of the tranced devotees, the two bearded sufis he'd seen in the café, the dervish angels, watching impassively. The older, whitebearded dervish rendering to Castle a smile: a faint, sweet acknowledgement. And then they turned to look at. . .

Castle's ex-wife, and Jeremy, holding her hand. The authentic Jeremy. She was engrossed by Winston; Jeremy was looking around in confusion and fear. A barefooted man in a suit, one of Winston's lieutenants, stood with his arm around Jeremy's mother; he was a tall, almost vulpine man with gold-tinted glasses and a dangling earring showing the hologrammed spiral-to-a-star Open Intuition symbol. He'd converted Jeremy's mother, Castle supposed. The man glanced with irritation at Jeremy when he tried to tug his mother toward the exit doors.

Struck to the heart by Jeremy's loneliness, Castle—now himself visible—was quickly wading through the tranced initiates, striding directly to his son. The old dervishes were at Castle's side, with them the angel who had been the "Jeremy boy" to Castle—all three of them working to open a path for him. The crowd parted without knowing why. They saw Castle, but the others were hidden to them.

Then Jeremy saw Castle and gave a cry of unfettered gladness and ran to him. Their embrace was a perfect fit, paternal and filial in an iconic connection that made Castle think of some lines he'd read somewhere—

—All I can hope to be
is a good design in the tapestry—

—and then Jeremy's Mom was there, frowning "what are you doing here?" at Castle.

Castle looked at Jeremy's Mom, and looked around, and saw she was etherically part of this, caught up, a living swirl in this New Age effluvium.

And then time's nautilus disclosed itself again, and he saw another Now, a vision of the future to come: everyone in this auditorium, along with 7,296,407 others converted through television. . .

Dead. They would die in history's most magnificent and most exquisitely engineered mass suicide—a Holocaust in which the victims built their own gas chambers, executed themselves. By Sri Winston's spiritual decree—an event Winston would call "the Sweet Armageddon" —and by the force of spiritual despair, a total of 7,296,407 people would be dead along with Winston three years hence.

Then Castle was back in this now, and certain that he would not trust Jeremy to her; she would be dead with the others, and Jeremy too.

So Castle struck the gong of his whole being, and said, "Jeremy will come with me while you're studying under this man." He said it on several levels and with just enough edge.

She started to demur, nudged by habit and pushbutton resentment, but then the white bearded dervish whispered in the ear of the man in the gold tinted glasses—through the man did not know, of course, that he was whispered to, that anyone was there to whisper—and the Winston devotee stepped promptly over to Jeremy's mother, and took her by the arm. And told her: "It's a good idea. Just until you've made the great Jump. No distractions. . . it's for the best. . ."

And Winston's voice rose melodiously, rhythmically, sending out another wave, that caught Jeremy's mother warmly up, so that she nodded vaguely, and turned away from her son, toward Winston, and just like that Castle was free to take Jeremy by the hand, and walk with him—the authentic Jeremy—out of the auditorium and into clean winds scouring from the Bay.

Outside, Castle saw more clearly now the two currents of being, one toward the way station of the sun, the apex of the Tree of Life— and one toward the spaces between the stars, the ground holding that tree's roots, and he saw lives pulled this way, or coming together to move that way.

Castle and Jeremy, the real Jeremy, hand in hand, went the other way, drawn on, into the other current. They followed the faint but growing sound of an infinitely refined music. . .